I0787970

SEASON OF THE DRAGON
Books 1-3

J.E. Taylor

Season of the Dragon © 2024 J.E. Taylor

Cover Art by Joolz & Jarling

SEASON OF THE DRAGON
Books 1-3

Monsters, trust issues, and a near death experience.

What else could go wrong?

The end of life as we knew it didn't come with a nuclear blast. It didn't come with the deadly impact of a hurdling asteroid. No. It came in a wave of illness that swept the world with fear, and in our quarantined silence, the monsters awoke.

Leviathans, serpent kings, and dragons came forth from the bowels of the Earth. The season of the dragon began with fire and fury and ended with a new world order. One in which these giant terrorists held all the power.

When Mikhail St. Clare betrays the monsters by saving me from death at their claws, I cannot trust the last remaining dragon shifter. Not when humankinds' survival is at stake, and he had a hand in our near extinction.

The only thing we seem to agree on is our desire to annihilate the leviathans and unseat the Serpent King. Our personal futures depend on ridding the earth of these murderous overlords.

We thought crossing the leviathan-patrolled city where every corner hides a hideous death was our most lethal hurdle. But building a bomb large enough to wipe out an entire species carries its own insane levels of danger.

One wrong move and we could destroy everyone living in New York instead.

Dragon Tempest
Season of the Dragon
Book 1

Dragon Tempest
Chapter 1

I CROSSED THE EMPTY road, approaching the point on the hand-drawn map I held marked with a black *X*, wishing I had technology like we used to before the beasts rose. Maybe then I would know what I was up against. I drew the short straw for this damn mission, and here I was, in front of the agreed-upon meeting place. I pocketed the sweat-stained map with hands that were as slick as an icy hill in January.

Today, I would either save mankind or damn them into extinction.

I rubbed my palms on the fabric of my pants, wishing I had formal military training under my belt. The pseudo-military unit I was part of was a mix of militia and left-over military relics. We were always the unit that had this task assigned to us. The more experienced units felt we were expendable.

"I'm here," I whispered into my comms before I unclipped the microphone and pulled out the earpiece, dropping both on the sidewalk before crushing them under the heel of my boot.

This was not part of the protocol, and I'm sure my superior officer was going ballistic, but everyone sent before me had been stupid enough to wear them inside the monster's den, even though they were explicitly told not to have any communications gear at all on the negotiators.

And every last one of them had been roasted alive and dropped in Times Square like a discarded bag of garbage.

I did not want to be another dead body.

You would think after surviving a global pandemic with a death toll of four billion people in a matter of months, I would be more prepared for this. But even the burning pyres of human flesh dotting the horizon was less unsettling than meeting with a monster.

You see, the end of times came crawling in disguised as Pestilence wiping out half of humanity before the creatures rose from the bowels of Earth to take over. They had been dormant for millennia and woke to the silence that befell the planet.

I remembered when the world was still digital. I remembered that first news report, when the serpent king slithered from the ocean with an army of leviathans on its scales. I remembered the horror at the sheer numbers and size of these creatures. And the terror as they issued their first demands.

Even then, they demanded unequivocal surrender.

But they were nothing compared to the dragons' entrance into the world. They came from the bowels of the Earth, breaking through the ground in fiery blasts that looked more like volcanic explosions. When they joined the serpent king and his armies, mankind shuddered but stood firm.

Then the monsters exercised their might. Their complete annihilation of every military installation across the globe was akin to us purging the lawn of ant hills. Coordinated attacks wiped out our ability to defend ourselves on a global scale. Our ability to launch air or sea strikes was decimated by the fiery beasts and our nuclear arsenals were all destroyed.

Now, all we had were a limited number of firearms, and even those only served to irritate the beasts.

So, here I stood, ready to negotiate humankind's submission, which irked me because I bowed to no one. I earned every medal pinned to my damn uniform—unlike our current commander, who plucked the ones off the dead body of our former chief just to make his uniform more impressive to the other platoon chiefs.

I would rather die in a fiery blast than kneel to these things, which was probably why that asshat insisted I go negotiate for our kind. He was hoping I'd be the next body dropped.

Although it was very tempting to tell the beasts to go to hell, I had to think beyond myself. I was not the only one left and had to act accordingly. Defending humanity was at the core of my soul, despite how much I hated these things for nearly destroying our planet.

I stared at the mammoth door constructed of wood and metal that replaced the human-sized doors that used to be the entry to Grand Central Station. The construction of the door twenty times the size of the original was a feat that I could not fathom. These creatures were smart, but I needed to outsmart them today, so the human race could survive.

I rapped my knuckles against the door. It creaked open a moment later, as though they had been waiting for my arrival with bated breath. Reptilian, citrine-colored eyes blinked at me from the darkness. A sniff followed by a low growl came from inside.

"They sent a female." A gravelly voice filled the air.

His voice sent a rattling chill through me, but I stayed still, even though my flight instincts engaged. If I ran, I was as good as dead. So, I stared at those eyes and stanched the need to rub away the goose flesh that covered my skin underneath the stained dress uniform I wore. Instead, I straightened my back and jutted my chin out, announcing with my body language that I wasn't someone to be fucked with.

The door opened more, and a reptilian arm waved me inside.

I obliged and stepped into the blackness with a list of reservations as large as the isle of Manhattan. The likelihood that I would end up a charred piece of meat they dropped in Times Square became much higher now that I was inside their fortress.

The door closed behind me, and I glanced over my shoulder as darkness fell on all sides of me. I gulped a nervous swallow and turned back toward the abyss, blinking rapidly to help my eyes adjust to my dim surroundings.

"Go on," the creature said impatiently.

The dim light along with his tone mixed with my adrenaline and brought out my snark. "I would but I'd rather not trip over anything you might have lying around."

"I forgot you creatures cannot see in the dark." His distaste bled through his words, as if I were the one infringing upon him. A plume of fire lit hanging lamps all the way down the corridor, and I glanced up at the dragon escorting me through enemy territory.

He wasn't as hideous as the leviathans and sea serpents. His scales glowed in the low light, giving him an almost iridescent look that spanned the color spectrum. I hadn't seen any of these creatures close up and found fascination had replaced the disgust coursing through my blood.

"Why are you staring?" he snarled, revealing teeth as sharp as sword blades and almost as long as I was tall.

I stopped and faced him. "I have never seen your kind close up. I am... curious." I picked my words carefully because he could smite me to ash with one breath.

"Curious as in how one studies a bug?" He narrowed his eyes and brought his head to the floor and huffed.

My hair flew back from his exhale, and I still had to crane my neck to meet his gaze head-on. I did not flinch at his inspection, either. Which I think he expected, especially with the way he recoiled when I stepped closer.

"No. Curious in the way two strangers are when they meet after so much hype has been made about the enemy." I couldn't look away from the beauty this monster emitted. It was like craning your neck to see a particularly nasty accident. He fascinated me, which could be detrimental to my life.

His head cocked. "I could just roast you like I have all the other emissaries sent by your kind."

His words were meant to be a warning, but the discomfort in his voice was enough to make me smile. I took another step closer, testing the boundaries even though my sense of self-preservation balked. "I doubt you would give me any warning if that was your intention."

A low growl emitted from between his teeth.

Truthfully, I was the first female officer our unit sent into the den to negotiate on our behalf. In all the briefings we had before we sent our men to do the negotiations, not one of them suggested they bow to the monsters. They were just ordered to take whatever deal was on the table. But my orders were to be submissive and to sign the damn peace treaty.

Submissive wasn't something I could do, but so far, I'd lasted longer than anyone else, so perhaps coy was the winning strategy. Although I did not want to get cocky and push this dragon into a raging inferno.

The dragon sniffed again and grumbled as he rose to his full height. "What game is this?" he growled as smoke drifted from his nostrils.

I moved forward, drawn to the rainbows reflecting in the light. "It isn't a game. Your scales are beautiful." Even I heard the incredulousness in my voice. I didn't believe these beasts could capture beauty. It was almost hypnotic.

"Move along," he said. But the hostility present in his voice before seemed to have faded, as if a compliment wasn't something he was at all comfortable receiving and he did not know how to properly react.

I could not help it. I reached out and touched his leg. The growl that emitted from above me nearly had me pulling my hand back. Instead, I pressed my palm to the cool skin of the dragon. He was smoother than a snake and just as soft to the touch, which was not what I anticipated. I expected hard and unyielding scales, but as I ran my hand down, each scale seemed to quiver under my touch.

He stepped away from me with another divisive snarl.

I looked up. "I'm sorry if I made you uncomfortable." I tried to muster up sincerity, but it just wouldn't come. I wasn't at all remorseful for my actions. Quite the contrary. If

I lived to see my platoon, I could now brag that I touched a dragon.

"Humans and their damned curiosity," he muttered.

I raised an eyebrow. "Others have done that?" I could not see any of the hard-core officers sent before me doing the same.

He lowered himself into a crouch with a low rumble that sent my heart into a fearful patter. "How would you like it if I touched you?" he hissed.

"It depends on what you look like when you shift." I crossed my arms and pursed my lips. I didn't even know whether these things could shift, but some intel suggested that perhaps they could. Some of our secrets had found their way to the monsters, which would have only been obtained by someone hiding among us in human form. The alternative wasn't anything I could consider. If they weren't able to shift, these creatures had crazy super hearing powers and we, as a species, were utterly doomed.

He pointed a deadly claw at my chest and drew down. Fabric ripped and I gasped, trying to gather my dress coat together before he had a chance to tear my blouse. The bastard seemed to be smiling. "You like it about as much as I do, so stop with the games," he growled, still in reptilian form.

I shot my hand out and before my brain was able to stop the actions of my body, my palm slapped the side of his snout. "That's for ripping my jacket," I snapped. Apparently, I had little ownership over any of my actions today.

The glare in his eyes knocked sense into me, but I did not blubber an apology. Something deep inside me told me not to. If I did, I would feel the dragon's wrath.

In one moment, he was a reptilian beast; in the next, he had a human hand around my throat, with me slammed against the nearest wall. The shit thing was, I recognized this bastard. I had seen him at least once a day patrolling the area outside the monsters' domain, as if he were human. I struggled under his immovable grip, staring into his golden eyes as they took me in with such malice I nearly lost my bladder.

"Paint me surprised when they actually followed through with sending one of their weaker species to negotiate with us."

Anger filled me at his duplicity, and I kicked his shin with everything I had. He winced and his eyes darkened. In human form, he radiated heat the way a furnace would, and it burned the areas of my skin that were exposed.

He squeezed harder, cutting off my ability to draw a breath. "Just because you have a pair of tits doesn't make you immune from our wrath. Understand?"

Despite the fury filling every pore, I nodded.

He released my throat, stepping away. "You will not leave here alive if you continue playing games. Your entire race must submit, or we will annihilate you." He pointed a finger at me as the words bled from between his clenched teeth.

I stared him down as my commander's orders surfaced in my mind. A bitter taste filled my mouth. "We are willing to concede." I hated myself for uttering those words.

The twitch of a smile appeared, and I loathed this spying beast with all my heart. He extended his large hand and opened it, palm up. Metal gleamed in his palm. "Show me."

I stared at the iron collar in his hand and then looked up at him.

"You are the last emissary we will entertain. Prove to me that you are willing to submit to our rule, and we will spare humans from extinction."

Oh, how I wanted to tell him to fuck off, but that evil glint in his golden eyes made me reach out for the damn collar. I plucked it from his hand.

"What the hell am I supposed to do with this?" I shook it at him.

"That is your new collar, designed specifically for the dogs that you are." He crossed his arms and the T-shirt he had on nearly burst under the strain of his muscles.

I blinked at him and then stared at the iron. But I could not bring myself to clasp it around my throat.

"If you are unwilling to submit, I cannot see the rest of the humans abiding either." He transformed back into the giant dragon. His chest glowed red as he stared down at me.

"God damn it," I whispered. Then, against everything that I believed, I clasped the metal around my throat. When the locking mechanism clicked, the dragon chuckled, and smoke rolled out his nostrils.

"You owe me ten extra-crispy meals, Mik." Another dragon stepped out of the shadows.

The dragon next to me hooked a chain onto the back of the collar, grumbling as he glared at the other dragon. They both shimmered in the light of the lamps. And then Mik dragged me forward with a vicious yank that nearly had me sprawling on the marble floor.

"Mik?" I asked as I caught my balance and stumbled after him.

"You have an issue with my name, slave?" He glared over his shoulder.

"I just didn't think you had human-like names." I bristled at being called a slave. "Especially after being relegated to underground caves for so many years." I held onto the chain so he wouldn't snap my neck with each stride. But the fact I wasn't fried to a crisp was a good sign. Or so I thought.

He chuckled. "You came here to negotiate for your kind and still find it appropriate to insult me?"

"I find it fascinating that you think small talk is insulting," I said without losing a beat.

"Where were these smart-mouthed ones when we first arrived?" Mik's cohort asked him as he studied me with eyes like emeralds. "Are they all like this one?"

Mik's laughter rang through the cavernous building. "Perhaps the leviathan ate them."

"Do you think they will eat her?" He eyed me in a way that made me stumble.

"Who knows. They haven't been all that communicative lately."

My eyebrow cocked as I watched the floor, praying I didn't stumble. Mik's tone held contempt, and I wondered if now that mankind was ready to surrender, whether there was trouble in the monster ranks.

We crossed into a wide-open room, and Mik yanked me forward. I fell and rolled right into the middle of what used to be Grand Central Station's famous entryway. Cold air flowed in through the empty windows. Broken glass littered the floor, biting into my exposed skin.

I blinked at the corral in the center of the room. Some of the men we had sent before us stood huddled together. Every last one of them wore the same iron collar as I had on. On the floor sat a torched carcass that had been torn into. But it remained half eaten. It took my brain a moment to identify what the hell it was.

A deer.

The monsters hadn't killed all the negotiators. Outside of the shackle around their necks, they did not look any worse for wear, but their expressions at seeing someone else dragged in were utterly horrified, as if my addition meant others would die.

My mind reeled at the ramifications.

Who the hell had these assholes dropped in their stead? Some innocent civilian?

The thought turned my anger into something almost unwieldy. *What kind of game were they playing with us?*

I turned and stared at Mik, and then waved at the spectacle behind me as if I truly had weight in what I said. "What the hell?"

Some of the officers in the pen said "Shush" to me. I ignored them, focusing on the giant dragon who held my leash.

Mik circled around me, hissing in a way that set my skin on fire, and I gulped down the fear, choosing to concentrate on the fury instead.

"Who are you to speak to me like that? On your knees, slave." His growling voice rattled the rafters.

"Fuck. You," I snarled back, nearly screaming loud enough to be heard on the street.

The men in the cage gasped.

Mik's mouth opened, baring his razor-sharp teeth, but I didn't move. I didn't drop to my knees. I just glared until something knocked into the back of my knees with such force it sent me sprawling onto the floor face first.

A hand grabbed my hair and yanked my head back, pulling me to my knees. Those citrine eyes stared down at me. "Be very careful as to what you say next, slave." His glare promised a world of pain.

I reached up and grabbed his wrist, digging my nails into his flesh. "Let me go!" My sense of self-preservation had fled like a scared child.

He actually grinned and glanced up at his dragon friend, and then looked at the men in captivity. "They all took a knee." He met my gaze again. "For humanity's sake. Now, they serve as the leviathans' next meal."

I growled and still tried to yank my head away. "Fuck you," I said. "I'm never going to agree to be your slave." I couldn't help my reaction. Being caged like cattle was not in my makeup. Even though I knew I was damning the human race, the rebel in me just could not submit.

He looked up at the other dragon and shrugged, as he spun me toward the cage of men. Fire flew from the other dragon's mouth. The men's screams filled my ears. I stared in horror as the green-eyed bastard cooked them to a crisp. Their charred bodies fell quickly.

I struggled in the dragon's grip as he forced me to watch their deaths. I was not going to go without a fight. When he pushed me forward, he picked up the end of the chain and dragged me toward a dark cavern on the other side of the station.

The crunch of bones behind me caught my attention, and I turned to see the other dragon feasting on the dead. My heart hammered in my chest as Mik pulled me into the dark.

Dragon Tempest
Chapter 2

HIS EYES BURNED IN the dimness as he threw me across the space. I slammed into a wall, knocking the breath out of me. But I remained on my feet and squared myself in the direction of his bright eyes.

The door clanged shut behind him, drenching us in total darkness, and my heart nearly burst through my ribs it beat so frantically. This was it. I was going to roast alive in this dark space.

"Scream like I'm hurting you," he said, so softly I didn't think I heard him right.

When I didn't make a sound, he huffed.

"For God's sake, do you want to die today?" His eyes glowed bright. "Scream." His hissed whisper filled the space, as if he had a stake in my survival.

I tilted my head back and screamed, putting all my horror, all my frustration, and all my momentary confusion into it. It echoed on the walls and made my throat raw.

He lunged at me, covering my mouth with his hand as he roared in a way that ringed my ears, and then he tossed me against the door so hard my head spun from the collision with the wood.

I was too dazed when he picked me up and pulled open a side door and gently set me down inside before he whispered, "Shh," in my ear. The door closed but a plume of flame reached under the door before it receded.

My mind couldn't grasp what just happened. *The dragon saved me. Why?*

The slam of the outer door made me jump, but for some reason I kept quiet. Maybe my self-preservation finally raised its head inside me.

"Dude, you turned her to dust? You know better. You just wiped out their next meal."

"She pissed me off." Mik's voice drifted under the door. "I lost control."

I stared into the dark, wondering what the hell was going on. This was not what I expected. Especially after they fried the other servicemen in the corral. It was as if I passed some weird test that allowed me to be saved from their wrath.

"They'll be back within the hour and be pissed that we've destroyed their meals.

Especially after keeping them alive for so long. They were looking forward to some raw human flesh."

"You left some of the crispy ones, right?" Mik asked.

Silence layered over the room.

"Seriously?" Mik sounded exasperated.

"I've been hungry for days," the other dragon whined.

"Well, you can explain that shit to them. I need to go find a body to drop."

"You know what they'll do to me. They won't hurt you. Let me do the body drop."

His panic sounded in his voice like a bullhorn. The entire ordeal had me questioning everything we had been briefed on. But they still had killed those soldiers without so much as a blink. It made zero sense.

Another beat of silence fell and then Mik's annoyed voice said, "Fine. Go. And give it a few days before you return because they will be pissed, and if you come back too soon, you'll feel their wrath. And I really don't want to be the only one left to deal with those assholes."

"Thanks." The sound of wings filled the air.

My mind swirled. There were thousands of dragons when the world went to hell. That wasn't that long ago, was it? I stared into the darkness, numb with questions.

The door opened and then closed behind the shadow that stepped inside. A small flame flickered, and Mik crouched next to me in human form with a fire dancing on his fingertips.

"Come on." He grabbed my arm.

I yanked it from his grip. I didn't know whether he was leading me to freedom or playing some twisted mind game before he killed me.

"Look. I'm sorry, but if we don't leave now, they will kill you and they will kill me and humanity's chance to survive their war will be gone as surely as those soldiers." His eyes certainly didn't look like he was playing a game. They were actually...pleading.

This time when he gripped my arm, I let him lead me down into the bowels of the subway system. A system that had not run for at least a decade. First the pandemic stopped all people's movement, and then the monsters came, so we really never had a chance to restart our lives again.

His grip loosened, and he slid his hand down so his fingers were intertwined with mine. It was strange and I stared at the union of our hands. This time, it didn't hurt despite the warmth radiating from him, as though he had some internal burn setting that he could turn on and off.

"Who are you?" I asked after we'd gone at least a mile. I was used to long runs, but this was tough, especially being dipped in darkness and trusting that the person leading you had your best interest at heart when just a few minutes before he was gung ho on killing you.

"Mikhail. The only surviving heir to the dragon throne. I guess," he said with a soft laugh. "Last of my kind."

"What about your friend back there?"

"Ricky?" He sighed. "He would rather see this world destroyed than side with the human race.

And he won't listen to me. He will go back and grovel like the fool he is. He'll be lucky if the leviathans just rip him apart for eating their food." He shook his head and actually looked a hair remorseful. "An unfortunate sacrifice."

I skidded to a stop and tried to yank my hand from his.

He turned toward me with flames still dancing on his hand so I could see his face. "The leviathans killed my family a couple weeks ago." He looked up at the ceiling, and I caught the sheen of tears over his yellow irises. "Did you not notice the lack of dragons burning things?"

I blinked at him, dumbfounded. I had noticed the absence of dragons in the air, but I thought that was due to the pending negotiations.

"And Ricky, he just stood by and let it happen. At one point, I considered him a friend, but he is no better than the sea serpents and leviathans who wish to see the utter destruction of life."

"Still, he is a dragon." It seemed too easy for this thing to turn on his own kind. Although, he could also assimilate with humans. He was a chameleon and one I should not trust.

He tried to move me from where I stopped. "We don't have time for this," he whispered and met my gaze. His teeth clenched when I didn't budge. "Do you know what would have happened if I let my friend take you into that room that I took you into at the station?"

Even the way he stated "my friend" reeked of hostility. "What?" I snapped, still not convinced that this creature was to be followed to God knows where.

His sharp eyes locked with mine. "Ricky would have raped you and then, if he wasn't satisfied, he would have slowly cooked pieces of your body. Feet. Legs. Hands. Arms. His idea of torture outshined all others, and that's probably why he is still alive. So, if I wanted you dead, I would have just let him do his thing, as vile as that is."

"What would he have done if I satisfied him?" I asked, curious whether that would have led to my survival. Sleeping with the enemy wasn't ever put on the table, but if it meant survival of our species, I would have done it.

He bit his lower lip and shook his head. "If you didn't die from having relations with a full-blooded dragon, you would have died in childbirth, because he would have continued until you were carrying a child. And bringing a dragon into the world is a bloody disaster. Believe me."

The way he pressed that point had me narrowing my eyes. "What have you done in the name of this war?"

He looked down. "Pulled the dragons from their sleep, only to lead them to slaughter. Betrayed friends. Failed family. And killed countless humans in countless ways." He finally looked up. "I'm not a saint, but I've been on this planet long enough to know what humankind is capable of, and I'm betting on you for *my* survival."

"We are just another pawn in your quest for dominance." I ripped my hand out of his grip. "I'm not playing into this game of yours."

"I'll haul you out of here over my shoulder," he warned as his eyes flashed into the danger zone.

"Why me?"

His teeth clenched, shifting to sharp shards instead of the blunt human teeth he had a moment ago. "Because you were the first female to be sent on a death mission and you killed your comms outside the door. That isn't an action of a sane soldier. Which means you, as a species, are just as desperate as I am."

"Fuck you," I growled.

"I could, but you wouldn't like being an unwilling participant." He didn't wait for me to take his hand. Instead, he hauled me over his shoulder and turned back in the direction we were headed.

I struggled in his grasp, but he clamped down harder, nearly crushing my ribs. I opened my mouth to scream, but it vanished the moment Mik started to move. He was like the wind and impressed me into silence as we barreled through the tunnels as fast as a freight train on high speed. All light disappeared as we flowed farther into the maze of subway tunnels. Occasionally, a shaft of light penetrated the darkness, but it wasn't enough to give me a glimpse of where we were.

It wasn't until the tunnels opened to a thruway that my mind grasped where we were. The Brooklyn Bridge, or what was left of it, stood in front of us. Instead of continuing to the water, he turned and headed back into the city to where the buildings still stood relatively unscathed.

He ducked into one of the near high-rises and traveled up the stairs to the top floor. "None of the monsters know this place exists." He put me on my feet outside a door. When he pulled out a pair of keys, I was even more dumbfounded. He swung open the door to a swanky penthouse, as if it were the most normal thing in the world.

"What the hell?" I said as he ushered me through the door and locked it behind us.

"I don't know why I was compelled to keep this part of my human existence a secret to the other beasts, but I did." He pocketed his keys. "I was born in the days humans were only in Mesopotamia. My father, the king of the dragons, came out of hiding to see if life had been restored topside. You see, my kind existed when dinosaurs walked the Earth. And we hid when we saw the meteor falling from the sky. Outside of my father, the rest of the dragons stayed in hibernation until I called them forth." Mik crossed to the windows overlooking the broken Statue of Liberty.

That meant this man standing before me was thousands of years old. I took a seat on the nearest piece of furniture so I wouldn't collapse on the floor.

His reflection smiled at my reaction. Then his focus went back outside this little haven and his smile faded.

"How many of you are there out there posing as humans?"

"I'm the only one who can shift. I guess it's because my father fell in love with a human woman. She died birthing me. He told me the story just before he died and cautioned me from ever falling into the same trap." He continued to stare out the window.

"And how did you form an alliance with the serpent kings if you were already here?"

"When I saw their arrival, I met them in my true form, and they said they wanted an alliance with the dragons. It was time for the ancient to rule this world again. I made the mistake of telling them I had lived among mankind as one of them. That I could shift between forms as easily as the wind strips a tree of leaves in the fall. That was my mistake. They used my skills."

My brain was slow to catch up and then what little military training I did have kicked in. I stared at the back of the traitorous dragon. He had to have valuable intel on these monsters. "How do we defeat them?" I found my feet and crossed to him. "You said you are our best bet on winning this war. How?"

His lips pressed together, and he sniffed the air before turning toward me. With him relaxed and not glaring at me, I noticed just how handsome he was. It wasn't as if I hadn't noticed him as he patrolled either, but being this close, without hostility radiating from him, I couldn't tear my eyes away.

"We decimated your ability to launch a large-scale attack," he said.

"No shit." I crossed my arms, waiting. When he didn't continue, I narrowed my eyes. "This isn't about saving mankind. This is about saving you."

He shrugged. "It's one and the same."

"Pretentious bastard." I glanced out the window, trying to rein in my aggravation.

He laughed. "I guess I am." He stepped closer to me, so I had to look up at him. "But I am your best chance at survival."

I had had enough of his macho shit. "And if I tell you to piss off?"

"Then it looks like humankind will have two different enemies to deal with." His eyes sparkled, and I didn't know whether it was from the tension in the room or whether he really did relish the idea of being on opposite sides in this war.

Frustration raked its claws down my back, and I went to throw my head back with exasperation, but the collar he had on me stopped my attempt at displaying my unhappiness. "Take this damn thing off and I'll consider it." I tapped the iron still clasped around my throat.

He rolled his eyes then twirled his finger. "Turn around."

Reluctantly, I did as he asked. He pushed my loose hair away and tinkered with the thing. Heat seared the back of my neck and then the metal clanked on the floor. He touched the sore area of my neck with a sigh.

I winced away from him, careful not to step on the open collar. "Thank you." Now that I was free, I headed toward the door. "I need to let my unit know I'm alive."

"Not yet," he said. "We need to wait it out for a few days, just like I told Ricky to do."

I spun on him and his audacity. "Excuse me?"

He leveled a cool stare. "You are still my prisoner, even without the collar."

I gritted my teeth at him, giving him my most hateful glare. But things could be much worse than being holed up in a high-end penthouse. I could be dead like the rest of the soldiers in Grand Central Station. Or I could be his friend's plaything and God knows how that would have turned out.

I glanced toward the kitchen and the glow on the stove caught my full attention. I blinked as the truth settled. I stared at the display on the stove. At the red numbers radiating in the dimness. When they changed, my heart leaped into my throat. It had been years since I saw a functioning digital clock. I whipped my gaze to Mik.

"You have power?"

His lips curved into a sly smile. "This is one of the buildings I purposely did not target. I told them it was inconsequential and empty. There were a few apartments on the lower floors, but the tenants decided to bug out of the city when the pandemic struck. The rest of the building was in the midst of being renovated, so really, only this floor was occupied. But to the outside world, it looks like just another demolished building due to the specialty glass I created. And as far as your question, yes, this penthouse is solar powered. Between the glass panes and the shingles on the roof that I also designed, as long as the sun exists, I will have power."

My eyebrows rose. This ancient dragon had quite the brains to go along with the brawn. I hated that I was impressed, and I turned away from his distracting attractiveness and mulled over his words.

It had been years since I'd seen anything electrical that worked, especially since the creatures ruined all the transfer stations and any energy sources we had. Even our solar panels and wind turbines had been ripped to shreds.

A working kitchen. It was just too tempting to resist, and I had to test it out because a large part of me scoffed at his information dump. No one had invented solar glass panels. I had heard about solar shingles, but that was some recluse billionaire's invention.

He didn't stop me when I crossed to the kitchen and entered through the galley door. He decided to lounge on one of the comfortable chairs facing the kitchen and study me with those piercing amber eyes.

He didn't seem all that opposed to my curiosity, so I turned and opened the refrigerator, expecting an empty, dark shell. But instead, I blinked at an array of fresh produce, among other things. A six-pack of beer caught my eye and I reached in, plucking one out without asking. If I was his prisoner and this was my cell, then everything inside was fair game.

Instead of searching the drawers, I used the edge of the counter and popped the cap off.

"What is your name?" he asked from far too close.

The beer nearly slid out of my hand, and I spun to stare at his chest.

He reached out and plucked the bottle from my hand.

I grabbed it back and glared up at him, and then tapped my nametag on my uniform.

"Woods?" His eyebrow rose.

"Sergeant Woods." I took a sip of the beer and shuffled back against the counter, putting space between us.

"What is your first name?" Mik crossed his arms.

I pressed my lips together. I did not want to reveal the biggest joke in my platoon. Hell, the biggest joke of my entire life. High school had been brutal. My parents must have been smoking something funny when they decided what my name should be.

I took another sip of beer, opting not to say anything. I did not want a dragon laughing at me, too.

He reached out and grabbed my arm with one hand, and took the beer from me. "Name or you do not get to finish this."

It had been a very long time since I had a cold beer. I sighed and rolled my eyes, resigning myself to being the brunt of whatever jokes this fool would dole out. "Holly," I mumbled and reached for the bottle.

His lips twitched into a smile. "Holly Woods?" He handed me the beer and let out a guffaw that was as warm as his penthouse. "You deserve the entire six-pack for that."

Although his laugh sounded musical and rich and his smile just about took me out at the knees, it burned because this wasn't a casual conversation. This wasn't a chance meeting. He had been party to the slaughtering of my kind.

He stood by as the heathens from hell demanded our eternal servitude.

I was his prisoner.

And I would do well to remember that.

Dragon Tempest
Chapter 3

AFTER HE LAUGHED AT my name, I chose to drink and sulk in a corner chair with a view of what was left of our world. The charred and twisted buildings across Manhattan were a stark reminder of the power of my captor and his kind. In the distance, the slithering march of the serpent king began through the city, toward the downtown area where we were holed up. From this vantage point, it was quite a horrific sight. The serpent king towered over the leviathan army, and the leviathans were at least three stories high to begin with.

I leaned forward, taking in their military-like formation and how they swept the streets as they passed. I stood and approached the window as that ugly thing passed by near enough for me to be able to see the top of his scaly head.

Mik stepped next to me and stared out the window.

His eyes blazed and he turned away from the vile destroyers. It was his turn to grab a drink, but instead of beer, he chose a single malt whiskey that matched his eyes. He returned to the space next to me, and I could feel the hatred radiating off him like a lethal nuclear meltdown.

It was time to ask the question burning a hole in my brain since he pulled me out of Grand Central Station. "There were thousands of you. What happened?"

He waved at the procession, as though that explained it.

His gesture did not answer my question. I waited for more, but he just leveled a murderous glare at the beasts below as the muscles in his jaw clenched.

If he hated them so much, why did he stand with them? Why didn't he switch sides sooner? It made no sense. "You obviously hate them, yet you still masqueraded as one of us and killed humans at every chance."

He stared out the window, took a hefty sip of the amber liquid, and then nodded.

His silence sent a flush of aggravation over me. "So, why the hell should I trust you?"

He pursed his lips and glanced at me. "You shouldn't."

Well, at least he was honest, but it did not squash all the questions flying around in my head. In fact, it made it worse. "Then what the hell am I doing here?"

He stared out at the monsters as they slid into the river, descending into whatever watery hell they called home. He recoiled as the last of the leviathans passed, dragging something broken and bloody.

I leaned closer to the window, squinting down to see what made my host flinch. I gasped at the torn body of a dragon being dragged behind the morbid convoy.

"Damn it." Mik stalked away, downing the liquid in his glass. Instead of refilling his cup, he grabbed the bottle off the counter and sucked down the entire contents before slamming the empty container on the counter, where it shattered into a million tiny fragments.

"You are here to help me avenge my kind," he said with his back to me. "And to make sure the same thing doesn't happen to your kind."

His low, growling voice seemed to echo in the apartment, filling it with such blackness that I shivered. I glanced back just as the last of the creatures disappeared into the Hudson River.

The procession was only a small fraction of the numbers around the United States and the world, based on the reports that filtered in from all over the globe before the satellites were taken out. Even with all our casualties, we humans still outnumbered these beasts. But if we continued to be stamped out in droves, our numbers would dwindle to the point of extinction.

There had to be more dragons somewhere. "There aren't any more of your kind in other countries?"

He shook his head, but this time it wasn't as sure, and his eyes reflected a mixture of doubt and a sliver of hope before it faded. "No. I would feel their existence in my bones. Just like I was able to feel each and every death until recently." He wiped his face.

"What do you mean, until recently?"

"Seeing and feeling so many slaughtered just numbed me to their existence and their deaths." He sighed. "I didn't feel Ricky's passing like I should have."

"What changed?"

He was quiet for a long time and then he turned to me, meeting my gaze. "My alliance. So don't make me regret my choice."

I COULD SEE HIM stretched out on his bed, snoring away while I lounged on the couch. I guess, as prisons went, this one wasn't bad, but I didn't plan to spend any significant time here. Not if I could help it. I slowly rose and headed to the front door to study the lock.

I stared at the keypad, trying to make out which ones Mikhail had touched. I couldn't distinguish any fingerprints on them in the low light. I leaned back to get a view of the bedroom to make sure he was still out. He hadn't moved an inch, so I reached into my pocket and pulled out my small face powder compact. It had saved my ass before, so although the guys gave me grief, they never had the right tools to get out when a keypad was involved.

I dipped the puff enough to scrape out excess powder and held it close enough for some of the powder to drift onto the keypad, then I blew softly. The powder clung to marks on six of the ten keys, and I closed my eyes. I had hoped for a three- or four-digit combination. At least having the ones with marks meant I didn't have to attempt a guess at a million different combinations. I had the numbers that made up the code, which was a start, but I was a long way off from solving this puzzle.

"You'll never figure out the right combination."

I jumped at his voice and my compact tumbled to the ground. I stood and spun around to face him as my fight reflex took hold. My adrenaline spiked and I squared my feet, clasping my hands into fists. I didn't dare budge with the reflection of aggravated amusement in my captor's eyes.

His eyebrow rose. "You think your attempt at a combative stance is intimidating?"

I pressed my lips against the automatic *fuck you* that wanted to escape. I was used to just leveling a glare to get my way. My reputation of being a badass was well known in the barracks, and perhaps I'd have to teach this dragon a lesson.

When his footing shifted into an equal fight stance, I swallowed hard. His little hand signal to engage me in a fight lit a fire in me. I did not like his arrogance, and I stepped forward as if I were entering a sparring ring back at the base. Except here there was furniture and glass tables that could shatter if a body slammed into them hard enough.

His lips tilted into a smirk and he lifted his arms, mirroring my stance. We danced around in a slow circle, sizing each other up, and then I stepped in and threw a left hook. He barely parried in time and the surprise on his face was enough to bring a smile to mine.

"I didn't realize you were a southpaw." He readjusted his stance.

I didn't answer but this time when I went on the offense, I threw a right hook aimed squarely at his jaw. My knuckles grazed his stubble.

A satisfied smile spread on my lips. "I'm ambidextrous."

He stepped in and grabbed me, sending me flying into the back of the couch, and then he was at my side with one hand clasped around my throat. "Well, my ambidextrous friend, I suggest you give up trying to escape and get some rest before I truly lose my temper."

I scratched at his hand as both fear and anger mixed in my blood and heated my cheeks. My lungs screamed for air. He hadn't threatened me since we left the main entrance of Grand Central. Burning aggravation scraped over my skin, clouding my mind as his hand released. I sucked a breath in and coughed.

How dare he treat me like this!

"Now are you going to be a good girl and get some rest?"

"Fuck you," I rasped.

He grabbed my arm and hauled me into the bedroom. My heart went on a rampage in my chest, and I tried to maneuver out of his grip. When I couldn't, I moved in closer and tried to flip him over my hip, but he was as solid as a rock mountain and all my resistance did was piss him off more.

He grabbed something out of his bureau drawer, and I fought even harder at the sight of the zip tie. It wasn't until my hands were secured on the headboard that he stepped away to inspect his arms.

His eyes narrowed at the welts I had inflicted. Some of my scratches drew blood. I smiled at my handiwork until his gaze snapped to mine.

"I really should, just to teach you a lesson, but I've never fucked in anger," he growled.

His voice was so full of malice that it triggered something deep within me. "You should try it some time. It really releases the endorphins." The words were out before my brain could stop them.

His gaze narrowed even more. "Is that an invitation?"

I blinked and my senses returned before I said something that caused him to follow through on something he could never take back. It would destroy whatever chance the human race had, because I would end up killing him at the first chance if he took it as an invitation.

"No."

"I didn't think so." He went to the opposite side of the bed and crawled under the thin sheet, rolling so his back faced me.

I stared up at the dark ceiling, wondering how this evil thing sleeping next to me could also show a measure of decency.

Dragon Tempest
Chapter 4

MY ARMS ACHED AND I went to lower them, but they wouldn't budge. I blinked my eyes open to a bright sunrise in an unfamiliar place. My head hurt as I squinted around the room.

"Ah, shit." My head fell back on the soft pillow. I was truly in the dragon's lair. It hadn't been a bizarre dream like I had hoped. And last night, I had drank more than a six-pack of cold beer on very little food. It had been enough to affect my perception.

How the hell had I thought I could take a damn dragon in a fistfight?

My entire face flushed hot. If I had the freedom of movement, I would have covered my face to hide the absolute mortification rolling through my sore muscles.

The bump next to me rolled and Mikhail's golden eyes took me in. "Are you going to behave today?" he asked with the gruffness of sleep still on his voice.

His condescending tone made me want to growl a no, but I needed to use the restroom, so I nodded. I wouldn't cause problems. At least not right away. But I was still hell-bent on getting out of here today.

He reached out. His nail grew to the dragon's sharp shard, and he swiped the ties binding me, releasing my arms.

I pulled my arms slowly toward my body, grimacing through the stiffness and pain. I rolled off the mattress and onto my feet. Gravity made my situation a little more dire than laying prone had.

"Bathroom?" The question squeaked out as I clenched my thighs together against the pressure.

Mik pointed to a door in the corner.

I hurried across the room and slipped inside, relieving myself on the pristine porcelain. The water in the toilet was clear, as if it worked, not stagnant with piss and poop like every other commode in Manhattan. I blinked as the clear water turned yellow.

Did he have a working bathroom?

I flushed and marveled at the spiral of water cleaning out the bowl. Another stellar perk of this penthouse. I glanced at the oversized shower stall with jets and a rain showerhead. The toilet cycled through, draining out the soiled water and replacing it with clean liquid. That clinched my decision. If I was going to be a prisoner here, I was going to take full advantage of all these benefits.

I couldn't get out of my dirty clothes fast enough.

Just before I stepped in the shower, the bathroom door opened. I didn't bother covering up, and Mik's eyes widened just before he looked away.

"Do you mind?" I asked as I turned on the shower.

"My apologies." He closed the door behind him, but not before his face flushed red.

Whether it was from embarrassment or something else, I didn't care. I stepped into the shower. My muscles just about melted. The water was warm and my current plan was to stand under this spray until there wasn't a drop of warm water left.

I used the soap and cleaned every crevice and then turned on all the jets. My head dropped back as my skin was pelted with heavenly streams from all angles. I don't know how long I stood in a stupor of ecstasy, but when I finally opened my eyes, my gaze fell on the shampoo and conditioner sitting on a corner shelf. I didn't care that it was made for men.

I used almost all of the shampoo, cleaning my hair as if it hadn't been cleaned in months.

When it squeaked, I used a small dab of conditioner to get rid of the knots. The water still remained hot, and the room was so full of steam that I knew the moment I stepped out of the water, I would break out in sweat, but it was so worth the long shower.

I turned off the water and grabbed one of the plush towels. I wondered whether Mik had laundry machines as I stared down at my crusty clothes. I did not want to put them onto my clean skin. It was worth asking as opposed to getting immediately grimy. Besides, the towel covered me from my underarms to my knees.

I wrung the water out of my hair and scooped up my dirty clothes before stepping out into the bedroom. Mik wasn't in the bedroom and the bed was nicely made. I found that strange. As I glanced around, I realized the dragon who torched the land was a neatnik.

The clang of pots drew me out into the living area.

"Do you have laundry machines?" I asked.

Mik looked up at me and then pointed toward a room on the other side of the apartment. I followed his silent direction and stepped into a modern laundry room. I emptied the pockets of my clothing and then dumped it into the washing machine, poured detergent in, and turned on the machine. I leaned against it with my eyes closed and drifted back to a time before the monsters.

While we were all quarantined to our homes, we had all these modern conveniences. Back then, the biggest worry was if we would be able to find toilet paper. This apartment brought back all those bittersweet memories, but it also layered it with a fury that nearly got the best of me. These creatures stole everything from us, and this poser still had all the modern conveniences that the human race designed.

I resecured the towel and waltzed back in the living area, ready to give him a piece of my mind. The words died on my lips as he pushed a plate of scrambled eggs and toast across the counter. I blinked at the hot meal.

"Where did you get eggs?" I met his gaze.

His secret smile irritated me but not enough to launch into the tirade I was prepared for when I stepped out of the laundry. I climbed onto one of the barstools, holding onto the towel until I was settled.

I dug into the offered meal and hated that it was as good as everything else in this place. When I finished, he pushed a glass of orange juice across to me. I sighed.

"No coffee?" I sent a glare in his direction, but I didn't refuse the juice.

"I don't drink coffee," he said.

"Seriously?" I had never met anyone who didn't drink coffee. Even without electricity, the platoons connected the wires to car batteries in order to get them to work. Coffee people were serious about their cravings.

"I learned early on that caffeine was not my friend."

Despite wanting to remain pissed off at him for keeping me prisoner here, his comment lit the seeds of curiosity. I downed the juice in the hopes it would dampen the burn, but it only seemed to make that itch all the more prominent.

"How so?" I set my glass on the counter and met his golden gaze.

"Caffeine turns my fire into something much more...deadly. Normally when I incinerate something, it just burns. But with caffeine in our system, our fire basically erases whatever it touches. It is much more than full incineration. It's almost as if it taps into whatever magic we hold and sets it loose on a scale that is beyond human comprehension. For instance, instead of just neutralizing a nuclear chain reaction, our caffeine-enhanced fire erases it from existence. We were all caffeinated up when we went after your nuclear missiles and power plants. It was necessary for us to preserve the environment. Otherwise, we would have ignited the destruction of this Earth."

This was more information than I had gotten the day before, but it still bred more questions. "So, why didn't you just load up on caffeine and take out the leviathans?" I crossed my arms over my chest and cocked my eyebrow at him.

"Because they have armor that prevents them from being annihilated by our fire. A few tried when they decided we were a danger to their plans. Even with caffeine, it did not work against whatever the hell their outer shells are made of."

My gaze narrowed. "If you couldn't beat them by making them disintegrate, why in the hell do you think we can?"

"Fire isn't the only means of destruction out there," he said. "You have killed a few, haven't you?"

I pulled back and stared at him. *How the hell did he get that intel?*

I had found a way to compromise their shields, but I wasn't about to reveal how. It was unorthodox, and I had stumbled upon it by accident, but it worked. It seemed leviathans had a nasty reaction to bleach. Unfortunately, there wasn't enough bleach in the States to kill the lot of them.

However, since that day, any time I was on patrol, I had carried around one of those kid's super-soakers filled with bleach with me. So did my platoon. But even if we were all armed to the hilt with bleach and launched an attack, that wasn't what ultimately killed the beasts.

And we didn't have enough bullets left to finish the job.

"Were those just rumors?" he asked when I remained silent.

"No. They weren't rumors." I allowed a confirmation of sorts, but the details would remain with me until I believed I could trust this bastard. Which, at the current pace, would happen about the time hell froze over.

"So, you figured out how to kill those things." He leaned against the far corner and smiled at me as though I were some hoodoo witch who could snap my fingers and our enemies would fall.

It was a lot messier and more complicated than that.

I just shrugged. His admonishment to not trust him was front and center in my mind. He was a dragon, after all.

He cocked an eyebrow.

I rolled my eyes. "Yes. I figured out how to compromise their armor so a bullet could pierce their fucking brain."

"How?"

It was my turn to smile. "That is my secret. And until you prove your worth to the human fight, it will remain my secret."

His teeth gnashed together, and he swiped the empty plate and glass from in front of me, forcing them into the dishwasher with the grace of a lumberjack hacking down a tree. He leveled a glare at me before he retreated to the bedroom and slammed the door behind him.

I took the opportunity to really inspect the apartment without his probing eyes on my back. When I walked into the room opposite the bedroom, I stalled a few steps in. Two walls were lined from floor to ceiling with books. A deep mahogany desk sat in the center facing the windows, and a comfortable, oversized leather gliding loveseat and matching ottoman occupied the corner closest to the shelves. A computer sat on the desk, with pictures cycling through. My heart lurched at the sight of electronics that worked. It was as if this entire apartment was its own grid. One that had never been compromised by the monsters.

A picture of Mikhail with a stunning woman and two children who were spitting images of Mik flashed on the screen. I stared at his easy smile and the way he looked at the woman instead of the camera. The picture changed again, and other photographs of his life flashed in a slow, rolling slide show.

I pulled the desk chair back and took a seat with my gaze glued to the screen as I watched his family age and branch out, the kids growing and finding spouses. However, there was no evidence of grandchildren in the pictures.

I could not reconcile these photographs with what he told me about humans giving birth to dragons.

He obviously did it, so either he was a liar or...

My eyes widened. *Or there were dragons in our midst for much longer than any of us knew.*

The squeak of the door made me swivel the chair toward the entry.

He leaned on the doorjamb, with his arms crossed and his hair dripping wet, leaving water marks on his neatly pressed shirt.

"You had children?" I waved at the computer.

He nodded. "Had being the operative word." His jaw clenched as the pictures continued. His eyes moved from mine to the screen with both anger and longing visible in the flare that bloomed in his irises.

Nothing added up with Mikhail. "I thought you said humans having children by dragons was deadly to the mother."

"Yes."

"And yet?" I pointed as the frame cycled to a younger version of his wife holding what looked like human children. The only indication that they were not human was the odd color of their eyes. Eyes that matched Mikhail's.

"That wasn't their birth mother." He met my gaze. "Their birth mother died in labor. Anna was with me when they were born."

I looked back at the screen. "They were like you?"

Mikhail gave me a nod. "Yes. They could breathe fire, but had a harder time shifting. Probably because they were more human than dragon, but birthing them still killed their mother."

"If they were more human than dragon, how did their mother die?"

"Dragons lay eggs and the babies break through the shell by using their fire when they are ready to come into the world. So, you can imagine what happens to a woman carrying a dragon in their womb."

I swallowed. "They think the womb is a shell?"

He nodded.

I cringed and looked back at the pictures, trying to block out the image of someone frying from the inside out. Instead, I focused on the apartment. It was not set up for a family. "This wasn't where you normally lived, was it?"

"No, this was an off-the-books experiment. It's the only place of mine that survived the culling. And by some miracle, I was able to keep this building from being targeted long enough for me to disguise it with what I wanted the outside world to see." His gaze moved to the pictures, and his lips curved into a sad frown. "They used Anna and my children to keep me in line. And then used the rest of the dragon federation to do their bidding. They had us take out your ability to attack from the air. When there were no more dangers of an assault by air, the dragons lost their usefulness. We were no longer allies in their bid for world domination. I was chained and forced to watch the slaughter of my family, of my dragon kin. They killed everyone, with Ricky standing by their side. He was spared to be my babysitter. To make sure I stayed in line." He let out a chilling laugh. "They thought I had alliances with him just because he shared dragon blood." He shook his head slowly and his eyes blazed with a red hue.

"Why were you spared?"

His tilted smile appeared. "I can shift and infiltrate your ranks. *I* was still useful. And with a single dragon left alive, they felt that was enough leverage over me. But they underestimated me, just as they underestimate you."

I turned back to the computer and my gaze drifted out the window. I didn't know how much of that was true or pure bullshit.

Especially considering he just admitted he could be a spy.

Dragon Tempest
Chapter 5

THE CONVERSATOIN LAGGED as neither one of us was willing to share anything more than what had already been discussed. I did not trust him, especially with the possibility that he could be playing me to get information. But the battered carcass of the last dragon kept surfacing in my mind, along with Mikhail's explanation of how his family died.

If he wasn't snowing me, I could understand the abrupt change in mind. If all my friends and family were executed in front of me, could I have survived such a thing?

I didn't have a good answer. If I had children and had to witness their slaughter, along with the one who had my heart, I think I would have struck right then and there, and gone down in a blaze of glory, along with however many I could take with me.

But in Mikhail's case, they could not harm their executioners. There was nothing they could do beyond watch and grieve.

It would have broken me.

I glanced sideways at Mikhail, wondering just how much of his sanity was left after something like that. It gave me a new appreciation for the beast. He not only survived a millennium or more and developed things to make life all that much easier for the human race, as evidenced by the building we were in, but he also survived the devastating slaughter of his people. His family.

Yet he still seemed to have some decency left.

Was that even possible with his most recent history?

Across the apartment, the dryer dinged, interrupting my silent lament. I shot to my feet, moving past him in search of the first truly clean clothes I've had in a long while. I pulled the garments from the drum and smelled the light lavender scent of the dryer sheets.

The towel I wore dropped faster than a whore's pants, and I slid my warm underwear and bra on.

I had to admit, it almost was orgasmic as I pulled my pants on. Warmth and clean all bundled up into one fine moment. My shirt came last, and I turned toward the living room and started threading the buttons together. Mikhail stood in the center of the room with an eye cocked at me. I smoothed the shirt and my cheeks heated.

I had no idea how long he had been standing there, witnessing my reaction.

"You have no idea how long it's been since I had machine-washed and dried clothing," I said as I finished buttoning up my uniform. I turned back to the machines where my belongings, including my switchblade, were still laid out where I had put them when I started the wash. He hadn't tried to remove the knife, which told me I wasn't armed enough to take him out. I stepped into the main room feeling more human than I had in years.

"It is a nice benefit of this place."

I glanced around and nodded. "As nice as it is, I cannot stay. They went back to whatever watery hell they reside in. That gives us a window to get to my team and let them know I am alive and figure out our next steps."

Mikhail sucked air in through his nose and slowly shook his head. "Not yet. Not until you tell me how you beat them."

"Fuck you." I squared my feet and glared at him from the entrance to the laundry room. He could kill me with a puff of fire. Turn me to ash. But I wasn't ready to trust him with my secret. That would cheapen whatever value I held. I removed my switchblade, holding it tightly out of sight.

His jaw tightened and his glare could have lit the room ablaze. Smoke came out of his nostrils with his exhale. He stepped toward me, and I brought the blade forward, flipping it open. It gleamed in the morning sunlight.

"I promise I will get more than a couple slashes in before you kill me," I snarled.

He clenched his fists and closed his eyes. "I would have never brought you here if I intended to kill you." When his lids snapped open, his irises were ablaze with dragon fire. "Ricky didn't heed my warnings either and look what happened to that sorry son of a bitch." He waved at the window, reminding me of the leviathans' retreat.

I slowly lowered the blade and relaxed as his words sank in.

"I don't want to be stuck here with you either. You seem to be nothing more than a petulant child who thinks she's been around." He pointed his finger at me. "You are nothing more than a shooting star. Bright and beautiful one moment and then gone in a snap." His fingers clicked together to bring home his point.

I stared at him, blinking. "Did you just call me beautiful?" My voice cracked.

He ran his hand down his face. "Jesus," he muttered and crossed to his office, slamming the door behind him.

The closed door mocked me with his non-answer, even as the rest of his rant sank in. I glanced back out the windows. We had seen the army disappear into the Hudson River and the sea serpent move out into the open waters of the Atlantic. Hadn't we?

I marched over to his office and turned the handle, swinging open the door. "Why do you think it is unsafe out there?"

He slowly turned the chair toward me. "Because I know them. They would not leave the city without dragging my dead ass off into the river, too." He crossed his arms. "I can't see all the patrols from here. Neither can you. But they are out there. Looking for the last dragon. The last beast that can ruin their plans. I know too much, and I have basically defected from their team. That makes me a traitor. You've seen what they do to those they feel are traitors." He waved at the window where the procession had passed.

"You told me not to trust you. And I'm taking that to heart."

He nodded and his gaze dropped to the floor. Without another word, he swung the chair back around to his computer screen filled with spreadsheets and went back to clicking the keyboard as he had been when I interrupted him.

I let out an exasperated sigh and turned to leave just as his printer whirred to life. Instead of exiting, I lingered.

He turned from the printer and handed me the paper. "A peace offering."

I took the sheets from him and glanced at them, shuffling through the pages. I blinked and crossed to the couch in his office and sat so I could truly digest the words and numbers he gave me. It was a breakdown of the number of armies across the globe and how many leviathans comprised each sector. There wasn't just one serpent king, either; there were dozens of them spread around the world. My mind stalled at the sheer numbers, hundreds of thousands of the beasts. I knew their numbers were massive, but at least we still outnumbered them. There were far more humans here in the United States than the total amount of monsters on the planet, even after the pandemic took out half of our population.

The only problem with the calculations on these pages was I didn't think there was enough bleach or bullets left to destroy them. Unfortunately, I didn't know the first thing about creating bleach, and without the internet, there was no way to search for the information. Libraries didn't carry much in hardcover these days, so even those resources were limited.

The next few pages were the current routes of their grid patrols and the timings of their rounds. At least their patterns were predictable, but it gave me enough heart palpitations thinking about my platoon out there on their own tours. I prayed they didn't encounter the filthy beasts because with the way they were covering the blocks, another one could flank them and take out my crew easily.

"This only increases my need to get back to my platoon." I waved the papers at him.

He nodded slowly. "As much as it pisses you off, we have to wait at least another day. I want them to think I've flown off somewhere they can't reach."

"You may be trying to save your own ass, but I'm trying to save my people." I threw the sheets onto the cushion next to me with a snarl.

"I am trying to save the human race as well, despite what you think. I know the decimation my kind caused to your weapons and factories that produced them. I can calculate the number of arms and ammunitions you have, and it is not enough."

His words echoed my assessment. I stood and crossed to the windows, staring out at the bright sky. "The longer I'm here as your prisoner, the more of my people will die."

"How did you take them out?" he asked again. This time his voice was soft.

I shook my head. Even with the military details he provided, I wasn't divulging my secret weapon until I was back with my platoon. "You haven't earned that information, yet."

"What do I need to do to gain your trust?"

I turned to him. "You have to bleed for the cause."

Dragon Tempest
Chapter 6

THE NEXT FEW HOURS were like being in a human pressure cooker. The tension between Mik and me crackled like electricity on the air. I set the stakes for earning my trust, but I wasn't sure I would ever let my guard down. I did not know whether this dragon was truly on our side or not.

Was this their way of wiping out my platoon? Have the dragon infiltrate and allow me to lead him right into our midst, only to have him cook us all alive?

I couldn't clearly see his angle. And I did not know whether what he was telling me was truth or lies.

The questions swirling in my head were maddening and I stood, crossing to his library to find something to pass the time. His bookshelves held a variety of genres, from Stephen King to Tom Clancy to J.D. Robb, along with some romance novels and even Shakespeare. An old Sidney Sheldon title caught my eye, and I pulled it down and settled into the glider.

A few chapters into the legal thriller, the scent of beef cooking wafted into the room. My mouth watered in response, and I folded the corner of the page I was on and left the book on the chair.

As soon as I cleared the door, the sizzle of meat reached my ears and I hustled to the island counter and sat with my rapt attention on the burgers on the griddle in front of Mikhail.

He slid the oversized patties onto a plate and turned off the burner, then he picked up the silverware on the counter next to the stove and headed into the living area without so much as a glance in my direction.

My jaw dropped. This was the first time he had been truly inconsiderate since he pulled me out of that dungeon of death inside Grand Central Station.

He turned his golden gaze in my direction as he took a bite of his meal, but he didn't speak. His stare seemed more of a silent challenge than anything akin to burying tensions.

I crossed my arms and leveled a glare with a derisive huff.

"I'm not your personal chef," he said. "If you want something, you are more than capable of cooking it yourself." He went back to eating.

I blinked and my mouth popped open. He just gave me full liberty in the kitchen, and I wasn't going to let that go to waste. I crossed into the galley and pulled both the freezer and refrigerator doors open. The icebox was full of meats, and the refrigerator had half a pound of hamburger, thawed, sitting on the center shelf wrapped in cellophane. The thought of a juicy cheeseburger sent me into action. I took a handful of meat from the package, forming a nice thick burger, and then plopped it into the frypan and turned on the heat. Before rifling through the refrigerator for cheese, I washed my hands and made sure to cover the remaining chuck with the wrap and put it back where I found it.

A thorough search of the refrigerator didn't uncover any cheese or buns, and I sighed. I'd just have to deal without cheese. Still, a juicy homemade burger and not one of those frozen flat patties that seemed to be the only thing left in stores sounded as delightful as a four-course meal.

I cooked the burger and slid it on one of the plates I found, grabbing a beer before I climbed onto one of the counter stools with my back to Mikhail's piercing gaze. I wasn't going to sit at the table with him.

The chair next to me scraped on the floor and his plate slammed down on the counter next to me. His form was hard to ignore, especially with heat rolling off him in waves.

I didn't dare glance his way. I wanted to enjoy my meal, not verbally spar with a damn dragon.

After a few more bites, he dumped the plate into the sink with a clang. I did sneak a glance and caught him staring at me with the creases of frustration in the area between his eyes and at the corners of his mouth. Sparks seemed to flash in his irises, which I guess was better than fire, but his aggravation was palpable on the air around him.

I refocused on the meal I cooked and continued eating, although the focused attention made it hard to enjoy. I finally slammed down my silverware and turned toward him.

"What?" I threw my hands in the air.

"Why won't you trust me?"

His soft question burned enough to set off my anger button. "Because your kind generally fucked up our existence, and you allowed those soldiers back at the station to be cooked alive. To you, we are expendable. Besides, you are keeping me here against my will." I took a cleansing breath. "And last but not least, you told me not to trust you." I stabbed my index finger into his unyielding bicep. "I don't know if you are truly on our side or if you are a plant to get information about us. War is about information. Whoever has the most wins." I focused back on my food, picking at it with my fork as I turned over everything in my head. "Were all those pictures manufactured? The sob story of your wife and kids? The numbers you so conveniently had at your fingertips?" I waved at the study. "Why the hell would I trust you after a few strategic acts of kindness?"

Each accusation darkened his eyes and his lips pressed together at the last string of questions. He did not speak at first, as if he were digesting everything I said. When he did, his voice was soft but strained. "I have not lied to you. I've shown you my sanctuary. The only place I remain safe from both the leviathans and the humans. I have put myself in a vulnerable position and at the same time, I've given you valuable information."

I wanted to heave the plate across the room. Acute frustration filled me and hung on the air, because a part of me did want to trust him. The stubborn soldier hung onto my doubt. "It is not enough. Besides, you think I'm just a weak woman who you can manipulate to do your bidding," I growled through clenched teeth.

He laughed loud enough to pull my gaze away from what was left of my burger on the plate.

"You are the furthest thing from weak." He went around into the kitchen to clean up the dishes.

My aggravation lowered to a simmer at his musical laugh, along with the compliment. "But you are trying to manipulate me." I resumed eating, even though my stomach was tight from the emotion swings.

He scrubbed the pan in the sink. "No more than you are trying to manipulate me."

"What the hell does that mean?" I was not trying to manipulate the man and for him to insinuate that just added to the burn in my stomach.

He paused his cleaning and looked up at me. "Our end goal is the same. We both want the monsters gone. But our short-term goals are vastly different. I want to keep us safe until the danger has passed so we have a reasonable chance of obtaining that end goal, while you want to run headlong into a death trap."

"Just because I want to get back to my platoon does not mean I want to run headlong into a death trap," I said around another bite of my juicy, medium-rare burger. "Besides, we do have that secret weapon you're hell-bent on getting out of me. But I can't risk my friends and family by telling you without proof that you truly are on our side. Numbers and beat routes aren't enough."

He cocked his head and raised his eyebrows in a universal skeptical scowl. "How are you going to explain me to your platoon? How do I know I'm not following you to *my* death?"

"Some of my troop members have seen you in this form during your patrol," I challenged. "Even I thought you were human." I took the last bite and pushed the plate next to his by the sink. But his questions festered inside my head like an incurable disease.

"True." He put my plate in the dishwasher after he set the clean pan in the drainer. "However, you need a viable story on how you escaped the dragons' lair. A body was dropped, saying you failed, and the human race was now doomed. So how do you explain that without compromising me?"

"How the fuck do you know that?"

"Because I wrote the damn notes pinned to all the bodies. And there are no more. No more negotiations. Their intentions have been declared. So again, how do you explain without compromising me?"

Mikhail leaned on the counter and narrowed his eyes, waiting for an answer that I didn't have. Especially considering my mind went numb with his last revelation.

"Well?"

My brain snapped back in gear. Saying he rescued me left a lot of unanswered questions. *Like, how had he gotten into their fortress unnoticed?* Dragons were more notorious for sniffing out humans than any of the creatures. *How did I get out of there before I was toasted? Why was a body dropped? What had I done that made the negotiations null, besides running?*

So many questions would come from my showing up, but I still couldn't let them think I was dead.

One of his eyebrows rose. "No viable story?"

I hated that he had already thought of this stumbling block before I did, and my mind still couldn't grasp a story that worked in any way without putting either of us in danger. "I didn't go?" I finally said.

He stood. "And seal humanity's fate to certain death? No one would buy it."

"I trashed my comms before I stepped inside."

"You'd go up in front of a firing squad."

"They wouldn't do that." I was quick to defend them, but if my commander thought I bagged out of the negotiations, he would probably court-martial me. He'd always carried animosity toward me, and this would give him the excuse to get rid of me once and for all. Which was probably why he sent me into the dragons' den in the first place. Besides, in any case, I would have to answer for the burned body.

"I had a chance to run when they torched the other prisoners?"

"What other prisoners? Every last one of them was a burned corpse dropped in Times Square. They were already dead when you were sent to negotiate."

I glared at him. "What is your viable story?"

He chuckled and shrugged. "I don't have one, which is why we are here and not in your encampment. This is my safe house. It's the place where I figure shit out. If we don't have this down solid, we have a problem. So, we can keep up this lack of trust game, or find a solution to our problem and chase those bastards back to where they belong."

Dragon Tempest
Chapter 7

AFTER MIKHAIL RETIRED FOR the night, leaving me to the comfortable couch, sleep evaded me even as he snored a room away. I glanced at the door lock again, wondering whether I could figure out the combination. Even if I could, where would I go? If I told my troops the truth, none of them would believe me, and it would put Mikhail in danger, which didn't settle well with me. I didn't trust him, but I didn't want him dead.

My brain kept turning things over. The next thought made me sit up with a gasp. *What if the leviathans already attacked my platoon? What if they are already dead?* I climbed to my feet and crossed to his door.

"Mikhail?" I said, loud enough to interrupt his snore.

He turned toward me and blinked open his eyes. For a moment, he just stared at me as if he didn't know who I was.

"What, Woods?" he said after a few blinks.

"Do you think they wiped out my platoon?"

He glanced at the darkened windows beyond me and shrugged. One look at the clock and he turned back to me. "Go to sleep."

"We could go now. It's dark out." There was no way I was getting sleep with that horrifying thought pinging around my head.

His eyes turned into bright infernos. "We are not going out there until you figure out a viable story that will not get either one of us killed. Now get out of my bedroom," he growled.

I closed the door and wandered back to the couch. My gaze kept going to the door, but I knew if I started playing around with the lock again, I'd end up with zip ties around my wrists and another night of fitful sleep. At least the couch was more comfortable than trying to sleep with your arms tied above your head.

The laundry room had a toilet and a sink, so I had facilities without crossing through the bedroom. But even with the comfort surrounding me, I could not get the thought of the leviathans attacking my friends out of my head.

And because I could not sleep, I crossed into the study and opened a document and started typing different stories of how I got away from the dragons. None of what I made up worked. I'd never be able to sell it and would end up at the bad end of the firing line.

I was not a good liar. I've never been good at fibbing, so whatever truth I could weave into the lie, the better, so I erased the prior ideas and wrote everything that had happened up to this moment.

Once I finished, I printed it off and started reading, looking for opportunities that would be realistic for an escape from the dragons' lair. With a pencil in hand, I went to town, jotting down ideas on the bottom of the paper.

If I said I never went to the meeting, I would certainly face the firing squad. What if Mikhail intercepted me and dragged me away to save me? Nope. I killed my comms before I went in. If I had been kidnapped at the doorway, they would have known about it and then Mikhail would be in front of the firing line.

What if I got away when they were torching their prisoners? How did I get away unscathed?

What if the dragon stepped out of the room long enough for me to find a hidden passage? Not realistic enough. And they would want to know how to get there and launch their own attack, especially if Mikhail had been telling the truth about the note. Besides, how did I find the passage? I would get totally tripped up on trying to remember how I found a hidden passage.

What if Mikhail rescued me through a hidden passage in that room? How did he find it? Could he show them how to get to that to launch an attack? How did he know I was there, and the dragon wasn't? Why didn't he save anyone else?

I erased everything but the second and last ideas. They stayed on the paper while the rest went to the garbage canister in my head.

I shuffled between the two. The second one put Mikhail in the hot seat, and I wasn't sure he would want that, especially considering the higher-ups would pump him for as much information as possible about the operations. And if they wanted to send people in, they would get slaughtered.

That wasn't the right option.

Which left me with the option of escape while they were preoccupied with the other prisoners.

Why wasn't I with them?

I'm a woman; they had other plans for me. I shivered, thinking about what Mikhail had said about his buddy, and I wondered whether, over the years, he truly had taken a woman or two hostage and had his way with them. The idea nauseated me. I shook my head and focused.

When did I have a chance to run?

While they were eating the crunchies. Again, I had to stanch the chill that rode my spine.

How did I get away unscathed? I couldn't have.

I leaned back in the seat and ran my hands through my hair. But I could possibly have survived in the subway tunnels. They wouldn't believe I had been in the subway tunnels for days. Not with my uniform so pristine from the washing machine.

"Damn it," I muttered and glanced down at my clean clothes.

And getting away unscathed wasn't realistic. I'd at least have gotten singed, at the very minimum. My eyes widened and my head snapped toward the main living area. I had a dragon at my disposal. I could still get singed and make this line believable. And then when I finally surfaced, Mikhail found me and nursed me back to health.

I crossed to the bedroom and swung open the door. "I've got a viable story, but it means you have to do something I'm not sure you are going to like."

He rolled over and cracked an eye open. "This better be good or I may just tie you to the post so I can get some rest," he snapped and sat up.

His exposed chest caught me off guard. Muscles flexed as he moved and the entire vision of him half naked stole my voice for a moment.

"Well?"

"You need to singe my back. Like I didn't quite outrun all of a dragon's fire."

His eyebrows arched. "You will get burned," he spouted.

As if I didn't already understand that. "Yes."

"You want me to burn you." He rubbed his face and then shook his head. "You are truly out of your mind."

"Hear me out. The story is I got away from you while you and your cohort were killing and then eating the other prisoners. I got down to the subway tunnels before a blast of dragon fire torched a good part of the passageway. I found an inset in the wall that buffered me from most of the fire, but my back got singed. I wandered the tunnels until I found an exit, and that's when you found me and took me in and put burn salve on my back and made me rest until I wasn't as bad as you found me. That's why it has taken me a couple days to get back to the barracks."

He chewed on his lower lip. "Let me sleep on it. I suggest you get some rest too, because if we decide this is the solution, you are going to need all your energy reserves. And it may mean we need more time here so you can partially heal."

I swallowed hard. "You can do something like a controlled burn, right?"

"There is no such thing as a controlled burn with dragons. If you insist on this insane path, I'll figure out a way to do it so I don't kill you. Now get some sleep." He rolled over so his back was toward me and within moments, his soft snore filled the room.

I closed the door and went to try to do as he said. Sleep found me but it was fitful and filled with images of me burning to death.

Dragon Tempest
Chapter 8

THE CLANG OF DISHES pulled me awake, and I blinked at the brightness surrounding me. Sleep crusted in the corner of my eyes and my bladder held a heaviness of a very long rest. The covers were bundled around my legs. I untangled myself and headed for the laundry room before I soiled my pants and the couch.

I wiped the crust out of my eyes as I relieved myself and then glanced at my watch. My eyes widened. It was after noon. Twenty after, to be exact. I had not slept that heavily or that long since I was a young teenager, before the world went to shit.

"Why didn't you wake me?" I asked a fully dressed Mikhail when I came out of the bathroom.

"Because you will need your strength if we decide that crazy option you put on the table is the best course of action."

"So, you have considered it?" I took a seat at the counter.

He sighed and met my gaze. "I'm not the one who has to make the decision. It is dangerous for you. You will be injured. This is not a sunburn or accidentally burning yourself on a hot pan. You do understand that, correct?"

I nodded slowly. "Yes."

He shook his head. "You are insane," he muttered under his breath, but I picked it up.

"Honestly, if I go back unscathed, I will be put in front of a firing squad for failing in the negotiations, regardless of whatever excuse we come up with. This is the only reasonable way for us to go back to my squad without putting either one of us in danger. It's a story that makes sense, and it's one we both can keep straight. Anything else I came up with would have too many holes and too much potential for our stories to vary."

"What were your other options?" He leaned back with a glass of juice in his hand.

"The other options either involved you intercepting me before I went into the negotiations, which would put you in front of a firing squad, or a secret passage from the room I was put in. Either I found it or after the dragon left me, you rescued me. But with that, they would want to know where it was and they would go on the offensive."

"The secret room was real." He raised his eyebrows.

"Yes, but that puts you in the hot seat to explain how you found it without getting caught."

He sipped his juice, mulling it over.

"But that doesn't account for all the missing time," I added.

"It's simple—we hid in the subway system for a few days, avoiding any of the patrols and the larger areas that the monsters could squeeze into." He drained his glass. "I like that option better than burning you."

"How did you find the passage? Why didn't you get anyone else out? What were you doing there? Who are you—or worse, we know who you are since you've been topside, so what the hell are you doing?" I rapid-fired questions at him. "Those are the easy questions. When the hard ones come about whether you are a sympathizer, how will you handle those? And what will you say when they want you to lead our army to that entrance?"

He bit his lip while his golden eyes locked with mine. "I would rather be the one under fire."

The hardness in his eyes made me sigh. He was trying to be a gentleman, but I did not need someone to swoop in and save me.

"I still think my solution is more realistic. I can sell that. I'm not sure if I can keep the stories straight on anything else. Besides, I washed my clothing. They would never believe we were wandering the subway system with these things so pristine." I waved at my wrinkled uniform.

His shoulders rounded and he hung his head. "For the record, I'm not thrilled about the option you seemed to be so resigned to. Especially if you aren't willing to tell me the secret to defeating the leviathans."

"It gives you incentive not to kill me," I said, and his gaze shot up to mine. A shadow passed over his eyes, and I kept the cocky smile plastered to my lips even though it wanted to slip away.

"Damn it! Don't you understand? I've never attempted this. You might die even though that is the last thing I intend." He ran a hand through his thick hair, looking every bit as exasperated as his voice sounded.

"I understand fully what is at stake. Both our lives. This is the only story that will hold water without putting either one of us at risk. Does the idea suck? Yes. But it is the only one that will pull us out from under suspicion." I took a breath to calm the escalating anger. "I'm already going to be drilled for killing my comms before I stepped inside. And, based on that note of yours pinned to the dead body dropped in Times Square, my apparent failure to negotiate effectively. This I can keep straight, and I can show them proof of being injured. Anything else will backfire. Trust me on this."

"Neither of us are long on trust." He crossed his arms.

I closed my eyes. "I'm trusting you enough not to kill me," I said softly.

"And yet you won't tell me your secret," he muttered under his breath.

"If I live through this, I am more likely to confide in you."

"You are a strange woman."

"Think you could cook me up some eggs?" I asked.

"Trauma on a full stomach?" His eyebrow arched.

Any ounce of hunger vanished with his statement. It probably was unwise to eat before I attempted to survive his dragon fire.

"So, how do we do this?"

"I have a place on one of the lower floors that I used to bring my kids to let off steam. This was our escape building in the old world, too, when things got stressful."

"Really?"

"I have a stainless-steel room surrounded by fire-retardant insulation. During their teenage years, it was a place they could go and just let all their frustrations out. It was much preferred to torching another classmate." His lip turned up on one side as his gaze became distant. When they refocused, pain flashed before he doused it and cleared his throat. "Before we go, I need you soaking wet, with the coldest water you can stand. And a wet towel over your head."

I blinked. "Won't the steam from the fabric burn me?"

He chuckled. "If it's not wet, the entire uniform will burn like that." He snapped his fingers. "This is the only way I can think of to protect you from third-degree burns."

"You don't sound so sure."

"That's because I'm not. This is risky. I will do my best not to kill you, but you will be burned. It will be worse than just a singe, but I do have access to medicine and burn protocols in this building. So, I do have what will be needed to keep you from getting an infection."

Doubts started to surface in my own mind, but I pushed them away. I would die in front of a firing line if I went back unscathed. I was certain of that. "When can we do this?"

"You know where the shower is." His jaw jutted in the direction of the bedroom.

"Oh. Now?"

"If you insist on this, yes. The sooner we do this, the sooner you'll heal, and we can meet up with your platoon."

I nodded and slid off the bench, heading toward the shower. I grabbed the towel off the rack and turned the water on warm and stepped under the spray, fully clothed, soaking both myself and the towel before I slowly dialed it to the coldest setting.

I stood under the spray until my teeth chattered. Mikhail hung by the bathroom door, waiting for me to finish. The minute I turned off the water, he stepped forward, picked me up, and then sped out of the apartment and down the stairs. Within a blink, I was put down in a corner of the room he described, facing the stainless-steel, with my back to the entrance. I still dripped cold water and my teeth still clicked as I shivered.

"Put your hands up, facing you."

I did as he said, and he draped the towel over my hands and the back of my head.

"Cover your face and ears and then remain very still."

He adjusted my hands once and then silence filled the room. One moment, I was freezing and the next, I was sweating. My wet uniform dried and heat wrapped around me. Before the heat turned into pain, a blanket covered me and strong arms held me as a hand gently patted the blanket in several places. And then I was hauled over his shoulder. The jarring movement brought the agony to life and I cried out.

"Damn it," Mikhail muttered, and the blanket was thrown off me as he gently set me facedown on my feet in the shower. He turned on the water to a low setting and dialed it to cool, not the frigid cold that I remembered. He held me steady as the coolness seeped over my form. It did nothing to calm the pain accosting me, and I was glad his arms steadied me.

What I could see of the front of my uniform carried no clue of what my back must look like. The edges of my hair that I saw were white and curled, as if the fire had stripped it of all color. I went to reach for some of it but moving pulled a moan from my chest.

The water shut off. Mikhail gently led me into the bedroom and laid me out on my stomach on the bed.

"Your bed," I whispered.

"The bed will dry. Do not move."

I turned my head in the direction of his voice just in time to see him disappear out the bedroom door. The act of moving even my head caused pain to stab the backside of my body like a thousand knives.

I marveled at how fast it had been. This was so different than when his friend torched the prisoners. They obviously felt the flame. Their screams still echoed in my ears when I closed my eyes. But today, I hadn't even felt the flames lick my skin. One moment I was damn cold, and the next I wasn't.

I'm not sure what would have happened if Mikhail hadn't had a fire blanket. Hell, if this had happened in the tunnels, I'm not sure I would have survived without help.

He stepped back into the room with an armful of ointments and medical bottles, needles, and enough gauze to cover my body three times over.

"For the record, my idea sucked," I muttered as his weight moved the mattress under me.

He cracked a smile. "Keep that sense of humor, because this is going to hurt even worse." He grabbed the garbage can and set it next to the bed before he started peeling my clothing from my body. Scissors cut the fabric at my sides. Charred fabric with regular strips of my uniform at each end dropped into the garbage, one after another. Some of the charred strips dripped with goop that I could only ascertain was part of my injuries. My stomach flopped but I bit back the bile. I didn't need to be throwing up right now and was silently relieved that I hadn't eaten yet.

"How bad is it?" I asked when I was sure my stomach wasn't going to betray me.

"You're alive," he said without answering the direct question. He just kept cutting away pieces of my clothing from my shoulders all the way to my stockinged feet, including the straps and backing of my bra and the back of my panties, both of which didn't look quite as charred as the actual shirt and military-grade pants. "I hope you weren't attached to your uniform," he said as he dropped the last piece of fabric into the garbage.

"I didn't think this through," I whispered and then began concentrating on counting breaths as the pain bit into my back like being dipped into the center of a furnace and alternately into the north Atlantic at the height of winter. Each shiver that traveled through me drew a hiss from between my teeth.

Mikhail didn't speak to agree with me. Instead, he opened a jar and spread a cooling substance on my back. The sweet scent of honey drifted around me. He kept slathering it on until he got to the back of my ankles and then he dropped an empty tub of honey into the garbage.

He moved to the side of the bed where my head rested as he wiped his hands on a clean towel. He slowly knelt and met my gaze. Worry lined his lips and eyes. He attempted a smile and that was enough to set off my alarms.

"How bad is it?" I repeated, holding his gaze.

He glanced at my back and winced. "Pretty much second-degree burns from just below your collar line to your socks. Your bra and panties gave you an extra buffer, so those areas are just red, same with where your socks were. But the rest is already blistering."

"Shit."

"At least I did get to you before the flames consumed you." He sighed. "But it is going to be a few days before you are in any kind of shape to take the hike to Midtown, even if I carried you." He rolled out strips of the gauze and started laying them gently over the honey-covered wounds. "I know that doesn't thrill you, but I can't have you overdoing it and getting an infection."

He reached over and picked up a vial. "This is all the penicillin I have left." He showed me a half-empty canister.

I didn't have the heart to tell him I was allergic to penicillin. "That won't be necessary."

He started to prepare a syringe for the antibiotic.

"Don't. That will kill me. I'm allergic to penicillin," I said as he fitted the needle into the vial.

He blinked and stared at me, his mouth popping open. And then he discarded the needle into the garbage can and recapped the bottle. "Anything else you are allergic to that I should be aware of?"

"Apparently fire."

He actually snorted a laugh and his smirk disappeared as fast as it surfaced. "Seriously, are you allergic to anything else?"

"Anything with 'cillin' in the word. Penicillin, amoxicillin. Other than that, I'm good." I toyed with telling him I was allergic to honey. But that would be too cruel, and I wasn't sure what he would have done, and I did not want the cooling substance to be rudely scraped off my back.

"Can I get you something to eat?"

Food was the last thing I wanted, especially eggs, but I needed some form of protein to help heal faster and honestly, the honey tickled my sweet tooth. He raised kids, so he had to have done something like pancakes in his lifetime. "Do you know how to make French toast?"

"Syrup or strawberries and confectionary sugar?"

For the life of me, I could not make a decision on which staple to have on my dessert-like breakfast. "All of the above."

The dimple in his cheek appeared and then he straightened up the remaining gauze and other remedies, placing all of it on the side table before he left me to wonder what the hell I was doing.

Dragon Tempest
Chapter 9

I CAN'T REMEMBER THE last time someone actually fed me. It must have been as an infant or early toddler. Mikhail sat on the edge of the bed and cut small pieces as if I were an invalid, but it was possibly the sweetest thing anyone had ever done for me. My eyes teared up enough for me to want to mutter curses under my breath, but I couldn't, not with him studying me.

"Does it hurt? I can put more honey on if you need it," he said at the first sight of a tear escaping the corner of my eye.

"No. It's fine." I sniffled. "Just keep the food coming until that plate is clear, if you don't mind." I tried my best to smile, but my emotions were not in control.

"Why are you crying?" He cut another piece.

"I have no fucking clue." I avoided his gaze. "I don't cry."

He didn't do a very good job of suppressing a smirk and fed me another bite of breakfast.

I took the next bite full of syrup and a strawberry. "This is really good." I licked my lips and sniffled as I swallowed. I glanced up at him, the movement making me wince.

"As soon as we are done eating, I'll change the bandages."

"Why are you being so kind?" I blurted before taking the next offered bite.

"Would you prefer I let you get up and make your own food and change your own bandages?"

I blinked at him and thought about what that effort would be like. "No," I finally said, but I bit off the part about actually liking this treatment. That would give him more leverage than I wanted him to have. I was still his prisoner, even though I felt more like his patient right now.

"I did the damage. It's my mess, regardless of whether it was your idea or not. So, I am taking care of you, as I rightfully should." He gave me the last bite on the plate and stood. "I also need to find you suitable clothes, since you can't very well walk through the streets at this time of year with no clothes on."

I belted out a laugh, even though it caused some pain. "I would appreciate that just as much as the care you are providing at the moment." I met his gaze and his soft smile nearly brought me back to tears.

He is a dragon, I mentally scolded myself as my insides melted.

He set the plate down and peeled back the gauze. In some places, it caused my breath to hitch and those were quickly drenched in honey before he added a clean layer of covering. When he was done, he glanced at me. "Can I get you anything else?"

"If you could help me up, I'd like to use the bathroom."

He put the plate on his bureau and pulled me to my feet. The front of my clothes remained on the bed and heat filled my cheeks, the embarrassment drowning out the protest from my back. He did not move to the front of me; instead, he kept his hands under my armpits and guided me into the bathroom, stopping in front of the toilet.

"I can get it from here," I said, even though I was unsure.

"I'll be in the bedroom. Call if you need help."

The minute his hands left, the pressure of my full weight nearly made me cry out, but I clamped my lips together and shuffled around, straddling the toilet. I slowly lowered as far as I could go without having my burns touch the seat. It was a hell of a challenge, but I was able to relieve myself without getting the bandages on my backside wet.

Straightening was another story and I nearly started to cry as I stood and shuffled to the side of the toilet, where I pushed the lever and watched the water circle around the bowl before it disappeared.

"You good now?" Mikhail asked from behind the partly closed door.

"Yeah. You wouldn't have something I could cover my front with, would you?"

A hand poked into the room, holding a deep-blue bathrobe that looked like it was made of the softest cotton. "You can slip it on backward, so you don't irritate the burn."

It took all my strength to shuffle across the room and take it from his hand. Moving to put it on took more energy, but I managed. I reached for the door and opened it to see Mikhail putting a new sheet onto the bed. The soiled bedspread and sheets sat by the door, and he looked up at me as he smoothed the fabric and folded back the sheet before he fluffed a pillow on top. He crossed and helped me back to the bed.

"You didn't need to..."

"Clean bedding will help mitigate any chance of infection."

He held the sheet up for me and held my hand while I did my best to climb onto the bed. Bending my knees pulled a groan of agony from my chest, but I made it onto my hands and knees. Lowering myself onto my stomach stung my back to the point my breathing sounded like a constant hiss.

As soon as I laid my cheek onto the soft down pillow, Mikhail put the sheet gently over me. It was enough weight to make my entire back tingle with sharp pain.

"I know it hurts, but we also need to keep your body temperature consistent."

“How do you know so much about burn care?” I whispered.

“Human wife. Dragon kids. Mistakes happened and we dealt with them.”

I gave a nod and closed my eyes. The effort of eating and using the facilities wiped me out.

“Take a couple sips of this before you sleep. Hydration is critical.”

I opened one eye and stared at a straw frighteningly close to my face. I did as he asked, taking a healthy sip and then a second, relishing the sweet sports drink he plied me with. Coolness followed it down and spread through me, calming the burn in my back. I had a moment to meet his gaze and then my eyelids drooped down, casting me into unconsciousness.

Dragon Tempest
Chapter 10

HOURS BLENDED AS MIKHAIL spoon-fed me and changed my dressings multiple times a day for what seemed like forever. When I finally was able to get up on my own and use the facilities, he seemed to back off on all the coddling.

The bright sun lit up the bedroom and I rolled off the bed, shuffling to the bathroom, where I did my business. Today, there was a very long and very soft T-shirt left on the counter. It was big and fell below my knees, but soft enough not to make me whimper as the fabric settled on my skin.

Walking across the bedroom took a little more energy. This was the farthest I had moved since the morning he set me ablaze like a human torch. Each step stretched muscles that hadn't really moved much since that day. My brain was so murky, it could have been more than a week at this point, but I wasn't sure.

He was rummaging around in the kitchen and glanced up at me. "We're going to try to shower today," he said.

"We?" My heart started at the idea, and it wasn't because I was repelled by the thought. He had seen more of me than most men had; although showering with him may have been in my fantasy dreams, it wasn't anywhere in my reality's comfort zone.

He rolled his eyes. "You need a shower. Your wounds aren't weeping any longer, so a warm shower to clean you off is on tap. If you don't think you can handle that alone, I'll help you."

"You'd like that, wouldn't you?" I narrowed my eyes. The coyness in my voice made me cringe. *Where the hell was that coming from?*

"Truthfully, no. It's not...pleasant." He chose his words carefully. "But it is necessary."

His rebuff actually sent my stomach plummeting to the ground in a freefall I didn't expect. "To ward off infection." I finished his sentence with what seemed to be his answer to everything lately.

"No. It's necessary because you smell like a diseased piece of honey."

I snorted a surprised laugh as he tilted the side of his lips in a half smile and slid a plate piled with French toast across the counter. Even though movement was still challenging, I moved to the counter as if I hadn't eaten in days. Mik's French toast was all the rage. I would run across a bed of coals for them at this point. I dug into the stack without taking a seat. Standing seemed to be easier anyway. I couldn't see sliding onto the chair with how badly the back of my thighs still hurt.

"Thank you," I said around the food.

He gave me a nod and headed toward the bedroom. The shower went on while I ate. By the time I finished my breakfast, the shower had gone off again. Mik came out a couple of minutes later with an armful of sheets, crossing to the laundry room before he returned to the kitchen. He began to clean up the dirty dishes.

"I can do that." I felt a pang of guilt at his pampering. Dragon or not, I could get used to being waited on by him for a long time. I stared at his hands under the water as he washed the dishes, mesmerized.

"Shower." He nodded toward the bedroom. "Everything you need is in there."

It wasn't a request I could deny. The thought of feeling clean won out over the nerves of having water hitting my burns.

"You are going to want to start with lukewarm water and then dial it up until you are comfortable. There is baby wash in the shower and a soft cloth. Use that, along with the baby shampoo. Nothing with harsh additives." He met my gaze. "And when you get out, softly blot. I have a nightgown in there for you as well."

"When did you get that?"

He wiped his hands on the drying cloth. "It was my wife's. She kept some things here for when we needed to get away from the grind."

"You had clothes here all this time?" I gawked. Despite not being able to handle the idea of putting pants on, the thought of clean clothing set me off.

He glared at me. "All this time that you had an issue with just a sheet being on your back?"

I lowered my gaze and heat filled my cheeks. He was right to snap back at me. "Sorry." I turned and headed into the bedroom, and took note that the bed was again made with the original comforter that he dumped my soaking wet form on. In the bathroom, he had set the bath wash and cloth on the bar on the wall of the shower and had a couple of plush towels on the bench by the shower entrance.

I stripped out of the T-shirt, wincing as the fabric scraped along my back. I stepped into the shower and stared at the controls. Trepidation swept through me, and I almost backed out of the shower.

"You can do this," I whispered to myself, and forced my hand to the knob, turning it slowly until a light drip came out of the rain showerhead above me. The water was too cool, and I dialed it warmer at a fraction at a time until the temperature seemed just right.

As slow as possible, I increased the water flow, allowing a little discomfort at the volume. But standing under it soon soothed both my mind and my back. I reached for the baby shampoo and soaped up my hair first because I dreaded the thought of swiping the baby cloth over my backside.

After I rinsed out the last of the soap from my locks, I dabbed some bath wash on the cloth and cleaned my front side as thoroughly as I could. Then, before I chickened out, I gently ran the cloth over the back of my shoulders.

That action produced tears that mingled with the water. I added more soap and continued to gently swish the cloth over my shoulders and then my lower back, butt, and legs until I shook from the exertion.

I turned the shower off and reached for the towels, first drying my front off, and wrapping my hair before I tried to blot my back and legs. All I could smell was the soft fragrance of lavender and yet my back and legs screamed as if I had ripped the scabs off and reignited my skin.

Nearly blinded by tears and agony, I crossed to stare at the nightgown. It was the lightest powder-blue silk fabric I had ever seen, and I slipped it over my head, letting the silk caress my skin. The coolness of the fabric soothed my back, and I hoped my wounds hadn't started weeping again. I did not wish to ruin this pretty garment that flowed over me and ended just above my knees. It fit as if it had been mine all along.

I felt clean, but I also felt raw, although my knees seemed to have loosened to the point that it didn't hurt quite as much. The shoulder straps of the nightgown lay where my bra straps would have rested, and although the straps were much thicker than a bra, it didn't irritate my back the way I expected.

I unwrapped my hair and ran the brush through it to get the knots out before I crossed into the bedroom. Mik's wife and I were not that different in build, and I opened both closet doors. The right side of the closet was all his clothing, from power suits to exercise clothing, to jeans and T-shirts. The left side of the closet was all women's clothing. I ran my finger over the different fabrics, settling on a pair of black jeans with a matching leather jacket toward the far end that were the exact size I wore.

A twinge shimmied up my spine. I guess I could understand why he didn't mention a closet full of clothing to me. These were his recently deceased wife's clothing, and I needed to show an iota of respect for his situation and a little gratitude for all he had done.

I stepped away from the closet, closing it softly before I opened the bedroom door. "I think I'm ready to go on that trek to Midtown," I said.

He glanced up at me and smirked. "You aren't going anywhere with that on."

I glanced down and played along. "Why not? It's certainly pretty enough."

"It's November. In New York City."

"But this feels so good against my back."

"That's because there isn't a lot of fabric on your back." He stood, crossing until he was towering over me, and then he gripped my shoulders and slowly turned me. He swept my hair to the front and leaned close enough for me to feel his breath tickle my back.

His fingers drifted over certain spots. The area where my bra had been didn't elicit a response, but when his hand went lower, over the core of my back, I winced.

"If my touch causes you to wince, anything in the closet would put you into a stressed, sobbing mess and you wouldn't make it ten feet. You aren't ready. And I'm not taking you through the city with just that on."

I jutted my chin out in defiance, but I didn't argue with him. Deep down, I knew he spoke the truth and I hated him for it.

Dragon Tempest
Chapter 11

THERE'S SOMETHING OBSCENE ABOUT tight-fitting pants and second-degree burns. After he left me to get some rest for the night, I went to the closet to see whether I could get into the jeans I had seen earlier. Although they were my size, I could not pull them up beyond my knees. Every attempt at pulling that fabric farther turned into a silent tirade at my captor.

I couldn't go through the city dressed as I was, and I couldn't put on a damn pair of clothes to make that trek.

I hated that he was right. The thing that burned the most: if it hadn't been for Mikhail, I would not be here alive and breathing and cursing a closet full of clothes.

It took another half a week before I was able to shimmy those damn pants on. And I stood, breathing hard from the effort, but it was definitely a win. Today was the day we were going to finally seek out my platoon and let them know I was alive.

"I'm ready," I said as I came out of the bedroom in the jeans and snug-fitting black T-shirt that I had eyed yesterday as I slammed the hanger with the jeans back into the closet. I balanced a leather jacket that I had coveted on my finger. I still moved slower than I wanted to, but I was able to get the clothes on without crying and moving in them wasn't complete agony.

Mikhail looked up from his book and his eyebrows rose as he took me in. He met my gaze. "Is there anything else of my wife's that you'd like to lay claim to?" he asked through tight lips.

I glanced down at the clothes and back at him, realizing that I really never asked whether I could pilfer her things. I just assumed that when he mentioned the closet, it was an open invitation. "I should have asked. I'm sorry." I started toward the bedroom.

"Don't..."

I turned back to him.

He shook his head with his eyes closed. "You don't need to apologize. I did say you could have anything in the closet..." He glanced at his hands. "It took me off guard."

When his gaze rose and met mine, I saw the grief clearly in his flaming irises.

"I'm sorry," I said softly and crossed, gingerly lowering myself onto one of the chairs. It was the first time I had put any weight on the back of my legs since our flaming adventure and it was not in the least comfortable.

He nodded and took a breath. "If we are going to go on a trek through the city, you may want to wear a pair of comfortable sweatpants. Those might end up ripping the scabs of your burns open. And that would not be good because I have a feeling where we are going, there isn't the best medical resources."

I had worn sweats occasionally since the day I took my first shower, along with the nightgown he had given me. But that was more because I didn't feel like flashing him as I read on the bed on my stomach. Even those had irritated my legs, but he had a point. Walking any distance in these pants might not be healthy, and he was right: although we had medics, we did not have the supplies he seemed to have.

"Okay."

"If there is anything else in the closet that you fancy, please put it on the bed and I'll carry it in my backpack. That way you will at least have a few outfits as I'm sure they have already divided your things up among the troops."

I blinked at him. "How would you know what we do with belongings of those who have been pronounced dead?"

He gave me a look that made me shiver. After all, he had been a spy before he had a change of heart.

I kept forgetting he truly was the enemy. "I have an odd question, considering everything that has transpired. Why did you save me?"

"I told you why." He stood and passed by me, heading to the bedroom.

"No. Not really. You said because my actions showed just how desperate we humans are and you took the opportunity to form an alliance. But you could have sought someone else outside of your lair, so why me?"

He stopped with his back to me. "I had heard several rumors about you. You are a legend within the human community and a feared adversary within the ranks of the leviathans. I'd met you before. I couldn't understand the reverence." He glanced over his shoulder. "Then you didn't follow protocol by killing your comms outside our doors. I saw that fire in you. The one that kept you defiant in the face of certain death, and I gambled. If you could defy orders to surrender, you might be able to overlook my sins and see that I could help us both in the battle against extinction. You're the only soldier I felt I could trust. I decided to bet my life on you instead of dying trying to take down monsters that I have no idea how to defeat."

"I'm betting you're regretting that choice right now."

He smiled. "On the contrary. This was probably the wisest choice I made since the pandemic hit."

I didn't know how to address his answer. Heat filled my cheeks and I forced myself to my feet, heading back into the bedroom to get into something worthy of travel instead of these tight jeans that felt as if they were cutting off my blood supply.

I grabbed a pair of clean sweatpants that were folded on the sitting chair in the corner of the bedroom before I stepped into the bathroom. I unbuttoned the pants and took a breath. Getting the fabric over my butt wasn't a problem, but the minute I hit my thighs, I winced. The fabric bunched and scraped the burns. I didn't have the reach to pull them slowly off from the bottom in the same manner I had pulled them on.

"Shit." I couldn't do this by myself like I had hoped. Not without doing damage to the healing process. "Mik?"

He stuck his head in the bathroom with an eyebrow raised.

"I can't get them off myself."

"Fine." He crossed and assessed the situation. Then he grabbed the waist of the pants and pulled them back up, smoothing out the fabric all around.

I didn't question him. What he did alleviated the sharp pains in the back of my legs.

"Stand with your legs together, but not tightly together. I need enough room for a roll of fabric to travel down."

"That sounds painful."

"It shouldn't be if I do it right. I plan on just peeling the fabric off until I get to your ankles, then I'll need you to sit on the commode and I'll get the rest without scraping the jeans on your skin." He inspected me again. "How the hell did you get these on?"

"Centimeter by centimeter, starting at my ankles."

He huffed at me and readjusted my stance before he took the top of my jeans and folded them down. Without yanking, he pushed, and the fabric rolled over on itself, creating a straight drop to my ankles. Jeans still wrapped around my lower legs, but my upper thighs were clear of fabric, and from the lack of oozing and blood on the jeans, it looked as if I was in the clear on any disruption of my burn scabs.

I was totally impressed, but I was also standing in the center of the bathroom and nowhere near the toilet. He leaned over and reached into the shower, grabbing the teak bench seat, and plunked it down behind me.

"Sit."

The order barked out of him with such authority, it surprised me enough to immediately obey. I lowered myself and gripped the edges of the bench, expecting the last of the removal might actually be a little more difficult.

"Legs straight out," he said with a softer tone. He kept his eyes on my feet now that my hoo-ha was visible.

He moved quickly and the rest of the jeans peeled right off, and he unceremoniously dumped the fully inside-out jeans on the floor behind him as he stood and met my gaze. "Stand so I can assess the damage."

Damage? "I don't feel like anything is damaged." Everything hurt, but nothing seemed to be screaming as though I had done any damage.

His glare told me I had better do as he said.

I got up and turned, fully aware that my lower half was bare. Even though he had taken care of me like a dutiful nurse over the last week and a half, something about this time made me want to shift my feet. It was the first time I felt self-conscious.

"Stay." He left the room and came back with a small jar of honey and gauze.

"But—" I started and glanced at the jeans. The darker color of some of the crumpled pants shut me up. I had not seen the center of the back of the pants when he pulled them off. Had I, I might not have been so quick to think everything was just fine.

He dabbed a little honey on the middle of both thighs and then handed me the jar. This time, he did a full wrap around each of my legs and taped the bandages instead of just laying them on me. He stood and took a quick glance at my lower back before he pulled the T-shirt back down.

"Next time you decide you want to get dressed before you are fully healed, let me pick out what you should wear. Pouring yourself into those skinny jeans undid the progress we have been working toward over the last week and a half." He snatched the honey from my hand and tossed me a pair of sweatpants as he stalked out of the room.

Dragon Tempest
Chapter 12

I OPTED NOT TO follow him into the living room. Instead, I went to the closet and started to look through his wife's clothing a little closer. Some of the clothes, like the tailored suits, were not my thing, but there were several T-shirts that were soft and probably snug like the one I currently had on.

Her pants were almost all of the skinny variety, but the only pair that I really liked were the ones with blood and puss streaked on the black fabric in the bathroom. Anything beyond that looked like formal wear. I took my stash of a whopping three shirts to the bed and folded them neatly in a pile before I fell onto my stomach across the bed.

Mikhail finally came back in the room and glanced at the meager pile of three shirts on the bed that I had amassed from the contents. He crossed to the closet and pushed the suits and the more formal attire that I had stopped at aside and pulled out a few items, tossing them onto the bed next to me.

I sat up and stared at the growing pile, especially the one dress that he actually placed in the pile that I hadn't gone far enough into the gowns to see. It was black velvet and long, with a princess neckline.

"What am I supposed to do with a dress?" I looked up at Mikhail, thinking he really did not know me at all, even with the few weeks we had been quarantined in this apartment together.

"My wife said it was the most comfortable thing she owned when the weather got cold." He reached down and slid a box toward the bed. "I think these might be your size."

I hadn't even thought to look at the shoes, but all I caught a glimpse of were pumps that were impractical for outrunning a monster.

I opened the box and blinked. In that moment, I wished to God I had met this woman because her tastes were impeccable. How did I ever miss these? Inside the shoe box were pristine designer cowboy boots with steel toes that shone against the black leather. The insides were lined with a soft fur. I glanced at the size, shivering at the accuracy. His dead wife and I had quite a bit in common where physical build was concerned.

And then he pulled out the one thing that rivaled the boots: a pair of fur-lined leather pants. These weren't skinny pants like the jeans, either. They were built for comfort and warmth. I stared at them like a child gawking at a giant lollypop.

"Pants like these kept her warm when we'd go riding up in the mountains." He let out a soft laugh as he caressed the leather. "She'd even wear them under that dress when it was really cold. With the cowboy boots." With a heavy sigh, he handed me the pants. "Both the boots and these leathers are new. She never got the chance to break them in."

I took the pants, and the leather was like soft butter under my fingers. I ran my thumb over the fur lining and sighed at the excess these represented. My parents wouldn't have been able to afford clothes like this, unless they wanted all of us to eat dirt sandwiches for months on end.

I glanced up at him. "Who are you exactly? I know you muttered something about being the heir to the dragon throne and all that shit, but this penthouse, the technology, and everything else you have just doesn't add up."

"Mikhail St. Clare."

"The tech giant?" My voice cracked. I had read about the billionaire recluse who had developed working solar shingles and everything else Mikhail professed this building utilized.

"I'm surprised you didn't recognize my wife from the pictures." He then looked at the pants still in my hands. "I'm equally as surprised that you didn't have those in your pile already."

"I, uh, I didn't even know they were back there. I stopped at the dresses, assuming the rest of the closet was more formal wear and I have zero need for anything formal." At least my mouth still worked, but the newest information he just dropped on me made me dizzy from the ramifications.

His brow creased. "You really did not know who I am?"

I shook my head.

"Does it make a difference?"

"Difference?"

"In trusting me," he said.

He just dropped a bomb on me. Knowing he walked among us for centuries and chose to align with the monsters still burned. The way he had cared for me over the last couple of weeks softened me some, but I wasn't sure whether he did it just to find out my secret, or whether he truly was on our side. But him being a billionaire tech giant had no impact on my reservations at all. "No, it has no impact whatsoever."

Mikhail took a breath and turned back to the closet, studying the contents once more. "I'm sorry I got so short with you earlier," he said with his back to me before he moved to his side and started making a small pile for himself as well.

"It's okay. I didn't know putting on the pants would do damage."

He just nodded as he finished his packing routine. He stuffed in an unopened jar of honey and some bandages, and put his hand out for the pants I still held. I handed them to him, and they went in the bag along with the rest of the clothing he had deemed worthy, including the dress. He glanced at the boots in the box at my feet. "Do you want to wear those or the boots you had on when you got here?"

I looked down at the boots, debating. "Do you have any socks?"

He crossed to the bureau and pulled out a pair, tossing them to me, before adding some to the backpack.

I put on the socks, making sure to fold the tops down so they didn't scrape against the healing burns, and then slid the boots on and stood. It was like stepping on a cloud. I walked across the room to get an idea whether my feet were snug enough not to slip, because all I needed were blisters on my feet to go with the healing burns on my body. Nothing scraped or shifted. These boots were the most comfortable things I had ever had on my feet, and I had some damn comfortable slippers growing up.

"I think these will be fine, if you don't mind," I said. "Can we tie my other pair to the backpack?"

"Sure." He left to retrieve the boots from the living area where I had set them the night before I came up with the idiotic idea of having him burn me. He tied them to one of the straps and gave me a nod. "I need to grab some food for the road before we go."

I followed him out to the central area, where he put down the backpack and went into the kitchen and pulled out another bag with clips on the sides. When he headed toward the front door, I cocked my head.

"Where are you going?"

He glanced over his shoulder. "I'll be back."

My face must have shown some level of the sudden swell of panic that accosted me, turning my face and hands cold, as if they had been dipped into vats of ice water.

"I'm not leaving the building," he added. "My food reserves are here."

A steel room for fire control, now food reserves? Man, I'd like to search each floor to see what else he had stowed away in this metal can, but climbing the stairs down did not seem like a happy endeavor considering my thighs were already screaming under the bandages.

He disappeared and the door closed behind him. That sense of claustrophobia kicked in. What if something happened to him? I'd be stuck trying to figure out his passcode on the door and truly, with the number of keys his fingerprints were on, that could take days. Although I had an unlimited supply of water, food in the apartment was a finite resource.

I crossed to the window, trying to get my unease under control, but the view did not help my mood. Leviathans were visibly patrolling the immediate area, slipping behind the taller buildings on their patrol, but I caught a few as they passed the lower buildings or through some of the demolished buildings. Although they weren't as big as the fabled Godzilla who towered over the tallest buildings in Japan, they did tower over most two-story homes in the suburbs and could squash single-story buildings under their muscled reptilian forms. What they did to humans was much like the T-Rex in *Jurassic Park*, except they had full use of their appendages. They did not suffer from tiny T-Rex arms and knew how to use their deadly claws.

I wondered whether their presence in Midtown was the same as what I was seeing here and if it was, human death was going to be rampant in the city.

Now was not the time to keep my secret. Not if we had any hope to cross the city. I did not want to go out into those streets without protection. Without a viable weapon, we wouldn't even make it to the subway down by the bridge. I glanced at the laundry room. With everything Mikhail had here, he had to have bleach. I crossed into the small utility room. While the laundry detergent and dryer sheets were on a small shelf above the washer and dryer, I headed for the small closet near the commode.

I swung the door open and scanned the shelves. Relief washed through me at the almost industrial-size bottle of bleach on the floor and solidified in my bones when I picked it up. I wasn't even sure it had been opened yet. I sighed and took a deep breath, looking at the other spray bottles lining the shelves. I tested all the stream sprays. Once I determined which bottle would give me the maximum distance, I emptied the contents in the sink and rinsed it out, filling the container with water. I cleaned out the spray nozzle as well, pumping until only water came out.

I emptied the water and then dumped the bleach into the bottle, filling it to the brim before I screwed on the spray top. I sprayed until I was sure only non-diluted bleach was coming out and then locked the nozzle. When I turned, I startled enough to almost drop my weaponized spray bottle.

Mikhail stood in the doorway, staring at me. His gaze jumped to the open container of bleach. "What are you doing?"

I opened my mouth and then closed it with a sigh. "You wouldn't have a super soaker, would you?"

His eyebrows arched and he gave me a look as if I had truly lost my mind. "A water gun?"

"Yes. You had kids. Do you have one or two lying around this building?" He seemed to have everything else, so it was worth a shot.

"No. Why?"

Damn it. I glanced down at my spray bottle and then out the window at the leviathans in the distance. "Do you have a regular gun?"

He shook his head. "Dragon. Remember?" He pointed to his chest as if I were daft. "Again, why?"

"What about that rifle you always had slung over your shoulder while you were patrolling?"

"That's not loaded. I've never had any shells for it." He still had that quizzical look etched into his face, even with the reddening of his cheeks.

I turned away from him, aggravated. Although he had not yet bled for the cause, he did an awful lot for me the past couple of weeks. Plus, I did not want to be in the streets with those things and caught without any sort of defense. I capped the rest of the bleach bottle and shoved it at him. "Then you may need to use that fire of yours if we encounter them."

His eyebrows knit together, and he looked from the bleach bottle in his hands to the spray bottle in mine.

"If I can't shoot them, you have to burn them. *This* is my secret weapon. They are patrolling. If they find us, we need a way to defend ourselves." I shook my bottle. "This is the leviathans' weakness."

"Bleach?" His voice cracked with a bark of a laugh.

"Yes. It breaks down whatever shell is protecting them, and then all it takes is a bullet to the brain. Or in our case, dragon fire."

He blinked. Then his gaze dropped to my spray bottle and returned to mine with narrowed suspicion. "Really?" He crossed his arms.

"Yes. I stumbled on it when I was washing my clothes in a tub by the river. I was caught off guard and threw a bucket full of bleach in the bastard's face. It was the first time I'd ever seen one writhing in pain and I took the opportunity to plant a bullet between its eyes. I was surprised when it toppled over. But there is a finite supply of bleach since the pandemic." I shrugged. "And a finite number of bullets. So, you see our predicament."

He met my gaze and slowly nodded. His head dipped in a sign of respect. When he raised his head, his eyes blazed in a way that made me swallow hard. A viciousness surfaced in those flames in his irises, turning them almost blue before it faded.

When he nodded toward the front door, I hesitated.

"Ready?" he asked with a gruff voice.

I wasn't sure after that flash in his gaze. I didn't think he would torch his home, but outside this apartment, if he chose to end me, all he had to do was take a big breath and incinerate me into oblivion.

Dragon Tempest
Chapter 13

AFTER MIKHAIL PUT THE backpack on and latched the bottle of bleach to one of the heavy-duty clips on the pack, he handed me the leather jacket I had brought out earlier. The moment I zipped it up, he hauled me over his shoulder and took off down the stairs in a flash.

He set me on my feet just inside the front door while I caught my breath. I took the opportunity to open the nozzle on the spray bottle to the stream setting. I tested it out, spraying a stream that hit Mikhail's jean-clad legs.

He glanced down at the thin line spreading over his pants and sent a glare at me. "You had to ruin the last pair of good jeans I own?"

I met his irritated gaze with a smirk and rolled my eyes. "God forbid I ruin your jeans. I was just making sure this works." I turned toward the door, away from the growing inferno in his eyes. "Ready?"

"No. The grid hasn't been completed yet, and if we go out now, heading toward Midtown, we will run into at least one, probably more." He stepped by my side and glanced at his watch. "We only have to wait a few more minutes."

I was just about to open my mouth to argue when a foot large enough to squash me appeared on the street outside the building's door. As it stomped by, I glanced up at Mikhail.

His lips moved as he counted down the seconds after the feet passed by. He nodded and met my gaze. "Time to go."

He pushed open the door and stepped out, holding the glass open for me before he closed it and punched in a code on a hidden keypad in the wall. The keypad recessed and a cover slid down.

The minute the door closed, I stared at the holograph emblazoned on the glass, showing me a demolished first floor that was not anything like the lobby we just left. I glanced up and what I could see of the building from sidewalk level gave the impression that the building was indeed not in live-able condition. It looked like broken windows and charred walls. I glanced at Mik with wide eyes.

He put his finger to his lip to shush me and took my arm, leading me the opposite way from where the leviathan had gone. I glanced over my shoulder when we were a few blocks away and I could not tell the building we had been in from the twisted, broken buildings surrounding it.

My appreciation for the tech genius next to me grew and then was immediately squashed when he manhandled me into a small side alley where there was little maneuverability. He covered my mouth and put his finger to his lips as he shimmied in the tight space, pushing me farther in. All I could smell was bleach. I looked down as he poured some of the canister on the ground, filling the space with enough to make my nostrils burn and my eyes bleed tears. He capped it before I could say anything and moved me farther into the ever-tightening crevasse.

The sound of the clip securing the bottle to the side of the backpack seemed to echo in the small space.

"Mik?" I whispered.

He shook his head and pushed me back another couple of steps into a corner where the two buildings met, towering over me when there wasn't anywhere else to go. Shadows grew darker and I looked up at the crack above us.

I realized Mikhail was blocking me from being seen but at the same time exposing himself or at least the backpack, if it could be made out in these shadows. It was black, so hopefully it blended in.

The leviathan sniffed the top of the crevice we were in and its nose crinkled as it recoiled. A massive sneeze rained leviathan snot down on us, and I nearly vomited at the stench of it. Although that beast couldn't fit into this small space, it certainly could knock the building down on top of us. It sniffed again but not as close to the opening as before, and then roared in aggravation.

My heart dropped.

Then it moved on, stomping away with extra force, like a child after being grounded and sent to their room.

Mikhail sagged against the wall and glanced at me. He leaned close. "Just a couple more blocks to the subway," he whispered in my ear, so low that I almost didn't make out what he said. He put his finger to my lips, shushing me without words.

We made our way back into the street and again, he took a grip on my wrist, dragging me along. I wasn't going as fast as he wanted and he turned, hauling me over his shoulder.

I closed my mouth on an argument when I looked up and, in the distance, I saw the leviathan who had passed us still sniffing alleys. I wasn't in any condition to run and that's exactly what we needed to do. We needed to run fast enough to break land speed records.

Mikhail turned on the speed and we were at the subway entrance in a flash, and he jumped over the railing, falling to the landing a floor below the asphalt. He kept going until we were in the subway tunnel itself and far enough away from where we entered to slow down.

When he set me down, I stumbled, and he caught me. My hand landed square over his heart and it hammered against my palm. I looked up in the darkened tunnel at his glowing eyes. He was even out of breath, but I wasn't sure whether it was from the sprint, the close call, or me in such close proximity to him.

"That was too close," he whispered and put his hand over mine, taking hold of my wrist before leading me down the tracks.

"You poured the bleach on the ground to cover our smell?"

"While it was a waste, it was necessary." His voice rasped in the darkness as he guided me at a pace I could keep up with.

The click of a hammer echoed against the walls, and then another, and another, and we halted. Bright lights flooded the cavern, making us both put our hands up to block the glare.

"Who are you and what are you doing in the tunnels?" a deep voice demanded.

It was a voice I recognized from one of the other platoons in the area. "Benny?" I asked.

A couple of lights lowered, as if emitting the name was like uttering a magic password.

"Woods?" Benny questioned, as if he did not believe what he was seeing.

Mikhail let go of my wrist, and I stepped forward.

"You mind lowering the blinders?" I asked, still shielding my eyes from the lights.

"You're dead," he said.

The lights went from my face, down the leather jacket, to the large sweats and sleek cowgirl boots, remaining on the tracks this time.

"Almost, but Mik here found me and nursed me back to traveling health." I hooked my thumb at Mik behind me.

"They dropped a body."

I inhaled with a nod. "They dropped a lot of bodies that weren't our negotiators."

"What the hell you muttering on about?" he snapped. The gun raised a fraction in my direction.

"They didn't kill those we sent. At least not at the time we sent them. I got the unpleasant entertainment of watching the dragons torch them and then argue over who was going to get a crunchy snack." I shuddered visibly. "They were preoccupied, and I took the opportunity to slip away. I thought I made it without notice, but as soon as I got just beyond the platform, dragon fire filled the subway tunnel. Luckily, I got into one of those little alcoves." I swallowed, trying to find the right words to spin the story the way I wanted to.

"I found her crawling on the tracks the next morning, near Penn Station. I took her back to one of the buildings down near city hall that I've scouted that isn't too badly destroyed, found a clean area, and set up camp to get her into travel condition," Mikhail said.

I turned and lifted my jacket and shirt so they could see the damage.

The lights all lowered.

"I would have come sooner, but..." I turned back to the group. "I wasn't capable enough until today. I can't move fast."

"How did you treat that?" Benny asked from behind the lights, directing the question at Mikhail.

"Honey, and kept it covered and as clean as possible."

Benny's dark features came into view as he stepped close with his flashlight illuminating the ground. His narrow-eyed glare made it clear he wasn't buying the Boy Scout routine. "Did he hurt you?" he asked me, swinging his gaze to me.

Benny always seemed overprotective of me any time I encountered him and it'd only gotten worse since his sister died from a direct hit with dragon fire. His arm still sported the burns of carrying her dead carcass away from the battle.

"No. And he was kind enough to share some of his wife's clothing." I waved at my mismatched outfit.

"Where's your wife?" Benny asked, his voice still laced with suspicion.

"The monsters killed her," Mikhail said in a voice that seethed with hatred for the leviathans. He hadn't even used that kind of venom when he told me the fate of his family. His jaw jumped as he clenched it and pressed his lips together.

Benny crossed his arms and studied Mikhail. "And you just happened to have clothes that look like they fit Woods here."

"Benny—" I started to interrupt him, but he put his hand up to silence me. He was a superior officer and rather than argue, I'd let Mikhail answer. Otherwise, the guns would be leveled again, and they'd force us back to their barracks and I would not get to my platoon for days while they sorted this out.

Mikhail straightened his back. "Do you have any idea who I am?" he nearly snarled.

Benny's flashlight moved back to Mikhail's face, illuminating Mik's eyes. They nearly glowed in the brightness. When the light lowered, Benny said, "No idea."

Mikhail wiped his face. "I'm Mikhail St. Clare."

Benny stared at him as if that name should mean something. And then his eyes slowly widened. "Like in St. Clare Institute."

Mikhail's lips twitched into a half smile and he nodded. I knew he was a tech genius. I just didn't connect the dots as to everything that fell under his umbrella. St. Clare Institute was a renowned school that committed to educate every child in the New York City region from kindergarten through college. He dumped millions into ensuring underprivileged children had a fair shake before the pandemic.

"Yes," Mikhail answered. "Are you familiar with the institute?" His voice softened in a way that lessened the confrontational stance.

Benny nodded. "I had a scholarship lined up for college before the shit hit the fan."

"Then you probably have seen pictures of my wife and me together." He kept fishing for how much Benny knew about him and when he received a nod, he continued. "Woods is about the same height and build as Anna was, and I never got rid of the things Anna made me pack when we left our home."

"I met your wife. She was a nice lady." Benny's demeanor became more conversational and less overbearing. "Where's the rest of your family?"

Mikhail wiped his face. "They were with Anna. Those monsters killed everyone I cared about."

Benny grunted acknowledgment of his loss. "We all have the same sad story. What are you going to do about it?"

"Build bombs full of bleach and shrapnel and launch them at the entire army of leviathans."

My gaze swiveled from Benny to Mikhail, and my mouth popped open. *In this small frame of time, he devised that plan?* I needed to pick his brain a little on that idea.

Benny's eyebrows rose, as did the rest of the group that I could see in the dimness beyond us. "Well, in that case, I think we can clear a path for you to get to it. I assume you're headed toward the—"

"Yes." I interrupted. I hadn't quite divulged the exact location of my platoon to Mikhail, and I didn't want Benny to let the location slip. "I need to let my platoon know I'm alive."

"Unless you'd like to come on over to our platoon. I'm sure our commanding officer wouldn't mind. I think we can all get behind your idea." He smiled.

"Thanks, but I've got to get home before I trade up." I winked at Benny and he gave me a nod.

"We'll make sure you get there." He turned and signaled for everyone to follow.

They headed out at a jog that I could not keep up with, not with my back and legs screaming at me as though I had betrayed them with movement.

Mikhail took my wrist again as he led me through the dark like a father would lead a child. It was odd, but I was thankful, because I couldn't see what was in front of me now that the ones with flashlights had gotten so far ahead of us that they were only a warm glow in the distance.

I think if Mikhail could have put his arm around my waist to make sure I was surefooted instead, he would have. But that would have left me wincing at the pressure on my wounds.

Dragon Tempest
Chapter 14

"THANK YOU FOR FILLING in the gaps," I said softly as we kept our slower pace. The rest of the squad had gone far enough so their glow was faint, but still visible. I was glad that they didn't hang around us so Mikhail and I could talk freely.

He grunted acknowledgment and kept walking at my slow pace.

"What's eating you?" I asked, barely making out his profile in the dark tunnel. His brow was a mask of wrinkled concentration, like his mind was going at an inhuman pace.

"I'm building the blueprints in my head." His voice was soft, like if he spoke too loud, what he was crafting in his head would shatter.

I had no idea what he meant. *Blueprints?* "For?"

"The bomb and the delivery mechanism." He glanced at me as if I were short a deck.

"You were serious?" His mention of a bomb had been delivered with such bravado that I thought he was pulling their legs. I didn't think he was truly serious. Especially considering it hadn't been more than an hour since he found out what compromised the monsters.

He glanced at me, and his eyes flashed for a moment.

He was serious as it gets. "How are you going to wipe them out? Bleach only compromises their shell."

"Shrapnel in the bomb followed by my fire."

That was an ingenious idea—with one exception. "An explosion may compromise the effectiveness of the bleach."

"Not if it's done right. We need to create this bomb in layers. The innermost layer is the explosive. Surrounding the explosive is our sharps. Nails, screws, knife blades—anything that will puncture. And all that shrapnel will be floating in bleach."

I slowed to a stop, meeting his gaze as hope flared inside me. I don't think any of us thought of something so effective. I mean, we did think of bombs, but after seeing the leviathans walk through a wall of grenades, we shelved that idea.

"How would you detonate?" Remote detonation wasn't available without the use of cell phones to send the signal, and radio signals were risky.

He started to walk again, tugging me gently along. "Walkie talkies. You can send a signal pretty far with the military-grade ones. We'd just have to make sure the frequency is not the same as the ones you use for your comms. The more pressing issue is delivery method. The detonation has to be at or above head level for maximum impact."

I followed along, digesting his thought process. How easily he seemed to formulate a way to do what we all wanted to but didn't have the technical know-how or the supplies to pull it off.

He drew up sharply, and yanked me toward the far wall, pulling me up on the side platform and into a small alcove. "Spray some bleach on the ground," he whispered with an urgency that bypassed my questions.

I didn't hesitate. I twisted the nozzle of my spray bottle and doused the floor around us just before the screams reached my ears. I froze, with my heart slamming in my chest. Leviathans had never breached the tunnels before. They were too damn big. And yet, I could not fathom what kind of monster could create such terrifying screams.

Mikhail shoved me into the alcove and stood with his back to me. The backpack pressed me into the wall, enough so I had to clench my teeth against a cry of pain. The rough cement seemed to dig into my burns like a set of sharp claws.

He reached back and stripped me of the bottle, and I did not fight him. The tunnel here seemed to be larger than the normal tunnels. The clacking of claws on the rails made me shiver.

"Motherfuckers," he whispered and raised his arm.

The smell of bleach filled the area, along with the cries of whatever Mikhail was aiming at. Based on the screams, it had to be leviathans. But how did they fit into the tunnels?

Mikhail's aim must have been impeccable, because he took a deep breath and sent a streak of blue flame into the tunnel. I caught sight of the miniature leviathans just before they burst into fully engulfed flame. I had never seen a leviathan as small as a large grizzly. Normally they were two to three times the size of the stuffed wooly mammoth in the museum.

The tunnels echoed with their death cries as they collapsed on the ground, succumbing to Mikhail's fire. Before the flames dissipated, Mikhail turned and hauled me over his shoulder. He headed in the same direction the small unit had gone before they were slaughtered. When the rails forked, instead of taking the left fork that would have led us by the dead and back to my platoon, he took the right arm, circumventing Broadway and heading toward what used to be the more upscale East Side of Manhattan.

Which took us closer to Grand Central than I really wanted to be.

When we were far enough away from the dead leviathans, he stopped and set me down on my feet, placing the spray bottle into my hand in the darkness.

"They sent their young into the tunnels," he snarled and then the clang of metal against metal echoed. I wondered how many of those things were down here with us and whether these chambers would end up being our tomb.

"We need to get to my platoon."

Fire flared and Mikhail held his hand out, with flames dancing across his palm. "If your platoon was located in these tunnels..." His eyes held all the horror of his unsaid statement.

Thankfully, we were not holed up in the subway system. We were stationed in what was left of the Museum of Natural History and points north and west. Some of us were as far as the western shore, just for the distance from Grand Central. That's where I stumbled upon my secret weapon while doing laundry by the river.

Other platoons were stationed near Times Square in the theater district. There were many lower buildings among the rubble of the towers that had not been fully destroyed by the beasts.

We did use the subway for traveling between squads. It was better than being caught on the surface. And the beasts must have gotten wise to the fact we were using it as an underground highway. A few of the tracks had been crushed by the leviathans on the surface, some from just their sheer weight on the roads above and some by angry leviathans that had gotten a whiff of our scents wafting up from the sewer grates on the sidewalks.

I shivered. "My platoon is not stationed underground. There was too much risk of compromise if they found our exact location."

"Well, the Museum of Natural History isn't exactly a inconspicuous location, either, and it's not that far from a subway entrance."

I blinked and looked at him. My mouth popped open. "You know where we are located?" And here I was trying to keep the location a secret when he knew all along.

He nodded. "I know where all the human armies are."

"Then why would you drop the bodies in Times Square?" All the bodies of what we thought were soldiers who we had sent were dropped in Times Square over the past few months.

We always got word of the charred body falling from the sky, usually with a new, more heinous note nailed in what was left of them. It was never pretty. And the demands and threats were getting worse by the drop, and now I knew why. They never had the intention of letting us surrender. Mikhail had said my note had already been written even before I arrived at Grand Central to negotiate. My note declared war as the penalty of my disobedience.

"I have lived among your kind for thousands of years. I have walked among you and witnessed your greatest achievements. I have also seen the hatred that has been bred in your hearts over the last half-century, to the point it wasn't as hard as it should have been to destroy your ability to fight back. Even with my wife and kids as their control chips, I still remembered the fighting spirit and how you band together when the world falls apart. I do not want to wipe you from existence the way they do."

"And yet you wanted us as slaves," I snapped at him.

"A slave that is treated with respect still has a life worth living. A slave has a chance at love and procreating and continuing the species. I sold the concept to the serpent king that we need the fruits of human labor. We need shelters built just as you do, and if the serpent king had any hope of ruling the world, he would need to rely on the ingenuity of the human race because God knows the leviathans don't have the skills."

My blood started to boil with every word that dropped from his mouth. "So, you are the one who sold us into slavery? You are the one who insisted we take a knee?"

"Would you have preferred extinction?" he growled as he leaned closer. "Because that was what I was fighting against. They wanted to rid the Earth of the stain that is the human race." The words spit like venom from between his lips. "And I still did not win the argument. They had no intention of following through. As I found out with the series of notes they insisted I scribe for them."

I recoiled from him. "And yet you killed us like we were the main course at a monster barbeque."

"I thought they would honor their deal and let my family live. So, yes. I killed when I had no other choice, just like back there. When there is no other way, it is a matter of survival." He pointed back toward the roasted baby leviathans and his eyes blazed in the darkness. "And now I am planning a mass murder to save humanity. So, leave the judgmental bullshit somewhere else."

I stepped closer, straightening my back in defiance to his growing anger. "Killing to survive isn't murder."

"Preplanned assault with intent to kill for the sheer sake of wiping a species out *is* murder," he replied. "But I'm willing to cross that line, because I know their game plan. And their game plan is the same. They don't give a damn about humans surviving their culling. All they care about is having enough to eat to sustain life, and they are intelligent."

"Smarter than dragons?"

His eyes narrowed. "Playing to my vanities, are we?" He took a step back as if my words defused the growing inferno inside him.

I cocked a half smile at him and shrugged. "Well, are they?"

"They are not smarter than I am."

I glanced back in the direction of the dead leviathans. "Do they know you travel the subway system?"

He shook his head.

"Well, they will now. There is no explaining charred bodies." I sighed.

"The army doesn't have flamethrowers anymore?"

"If we were a military-grade army, yes. But we are just citizens who trained to defend our country. We have some military people in our ranks, but your kind saw to it that all military installations were destroyed. So, no. We do not have flamethrowers, or assault weapons, or anything larger than shotguns and handguns." My hands found my hips, matching my current attitude-laced words.

He stepped back, giving me room to breathe as his demeanor calmed. "I thought you were armed..." he started and stopped, shaking his head. "It doesn't matter. We have something that can be weaponized. I just have to work on the how." He met my gaze.

"Fine. Can you take me to my platoon?" I pointed back the way we came.

"I am, but not that way. I don't want them to be able to track us, because if we walk through that mess and the blood of those they killed farther down the tunnel, they will be able to find us. As of right now, we have bleach on our shoes. They won't follow that smell, and as long as we periodically spray our boots, we will be relatively safe." He didn't sound so sure.

I nodded slowly as his words sunk in. "But this will take us through Grand Central."

"I know. It's risky, but I think that will be the last place they look for me. Besides, I'm keeping us in the deeper tracks, and I'll carry you through in case I have to turn on the speed. You just man that spray, because if there are more of those things down here, your life will depend on how good a shot you are." He pointed at the bottle in my hand.

"Fine." I sighed, even though I was not comfortable with this. *What if he was leading me back into the lion's den now that he knew my secret?*

Dragon Tempest
Chapter 15

MIKHAIL RAN THROUGH THE dark. The speed made me dizzy but then he skidded to a stop as Grand Central Station came into view. His breath caught and he slowly maneuvered off the tracks, careful not to step on any crushed tiles littering the floor. I didn't dare speak. I just held the spray bottle at the ready as we passed by a ramp that let light down onto the platform.

Instead of dropping back into the black of the subway tracks, Mikhail headed toward a door in the wall at the far end of the platform. Before I could say anything, he had us inside and me sitting on the ground, away from the door. The darkness swallowed us and a soft scrape on the floor set my heart on overdrive until Mikhail sparked a small flame from his finger.

My eyes nearly pulsed in my head. We were in a stock room full of shelves of cleaning supplies. My heart jumped at the view of the back wall. At least a hundred bottles of bleach lined the shelves.

Mikhail held up his wrist, nodding toward his watch. "Take the watch," he whispered as softly as possible.

I peeled my eyes away from the obscene display of leviathan killer products, and looked at Mikhail's watch before I met his gaze. "Why?"

"You can see the hands in the dark and if you press the button on the side, it has a small flashlight."

I still didn't understand why he wanted me to have his watch, but I took it anyway. Maybe he thought I needed something to focus on when we were in the pitch-black tunnels, especially after a day drenched in darkness and death.

"If I'm not back by the time the minute hand passes the hour, then grab what you can and go."

My brain stalled. *"If I'm not back"? Where the hell did he think he was going?* "Wait. What?" I grabbed his arm as he moved away.

"There is something I need to get before we leave, and I need to find a cart of some sort so we can transport that out of here." He pointed at the wall. "Because we only have one shot at this."

My gaze moved from his to the wall. The sheer number of containers made my mind reel at the possibilities. Of course, it was not enough to wipe out the army of leviathans, but it would do a significant amount of damage.

We needed something to carry it in because neither of us could hold all that in our arms and have a prayer of making it ten feet, never mind a half mile or more. I glanced back at Mikhail.

"Okay," I said quietly, but I was not thrilled to be alone and so near the place I rightly should have died.

He tapped the watch. "I'm serious. If I am not back, something went horribly wrong, and you need to leave. Understand?"

I swallowed and nodded, gripping the watch tighter.

He unzipped the food pouch and handed me an energy drink. It wasn't going to hydrate me, but at least it would give me some zip if I had to make the trek across the city on my own.

"If I'm not back, dump what you don't want out of the backpack and take what you can carry." He took the spray bottle and sprayed a patch near the base of the door before setting it down within my reach. "That will drown out your scent." Then he took the already opened bottle of bleach attached to the backpack and met my gaze, waiting for me to acknowledge his words.

The thought of strapping the backpack on my burns didn't settle well, but I would do it if I had to. "Fine. If you're not back by the top of the hour, I'll grab what I can and make a break for it." I didn't have the heart to add that on my own, in my current condition, it was as good as a death sentence.

The flame on his fingers disappeared. I didn't even hear the door. It took my eyes a moment to adjust to the dark. But I was finally able to make out the hands on the watch I gripped. I stared at the four single diamonds and bit my lip. If I remembered how to read a clock with hands, I had a little less than a half hour before I needed to go to his plan B.

I cracked open the drink and chugged a good part of it down. The coolness drenched my throat, soothing the parch. I sighed, recapping the bottle. I didn't want to drink too much without a bathroom or outhouse at my disposal. The inconvenience of being a woman burned from time to time. At least a man could discreetly stand and void. But I had to peel off clothing and cop a squat. I shook my head and slid the bottle into one of the mesh pouches on the backpack before gender differences truly turned to a disgusting mini-mind rant.

I refrained from turning on the flashlight feature, using only the little green lines to keep me company in the blackened room. Time moved slower than I remembered. Each minute resulted in the smallest of movement on the watch, but it was movement toward the unthinkable. The closer to the cutoff time, the more my heart pounded in my chest. Losing Mikhail meant we were doomed.

No one on my team would have the scientific sense to make a bleach bomb big enough or effective enough to take out a majority of the leviathan horde. The mounting panic flushed hot, making my back burn uncomfortably under the fabric of the shirt. I shifted and the watch ticked off another minute.

I wanted to get up and pace, but I didn't dare. My boot-clad feet would echo on this floor and draw whatever monsters were within hearing range right to this storage room. So, instead of pacing, I decided to gnaw on my fingernails. It was an awful habit of mine when I was nervous, but I never could quite kick it. Even in the days of fancy manicures, my nails looked as if they'd been chewed up by a woodchipper.

As the minute hand got closer to the get-out-of-here mandate, I had to get to my feet and move, if only to try to stretch out the tight skin on my legs and back. I flipped the flashlight on, and a dull light filled the room enough to create shadows. I made sure I aimed it toward the wall of bleach and not toward the door for fear that if light bled out into the concourse, the monsters would come and any hope for humanity would die with me.

Of course, there was no guarantee that if he didn't come back, I would be able to get all the way to my platoon, either. I glanced at the clock hands and swallowed hard as the minute hand landed straight up. As much as I wanted to wait a few more minutes, it was time I did not have. The hour hand on the watch hit the move mark. I needed to get physically and mentally prepared to make a run for it because he was not back yet.

His last words echoed in my mind. *Something went horribly wrong.*

A sense of loss engulfed me like a tsunami hitting a crowded shoreline. Devastation crashed into me, making my muscles weak with it. I could hardly put one foot in front of the other, but I forced myself to remain standing. If I crumbled into a sobbing mess on the floor, my chances at survival fell to zero. This sensation of emptiness inside me was not warranted. I only had known him a short time and most of it was filled with a tension so thick I nearly gagged on it.

I shook myself out of the momentary paralysis and crossed to the shelves, taking two of the heavy bottles in each hand as burning tears stained the back of my throat. I straightened my back against the emotional blow.

Mikhail was not back, and time had run out.

I sniffled and wiped my nose on the back of my coat sleeve, irritated at my reaction. It felt as if I had lost one of my squad, my family, and not a walking death machine.

How the hell could I be this emotional over a dragon?

Dragon Tempest
Chapter 16

YOU WOULD THINK REARRANGING a backpack to make room for bleach would be easy, but it wasn't. Every item of Mikhail's that I drew out created a web of feelings I did not anticipate. Even folding the clothes neatly and putting them in a stack on the shelving as though he might make it back and be appreciative that I didn't just toss them in a corner carelessly caused a reaction. The entire ordeal took much more time than I expected. When I finally had the pack brimming with bleach bottles, I secured it tight enough so nothing would inadvertently slip out if I had to sprint from certain death.

After closing the backpack, I attempted to haul it onto my back.

Brutal pain ripped through my muscles. The pressure of the pack tore at my more tender burn areas around my shoulder blades. I pressed my lips against the cry that wanted to escape, closed my eyes, and braced my knees from buckling. I took a step toward the door and couldn't hold my weight. I went down on one knee and the thud on the floor made me freeze despite the agony in my knee.

The door blasted open, and I could not get my hands up to defend against whatever entered. The backpack was nearly ripped off my arms and then a strong pair of hands gripped my shoulders, pulling me to my feet.

Bright citrine-colored eyes shined down at me. "What are you doing?"

I blinked up at the familiar eyes filled with such aggravation that it triggered my defenses. "I'm following your instructions and trying to get out of here." I stared up at him as my blood both boiled and cooled with the mixed emotions of relief and irritation accosting me.

He took the watch and pointed to the opposite side of where the minute hand sat. "When the minute hand gets here." He wiped his face and took the watch from my hand. "You're a half an hour too early."

My gaze dropped to the clock and I blinked. The damn thing didn't have numbers. Just diamond chips. "How the hell was I supposed to know which side represented the hour?" I snapped and ran my hand through my hair. Moving my arm made me wince.

The pair of industrial-sized laundry carts sat by the door, making me forget about my pain and embarrassment for just a moment. "Where did you find those?"

He must have taken my redirection as just that because he became all business. "In the Grand Hyatt." He rolled them to the wall and took out a duffel bag, setting it gently on the ground as if it held the crown jewels.

"What's in the bag?" I unzipped the backpack and reached for the bleach bottles inside. I needed to rearrange the bag yet again, but this time it was much easier. There wasn't the emotional toil of the task now that he was alive and well and issuing orders as if I were his actual slave.

"What is left of my wife and children."

My mouth popped open and after a moment, I closed it and glanced at the bag, wondering whether he was serious. *Did he really have bodies in there or was he being sarcastic?* I couldn't tell.

Before I could ask, he started swiping his arm across the shelves, dumping the contents into the carts. Plastic banged against plastic, making enough noise for me to glance at the door and wait for an impending attack.

"No one was there?" I asked, because if there were monsters in Grand Central Station, he would not be making this kind of racket.

"No. And I dumped the bottle of bleach across the floor leading back down here, so even if there were any sentries left in the building, they would think twice about following me."

I dropped the bottles I had put in the backpack into the bin as well and re-packed his clothing.

He gently set the bag on the pile with the smaller amount of canisters and then nodded toward the exit. "Hold the door for me." He dragged the carts toward the doorway.

I opened the door he pointed to, and he unlatched a second panel from both the floor and the ceiling, creating a double wide opening so he could actually get the carts out side by side instead of one after the other as I assumed he had come in because the single door could not accommodate the width.

The darkness swallowed him along with the carts, but metal on metal reached my ears. Before I processed what I was hearing, he was back by my side with flames licking his fingers to light up the supply room.

"Is there anything else in here you think would be useful?" He scanned the amply stocked room.

I examined the shelves, going from one to another, handing him items as I went along. Unopened industrial rags, rubber gloves, safety goggles, and a couple of empty spray bottles that looked brand new. I stopped at the far side of the room, where all that lined the shelves was toilet bowl cleaner. As tempting as grabbing a few of those was, we really didn't have a use for them. Most of our toilets had long run out of swirling water.

Well, at least I knew where to come to get toilet cleaner if the world ever turned itself around. But for now, that would be a pass.

He made room for the items in the backpack, secured it closed, and strapped it onto his back. He turned to me and without asking, he hauled me over his shoulder. Before I could admonish him for manhandling me, we were out the door and moving with the two carts rolling ahead of us. I had no idea how he could race while pushing the carts and keep me balanced on his shoulder, so I held onto the backpack as though it were the only thing keeping me in place as we cruised through the tunnels, making a racket that probably could be heard on the surface.

His lack of caution left me as breathless as his speed. When he finally veered out of the subway tunnels, the 125th Street station sign stood to our right. Mikhail slowed after we passed the platform and, with a quick turn, we were off the tracks and onto a smooth surface.

The partial moon lit up the sky and I blinked at the night. It did not seem as though we had been moving that long, but I hadn't been walking most of the day, so the fatigue of marching for twelve hours or more was blissfully absent.

Mikhail found a parking garage that had underground floors and rolled the carts into the absolute darkness. When we stopped, he set me down and lit a small fire with some of the debris. I didn't even know concrete could burn, but apparently between that and some car upholstery, it provided enough fuel for a fire.

The fractured concrete pieces heated the small space, taking away the wet chill in the air.

We were in the farthest corner of the parking garage and the sparse pickings of cars relayed a story all its own. Before the pandemic, this garage would have been packed, even at night. Because New York City never lay dormant in the old days. It was party central, with all-night diners and bars hopping until three in the morning. Now it was a ghost town filled with the dead.

I sighed and stood near the fire, warming my hands over it as I tried to avoid the direct stream of smoke. Mikhail cleaned up the rest of the debris, pushing it into the small fire. He positioned the carts on the outer edge of our small concrete camp, creating a barrier against anyone who might investigate smoke coming from the lower garage floors.

With the backpack leaning against the wall and the bedroll in his hands, he turned to me. "I need to see what damage you did to your back." He unrolled the sleeping bag, pointing to the soft bedding. "Jacket and shirt off, now." He yanked the honey from the recesses of the backpack.

I peeled the coat off, which was the easier of the two garments. The T-shirt stuck to my back, and my muscles protested as I tried to peel it off.

"Turn toward me," Mikhail said.

I followed his order.

He handed me the honey and then promptly ripped the shirt down the front and then tore the shoulders from the collar to the hem of the sleeve and pointed to the mat. "Lie down." He plucked the honey out of my hand.

His clipped tone and sharp mannerisms struck like a physical blow. He didn't even blink at my exposed chest. But then again, he'd been nursing me back to health for over a week, and I wasn't sure I really wanted him to notice me in that way. Although the lack of acknowledgment of my endowments irritated me, and I hesitated.

He met my gaze. "Why aren't you doing as I say?"

The emotional rollercoaster of the day hit with the force of a falling building. I crossed my arms over my chest, hung my head, and cursed the sudden flow of heat from my eyes. "I thought you died."

Silence fell over him, as if my words stunned him. He didn't move a muscle for a good minute, and then his finger hooked under my chin and tilted my face so he could see me.

"And...you are crying?" Surprise layered the husky tone of his voice. "For the enemy?" His head cocked as he tried to digest the sadness I knew reflected in my eyes.

It confused the living shit out of me, too. "An enemy wouldn't have nursed me back to health," I spouted back at him and wiped my face. I turned and marched over to the bedding and laid out on my stomach, pulling my hair to the side so he could see what kind of damage I had done.

He glanced at me and then his gaze moved away from me. To the duffel bag on the ground next to the bleach bins. He closed his eyes and pressed his lips together as if silently praying for something. Patience, forgiveness—who knows what. But when he opened his eyes, that steel resolve was back and he approached the mat. He knelt next to me, remaining quiet as he focused on my back. Most of the shirt peeled away without issue, except for the band across my shoulder blades. His audible sigh made me glance over my shoulder at him.

"This is going to hurt."

Before I could acknowledge the words, he ripped the fabric away, tossing it toward the dying fire. At first numbness settled, but that was short-lived, and my eyes widened at the sudden onslaught of burning pain. "Owww," I whined, glaring at him.

"I wish you had been more patient," he muttered as he tore open the honey and dug some out on his fingers.

The moment the sweet confection touched my back, tears squeezed from the corner of my eyes. It wasn't soothing like it had been when I was first burned. This time it stung like a thousand bees.

He pulled the gauze from the backpack and laid a couple of strips across my back. Then he stretched out next to me on the mat, staring at the ceiling as if he were a thousand miles away.

"Did you forget something?" I asked. The quickly cooling air brushed against my exposed skin, sending a chill that made my skin break out in bumps.

He glanced at me with open hostility, as though I intruded on his very thoughts.

"Clothes? Or a blanket?"

"No. Your back needs air and anything you put on that oozing mess will stick."

"But I'm half naked and it's pretty damn cold in here."

His eyes closed. After a moment, heat blanketed the area much more effectively than the sputtering fire, which at this point was only filling the space with reeds of smoke.

"Thank you."

He glanced at me with a crease between his eyes. "You were honestly upset at the thought of me being harmed?"

"Shocked the shit out of me, too." I turned my head away. I did not want to get into my precarious emotional state. Especially because I did not understand it one bit. Of course, most women would throw themselves at him. He was a gorgeous specimen. But he was a dragon and one that had sided with the real enemy. Albeit under duress. *Damn it.* My mind wouldn't let go of this.

When I turned back, he was still looking at me. "Don't confuse transference with true feelings."

"What the fuck is that supposed to mean?" I snapped and pushed myself up onto my elbows. The stretching of the skin on my back reminded me I shouldn't move with such speed. Not when the skin covering my shoulder blades seemed to be flayed. I clenched my teeth against a wince.

The crease deepened between his eyes. "Why are you getting so hostile?"

I wanted to slam my fist into his perfect cheek. I couldn't pinpoint what was setting the fire inside me to an inferno. It was a mix of anger and disappointment that made me want to get away from him. But being completely naked from the waist up left me at his mercy.

But he wouldn't take advantage of that. And that little tidbit added to the rage.

"You didn't even blink when you ripped my shirt," I muttered as I laid back down, looking away from him. His soft chuckle made me whip my gaze around again.

"You're upset because you don't think I find you attractive." His voice was filled with mirth. When his laughter faded, he said, "Considering I just collected my wife and children's heads from the spikes the leviathans propped them on, mustering up any level of attention was the last thing on my mind. So, forgive me if I seem disinterested." He rolled away from me, but the tension in his back was visible even under the leather fabric of his coat.

Way to make me feel a half-inch tall.

I closed my eyes and put my forehead onto the ground, disgusted with myself for not being more sensitive to what he must be going through. The thought that his family's decapitated heads were in that bag made my entire reaction even more juvenile.

"I'm sorry," I said with a sigh.

He grunted. He had every right to be angry. If the situation were reversed, I would have left my sorry ass in the cold, and gone for an extended walk to get my aggravation out.

I reached out and touched his back.

He arched away from my fingers. "Now is *not* the time."

"I am so sorry," I repeated and pulled my arm back, tucking it under me as the last of the light emitted by the fire faded away.

Dragon Tempest
Chapter 17

I MUST HAVE FALLEN asleep at one point during the night because when I woke, my teeth were chattering and even though a thick blanket had been draped over me, I couldn't stop shaking. I reached out and all my hand hit was the cold concrete. My heart jumped in my chest. I leaned farther, but Mikhail was no longer on the ground next to me.

The blackness of the underground garage pressed down on me and the chills reached my core. I propped myself up on my hands and knees and tried to remember where Mikhail had put the backpack. Inch by inch, I crawled until my hand grazed the wall. But I couldn't find the bag. Although I did find remnants of my shirt among the cold ashes of the fire. At least I thought it was my shirt, but I couldn't see to identify it. I crawled back to the bedding and the feel of the soft down confirmed I had not totally lost my mind.

I crawled beyond the bedding to where he had lined up the carts, but the farther I went away from the bed, the more certain I was that Mikhail was gone and he took the bleach with him. The cold of the concrete bit at my knees. I turned to head back, and my hand brushed nylon.

My breath locked in my throat. I ran my hands over the bag, nearly gagging at the three round shapes. I shuffled back until I hit the bedding. *Why would Mikhail take everything but his family?*

My mind reeled as I sat on the thick pad and reached around me, looking for anything. Soft leather brushed my fingers and I grabbed at it, pulling whatever it was into my lap. I felt in the dark and realized this was my jacket. Struggling through the tremors racking my body, I pulled it on and zipped it up. I forced myself to my feet, and my stomach dropped and rolled. I clamped my teeth closed against the bile clawing at the inside of my throat.

When I was sure I wouldn't vomit, I crouched down and grabbed the blanket, wrapping it around my shoulders. I needed to find light. My boots sounded like sandpaper drawn against rough wood as I shuffled forward with my arms outstretched.

My hand ran into the wall and I slid it in the direction I thought the ramp upward would be. When I rounded the corner, I tripped over something blocking the path. I caught myself, but the fall jarred my back and scraped my palms. Whatever caused me to fall let out a groan and I scuttled away.

"Woods?" a raspy voice asked.

I froze in place and slowly turned in the direction of the sound. One azure eye glowed in my direction. My skin flushed with the sudden rush of adrenaline, and I shuffled to him.

"What the hell happened?" I asked as my hands traveled over his shoulder and the side of his face. Tacky wetness covered my fingers as I got to his temple.

"You were having a rough night, so I went to find some antibiotics. I was too preoccupied with getting you help that I rounded the corner right into something hard. Based on the multiple contusions, I'd say it was at least two people, maybe more."

"Everything is gone."

His eye focused on me, widening. "Everything?"

The horror in his voice made me amend my statement. "Well, not everything. The duffel bag is still there and the bedding, but everything else is gone."

His eye disappeared and his shoulder sagged under my hand. "Did they harm you?"

"I, I don't think so." I had no recollection of anyone at all. The last thing I remember was

Mikhail turning his back on me. "I just woke because I was shaking too much, and my teeth were chattering hard enough to make my jaw ache." I wrapped the blanket around me a little tighter.

Mikhail let sparks ignite on his fingers, illuminating the area, and I gasped at the blood and bruises on his face.

"Oh, Mik," I whispered and reached to help him sit up. Seeing him in such rough shape made me realize that dragons could get hurt. They could die just like the rest of us, and Mikhail in human form was just as vulnerable as I was. It made me shiver.

The fire went out, plunging us back into the dark when he had to use both hands to push himself up. A moment later, the sparks lit up the area again. "We need to find those assholes." He leaned against the wall.

"And do what? Neither of us is in fighting shape." As much as I wanted to hunt the bastards down too and get our stuff back, about all I could do was cut them with some sharp words.

"I can shift and then all this goes away." He wiped his hand against his face and brought it into view of his flaming fingers. "Damn it," he muttered and ripped his shirt, pulling a strip long enough for him to wrap it around his head. He looked a bit like Rambo now, although his hair was much more clean-cut than the fictional character.

"You can still be taken down by a bullet." I wasn't going to let him step into something that could get him killed. Not when I needed him to help us defeat the monsters. At least, that was what I kept telling myself.

"They have the bleach." He cocked an eyebrow at me. "And those leather pants you like."

I pressed my lips together. As much as I wanted both the bleach and the pants, I wanted Mikhail alive in order to build that bomb. Without him, we were just picking off one at a time and losing people along the way. We couldn't afford to continue sacrificing ourselves for the cause, especially when it was a losing battle without the big guns.

And Mikhail was a very large, very deadly gun.

"We'll get the bleach back at some point. But it looks like we both are in need of medical attention now."

"I'll heal." He climbed to his feet and leaned against the wall. "Stay put. I'll go grab what's left of our things and be back in a flash."

"A flash?" Like either of us could move fast right now.

He gave me a half smile and took an unsteady step around the corner.

"You need a hand?"

"Just stay so I know where to find you." He gave me his palm and then closed his hand on the flames lighting the area.

I leaned against the wall in the dark as his footfalls became more solid. The scrape of the bag across the floor gave me chills and then footsteps approached from his direction. When he came around the corner, he put his hand out, lighting up the area so I could see. He moved faster than his condition suggested.

"I already miss my shower," he muttered and wrapped his free arm around my lower back in a gentle hold that offered support as we walked up the ramp.

"I do too," I agreed. There were a lot of things about his self-sufficient apartment that I would miss for a long time. And perhaps when this was all over, I would visit there again and cook him a dinner instead of being the one being spoiled by his culinary expertise.

He studied my profile. "We need to find you some antibiotics. You are too pale."

"Just what a girl wants to hear."

"I'm sorry for getting angry with you last night," he said as we rounded another corner. Light bled down the far ramp and Mikhail closed his hand, dousing the fire from his fingertips. "I'm sorry for being such a dick. I should have had a little more compassion, but I wasn't thinking clearly at all."

He gave me a squeeze. "Neither of us were at our best."

I glanced at him. The rough edges of his personality seemed to be smoothed out, and I couldn't help but think maybe he had been clocked much harder than either of us realized. "Exactly how hard did you get hit in the head?"

He let out a soft laugh. "Hard enough to knock me out. Why?"

"Well, you're actually being nice and it's not because I'm withholding information you want."

He gave me a sideways look. "I am attempting to treat you with the respect you deserve. You aren't my prisoner anymore. You're more of a partner in crime now. Our goals are aligned."

"What happens when our goals diverge?" I asked, curious to hear what he would say. This amicable side of him was refreshing, especially with no real strings attached. He could have left me to my own devices and taken the bleach to carry out his own revenge without me slowing him down.

"I highly doubt they will." He kept walking. "Besides, I guess thinking you might not make it through the night gave me a heavy dose of reality, along with some perspective."

My eyebrows arched. "I was that bad?"

He nodded. "You are still feverish, but at least you are coherent. Unfortunately, honey isn't going to heal the infection on your back, and if we don't get you something fairly quickly, that infection is going to travel into your bloodstream and then there is nothing I can do for you. I thought it had already traveled into your blood, but apparently you have much more resilience than I give you credit for. So, our first priority is finding a pharmacy that still has antibiotics."

"That's a tall order." We shuffled up the ramp and into a sun-drenched level. The brightness of it made me squint to relieve the sharp pain in my eyes. I stumbled and Mikhail's grip around me tightened, steadying me even though he winced.

"I'm tempted to leave you here where it's safe," he said as we headed toward the exit.

"No way. If I'm going to die, I'd rather it be by your side and not alone on a concrete floor."

"It's a real possibility out there. We are ripe enough with blood and whatever the hell is seeping out of your cuts to attract all sorts of predators." We limped onto the street and Mikhail glanced both ways. His gaze locked on something to our right and he pulled me in that direction.

Getting to the ground floor of the garage had been difficult but walking along the buildings like thieves was downright intense. With every muscle on high alert, each movement scraped my back like a tiger's claw. Two and a half city blocks later, Mikhail pulled me into the entrance bay of what looked like a demolished emergency room. He tucked me in a corner away from the road.

"Stay here."

I wasn't going to argue with him this time. I was tired enough to want to lay down right there, but I knew I couldn't. Besides, sitting or leaning on my back in any manner wasn't going to bode well for me. I leaned my forehead against the wall and closed my eyes. My back was to the building and the little alcove he put me in was secure enough that I shouldn't expect an attack from behind.

Still, although I wanted to let myself fall into oblivion, I held my ground, keeping myself awake, despite the lull of sleep. My stomach rumbled, but I ignored it. It was only when I felt the sting in my shoulder that I lifted my head. I expected some sort of bee. I did not expect a needle plunging into my skin or the burn of the injection.

My gaze snapped to Mikhail above me. I blinked and glanced around. Last I knew, I was leaning on the wall. But I was clearly on the ground now and my jacket was unzipped and pulled down to expose my shoulder.

"What the..." I started and then my stomach rolled. I clamped my mouth closed, swallowing the vile acid that wanted to be expelled from my insides, but I didn't think I had the strength to roll. A medical bag was close enough to my head for it to distract me. The open bag contained all sorts of bottles and packaged needles; gauze and bandages stuck out the far side as well. Mikhail had hit the mother lode of medicines. Something we had failed at miserably. Or what we found, no one knew enough about to actively use. We were just sorely prepared pseudo-medics who didn't have a prayer against serious injuries.

But it looked like the dragon was a bit more prepared than we non-medicine-bound people were. Even with the textbooks we pilfered from Mount Sinai medical school, we were still not at the level Mikhail seemed to be for burn treatments. He understood more about the human body and reactions than we did. But I guess if you lived since nearly the dawn of civilization, that would be the case.

He sat back on his haunches and pitched the needle into the garden beyond the alcove.

I raised an eyebrow.

"What? You want me to find a sharps container for that so someone can dispose of it properly?" He mocked me and the corner of his mouth cocked into a half grin.

I knew I was being ridiculous, but I still didn't like dropping garbage on the streets. Although there was no other place for it considering there were no garbage trucks regularly collecting the trash like in the days before the pandemic. "Yes."

He hung his head for a moment and then retrieved the needle, snapped it and then tossed it into an overflowing garbage pile. "Better?" He came back and rearranged the medical bag so it would snap closed. Then he put the shoulder strap for the duffel over his shoulder; the medical bag followed, and then he hauled me over his shoulder. "Come on, soldier. It's time to get you home." His voice didn't sound his normal strong self. It was strained and his gait was slower than normal.

"I can walk." The bouncing wasn't doing my stomach any favors, and although I had my doubts about walking, I didn't want him to do something catastrophic to himself.

"You need rest," he said.

"This isn't going to give me rest." Although the moment the words were out, I yawned. Whatever he had poked me with was sapping the energy out of me quicker than the walk had.

"Well, in less than an hour, we'll be at the museum, and you can rest on a cot or whatever bedding you have there."

I didn't have the heart to tell him soldiers slept on the floor. The accommodations he had at his apartment were like a five-star hotel in comparison. And we had hotels in the vicinity that we used in the early days, but they had become a constant target for the monsters.

Dragon Tempest
Chapter 18

A COUPLE OF BLOCKS away from the museum, Mikhail put me down. "I need to hide this somewhere safe until I can give them a proper send-off." He held the duffel bag with his family's heads in it.

I agreed. If he walked in with a bag of decapitated heads, there would be questions that neither one of us could answer. Maybe I could help him do what he needed to say good-bye. I glanced at the park. There were plenty of places to bury bodies in the park. "What constitutes a proper send-off?"

"Ashes on the wind. And I can't very well turn them into ashes here and bring them into the clouds, now can I?" He met my gaze as if my question set off his irritation spectrum. He took a breath. He pointed down the stairs behind me and handed me the medical bag. "I'm going to go down into the subway, and I'll be right back."

Before I could protest, he was down the stairs and out of view, leaving me exposed on the street. I did not like the feeling of being alone in the open, especially in my condition. If I had to run, I wouldn't be able to.

It was as if the universe felt my apprehension and decided to slam me with more angst. The ground shook and I stepped into the shadows to cloak me, but I didn't think it would be enough. When I turned toward the south, I swore I saw reflections of the monsters in what was left of the glass on the high-rises.

Home base was so close, but I wasn't sure we would make it. I made my way around the iron railing and glanced down at the blackness below. Underground seemed much safer than on the street, where I had nowhere to run and nothing to defend myself with.

I took the first step down, gritting my teeth, and then the second. Mikhail came racing up and slung his arm around my waist, yanking me backward. We crossed the distance to the front entrance of the museum in nanoseconds, and the way Mikhail held me against his chest allowed me to feel the hammering of his heart.

He was just as frantic as I was and I'm sure he felt my rising panic.

He reached for the door and I grabbed his hand, shaking my head. We never went in the front door. Anyone entering this way was considered an enemy and would be fired upon. We would not make it past the defunct metal detectors.

"Back. You have to go around back." I pointed toward the right side of the building. "We need to enter through the loading docks, or we are as dead as we will be staying out here."

He glanced at me and then over his shoulder at the monsters, and my breath caught at the sudden burst of speed he sprinted at. I nearly dropped the medical bag, but grim determination had me holding on. We couldn't afford to lose what he had found in that hospital, especially not with both of us in such crap shape. Although Mikhail could still run like the wind, even with his injuries. If I had to run, I would have been dead right after we left the apartment.

At the loading bay door, I put my hand on the plate, trying to remember the pattern of the presses to get inside. Middle finger, thumb, pinkie, then all five. The click of the door told me my memory wasn't as shot as I thought.

Mikhail grabbed the handle and rushed us inside, pulling the door closed before he leaned against the steel with me still plastered to his front.

"We made it," I said with a voice that I hardly recognized.

"We certainly did." His voice was as winded and tired as mine. "But why isn't anyone here to greet us?"

I pulled away from him and turned toward the darkened interior. The war room wasn't on this level. And only sporadic patrols came through the museum proper. I handed him the medical bag and then took his hand, leading him toward a back stairwell that led to the lower floors of the museum.

When we approached the door, a sentry stepped out of the shadows with a gun aimed in our direction.

"Freeze," the sentry ordered, and the muzzle of the gun lowered a fraction. "Identify yourselves."

"Sergeant Holly Woods," I started.

The gun came up again. "Sergeant Woods died a couple weeks ago," he snarled.

"Jesus Christ. I didn't die. I got away, but not without injuries, and Mik St. Clare helped me when he found me in the subway tunnels." I hooked my thumb over my shoulder at Mik. "We are both still in rough shape, so if we could go downstairs and lay down, that would be appreciated."

A flashlight blinded me, and I squinted. I refrained from lifting my hand, knowing any movement right now might make him squeeze the trigger of the handgun still aimed in our direction. The flashlight lowered and all I saw were white spots.

"I need to get her another round of antibiotics," Mikhail said from behind me, "and if there is a doctor here, he really needs to look at her burns to make sure the one on her back is the only one infected."

The distinct sound of a gun sliding into a holster filled the space and the flashlight beckoned us forward. The door opened and light filtered from below, making me dizzy enough to wobble on my feet.

Mikhail caught me and hoisted me over his shoulder. "Lead the way," he said to the sentry.

We followed him down to the archives, which was just a fancy warehouse under the entire building. There were two levels and this one held the war room area and general lounges for the troops. The sentry continued down to where the living quarters were and the makeshift hospital.

I glanced at some of the people from my precarious view over Mikhail's shoulder. When my gaze fell on a certain backpack leaning against the wall and a group of men sitting around, sharing food, I snarled, "Stop."

Mikhail halted and when I pointed, he put me down and crossed to the group of men eating our food and drinking our water. He reached across them and grabbed the backpack, handing it to me.

The men stood. "That's ours!"

"You stole that from us." Mikhail's growl sent a chill up my spine. If they had any wits about them, they would get the dangerous edge to his tone and back off.

"Bullshit!" One of the men went to grab it from me.

Despite my injuries, I wasn't about to let this asshole get away with taking it again. I grabbed his hand and twisted it back until it popped.

Before he could react, I punched his throat with intent to do damage. "That is for stealing our bleach," I snarled and drop-kicked his balls.

He went down gasping and wheezing and holding his groin.

I turned on the rest of the men, surprised I had enough energy to drop the asshole in the first place. But I kept that to myself and glared with my best poker face. "You heathens don't belong here!"

"They brought—" the guard began.

"They stole our things after they nearly beat Mik to death." I turned on the guard. "We do not attempt to kill our own. And we certainly do not steal from our own." I refused to collapse in front of these men. Even though the adrenaline rush that gave me strength had decided it was done, the raw anger remained.

The guard opened his mouth and looked between me and the four brutes behind me.

"Did we somehow lose our humanity?" I asked when no one spoke. I turned back and slashed my finger toward the exit. "I did not get my ass fried for dicks like you. Now get out. You do not belong here."

"I should have fucked you when I had the chance," one of the men growled.

He didn't get farther than a step when Mikhail's fist smashed him square in the face. The asshole went down, and I wasn't sure what kind of damage Mikhail just doled out until the body twitched on the ground and the front of the man's pants darkened with death piss.

Mikhail killed him with one square punch, and he glared at the rest. "You heard the lady."

The muscles in his arms twitched, and the others flinched.

"I'm taking the bleach," the last one said as he turned to leave.

"We were the ones who risked life and limb to get that bleach. It stays with us." I wasn't going to stand by and let them steal the one thing we needed to wipe the leviathans out.

"We earned those fair and square." The man's voice squeaked, like he might be losing his nerve at the way Mikhail's glare burned through the distance between them.

"Were you the coward who knocked me out with a piece of concrete?" Mikhail said. "Is that your idea of earning it fair and square?" He lifted his hand and ran fingers under his makeshift bandana and showed his bloody fingers to them. "Or were you the one who decided to kick me in the chest while I was unconscious?" His voice turned into a growl and his hands balled into fists.

I reached out and put my hand on his arm. He had already killed one, and I was sure we would have to answer for that. "Maybe we should let the court decide," I said.

The men paled. The court of law under this particular unit was brutal, and they would side with Mikhail. Being coldcocked and beaten just for giggles was inexcusable. And then stealing that person's belongings was another strike against them.

What they did not know was that both Mikhail and I would now be under the scrutiny of the court. Mikhail killing someone with one punch would certainly be questioned, but he was big enough to carry that power, even after being beaten. My interrogation would be much more thorough. After all, I had not followed orders. I had killed my comms and I was alive, despite a body drop.

"Fine, but if I ever see you on the streets..."

Mikhail's eyes narrowed. "If we ever come face-to-face out there, boy, you better turn tail and run, or you'll end up like your buddy." He pointed at the body on the ground.

The man swallowed and scurried away. The guard was still staring at us with an open mouth until my legs gave out. Mikhail grabbed me before I crumpled to the ground.

"Where is the medic's office?" he asked.

That seemed to knock the sense back into the guard and he turned, leading the way. I could have told Mikhail, but for some reason, my words were not forming anymore. My vision was the next casualty as it shrunk into a tunnel no bigger than a pin head.

Voices came from a distance and then faded away.

Dragon Tempest
Chapter 19

THE STEADY BEEP OF a monitor broke through the darkness. I blinked my eyes open to one of the rooms we reserved for the critically injured and one of the only rooms that we chanced running a battery-operated generator for. I had helped carry men and women in here countless times. But this time, I was the one lying on the bed with tubes and wires running from me.

The ceiling confused me. It looked more like stone tile. I didn't remember a room made of stone, but then again, I hadn't been in a room long enough to study the ceiling. I went to turn my head, but something soft prevented it. My brain grappled with the stimulus surrounding me. It was only when I tried to peer to the side that I realized what I was lying on.

This was one of the massage tables we found and brought back to the museum. It had been procured specifically for back injuries. I used my arms to prop up my torso despite the sharp pains scraping at my back. The room was darker than the view from the table, and I glanced around.

In the corner, a body slumped in a chair. A soft snore competed with the machines feeding me medicine and recording my vitals.

"Mikhail?" My voice was weaker than I liked. All this treatment meant I had been more on death's door than I cared to admit.

Citrine eyes blinked open, and I swore I saw relief wash over him before he put on his poker expression. He mopped his face with his hand.

"You should be resting. Not doing some lame upward dog," he said.

I snorted a laugh. "You've done yoga?"

Dimples appeared in his cheeks and he nodded. "It's very relaxing." His teeth flashed for a moment and then he turned serious. "We apparently have a date with the military court once you are well enough."

"The punch?" I asked. Killing another service member was as serious as stealing and beating one of us.

"No. They are trying you for treason because you did not close the deal with the monsters."

The disgust bled through his voice. "And because I saved you, I apparently am guilty of collusion." He leaned back in the chair and glanced around at the marble walls. "This room is pretty damn secure, too."

When his gaze came back to mine, I shivered. Anger bled through his eyes, making them almost glow in the low light.

I knew this was a possibility. After all, I was supposed to surrender to the monsters' demands. But what they didn't understand was giving in meant extinction. They had no intention of taking us as slaves. Mikhail made that perfectly clear.

Instead of continuing the conversation, I lowered myself back down. If we were found guilty of treason, my hope was we would be exiled, with nothing to defend ourselves. But that was wishful thinking. They would put us in front of a firing squad.

A warm blanket draped over my back, and I turned my head. Mikhail stepped back.

"You were shivering."

I wasn't about to tell him I wasn't cold. A firing squad terrified me, and dying wasn't the thing that had me so damn unnerved. It was Mikhail. *What would his reaction to a firing squad be?* That drove a chilling fear right to the center of my being.

I gave him a nod and the stress of both my injuries and the unsettling thoughts swarming in my head bled the energy right out of me. I welcomed the dark stupor that took over.

IT TOOK ANOTHER WEEK of antibiotics and intravenous saline to get me back to form. Although my back was a legion of scars and scabs, it was better than the oozing pustules that had covered my skin when we arrived.

Every time a medic came in to dress my wounds, a pair of armed military police accompanied them. I guess they were a little leery of us trying to break out of confinement. It wasn't until they changed out the massage table with a regular hospital bed that I knew the remainder of our time was limited. We had the story I concocted in the apartment before I let him burn me.

"What happened?" I asked Mik for the hundredth time this week.

Instead of going through the story again, he raised an eyebrow. "Why don't you tell me this time."

"I ran while they were preoccupied with torching the prisoners. I still don't know why they didn't just throw me into the pen with the others, but they didn't. And I saw an opportunity to break free, but I didn't get away unscathed. They blasted the subway tunnels and the fire nearly killed me. If it wasn't for you finding me, I would have died in those tunnels."

"How long after your escape did I find you?" This was a new question, and I blinked at him as my mind grappled with an answer.

"I don't know. I crawled down the subway tunnels from Grand Central. I don't have any idea of how far I went or how much time elapsed. The darkness didn't help with the passage of time, either. It could have been twenty minutes or twenty hours."

His lips turned up at the sides for a second. "Do you remember where I took you?"

Mikhail was good at this. Better than me asking him to tell me what happened. I had to think before I spoke. "I'm not sure. It was somewhere that was dark. You had something soft for me to lay on and some honey and bandages to put on my back. You fed me and kept me hydrated. When I was well enough to move, you found some clothes for me and here we are."

"Where did we find the laundry bins full of bleach?"

I stared at him. That wasn't part of the story we had discussed. Nor was it part of his recounting of what happened either. I looked down at my hands fidgeting in my lap and stilled them.

"We found the bleach at..." I met his gaze. "It's why you found me and why when I was able enough, we went back despite the danger. You knew there were cleaning supplies there, and you had already procured the laundry bins when you found me."

A dimple appeared. "Why were we found by those assholes so far away from Grand Central?"

I didn't have a good answer for that, but that begged a pretty horrific question in my mind. If those men had told them where they found the bleach and where they got their supplies, would they have also said anything about the duffel bag they didn't take?

"If they know where those men stole our bleach, they might also know about where the rest of our belongings are."

His smirk faded and his eyes went a fraction wider. He glanced at the door and then back at me with eyes filled with worry.

My question caused him distress. That wasn't on his mind but it was a solid question, because you could bet if those men said anything about us being there, they included the bag of heads in that conversation. There was no way to explain his family's condition. Not without disclosing Mikhail's true identity, which would mean his certain death.

"I'd kind of like to know where that landed."

"I'd like to know, too." He chose his words carefully, as if the room might be bugged, which was probably likely, but not with anything fancy like those of the old days. There might be a walkie talkie in the air duct, but that was the extent of the eavesdropping capabilities.

"Well, at least you were able to get medical supplies to bring here after we were attacked." I offered my best smile of support.

He took a deep breath. "I can't fathom them finding you guilty," he said with a quietness that made me almost miss it. "But your superior was as aggravated as I imagine the serpent king was after we escaped their wrath."

"Well, he had different expectations of how the whole thing was supposed to go. Having another charred body landing in Times Square and then me showing up alive solidified his theory that I screwed up. After all, I killed my comms before I went in. They weren't destroyed in the confines of the building like the others. So, he thinks I chickened out."

Mikhail let out a small laugh. "You don't have it in your blood to back down."

"No. I don't. Which was why sending me on this mission was such an asinine choice. He knows damn well I'm not capable of surrendering to those monsters."

"But you actually were going to and then the shit hit the fan."

"Yeah, seeing those other emissaries still alive threw me for a loop. And having them charbroiled before me was another shock that tripped my survival mode into high gear." I sent a cross look in his direction. It had actually frozen me in place, but if ears were listening, they'd need to understand why I ran.

"I'm glad you finally came to your senses. There is no negotiating with them. Especially since their only goal is to rid the world of humans."

I stretched out on my side. The conversation took a lot of energy out of me and I needed rest before they came to drag us before the farce of a court.

Dragon Tempest
Chapter 20

A KNOCK INTERRUPTED MY ATTEMPT to get comfortable. Even before Mikhail was able to get to his feet, the door swung open, and Commander Abrams stepped inside the room, with the medics scrambling after him. The commander stood almost as tall as Mikhail, but he was scrawny. If Mikhail blew on him, he would fly off in the wind.

Commander Abrams had his dress uniform on, with all the medals from the prior commander glistening in the light. His dress cap covered a balding head with tufts of blond hair on the sides that made him look more like Larry from *The Three Stooges* than a true military officer. His sharp, dark eyes pierced into me. He slashed his finger in my direction like a silent accusation, and I refrained from any response until asked.

"You screwed up." His growl held exactly the contempt I expected.

"No, sir." I did not screw up, despite what he believed. I didn't have a chance to negotiate before I was whisked away into that room. "All the other emissaries we sent to negotiate were alive and locked up in a pen like animals."

"Bullshit. We have their bodies."

"Just like you have mine?" I cocked an eyebrow at him.

He opened his mouth to speak and then snapped it closed. "Point taken." His tone softened a fraction, but not enough to let me off the hook. "Why didn't you try to free them?"

"If I had, I would have ended up just another extra-crispy snack for those bastards. I was made to watch their deaths and as they were feasting on the charred remains, I saw an opportunity to get away and I took it."

His gaze narrowed at me.

"I would have died if I stayed and tried to negotiate. They have no intention of letting us, as a species, live."

"And how do you know that?"

"Because that's what they said just before they torched the other messengers." That part hadn't been in the scripting we had gone through, but Mikhail had said as much at his apartment, so I threw in a little more sprinkling of truth.

He turned toward Mikhail. "What were you doing near Grand Central, knowing we were trying to negotiate a peace deal?"

Mikhail traded a glance with me. "Her body had already been dropped, so I assumed we might need all the bleach we could get our hands on and went to search for the custodial closets. I found her before I got to the ramps going up into the lower levels of the station."

"Sounds more like a suicide mission."

"Perhaps, but the monsters had already declared their intentions and they need to be stopped. Besides, they murdered my family, so I had nothing to lose by going after the one thing that can compromise their iron skin." Mikhail crossed his arms and squared his feet. His stance screamed contention, as if he welcomed the mounting tensions in the room.

Commander Abrams turned his attention back to me. "The court is expecting you momentarily," he said.

"I need clothes."

He snapped his fingers, and the backpack we had retrieved from the thieves was brought into the room and propped against the wall and then they took our breakfast tray out. The tray pulled my attention for a moment. There were two coffee cups. I didn't remember having a second cup.

"You don't have anything from my room?" I asked as the tray disappeared out the door.

He shook his head. "You know the drill. We believed you were dead, so the items were up for grabs."

I nodded. Nothing would be left. Not even my underwear, especially considering it was the nicer brand. I was never afraid of sneaking down to Fifth Avenue and slipping into the boarded-up stores. At least the ones I knew were hiding places for people too afraid to go back to their homes. Money was nothing more than fire kindling, so I had to bring things worthy of trading. Like food or spray bottles or soap or knives.

One time, I brought a bow and a dozen arrows, and they let me have an unlimited choice of the picked-over undergarments. I only took a couple of bras and a few pairs of underwear that were too big, but something was better than nothing. They made me take a package of a dozen socks too. Most of those items were in my secret hideaway on the West Side. Near where I first found out bleach worked on leviathans.

"Fine. Give me a minute to get presentable."

The commander stepped out of the room, followed by the medics. Mikhail was already crossing the room. He pulled out the clothing that he had packed for me and handed me the dress.

"No. Give me the leather pants and one of the T-shirts, along with the jacket."

Mikhail took a deep breath and met my gaze. "This is more appropriate for a court."

"No. The leather, please."

"You really want to reinjure yourself?" He remained with the dress extended toward me. His fiery eyes told me not to push him on this.

This wasn't an argument I was going to win. As much as I wanted to present myself as a badass, I did not want to end up in another medical bed. I was ready to fight the monsters, not battle my own body.

"Fine," I muttered and tore it from his grasp. I didn't bother making him turn away. My hospital gown dropped to the floor and the crushed velvet flowed over my body, surprising me with its softness and warmth. I could see why his wife dubbed this her favorite outfit. Now that I had it on, I didn't really want to take it off.

"You'll get to wear the leathers soon." He reached for the door.

"You should probably change." I pointed at his soiled clothes. He hadn't changed since we got here and was not really presentable to a court.

Mikhail glanced down at his filthy clothing and then, after handing me the boots I had coveted, he rummaged at the bottom of the bag below the clothing he had stowed for me. Out came a pristine pair of blue jeans and an equally comfortable sweater.

I sat on the edge of the bed, trying not to notice him as he undressed and redressed nearly as quickly as I had, but not without a very full view of his perfectly sculpted ass. *Damn dragon.* I looked away and hopped off the gurney. He left a neat pile of dirty clothing on the chair and then reached for the door.

Outside our room stood two military police officers. They promptly took each of us by the upper arm, leading us to the theater where they held their court proceedings. We were forced into the first row of seats in front of the elevated platform, where six men sat at a luncheon table dragged in from the cafeteria.

Commander Abrams sat at a side table reserved for the prosecution instead of at the jury table. When no one came in to represent us, I raised my hand.

"Speak," Nigel King, the second-in-command, said from the middle of the table. He was more distinguished than Commander Abrams. He would have been a much better leader, but Abrams had claimed the command first and no one wanted to argue with him.

Well, no one but me. I had adored our prior commander and the spineless way Commander Abrams handled himself felt like complete disrespect to our former chief.

"Where is our defender?"

He pointed at Mikhail. "Your friend said he would rather represent himself and you than have someone who did not know the facts representing him."

My gaze whipped to Mikhail. He wasn't a lawyer or a military person. He had no clue how this worked.

"I've got this. I had my coffee this morning." He looked at me in a way that left me cold. His smile did not reach his eyes, and I swallowed hard.

The layout of the court put the military police, the jury table, and the commander in front of us, and no one behind us. One sweep of his fire and everyone in front of us would be annihilated. His little warning about being fueled with caffeine made him the most dangerous thing in this building. Maybe even in the city. Caffeine was what allowed him to take out the nuclear arsenals.

I tried to smile and hide my unease. He patted my hand and stood.

"Do you know who I am?" He addressed the members of the court.

I wanted to stop him right there. His former life would mean nothing to these people.

"Mik. We've seen you patrolling the eastern quadrant from time to time," Commander Abrams said, as if it were not a concern of his. His tone held the contempt forming his lips into a scowl.

He let a half smile pass over his face and glanced at me. I tried to impress on him the uselessness of this with my eyes, but he either didn't know how to read me or didn't care.

"Do you know who I was before the world went to shit?" he asked, as if it mattered a great deal.

"No, and we don't particularly care. This is a trial for treason." Commander Abrams sent a glare in my direction.

Right then and there, I knew what our sentence was going to be. He wanted me dead. That was clear in his glower.

It was Nigel who asked, "Who were you before all this?" He leaned his forearms on the table. His dark complexion and the bill of his hat hid the sharpness of his gaze.

"My name is Mikhail St. Clare."

Commander Abrams didn't react, but the six men on the board did. They all leaned back in their seats and a few of them opened their mouths, announcing their surprise.

"The billionaire?" Nigel pushed his cap higher.

Mikhail nodded. "Yes."

"What does this have to do with Woods selling us out?" Commander Abrams growled the question as his fingers drummed the desk with impatience.

"Woods didn't sell out the human race." Mikhail matched the commander's glare.

"And how would you know?" Nigel shot back, pulling our attention back to the main table.

"Do you really think those animals would honor their deal?" He reached into his pocket, pulling out a small recording device. He set it on the table and pressed play.

The sound warbled as though the recorder was on its last leg, but then the unmistakable gravelly voice of the serpent king came on.

"Those fools keep sending more of their herds into our midst like they believe we are willing to strike a deal. Ha. They are our primary food source and once we have them corralled into one place, you dragons can cook us up a feast."

The laughter that followed made me tense up. I didn't know how long ago Mikhail recorded that, but it sounded as if there were more dragons there than just Mikhail and his doomed friend.

How long had he held onto that recording?

Mikhail turned off the recorder and pocketed it. "Since you know who I am, you also know I'm a technology genius. I didn't have a chance to get this to you before because I was going for the bleach I knew was stored in the custodial closets. That's when I happened on Ms. Woods in the subway tunnels just outside of Grand Central."

My brain focused on the recording and the sounds of many responding to the serpent king. It falsely gave the impression that dragons were still in play, that their numbers had not been decimated. It struck me as odd, but then the commander opened his mouth again.

"Do you have the recording of what happened there with Ms. Woods?" Commander Abrams leaned forward.

I couldn't tell whether he was interested in a recording or whether he was disappointed there might be something to exonerate me.

Mikhail looked at me and sighed, shaking his head. "I made the mistake of using a watch battery I had tucked away, and it died soon after I caught the serpent king's speech." His cheeks bloomed pink with embarrassment. "I may be a genius, but I have my moments of stupidity, too, just like everyone else."

Mikhail St. Clare was quite the actor. I glanced down at my hands as unease filtered into my blood, making my healing back itch. I forced myself not to fidget in the chair.

Commander Abrams narrowed his eyes. "How convenient."

"I'd say it was damn inconvenient, because then I could prove she didn't sell you out."

Mikhail's hands clenched as he glared at the commander. He refocused on the body of judges who would determine our fate.

"Sergeant Woods, why did you kill your comms before you entered the lair?" Nigel asked.

"With all the others, we never picked up anything beyond the first minute or two. We heard the door shut and then everything went dead. So, either these creatures are more advanced than we give them credit for and have figured out a way to block signals, or they stripped the soldiers of their comms. The latter seems more likely, considering the tape Mikhail just shared." I crossed my arms. "And I really didn't want one of those things touching me."

Mikhail glanced at me, and I saw the flash of something cross his eyes. I couldn't be sure whether it was hurt or surprise. I couldn't exactly blame him, especially after how I acted when I first saw his scales, but my only close encounter had been with a hideous leviathan.

"So, what happened next?" Nigel asked.

"They brought me into the main concourse, and I saw the last dozen soldiers we had sent to do negotiations in a pen, like caged animals. When the dragons ordered me to kneel, I...I refused." I stumbled on my words.

My commander's orders echoed in my head. *"You do whatever they tell you to. If they ask you to suck their dick, you do it if it means the solidification of the peace treaty. Understand?"* I had never verbally acknowledged his order. I just nodded like a damn fool.

"And how did that work out?" Commander Abrams asked.

"Not so good. I was forced to my knees and then they breathed fire on the other soldiers. There was nothing I could do to save them. And after, there was an opportunity when the dragons weren't watching me. I reacted. I sprinted to the closest subway ramp and down to the tracks. But before I got out of their range, they blew fire into the tunnels. I dodged into one of those little alcoves in the wall and that saved me from being just another crispy fried soldier."

"Why would they wait until you showed up to kill the others?" Commander Abrams asked with a voice laced with skepticism.

"I don't know. Maybe they just wanted to scare me before they tortured me to death. Or maybe it was because I didn't agree to the iron shackles they wanted me to put on. Or it's because I didn't grovel when they demanded I bow down to them."

"So, you caused the death of those soldiers."

I blinked and glanced up at Mikhail for help, unsure whether or not I was the one who signed their death warrants. Regardless, the commander walked me right into that one. It made me wonder whether he had been a lawyer before all this went down.

"If she had groveled and done everything they demanded, she would have likely ended up in that corral with the rest of them until the monsters got tired of hearing their complaints or decided they didn't feel like hunting for their food. And she would have died right alongside the rest at that point."

"You don't know that!" Commander Abrams snapped.

"Then what would you have done given the same circumstances?" Mikhail crossed his arms and they flexed under the sweater, pulling the fabric taut.

"This isn't about what I would have done. It's about her inability to follow orders." The commander's voice bellowed out over us. "Her orders were to surrender, no matter the cost."

Mikhail's hands remain fisted and he lowered them to his sides, as if he were near the end of his patience with this asshat. Anger radiated from him.

"My actions may have precipitated their wrath," I allowed. "But I think Mik's right. If I had just succumbed to their demands, I would have been dragged into the cage and left there with the rest, and you would have still had a dead body dropped in Times Square, along with the declaration of war for our failure to meet their demands."

Commander Abrams pressed his lips together. "They declared war and then they decimated a dragon to show their superiority. Why the hell would they do that?"

"Perhaps they were pissed that the dragon ate their food," Mikhail said. "Either way, Sergeant Woods never would have been allowed to return. Not since she actually saw the other prisoners."

"And you aided her in those tunnels," he snapped at Mikhail.

Mikhail studied him and then the table of judges. He glanced at me and took a deep breath. "Her fate has already been decided, hasn't it?" He returned his gaze to the table.

"She did not obey, and we are at war because of it."

"We've been at war since those things slithered out of the deep. Taking negotiators hostage and demanding more proves they never intended to honor a peace deal. They aren't interested in slaves. They want to wipe humanity off the face of the Earth. It's not because of one soldier who had the guts to not fucking grovel like the rest."

"She was sent to broker a peace deal."

"She was sent to her death and you fucking know that," Mikhail bellowed at them. "Doing the same thing over and over, expecting a different result, is the definition of insanity. How would her negotiations be any different than the other soldiers you sent to die? There is *no* negotiating with terrorists. Have you forgotten that simple creed?"

Mikhail's eyes seemed to glow with his contained fury. I reached out to touch his hand to try to calm him with a human connection. The minute my palm connected, I knew I had made a mistake. I yanked my hand back from the near burning inferno of his flesh, wincing.

My hand throbbed from it, and Mikhail's gaze darted to me and dropped to my reddened palm. I quickly turned it and rested it on my leg. "Sorry," I muttered.

"Your burns still bothering you?" he asked after a beat.

I nodded.

"Your medical report said nothing about your hand," Commander Abrams said with narrowed eyes.

"It's just tender at this point." I prayed he wouldn't tell me to turn my hand over. The throb of the burn continued and even the dress's soft fabric hurt. I was sure if I turned it over, there would be newly created blisters and there was no explaining that away.

Mikhail met my gaze and took a deep breath, unclenching his fists. He turned back to the ones who held our lives in their hands. "Is our fate already sealed?"

They wouldn't meet his gaze and a chill encompassed me.

"You cannot put Mikhail in front of a firing line," I said.

"You are not in a position to dictate protocol to us." Commander Abrams pointed a finger at me.

"He is your last hope to beat those monsters. He has the technological know-how to build a bomb," I spouted, unable to contain this information. Especially if they had their minds already made up. They had to spare Mikhail.

"Lots of people here know how to build bombs. They won't do a damn thing and you know it."

The commander was right. There were enough munitions experts still around to build a normal bomb. But we weren't talking a normal device. "No one knows how to build a bleach bomb big enough to compromise the leviathans en masse."

Commander Abrams blinked, as did the members of the judicial court. Their eyes turned to Mikhail.

"Can you do what she says?" Nigel's eyebrows lifted with interest.

"Yes. But I won't help you if you harm her." He pointed at me. "Do we have an understanding?" His gaze shot to Commander Abrams. "Or is your personal vendetta against her too big to consider the rest of humanity?"

Dragon Tempest
Chapter 21

"WHAT THE HELL DID you do to piss off your commander so much?" Mikhail asked as he paced in the marble room.

I sat on the edge of the bed, staring at my red palm. Thankfully, it hadn't blistered. But it was sore enough for me to not be able to close it into a fist. "I found a way to kill a leviathan." I glanced up at him.

He stopped and looked at me, and his eyebrows rose. "Bull."

"I got accolades for the discovery. He thinks I stole his thunder." I shrugged. That was the only logical reason I could think of for his animosity. "I also argued with the tribunal against him taking over. He wasn't the original commander of this platoon." I missed our original commander. He was a true leader. Not like this horrible, petulant child of a man.

Mikhail shook his head. "His hatred of you runs deeper than just your arguing against him being commander. You sure you didn't wrong him in some other way?"

I shrugged. "Not that I'm aware of."

"I really should have toasted their asses," he muttered under his breath. He swung around to face me. "This is what you were so hell-bent on getting back to?"

I sat back in the bed at the venom spewing from Mikhail. "My commander is not what brought me back. My soldiers are the reason I'm here."

"Where are these who you are so loyal to? I don't see anyone covering your back here but me."

His words slapped like a punch to the gut. I opened my mouth to answer him. But no one *had* come to our rescue. No one seemed to care. My squad would never let me rot or be court-martialed by the commander. Not in a million years.

My eyes widened and I moved to the door, but we were still locked up. I pounded against it until the military police guard opened the door. "Where is Unit 67?" I asked.

He blinked at me, and the frown that appeared braced me for the facts that followed. "They all died. Ambushed by the leviathans on their watch. A lot of the squads have been picked off since you were sent to negotiate that deal."

From his tone, I gathered he thought I should be put in front of the firing squad.

"They aren't going to stop," I said, compelled to make even one of them understand that the offered peace deal was as much of a farce as the trial we just participated in. "They want the Earth wiped of us. Like we are ants infringing on their world."

He met my gaze. "We could have survived if you had done your job."

"You're wrong," Mikhail said from the far side of the room. He stared down the guard. "They want this all gone from the Earth. They want their own civilization, and you are nothing but pests that need to be exterminated."

"Can you really build a bomb to stop them?" He met Mikhail's angry glare.

"With the right ingredients, I can build something that will do a great deal of damage to their army."

"Damage like a nuke?"

Mikhail took a breath and shook his head. "No. I'm not interested in annihilating everything within a thirty-mile radius. I'm just looking to do the maximum amount of damage in a small setting. I'd hate to take out this city, even in its current sorry state."

He nodded and glanced at me in a way that conveyed disgust. His eyes flicked to the dress and then to my face, as if I had somehow harmed him personally.

Then it dawned on me. "My uniform was ruined by the dragon's fire. And since you all thought I was dead, I no longer had any backups."

His gaze remained hard.

"I would have preferred to wear pants, but my back and legs are still healing, and pants were not recommended." I turned and pulled the dress up so he could at least see my calves and the backs of my knees. "My thighs are worse. Same with my back."

When I turned back to face him, his eyes softened a fraction, and he gave me a nod of acknowledgment.

I had never seen this cop before either, so he didn't know my history or my impact on this platoon. He only heard what he was fed by his commander in the month I had been gone.

His words finally sunk in, and the truth nearly stole my breath. "They're all dead?"

"Yes, ma'am," he said quietly. "The last couple of weeks have been rough. A lot of the troops consolidated after the first wave of massacres. Soldiers weren't the only targets, either. Civilians, basically any human out on the streets, no matter the age, was slaughtered."

My hand rose to cover my mouth as the reaction finally came in with the force of a wrecking ball. I blinked back the tears but a few escaped, tracing hot paths down my cheeks. The loss hit harder than a swipe of an angry dragon tail.

"They are soulless bastards," Mikhail said from behind me. He had moved closer, and I turned right into his chest.

I hated crying in front of people, but the emotional impact of my friends torn to pieces by those monsters really set off the tears. I buried my face in his soft shirt. He gently cupped my shoulders and squeezed in support. I now understood his need for revenge. When everyone you cared about was violently stripped from your life, you wanted those responsible to pay.

The door clicked behind us, leaving me in the quiet to mourn and wait for news of our fate.

It didn't take them long to make the decision. The walk from the rehabilitation room to the makeshift court was not long, but it seemed more like the green mile than a leisurely stroll. Every muscle in my body was strung tight enough to pull at the healing scabs on my back with every step.

When we entered, everyone, including Commander Abrams, sat at the table on the elevated platform.

I stopped at the gruesome view at the base of the table they sat at. Mikhail's wife and children's heads were placed on the floor in front of them, staring out at us as if we were their murderers. Mikhail tensed next to me, his eyes almost glowing with anger.

The military police pushed us forward.

We were escorted to the spot in front of the seats we had for the court-martial and the military police flanked us, with their hands remaining on their weapons.

The oldest man at the tribunal table stood. Colonel Vince Stallworth had been a high-ranking officer in the marines before the world went to hell. He had trained a good number of the troops, although I had never been in one of his training classes. He stared down his nose at the two of us.

"Care to explain these?" He waved at the heads.

"Not particularly," Mikhail said. The tone of his voice should have warned them off.

"I think you need to." Nigel's voice left no argument.

Mikhail glanced at me, his eyes nearly blazing and his hands in fists. Someone had been watching us when we approached the museum. I gave him a nod to explain.

"They slaughtered my family, and the monsters had their heads on pikes as a warning."

"A warning for what?" The commander leaned forward with a growl.

Mikhail took a breath, and I could see his mind working. "To understand the consequences of trying to enter Grand Central Station uninvited." His eyes narrowed. "Unfortunately, I did not know about bleach at that time. Otherwise, we would be having a very different conversation."

"If they are dead, why aren't you?" Nigel asked, his voice more of an accusatory bark than I had ever heard.

Mikhail pressed his lips together and ground his teeth. "I didn't know they followed me until it was too late."

The judges traded a glance, but no one said a thing.

"That does not sway our judgment." The colonel turned his attention to me. "Sergeant Woods, we find you guilty of treason."

My knees wobbled, and Mikhail reached out to steady me.

The colonel looked at Mikhail next. "Mr. St. Clare, it seems you have an affinity for getting those around you killed, and you did not use your best judgment in aiding Sergeant Woods. We find you guilty of aiding a traitor."

The MP grabbed my arm and the one next to Mikhail went to do the same to him.

"Do not touch me," he growled in a way that made the officer step back.

The officer's gun came out of his holster and he pointed it at Mikhail.

"Because of the circumstances, instead of sentencing you to a death by firing squad, we will give you a choice of how you will die," Colonel Stallworth said.

"How kind of you," Mikhail snarled.

I could feel the heat radiating from him.

The colonel glared. "The firing squad or death at the monsters' hands."

I stared at them, dumbfounded. Death by leviathan was never pretty. Neither was death by fire. But these people did not know just how dangerously close they were to becoming dust particles.

"We can shoot you dead in the museum gallery where the troops can witness your executions, or chain you to the General Sherman statue and leave you for the monsters."

Mikhail straightened his back. "I'll take my chances with the monsters." There was no hesitation in his choice. It was as if he did not want to harm anyone, and the firing squad would likely annihilate the entire building and everyone here, including me.

"They like to play with the prisoners," Nigel said. "It's a slow and agonizing death."

My gaze narrowed. "How do you know they like to play with the prisoners?" I had heard that they occasionally did chain the guilty to the statues to be dispatched by the monsters, but that was only reserved for the truly vicious criminals.

"We have a few of those camcorders that still work," Nigel answered. "Only the upper brass has access to them," he added.

"I still would prefer my chances out there, rather than give you sorry excuses for human beings the satisfaction of planting a bullet in my brain." Mikhail stood tall, glaring at the commander. He knew as well as I did, this was a personal vendetta and not a true military judgment.

"No one has escaped." Commander Abrams glanced between us with a measure of satisfaction, as though this were the true outcome that his twisted mind wanted. "And if by some miracle you do, we will hunt you down and kill you on sight."

Mikhail stared him down until the commander lowered his gaze.

"I'll go with Mikhail," I said, but my voice wasn't as strong as Mikhail's had been. Even though he was a dragon, I still had my doubts. If the monsters were within distance of the park, there would be little time to get free of whatever bindings they restrained us with.

However, Mikhail had easily burned through the neck shackle he put me in as if it were made of play dough instead of iron. If I was going to survive this, it would be by Mikhail's side. There was no mistake. If he had chosen the firing line, everyone in the building, me included, would have been disintegrated with his dragon fire.

Dragon Tempest
Chapter 22

WHEN THE ALL-CLEAR was given, we were marched out to the statue. I hadn't seen it up close, and I shivered at the sight of the blood-splattered granite and bones littering the ground. Hands attached to varying lengths of arm bones spread out at the base of the statue. Some had bits of flesh still attached, but most of them had been picked clean by the vermin.

It was enough to make me cringe.

One of the officers leaned a ladder in the middle of the statue and waited. When the military police officer opened one of the wrist shackles to put on me, I moved away at the sharp spikes on the inside. They were meant to impale the wrists of the prisoners. My gaze jumped to Mikhail's.

Mikhail just shrugged, like it was just one more injury that we'd have to deal with. Not a big deal to him, but if those spikes tore through a vein, we could bleed to death before we got back to his place downtown.

"That's so you can't pull a Houdini," the commander said from behind and pushed the end of a pistol into my back. "You can still choose the firing line."

My skin went numb at the thought of spikes in my wrists, and I almost took him up on the firing line. Mikhail, on the other hand, stuck his wrist out as if he were being fitted for a watch. No emotion leaked into his expression except the clenching of his teeth as the shackle clamped down on his wrist.

He didn't back down from this insanity.

They pulled him closer to the statue and tossed the other shackle to the soldier on the ladder, who threaded it around the bronze statue's leg, yanking it tight enough so Mikhail had to stand on the tips of his toes with his arm stretched to avoid the spikes tearing into his flesh further. A thin trail of blood ran down his wrist and under the sleeve of his arm.

The military officer pushed his other arm up so that the soldier on the ladder could secure Mikhail's wrist in the other shackle.

The commander jammed the gun in my back as the soldier moved the ladder toward the front of the statue. My chain would wrap around a bronze woman's foot and I was far enough away from Mikhail to bring sweat beads to my forehead.

I looked at the height of my shackles. I would be lucky if my feet touched the ground. My alternative was certain death. At least this gave me a chance.

I swallowed and stepped forward, resigned to another level of pain. And it ripped a yelp from me as the first restraint bit into my wrist. I was right about the height of these things, too. Even with only being wrapped once around the statue, my toes barely scraped the ground and the pain in my wrists was unbearable. Yet I clamped my mouth closed against the screams that wanted to come out. Mikhail hadn't uttered so much as a whimper, so I needed to suck it up.

I didn't dare fight against the binds holding me in place. I did not want to do any more damage than the spikes had done. Struggling would only tear more of my flesh.

As soon as the rest of the soldiers and military police had headed back in the direction of the museum, Commander Abrams leaned close. "Things could have been different if you had said yes to me all those years ago."

His eyes fell to the vee in my dress and back, in an insinuating manner that turned my overheated skin cold. I had no idea what he was talking about. He never approached me in any way other than irritation and outright hostility.

"Tenth grade," he said. "Before the monsters came." He raised an eyebrow.

High school? I had no clue what he was talking about.

"Junior prom?"

I blinked at him without any memory of a John Abrams in high school. I had been asked by a handful of guys, including a couple of geeks, but I wasn't really into dancing or being groped by pimply faced boys. Besides, my boyfriend had dumped me to go to the prom with the cheer captain, and I really didn't want to see that all night.

He growled at me and turned away. "Figures you wouldn't remember the biggest disappointment of my life," he mumbled over his shoulder. "Enjoy being mauled by the beasts." He left me to figure out what the hell I did to him in frickin' high school.

"Now that makes more sense than jealousy over figuring out the bleach angle," Mikhail's voice rasped harshly. He glanced toward the museum.

"Any time now," I said through gritted teeth. My wrists felt as if they were breaking. At this point, the spikes were not only shredding the skin of my wrists, but the way they were embedded between my bones was nearly blinding as my weight shifted in them.

"Metal takes a bit to melt. Especially when it's inside me." His head leaned back against the concrete. "If I transformed, it might be different, but that's an automatic death sentence for both of us."

"What do you mean? You could fly us out of here."

He laughed at me. "To where? Anywhere I fly you to will be inundated with leviathans. And that's if some hotshot soldier doesn't decide to shoot me out of the sky. I have to get us out of here in this damn human form if we want to have a prayer of survival. And I cannot take your shackles off until we get to someplace where you won't bleed to death."

My lower lip started to tremble.

"I know they hurt," he said, softly enough for me to look at him. His eyes glowed almost like a hot fire with reds and yellows, oranges, and even blues. It was beautiful and the concentration on his tightly clamped lips impressed me.

The wind shifted and I got a whiff of burning flesh. I glanced up at his hands. I prayed the camera on the bench nearby pointing directly at us had black-and-white film because the iron around his wrists glowed like the fires in his eyes. He was burning himself to save us.

"Mikhail," I whispered and even though my voice held pain, it also held awe.

Tremors in the concrete behind me had me staring toward the downtown area.

"They smell fresh human blood at least ten miles away." He sighed. "And dragon blood is even more pungent to them. So..." He yanked downward and the clasp holding the shackles to the chains snapped. "While these hurt like a motherfucker, I can't remove mine either."

He crossed to me and reached up, slashing his pointer finger across the lower link, severing it.

I dropped to the soles of my feet; he hauled me over his shoulder and turned on the speed toward the western shore before either the leviathans or the soldiers could come into view.

He only went down a few streets before slowing down. "You said you had a place on the West Side?"

"On West Seventy-Seventh, near Riverside Drive."

He turned in that direction and soon we stood on the corner of West End Avenue and West Seventy-Seventh Street.

"Which one?"

"Third building in. Apartment three-twenty-one."

The building had long been abandoned and although half the building was demolished, the other half still stood, along with the stairwell. My place was largely untouched by the destruction around me. So were a few others in my corner of the building. Within a blink, we were inside and in front of my apartment. He gently put me on my feet.

I didn't have a key with me, and I glanced at Mikhail.

"Can you break down the door?" I asked, even though I really didn't want to leave what little belongings I had up for grabs. But I wanted my private stash of clothes and trinkets. It wasn't much and probably could fit in a backpack, but it was mine.

He glanced at the door and then around him at the hallway before he jumped up in the air and slammed the sole of his foot into the door right next to the deadbolt keyhole. Both the door and the jam splintered. Thankfully, it didn't sail off the hinges, but it would never lock again with the damage to the deadbolt. The door swung in and I caught it before it slammed closed again.

The windows were still covered, and the collection of candles still sat on the table, along with the book I was reading the last time I needed space to think. It wasn't a pristine, glitzy apartment like his, but it was my private studio apartment that the service had no idea I still had access to. It held a pullout couch and the coffee table that I slid to the side when I wanted to sleep. My bureau full of the clothes that I adored and would wear around the apartment instead of my army-issued khakis, and my bookshelf of my favorites that I could re-read over and over and still fall in love with them. My little kitchen covered the wall next to the door and was comprised of a dead refrigerator and a stove that hadn't worked since the electric grid crashed, leaving most of Manhattan in the dark.

Mikhail closed the door behind us before turning to me in the dimly lit room.

My wrists throbbed, but I still crossed to the box of matches and attempted to strike one. It hurt too much to get the damn thing lit.

Mikhail crossed and leaned over. With a light breath, all the candles lit. And he didn't melt them into a puddle of wax. Although I was impressed, I still sent a glare up at him at his excessive display.

He gave me the edge of a cocky smile. "Do you have towels and bandages?"

"I don't think there is anything in the linen closet." I nodded toward the small bathroom.

He disappeared and came back just as quickly with a small box of Band-Aids. "For an escape lair, this is poorly stocked. Although you do have a half a bottle of bleach in the closet, so there's that." He set the box down on the table. "Does anyone else live in the building?"

I laughed. "No one has dared to come back inside with half the building basically crushed."

"Then I'll be back." He reopened the door and slipped into the hallway. The same smash to door after door occurred. When he came back, he had a half dozen of those reusable shopping bags that were all the rage before things went to hell. He placed them on the floor before he closed the splintered door to my apartment and slid the refrigerator in front of it.

He pulled out enough towels to cover the entire floor end to end if we wanted, Ace bandages, a half dozen Liquid Skin tubes, Band-Aids, antibiotic ointment, over-the-counter pain pills, and a mega pack of baby wipes that hadn't been opened yet. The last items he pulled out made my stomach growl: a couple of cans of SPAM along with three cans of soda. And he hadn't even emptied all the bags.

He licked his lips as he placed the food on the table. "It's not a lot, but..."

"Are you kidding? It's a feast." I went to reach for it, and he pushed it farther away with a shake of his head.

"We'll both need a little nourishment after I take these things off. But if we eat now, we both will likely lose it."

I stared at the food and then at him. It was the first time I saw the discomfort in his eyes. I was so preoccupied with my pain, I didn't consider his. After all, he burnt his flesh in order to break the shackles from the chains.

"This is going to hurt, but I need you to hang in there, because I am going to need help when I take mine off. Think you can do that?"

"I can stay conscious. But I have no idea if I will have any dexterity to do anything requiring fine motor skills—as you saw with the match."

He bit his lower lip and nodded. "You will have to, because if I bleed outside of a towel, we will be surrounded in a matter of minutes and we do not have nearly enough bleach to survive."

"Is that what's in the other bags?"

"One of them."

"What's in the other?"

"Clothes that look like they'd fit me. I didn't look for anything for you because I assumed you had something here."

"Your assumption is correct," I said. "But nothing like the leathers you had given me." The disappointment I felt at that loss bled into my voice.

He met my gaze. "I am going back as soon as we are done here."

"If you go there, you will be shot on sight."

"They have things that belong to us." There was no leeway in his tone. "And anyone who chooses to try to stop me will meet their maker. I had coffee this morning for a reason." He laid a clean hand towel on the table and nodded toward my wrists. "Put your hands on the towel with the insides of your wrists facing the ceiling."

I did without hesitation, even though his eyes drew closed as if preparing himself for something unpleasant. He reached out and put his index finger on the metal, slicing across it from one side to the other. The path of his finger left a fiery red line in the metal. Heat seeped through to my skin, and I forced myself to remain still.

He closed his hands and opened his eyes before doing the same on the opposite side of the wrist. Then he slid his finger under my hand, sliding it between the bottom half of the clasp and my wrist. With his other hand, he pulled straight up.

I let out a whine between my clenched teeth as he freed my right wrist and then did the same on my left wrist. My right wrist seemed less of a problem than my left one. The minute the spike came out, a huge well of blood bubbled out.

Mikhail put his finger into the cut, which nearly ripped a scream from my chest. Not only did his finger feel like a hot poker, but it was actually in the damn spike hole. He pulled it out slowly and the room filled with the awful scent of burnt skin.

"Turn your hands over, please."

My brain stalled, with tendrils of pain blocking my ability to comprehend his words. Gently, he reached out and turned each hand over. Then he pressed one hand over my right hand and yanked the remaining half of the shackle out.

At this point, I kind of wished I had been slaughtered by the leviathans, because the agony that gripped my right wrist soon echoed in the left as Mikhail repeated the process.

He brought my hands together in the towel, applying pressure around both my wrists.

I looked at him through a haze of darkness. A high-pitched buzz overwhelmed me, and I squinted. His lips were moving but I couldn't hear him over this weird din in my head. I took a deep, slow breath to get a grip on the panic filtering into my head. The buzzing faded.

"That's it. Take another breath."

I followed his directions to breathe, keeping eye contact until the noise filling my mind along with the fog blurring my eyes disappeared. His grip on my wrist was tight enough for my fingers to go numb.

"When you are good enough for me to bandage you up, let me know."

"I'm, I'm good."

His soft smile appeared. "No. You aren't good yet. When you get a little color back in your cheeks, then you can tell me you are good."

"I'm fine," I insisted, but my head still felt light enough for me to doubt my certainty.

He shook his head. "You aren't good enough for me to release the pressure and you sure aren't good enough for me to cauterize anything else. Give it another few minutes and keep taking those deep breaths."

I thought about trying to pull my wrists free, but the fear of the pain that would follow brought blinding tears to my eyes. Blinking them back, I willed them not to escape and was rewarded with the salty aftertaste of unshed tears. Normally when someone corrected me like that, I would get angry to the point of obstinate, but for some reason, the softness in Mikhail's tone was enough to diffuse the raging bitch.

"I'm good now," I said after another few minutes.

He nodded and slowly released my left wrist and reached for the package of wipes, tearing at the plastic wrap holding the three tubs together. They tumbled out and he caught one in his hand, putting it on the table. When he flipped the top open, he threw his head back in exasperation. The wipes were packaged in another challenging wrap.

His attempt at opening the wipes with one hand failed and he bit his lip like he was contemplating using his teeth. With a minute shake of his head, he slowly released my right wrist and then tore into the wipes, dumping them into the plastic container with the pop-top dispenser.

It was probably the funniest thing that I had seen with him since we met. And we had had a few comical moments in between all the stress and injuries. But seeing him open baby wipes just made everything we were going through surreal in a mind-bending way.

I snorted a laugh.

He glanced up at me and his eyebrows rose. "Are you laughing at me?"

"Just a little," I said. "You considered tearing it open with your teeth, right?"

"Yeah, but baby wipes taste awful, and I didn't want that lingering in my mouth."

He pulled out a half dozen and then peeled the bloody towel away from my left wrist, wrapping the remaining hand tightly in the fabric. The slow and steady way he cleaned the blood from my wrists, hands, and arms was quite endearing. He inspected the oozing spike cuts and instead of using his finger to cauterize them, he used Liquid Skin and then put Band-Aids over each puncture wound.

When he was finished cleaning and patching up my left hand, he asked, "Can you easily move that around or do you need one of the wraps?"

I flexed my left hand, and other than some uncomfortable pulling, I didn't find it too unbearable. Even clenching a fist. "This hand's good. Where did you find all that stuff anyway?" I nodded my chin at his stash.

"The last apartment on the floor by the stairwell. They obviously had kids, and, based on the fact they had Liquid Skin and all this other crap, I bet someone there was in construction of some sort. Or they were just accident prone. Either way, we got lucky."

He eyed my other hand and my gaze followed. "I hope you don't have to do whatever you did when you took the shackle off," I said.

He huffed. "Yeah. I think you might be shit out of luck there, sister." He unwrapped the bloody towel and started the same process of cleaning wounds and skin to ascertain the extent of my wounds. Any time he turned my hand, I winced. The hole in my wrist that he cauterized still had a slow trickle of blood. The puncture on the back of my wrist was a little more insistent.

"I'm going to have to do something with that," he said.

"Can't you just use that Liquid Skin stuff?"

"I can use it after I cauterize it, so nothing gets in while you heal, but I can't put it in the open wound." He handed me the bottle so I could read the instructions.

The bastard used that moment to do the same thing he had earlier.

My breath hitched and my eyes widened, but this time I wouldn't look down. It was as quick as the last time, but the burning locked my breath in my lungs.

"Breathe," he reminded me as he went about cleaning up the blood and applying Liquid Skin and then Band-Aids like he had with the left hand. He reached for an Ace bandage, and I pulled my hand away, trying to move it around like I could with my left hand.

Each motion felt like bone crunching bone, so after I did my pitiful attempt at moving it, I extended my arm out to him in surrender. He wrapped it tight enough to provide support, but not too tight where my fingers would turn purple.

He used an entire tub and a quarter of the second while cleaning me up. I hadn't reacted the second time he opened the inner wrappings around the wipes. Grabbing one of the empty bags, he dumped the soiled towel and all the bloody wipes he had tossed onto the ground before taking a new wipe from the tub to clean up the table.

He laid another clean towel down and glanced at me. "Think you can pull the shackles out of my wrists the same way I did for you?"

"I think I've got enough dexterity in my left hand to grip and pull as long as you do your thing with the sides like you did with mine."

"It may take some force, and it has to be straight up so you don't tear any more flesh in the process."

I nodded and swallowed the nerves cropping up.

"Just be careful not to smack yourself in the face, either." He drew his right finger along the seams of the cuff on his left hand, leaving those same fiery red lines. "And try not to touch the hot metal." He looked up at me and nodded at his wrist.

"Oh." I wrapped my fingers around the center of the cuff with my left hand and pushed my finger between the back of his hand and the other side of the cuff below so I could keep it steady.

He relaxed his wrist and closed his eyes with a quick nod.

I took a breath and pulled straight up. This wasn't as easy as he had made it seem. The muscle in my arm burned from exertion. It wasn't until I put my body into it that the upper part of the shackle dislodged with almost a pop. I nearly smacked my chin at the sudden release of tension.

Mikhail pulled his hand away from mine and turned it over on the towel before I had a chance to inspect his wound. "Hurry. I need to get this covered with the Liquid Skin as quickly as possible."

I took the back half with both hands and yanked upward. With the leverage I had from using both hands, it came out with less effort than the first one. I tossed the metal into the garbage bag and grabbed for the wipes at the same time Mikhail flipped them open and grabbed a few. With both of us working to clean up the blood, it was only a minute or two before he swabbed Liquid Skin over both the cuts on his wrist, covering them with Band-Aids just like he did with mine.

He leaned back and mopped his face with a towelette, taking a few deep breaths in the process.

"You didn't bleed as much as I did," I said as I collected the dirty wipes and threw them away.

"I cauterized my wounds trying to compromise the chains."

I nodded. I remembered the smell of burning flesh, but his wrists didn't look burned like mine would have been with that much heat radiating through them. "It's a wonder the metal didn't melt."

"It did. Which is why I'm bleeding again."

My gaze dropped to his wrists. "It melted? Inside the puncture wounds?"

"Yes. At least the spikes remained attached to the cuff. Otherwise, we'd be doing some fancy-ass surgery to get that out of my wrist."

I smirked at him. He usually didn't swear so casually. At least not in my presence over the past few weeks. "I think I'm rubbing off on you." I tossed the last of the dirty wipes away.

He huffed a laugh. "I'm not sure that's a good thing. You're a bit suicidal."

"I'm not suicidal. Trouble just tends to find me." I pointed to his other wrist. "You about ready to be de-shackled?"

He laid his hand on the towel and did his laser-heat thing with his finger again and then he reached under his wrist. "I've got the other side. Use two hands on this one."

I did as instructed, but this was just as difficult with two hands as it had been with one, especially because my right wrist was compromised. When it finally popped free, the wet sound it made curdled my stomach.

Mikhail turned a little green and he swallowed before turning his wrist down. He moved so quickly that I didn't get a good look at the wound, but the blood spreading on the towel told me I had ripped something critical.

"You need to cauterize that," I said.

"After." His voice was as rough as I expected.

"But..."

"I can't with this hunk of metal still in me," he snapped and clenched his teeth.

"Oh." I reached down and did the same thing with the last half of bindings left. That same awful, wet ripping sound filled the room, and the shackle came free. I tossed it into the bag with the rest of the trash.

When I looked back, an orange glow emanated from his wrist. Mikhail's face bled of all color and he met my gaze. His eyes held dragon flame and he shook with the force of it coursing through him, as if fighting something.

"Shouldn't have had caffeine." He groaned and bolted from the apartment, tossing the refrigerator as though it were a cardboard box.

The roar that followed made me cover my ears and then silence descended like a lightning bolt.

My heart thundered and I scrambled to my feet. I turned toward the window and pushed the curtain aside enough to get a view of the river. Nothing stirred. I swallowed the sudden surge of bile, forcing it back down. My body shook from both aftereffects of adrenaline and the pain that crept in like a thief, stealing my strength away.

I managed to get the door open. Mikhail had torn the door of the opposite apartment right off its hinges and disappeared into the wreckage beyond. The fading daylight made every shadow a suspect until one passed over the building in the shape of a dragon, catching my breath in my throat. He had shifted, which meant he was in more danger now than he was in human form.

"Mikhail!" I screamed, trying to stop whatever destruction he had in mind. But I was too far away, and his roar was too loud, like a battle cry warning the residents of New York to flee.

The fire that followed stripped me of strength. It was white, like the light of a nuclear explosion. Dust filled the air in the path of his destruction until he finally flew straight up until he was a speck in the sky.

I never saw him fall back down from the sky. I waited and wondered whether maybe he flew right to the moon instead. Hell, if I were him, I would choose any place but Earth right now, too. My gaze fell to the path of his destruction and my breath caught in my throat.

A clear path burned straight through to the park. Buildings that once blocked the view of the city were dust blowing on the wind, including where the Museum of Natural History once stood.

I grabbed the splintered doorframe, gasping for breath from lungs that struggled to bring in air. The awful truth weaseled its way into my mind. I frantically tried to deny any sense of betrayal, but I had led Mikhail to our headquarters. I had signed the death warrants of everyone inside that building the minute I pushed Mikhail to bring me back to my platoon.

As much as I disliked my commander and his childlike behavior, I did not wish him dead. And yet they were all dust particles on the wind. So was the massive amount of bleach we brought into the building.

I stumbled back into my apartment and pushed the splintered door closed. I stared at the bags on the floor and kicked the one containing all the soiled wipes. The bag flew across the room, littering bloody rags in a path to the window.

He had been the one to tell me not to trust him.

"Stupid girl!" I ran my hands through my hair and fell to my knees. My gaze landed on the last two bags, and I pulled them close. One did indeed have a couple of bleach bottles under a pair of men's jeans and a chambray work shirt, along with a good pair of socks that did look like they would fit him.

My mind reeled, trying to figure out whether he was on our side or not.

I lifted the T-shirt off the top of the second bag and just stared at the box that sat below it. My chin quivered. He had found a box of unopened chocolates and grabbed that along with another box of Band-Aids and bandages and a package of new women's socks that had never been opened.

I put the chocolates on the table and blew out the candles, stretching out on the couch as the exhaustion stripped me of logic. Tears flowed in a steady, hot stream down my face, and I curled into a ball, cursing him and wishing he was here at the same time.

Dragon Tempest
Chapter 23

AFTER EATING ONE OF the tins of SPAM and downing the sodas, I stripped out of the dress, tossing it on the chair in the corner before I used the tub of wipes to try to clean myself up. My back was still tender to touch, but at least it wasn't as wincingly awful as it had been.

I opened my delicates drawer and drew on a pair of nice, clean cotton underwear. The feel of it was like stepping into Mikhail's shower. I paused and glanced at the fractured door. I knew where he lived, but getting down the length of the isle of Manhattan would be a challenge.

I dressed in a pair of moisture-wicking pants and matching tank top that I used to jog in. It would at least keep my burn scabs from getting moist and sloughing off. Plus, they worked as an alternative to long johns under a comfortable pair of black jeans and a cotton long-sleeve T-shirt.

I had a worn leather jacket in the closet. It wasn't black or fur lined like the one Mikhail's wife had, but it would keep me warm enough for the time being.

Tucked away in the closet, I had an old backpack that I used to use going hiking. It was nowhere near as heavy-duty as Mikhail's but it would at least store a few changes of clothes, the food, chocolates, and some of the bandages and wipes.

I rummaged in the corner of the closet for my weapons. My knife sheath slipped easily onto my belt and the heavy hunting blade felt good at my hip. I just wished I had one of those super soaker toy guns here. At least I wasn't completely defenseless. I did have a spray bottle half full of bleach, which I put on the floor next to a growing pile of must-haves that would go with me.

The last thing went into the other holster on my right hip, although with my right hand in such rough shape, I doubted I'd be able to draw and shoot. The extra clip was still full, but I only had a dozen more bullets in the last package. That went into the pocket on the side of the pack for easy access if I needed to reload.

I packed my clothing first, pulling out my favorite shirts and yoga pants because they took up less room than jeans. The unopened bag of socks went on top of that, and then some of the bandages and the wipe tin with the last unopened package of wipes. The Liquid Skin that we hadn't opened went in, along with a package of nearly full Band-Aids and antibiotic ointment. The last to be dropped in was the SPAM and the chocolates. I zipped up the backpack, clasped the weatherproof flap over the top, and secured it before I strapped it on my back. I then armed myself with the spray bottle, filling it up with one of the bleach bottles. The grocery bag of bleach would be a pain, but I still hauled it over my shoulder like an oversized pocketbook the women used to carry around before everything fell to pieces.

I was ready for the streets of New York.

I was ready for the monsters, and I was more than ready to find Mikhail St. Clare and give him a piece of my mind.

The End

Continue Reading Book 2 on the next page.

Dragon Storm
Season of The Dragon
Book 2

Dragon Storm
Chapter 1

I STARED OUT MY window at the raging river. It seemed to capture my turbulent mood accurately. The setting sun sent prisms of light off the chaotic waters, and I turned away from the stormy view. Too many monsters lived under the surface to have calm seas. It was as if they knew the last dragon had fled the city and they could not follow to drag him down into the deep to his death.

Mikhail St. Clare.

Savior.

Traitor.

Monster.

There were so many other words to describe him, and each one sent a twinge of fiery fury through me. He had told me he was the last dragon, but after his betrayal, I couldn't trust a thing he had said.

But I did know where his hideout was. He had his very own safe house here in the city, near the Brooklyn Bridge. The shit thing about being on the west side perpendicular to Central Park was the sheer distance the bridge was from where I stood.

And between me and my goal was an army of leviathans.

As much as I wanted to just curl up and ignore the rest of the world, I couldn't. I hadn't laid down to die when the monsters came, or when they declared war on humanity, and I certainly wasn't going to give up because I had been duped by a dragon. My grim stubbornness kicked into overdrive and I was now much more determined to wipe them off the map.

I had a goal: come leviathan or Serpent King, I would blast through anyone who got in my way just to get my hands around Mik St. Clare's throat.

He was mine to extinguish, and I would fight all the monsters to let my revenge loose.

I turned and stalked out of my apartment. I was all piss and vinegar until I got to the stairs. Walking down the steps reminded me of all my injuries sustained over the last few weeks in an excruciating crescendo.

Taking stock of my ailments brought a wince with each step. The backpack irritated the healing burn scabs on my back. Holding the railing was tough with the wrist puncture wounds from the shackles that had held me hostage so the leviathans could tear me to pieces.

If it hadn't been for Mikhail... I stanched the thought before it could fully form. Mik St. Clare was not a man to admire *or* desire. He was a dragon with the magical ability to shift. I forced the thought of him out of my head and focused on the stairs in front of me, cursing Mik under my breath with each painful step.

If he hadn't whisked you away from Grand Central Station, you may have been able to truly broker our surrender.

I stopped.

Did I really believe that? Had Mikhail somehow orchestrated the failure of our negotiations, or had he at least been telling the truth about the dark intentions of the Serpent King?

My thoughts swarmed, keeping me frozen in indecision. I forcefully shook Mikhail from my head. I'd drill him for information before I dealt the mortal blow. But for now, I had to get to his building shrouded in destruction before I could extract the truth from the bastard.

The only thoughts I would allow would be those that relished his violent end. He had torched the Museum of Natural History, where my platoon gathered. It did not matter that the commander had sentenced me to death alongside Mik. What mattered was Mik killed them all, and the dust of the dead swirled on the air, choking those near the epicenter of destruction.

He vaporized our only defense against the leviathans.

Our stockpile of bleach was as gone as everything else in the path of his raging fire. Now we would have to scrape and scratch for every available container of what was the equivalent of liquid gold. The pandemic depleted our reserves to begin with. Everyone panic-bought bleach, believing it would kill the virus. Nothing, not even the sterilization properties of bleach, killed the virus.

That motherfucker just had to die out on its own, along with half of humanity.

Then came the monsters from wherever they had been hibernating. And our numbers have been dwindling since they arrived. We were truly at their mercy. And the creatures did not have merciful bones in their disgustingly vile bodies.

Without bleach to penetrate the leviathans' iron skin, we were a doomed species. Mikhail toasting our massive stockpile, a stockpile *we* hand delivered to my base, made his duplicity all the more painful.

Dragon Storm
Chapter 2

IT TOOK ME MUCH longer to climb down three flights of stairs than it should have, and by the time I reached the ground floor, my injuries sapped my energy. I leaned against the wall next to the door leading out to the street, second-guessing my plan. I was not sure I would make it down the length of the island of Manhattan.

One glance in the direction of Mikhail's path of destruction gave me a second wind. I had to see the damage firsthand. Hopefully, it would add to my dwindling reserve of strength and give me another blast of adrenaline to get me moving. The silence of the city struck me. What once was a bustling mecca now stood like a sepulcher. My footfalls on the blacktop echoed enough to keep my head turning and my muscles tense as I waited for predators to slink out of the dust and shadows. The tunnels provided darkness and stealth, but out here on the streets, the city that used to never sleep remained catatonic.

It was creepy on most days, but we were also running for our lives from the monsters, so really hearing the stillness made me pause. Even the river roiling behind me didn't break the quiet settling over Manhattan. Not even the footsteps of the monsters reached my ears.

"Damn," I whispered, just to make sure I had not somehow lost my hearing. My voice fell in a dive that hit the pavement, driving my steps forward. Two blocks away from the museum, the destruction started. One moment, I was in between the buildings and then, nothing. A desolate, dust-ridden scar broke the street, swallowing up everything in its path. Beyond the park, the scorching veered to the right, bypassing the park, and heading south, southeast. I couldn't see where it ended but it was a longer path than I had formerly thought. I swallowed hard.

The other platoons were farther south.

Could he have destroyed them, too?

That ominous thought quickened my pace and my heart. I kept a few feet from the edges of where Mikhail raked his fire over the land as the earth still radiated heat as if I stood next to a living lava flow.

I glanced at the smoldering path and picked up a small piece of metal debris from the road, tossing it into the scar. The metal bubbled and burst into flames.

Well, there goes a potential escape path.

If a leviathan came from the downtown direction, I had nowhere to run. Yet another reason to curse Mikhail St. Clare. Damn that dragon. I would make him pay for every slight, even if he could turn me to dust in an instant. I'd make sure I took him with me straight to the gates of hell.

The ash in the air made me cough, and my mind kept circling around what I might be inhaling. After all, when the towers came down that awful day in September of 2001, the dust from that caused cancer in survivors who were closest to Ground Zero. I rummaged in the depths of my inside pocket of my coat and pulled out a cloth mask, as if I were producing a rabbit out of a hat. Leave it to me to keep one of these silly things shoved in my pocket. But I was glad I had been diligent on the mask wearing protocol, even though I thought it was crazy and really did nothing in the height of the pandemic.

I slipped the mask on, praying it was enough to filter out the dust so I could avoid a debilitating disease later in life, assuming I lived long enough. Especially with the deadly trek I was currently on. Maybe the dragon was right. Maybe I did have a death wish. But, right now, an anger burning hotter than the scorched earth drove me forward.

I kept an eye in the downtown direction, but nothing stirred. It was as if Mikhail's actions silenced the monsters. His fiery scar stretched across the park and as I made my way around the pond, to the far corner where we had been left for dead, I blinked at the absence of the statue that we had been chained to. He destroyed it along with some of the buildings on Fifth Avenue. But the Plaza Hotel was left untouched.

The skyline of this area of the city had been transformed. I don't ever remember being able to see the Chrysler Building sparkling above the dust cloud like a beacon from this specific point at the edge of the park. It was usually hidden from view by the MetLife Building. But the path to it was clear now.

My heart leapt into my throat and instead of a brisk walk, I put on some speed despite my body's protests. It took me fifteen minutes at a light jog to reach the destination that had my pulse pounding. I stopped and stared at where Grand Central Station had been, almost in the same spot I had stood weeks ago to negotiate for our lives. But all that was left was half the hotel, and beyond the station the Chrysler Building towered untouched by dragon fire.

Mikhail had destroyed the monsters' home base and probably all the subway paths for miles. I shivered and glanced around. I was exposed standing here, just gawking. My mind could not grasp how far his fire could have gone underground. Especially with the sheer destruction topside.

God, I hope no one was down there.

But even as the thought formed, I already knew their fate. They would have never known what hit them. If I had to choose a death, that would be much preferred to being toyed with or torn to pieces a little bit at a time while the monsters laughed at your pain.

My head turned toward downtown. I needed to get to Mikhail's hideaway and confront him. I needed to know why before I plunged a knife into his chest.

Dragon Storm
Chapter 3

I MADE IT TO the beginning of Union Square before I felt the first disturbance on the ground. The subway entrance was too far from where I stood to make a break for it. I pulled my spray bottle of bleach from the holder on the side of my backpack and held it at the ready. Unfortunately, I would have to let the damn monster get close in order to douse it. The spray bottle did not have the distance of a super-soaker.

A ball of fear formed at the back of my throat, constricting my chest. I gulped it down, forcing myself to take long, slow breaths despite the pounding of my heart. One swipe of the leviathan's claws could slice me in half, especially if I stayed out here in the road. I slid into the park and found a tree that was wide enough to hide me from view. I contemplated climbing it, but the leaves had all shed and I would be as easy to pick as a piece of meat from a shish kebab.

A shiver climbed up my spine as the ground rumbled again. This time the vibrations were closer than before, but I could not tell the direction it came from. I scanned the city toward the downtown area from around the tree, even looking behind me from the direction of the devastation Mikhail had left. Although I didn't think that was the direction they came from, I couldn't tell. It was as unspecific as pinpointing the direction an earthquake came from while you were in the midst of it.

I pulled my hood up over my head and sprayed the back of it along with my backpack and down to my pants and shoes. If there were more than one, I did not want them to get a whiff of me. But if they already had, very little would deter them. They would search me out like a cat stalking a mouse.

With a deep breath, I glanced around the tree and froze. The Serpent King slithered up Broadway with the army of leviathans marching behind him. The closest I had ever been to the Serpent King had been from the window of Mikhail's safe house. But being at street level made my body tense hard enough to almost squeeze the piss out of my bladder. I crouched down closer to the ground in an attempt to make myself invisible.

But as they marched by, nearly half a football field away from where I crouched, I saw what they dragged behind the Serpent King. My heart stopped for a moment at the chained dragon. Its wings were shredded, as if the entire leviathan army had a swipe at them. They flew in tattered bloody pieces, but he was alive, despite the damage.

The dragon's nostrils flared, and Mikhail's citrine eyes flashed my way as they passed, as though he knew I hid among the trees. If there had been foliage, I would have been well hidden, but even with my crouching in the leaves, I knew he saw me. Yet, he did not alert the army to my presence. He just turned his head back in the direction they were dragging him.

I stayed down until the last of the procession passed. Then I looked toward the downtown area. Toward Mikhail's safe house, remembering what they had done to his friend. They made a spectacle of killing him and then dragging his dead body through the streets as a warning.

My hands clenched as tight as my teeth at the thought of Mikhail's dead body being dragged through Manhattan in the same manner. It burned in a way I did not expect. I wanted revenge, at my hands. I did not want the monsters to kill him for me.

I turned and sprinted, cursing my slow pace and my screaming injuries. If I ran headlong into a leviathan, I was prepared to do as much damage as possible. But they were not doing their grid rotations. Instead, they stayed on course. I made it to a side street near Times Square in time to see a leviathan pound a stake into the ground. The stake held the iron chain that ended around Mikhail's throat.

When they stepped away from the damaged dragon, the Serpent King's gravelly voice echoed through the silence, loud enough to be heard for blocks. "I give you an offering. The one who disrupted our peace treaty and left the path of destruction across your city is yours to deal with. We will not intercede."

I stared from my hiding place, watching in horrified fascination as the monsters withdrew down Broadway and then dispersed out of view. I crept forward, wondering what type of trick this was. The monsters seemed to relish our cries of terror and pain just before they snuffed out our lives, so this did not feel right.

As much as I did not trust Mikhail, I couldn't help but hear the Serpent King's same rasping voice proclaiming his true intentions of wiping us all out.

Did Mikhail have the equipment to fabricate a recording?

The thought scraped at my skin, making it itch and ripple like it wanted to retreat inside me. I glanced at the dragon, wondering whether anything he told me had been true. A flare of hot pain struck through my chest, as if an evil cupid had pierced me with a bitter arrow.

When the last of the leviathans had slunk out of view, I moved forward with my spray bottle still in one hand and my revolver in the other. I wasn't the only one approaching Mikhail St. Clare, either. Soldiers came from the direction of the nearest subway entrance, pointing weapons at Mikhail.

And the dragon's chest turned red.

I sprinted forward, holding both weapons in the air. "Don't!" I yelled. I wasn't sure whether my command was for Mikhail to not unleash his fire, or for the people not to harm the dragon.

I was conflicted at seeing him so vulnerable. Plus, I had too many questions that needed answers before I'd allow anyone to kill him.

Mikhail's chest was orange now as if he held in the rising flames. "Run, Holly," he hissed at me.

I slid to a stop a few feet to his right unfazed by the troops surrounding us. I pointed my gun at Mikhail, letting my fury surface. "Why?" I growled through my teeth.

"Because you are in grave danger." He looked to the south.

"No, you insensitive idiot. Why the hell did you destroy our only chance?" I snarled. "Why did you kill my entire platoon?"

"For the love of everything sacred, run. Now," he hissed louder.

Mikhail's voice was so full of pain and urgency that I finally registered what was happening around us. Others approached the dragon with their weapons drawn as well, except they were not facing Mikhail anymore like they had been when I first ran out into the square. The soldiers faced the streets to the south, east, and west.

Leviathans stood with their mouths salivating at every street entrance surrounding us. A few blocks down Broadway, the Serpent King came back into view with a smug look on his reptilian face, as though we had walked willingly into their all-you-can-eat buffet.

And we were the main course.

At least there were only a half-dozen leviathans as opposed to the entire army of them, so those of us gathered around Mikhail might have a chance to get out of this alive.

But it still made my mouth run dry and my palms sweat.

I traded looks with the soldiers surrounding me. They had heard the dragon call me by name. They had heard the warning. Although I didn't comply by turning tail and leaving them to fight the monsters alone, their eyes held a level of doubt in me that my superior officer had also shown right before he declared me a traitor and sentenced me to death.

Some of these soldiers recognized me from the multiple fights we waged in the past. They knew my reputation, and they stood fast, with their weapons aimed at the hungry beasts, looking every bit as scared as I felt. We were only ten wide, and I had a moment to wonder whether this was all that was left after Mikhail's destruction.

Only two of the soldiers carried super soakers. It would have been better odds if everyone carried the magic juice that disabled leviathans. Bullets wouldn't do a damn thing but irritate them unless we could compromise their defenses. Which meant bleach on their iron skin. It was the only way to make them vulnerable. However, with Mikhail behind us, if we could soak the mothers with bleach, Mikhail's fire could kill them without anyone wasting bullets.

Assuming he isn't a complete murderous dick.

I glanced over my shoulder at Mikhail. The orange in his chest turned red and yellow as he stared downtown. His gaze moved to mine, and he gave me a nod, as if he knew I was expecting him to have my back. I glanced at the growing pool of blood surrounding him and turned back to the ones who had done him harm. If I could, I would torch every single one of them myself.

I need to get hold of my emotions before they give me whiplash.

We only had one shot at this. Even with my misgivings of Mikhail's alliances, I assumed he wouldn't cook the soldiers while I was among them. I shifted under the weight of his duplicity. He never put me in harm's way before, so I had to trust he would keep that pattern now, despite still wanting to thrash him raw for what he did.

Instead of dwelling on whether or not he was on our side, I made sure my spray bottle was on stream. I pointed it at the nearest beast and squeezed the trigger. My stream fell short, but the beast crinkled his nose and stepped farther away. Instead of moving forward, I squeezed again, creating a barrier around us that the beasts stepped back from.

They roared at us but did not rush us like they had done in the past. I wasn't sure whether it was the neat line of bleach or something else.

"Hit them in the face or the chest if you can,"
I said to the ones with the soakers. I received
curt nods as they pumped the guns, ramping up
the pressure.

I glanced behind me at Mikhail. Was he the
reason the beasts weren't charging? The blaze in
his chest had turned blue, and smoke drifted
from his nostrils. He wasn't looking at the
leviathans like earlier; instead, he looked at the
soldier on the right with a super soaker.

I moved in behind the soldier, facing Mikhail
while I handed off my bottle of bleach to the
soldier next to the one with a super soaker. I
switched the gun from my right hand, which had
been compromised, and steadied it in my left
hand, aiming it right between Mikhail's eyes,
shaking my head slowly.

He met my gaze, and his eyes flicked up at
the Serpent King and then back at me as if some
sick deal had been made between them.

"Go!" I yelled. The bleach ripped out of both
soakers, followed by the roar of the leviathan.
"So help me God, Mik, I will shoot you if you
don't take out the monsters," I growled, low.

His glare told me more than I wanted, but he
let his fire loose, sweeping his head above our
heads and across the line of monsters. The
screams of the leviathans were much louder
than the death cries of the baby leviathans in
the subway had been. But when they all fell
silent, followed by thuds that shook the ground,
I chanced a glance down Broadway at the
Serpent King.

The Serpent King hissed, and his glare was
aimed right at Mikhail, as if he had done

something unforgivable this time. I had heard that hiss before. It was his call to arms. Which meant we had very little time to move before we were overrun by monsters. And this time, a small barrier of bleach would not hold back the herd.

"Retreat!" I yelled. The soldiers listened, ducking toward the west end subway entrance. I went to follow and then whirled around, meeting Mikhail's resigned gaze.

"Go." He nodded his head toward the soldiers.

Mikhail would be ripped to shreds if I left him to the beasts.

I aimed my gun at the clasp on the anchor in the ground and shot three times, praying the bullet wouldn't ricochet and harm either one of us, This was my only choice to break the iron hold on Mikhail. He couldn't fly away, not with his wings so destroyed. But he could run with the rest of us.

I grabbed the mangled chain and yanked him toward the subway entrance the rest of the team had ducked into. Mikhail in dragon form would never fit down the stairway and I spun, waving the troops down to safety before I turned to Mikhail. I pointed the gun at him. "Shift," I commanded.

"I can't." He met my gaze.

"You can't fly away either, and you can't fit down in the tunnels in your current form. So, shift, damn it."

"I cannot shift." He held out his shredded wings. "I need to heal first, or I will bleed out."

"Then figure out how to fucking fit down these stairs!" I yanked on the chain, pulling him with me as I hobbled down the steps. I focused on moving as fast as I could because the ground shook as thousands of leviathans raced up the streets of New York. Mikhail had to know death was coming at us at a speed we could not counter. I would pull him down here if it killed me because although I wanted to strangle the man, I could not let the dragon be ripped to pieces on my watch. "If you don't figure out a way to downsize, whether it's shifting, or becoming the incredible shrinking dragon, I will die with you. I can't leave you behind, no matter how much I want to."

The sound of metal clanking on the ground spun me back around. A mini-dragon the size of a wild turkey lay on the top step, caught underneath the large iron collar that had fit his massive form.

I hurried back up the steps and maneuvered the collar so he could get out. The moment he was free from the weight of the iron, I scooped him up under my arm, ignoring the stretch in my back. I limped quickly down the stairs and jumped the turnstiles, sprinting past the waiting soldiers. They followed me down onto the southbound tracks and I turned south, running as fast as I could into the deeper tunnels, flying blind in the near total darkness. The meager flashlights tried to pierce the blackness, but they only lit a few feet in front of us at a time. Tile panels fell from the ceiling as we ran, and the entire floor shook as if an earthquake ripped the ground apart.

When my adrenaline started to fade, my pace slowed until I couldn't take another step. My wrists throbbed and my back and legs felt as if they were on fire. I was sure I had done damage to my healing body again, and that knowledge sapped the strength right out of me. The rest of the soldiers surrounded us, but it was the darkness of the subway passage that pressed down on me until I couldn't take another step.

"I need to rest," I said.

"Will do, Sarge," one of the men said.

Then a dull light swung back in my direction, blinding me.

My eyes slowly adjusted enough to make out the shapes around me. I blinked at the line of soldiers in front of me, all of which had their guns pointed in my direction.

The largest one, with bright, accusing eyes, stared at me. "That thing knew your name." He nodded toward the dragon nestled under my arm.

I nodded and took a breath. How was I even going to explain this without them pulling the trigger? I slowly lowered to the ground and put Mikhail down at my side, protecting him with my arm. "It's a long story and one I do not have the energy to recount right now, so if you are going to shoot us, go ahead. I'm too tired to argue at the moment."

"I saved her," Mikhail said. "She is just returning the favor."

"How did you save her?" the soldier asked.

"She was sent to Grand Central and did not know that the leviathans and Serpent King were not interested in a peace treaty. They want to stomp out the human race, and I do not agree with them." He raised his fractured wings. "As you can see, they did not take too kindly to my traitorous acts."

Mikhail's wings did not look quite as bad as they had on the street. Some of the webbing had reformed, but it was translucent like a baby bat's wing and traversed by bloody scratches. He was still stunning to look at in the low light. His scales rippled with colors every time he moved. It was surreal, staring at him while he was so small.

One kick could send him careening down the tunnel, and I had a moment to relish that vision. Then I shook the image out of my head and took another look at his damaged wings. A slow realization hit, and I had to ask.

"How many times have they shredded those?" I asked, interrupting their interrogation.

He turned his citrine eyes on me. "Once before."

I closed my eyes. It all made sense now. I couldn't understand why he didn't fight back when they killed his family. He physically could not, and dragon fire, like bullets, only served to annoy the beasts when their armor wasn't compromised.

"Why did you destroy the museum and our stash of bleach?" I asked, coming back to the reason I wanted to see him suffer by my hand and no other's.

He looked down at the ground. "I told you. I had coffee before that farce of a court-martial."

The cock of a gun drew my attention back on the soldiers.

"You were court-martialed?"

"I can torch your asses before you pull any one of those triggers, so I suggest you put away the damn guns before I lose my patience." Mikhail's chest started glowing orange.

"Do not threaten them," I snapped. "You violated my trust and killed my platoon and who knows how many others with your caffeine-induced fire path."

Mikhail's wide eyes turned to mine.

"I don't give a flying fuck that you are the last goddamned dragon. You fried all that bleach we brought back from that stock room. Did you even think about that while you were leveling Manhattan?"

Gun barrels slowly dropped to the ground as the firing line in front of us witnessed me tearing the dragon a new one.

Mikhail pointed his wing at me. "I lost control and aimed my fire away from where you were. If I hadn't, you would not be here. And yes, I focused it on the bastards who tried to kill you. They would have tried again had I not taken them out. Unfortunately, the bleach went up in flames, too."

"I could wring your neck," I muttered and unclasped my backpack, setting it down so I could lean on the sturdy fabric. I wiped my face and glanced up at the soldiers. "We were court-martialed for treason." I pointed between me and Mikhail. "And chained to the statue at the entrance of the park."

They looked between us, cocking their heads like confused puppies. Their gazes jumped from the mini-dragon to me.

I held out my wrists so they could see my latest injuries. "Did you know those chains had spikes to keep people from escaping?"

Their eyes widened enough for me to see the whites clearly in the minimal light.

"Yeah. I guess that must have been something new, courtesy of Commander Adams."

"Commander Adams was a dick. I saw him steal the medals he didn't earn off your former commander's uniform." The soldier who seemed the youngest spoke, but from his mannerisms, I guessed he was actually one of the more senior members of this little platoon. Although I had never run into him on the streets. "But I still don't understand how they chained a dragon to the statue with you."

"The dragon is Mikhail St. Clare." I hooked my thumb toward Mikhail.

"Big Mik?" one of the ones shrouded in darkness asked, his voice cracking.

"Yup. Imagine my surprise when he shifted at Grand Central Station." I huffed and sent a sideways glare at the one who had actually saved my life multiple times since that failed negotiation.

"Dragons can shift?" the young leader asked.

"Apparently only Mikhail can shift. So no, not all dragons, only this arrogant asshole here." I waved at my cohort.

Guns cocked again, and I caught the nuance of change from interested to betrayed. I knew that feeling. I wouldn't blame them if they blasted him into next week, but I couldn't let them. I still had that small seed of hope that he would follow through on his promise to rid Manhattan of the terrorists.

"He is our only hope to take down the leviathans. You've seen his path of destruction and he's a tech genius from the old life. So, he knows how to make a bomb made with bleach," I added and then glared at him. "But we need to find more bleach now that he destroyed our stash."

"Do you trust him?" Hard, bright eyes peered over the barrel of a gun.

I glanced at the soldier who asked the million-dollar question and bit my lip. Did I trust Mikhail after what he did? It was not an easy answer, and I was too tired to care.

"I don't know how to answer you. I was marching downtown to find him and skin him alive after what he did to the museum. But seeing as he has not turned *you* to dust yet..." I shrugged. "I don't know his endgame, but I do know he has walked among us long before the monsters came. Hell, long before any of us were even born. So, it's your call." I waved at the guns. "Your choice to possibly save humanity or doom us to extinction."

Dragon Storm
Chapter 4

I GUESS MY "DONE with this shit" attitude impacted the soldiers in a positive way. They backed off and let us be for the moment, shuffling enough of a distance away so their quiet voices didn't carry to my ears. But I was sure Mikhail could hear because his ears twitched quite a bit and he kept his head so that one of his ears faced the group.

"You really thought I did that on purpose?" he asked softly.

My gaze fell on him instead of the shadows down the tunnel. I nodded. "You *are* a dragon."

He sent a cross glare in my direction and then looked away. "Have you learned nothing over the past month?"

I went to make a snide remark, but I closed my mouth. Mikhail had shown me more decency than my own platoon leader, even after he finally pried the secret of the bleach out of me. He could have easily turned me to ash along with everyone else, but he didn't. I glanced at my wrist and could just make out the bandage in the darkness. The bandage Mikhail had put on me before he set the city on fire.

Instead of dealing with the swirl of emotion building inside me, I focused my attention on our little band of soldiers. "Where's the rest of your platoon?" I called loud enough for them to turn toward my voice. If we were going to make it out of this alive, we would need more manpower than ten bodies and an injured dragon. Although, if Mikhail healed up quickly, he was like his own army.

What appeared to be the leader of the group came forward. "This is all that's left, ma'am." He was young and did not act like a militia member. He stood at attention like a true military soldier.

Damn. "I'm sorry." I didn't know what else to say.

"The past few weeks have been bloody." He glanced at Mikhail and then back at me. "They wanted to know where the last dragon was, and they slaughtered civilians and militia alike trying to find your... friend."

I jerked at the term and glanced at Mikhail. "I'm not sure I'd categorize him as my friend." I spoke slowly, trying to work this all out with a mind that was overtired and trying to catch up with everything that occurred since Mikhail whisked me away from Grand Central Station.

The soldier let out a small laugh. "If nothing else, the dragon considers you a friend. Or an ally. He wouldn't have told you to run otherwise."

I noted an underlying tone of disgust and met the soldier's sharp and accusing eyes. "If I *had* run, none of you would be here." I slid my gaze to Mikhail. "Isn't that right, Mikhail?" They needed to know what he almost did at the Serpent King's bidding.

Mikhail's head lowered. If he had been in human form, his cheeks would have burned red with embarrassment. "I agreed to their terms. I agreed to be bait so they could extinguish whatever resistance was still out there. If I died, they didn't care, but if I agreed to torch any humans who crawled out of the tunnels, I would be allowed to live as their..." He swallowed and his throat seemed to constrict. "As their pet," he said softly enough for the air to chill around me. "It was a matter of survival." His eyes lifted to mine. "But if they ever get their hands on me again, there will be no bargaining for my life."

His words caused a red veil to fall over my eyes, and my left fist shot out, smashing into the side of his snout, knocking him over. I shook the sting out of my hand and looked up at the soldier as if I didn't just punch a dragon.

"What's your name?" I asked as he stared with his mouth open in shock.

"Um." He looked between Mikhail struggling to get back on his feet and me. "Troy Harrington," he said. "And you just punched a dragon. You have a death wish or something?"

Mikhail chuckled as he rubbed his jaw with his tattered wing. "I think she does, but she'll never admit it."

I glared at Mikhail and pointed my finger at him. "You don't know a damn thing about me, so don't profess to know me just because you took care of me for a month."

His eyes narrowed. "Don't test me, human," he growled.

"Fuck you, dragon," I snarled back at him, ready to strike him down again.

Troy slowly backed up a few steps facing his palms toward the two of us. "I'm not sure either of you are safe to be around. I think I'll just take my men somewhere…"

"There *is* nowhere to go," Mikhail snapped. "The minute you show yourselves on the streets, they'll slaughter you. She is your best bet on surviving. And as much as it pains me, she is mine as well."

I huffed and turned my shoulder away from Mikhail, meeting Troy's sharp gaze. "You asked me if I trusted him?" I shook my head slowly. "No. But here's the shit thing. He has the brains and the fire capacity, along with a hell of a strong motive to destroy the leviathans and the Serpent King. And that is what I'm betting on here. Not his loyalty to the human race, which is fleeting at best, but his desire to strike the monsters down himself."

Troy pursed his lips as he digested my words. "I still think you two are a breeze away from an explosion." He crossed his arms. "But I will follow you since the dragon also thinks you are the one who will be our savior. However, if I think either of you are putting my men in danger, I will not hesitate to take you out."

I would have done the same for my team had they still been alive. I gave Troy a nod and then leaned against the backpack as exhaustion took over. "You might want those bleach barrels aimed in both directions. The leviathans have sent their young into the tunnels before," I said through a yawn, and then lay my head down, leaving my welfare in the hands of these strangers.

Dragon Storm
Chapter 5

THE SOUND OF HISSING cries filled the space, jerking me from sleep. The brightness in the tunnel made me momentarily wonder whether the leviathans punched through the pavement above us. But the stench that followed made that idea die as surely as the baby leviathans succumbed to Mikhail's fire.

Gunfire erupted in the opposite direction and Mikhail spun and ran weaving through the legs of the soldiers to the front of the line before spewing out another blast of fire that decimated the new attackers. Baby leviathans screamed, and I covered my ears.

When the noise faded, silence followed, and the team gathered closer around me. Once Mikhail breached the tiny circle, I stared at him. His wings were more solid now and he looked steadier on his feet than he had when I fell asleep.

"We need to get them to a safe space," I said, unsure he would agree to have a small delegation of strangers in his home base.

He nodded and looked south. He glanced at the soaker guns and the half empty spray bottle. "We need more bleach. Otherwise, we won't make it. I can guarantee they are feeding their young into the subway systems downtown, so the closer we get, the more we will encounter."

Hitting up another custodial closet at Grand Central was no longer an option, but that wasn't the only hub in Manhattan. "Are there custodial closets at Penn Station?"

His eyebrows rose, as if I had surprised him. "Probably. But wouldn't you have hit those places already?"

I know our platoon never thought of hitting up custodial closets in the subway stations. Schools, yes, but subway stations, not so much. We didn't even try hotels, either. I glanced at the soldiers. "Have you?"

They shook their heads. "We didn't even consider subway stations for having bleach." Troy's eyes lit up at the prospect. "Schools and hospitals we emptied out as soon as we found out about the leviathans' weakness."

They were just as shortsighted as we were. "Did anyone bother to search hotels?" Heads shook. There were plenty of those around. "Or the convention center?" Again, heads shook. So, we now had some other locations to search for our new form of ammunition along the way to Mikhail's.

I glanced at Mikhail. Having him on his feet in the front of the pack would be beneficial, but seeing as we were attacked from both sides, we needed more bleach delivery options. Otherwise, we would run out of firepower pretty quickly. We needed more hands to carry stuff, too, if we happened on another stash like we found at Grand Central.

"I think we are going to need you in human form. Can you shift yet?" I asked him, eyeing his mended wings.

He stretched them out and glanced at the whisper-thin membranes and red lines still traversing the material. "Not quite there yet," he said. "I'd be a hindrance to the team in human form right now." He met my gaze. "Another day and I should be good."

"In another day, we'll be knee-deep in leviathan babies," I snapped. I didn't have the patience for his healing that he had had with mine. The longer he remained as this tiny dragon, the more danger we were in, and I certainly wasn't in fighting shape. I just wanted to get to a place of safety before we encountered something unsurmountable. I narrowed my eyes and pointed at him. "Are you trying to sabotage our efforts?"

"He gave us a heads-up before the leviathans arrived." Troy waved at the cooked messes on both sides of us. "He didn't have to do that," he added.

Troy sticking up for Mikhail did not help my mood.

"We wouldn't be in this predicament had the damn dragon not destroyed our stash of bleach," I grumbled at them and turned away, checking my emotions. I took the time to dissect my response to make sure I wasn't reacting with feelings alone. I could not wrap my head around a vulnerable Mikhail. I mean, when he had been knocked out in the garage, when he came to, he took control again. Even as an injured mini-dragon, he was still a force to be reckoned with. But I didn't know how fast he could move, and if he held us up, that would only make it easier for the leviathans to multiply and send their offspring to their death in the hopes that we would run out of fuel or firepower in the process.

And looking at our reserves, that was a very high possibility. It was like being buried alive and watching as the last of the oxygen bled out, snuffing out the last match and plunging your last struggling breaths into darkness and despair.

I shivered at the thought and refocused. Although I would push myself for the cause, I did not think Mikhail would do the same. Not if it did not suit his end goal. He only had one focus in mind, and if we jeopardized it, he would sacrifice us to get his revenge.

The one thing we had in our favor: like us, Mikhail was now a prime target for extinction.

Dragon Storm
Chapter 6

MIKHAIL AND I TOOK the front of the pack with Troy on one side of me and Jenny with her super soaker on the other side of Mikhail. Karl, the other super-soaker soldier, took up the back along with Adam, who manned the spray bottle. The rest of the soldiers were sandwiched in between us.

We followed the Seventh Avenue express tracks south from Times Square. I hadn't run as far as I thought I did when we escaped the monsters. I hadn't even come close to the eight blocks to reach Penn Station. We made our way past the signage for the station, which seemed like it was only a few city blocks from where we left the dead leviathans.

"Stay put. Let me scope out the station to see if I can locate the custodial closets and anything we can pirate to carry bulk loads of bleach with," Mikhail said.

"Bullshit," I spat back. I wasn't about to trust him on his own.

"Excuse me?" He gawked at me, and so did a few of the soldiers.

"You are not stepping out of my sight. And if I catch you signaling to your monster friends out on the street, I'll put a bullet in your brain." I narrowed my eyes in a glare. "And where you go, we all follow. I'm not leaving these soldiers down here in the dark to be massacred by baby leviathans."

That earned me a cocked eyebrow from Troy. "We can handle..."

I turned on him, pointing my finger like a teacher who caught her student cheating on a test. "Nope. I'm not sacrificing anyone. Understand?"

"No disrespect, but that is not your call." Troy crossed his arms. "These are my soldiers, my responsibility. It's our war, too."

I gave him the once over. "How long have you been leading troops?"

His lips twitched into a smile. "Ten years. You?"

He was out of his mind. There was no way he led troops for ten years. We hadn't even been at war that long. "No fucking way. Not unless you started while you were still in grade school." My response earned me some snickers from his group.

"Sweetheart, I'm almost forty. I went into the Marine Corps the day I turned eighteen and worked my way onto the Delta Force."

I stared at him, and he smirked, causing me to realize my mouth had dropped open at the declaration of his age. I wouldn't have put him at even close to thirty. He looked damn good for his age. I popped my lips together, trying not to blush, but the heat in my cheeks told me I failed.

He continued, "When the world turned to shit, my mother fell ill, so I was on leave here in the city. Everyone else in Delta Force had been on base when the dragons came, but I wasn't there." His lips pressed tightly together. "I am the only Delta Force member left." He glared at Mikhail as if it were his fault, which was likely the case, because he commanded the dragon forces before they were slaughtered by the Serpent King. "Instead of joining one of the other militias that were being formed, I took a different route. I had no interest in businessmen and women thinking they knew tactical warfare better than I did, so I built this team from the inner-city gangs. They had the knowledge, skills, and raw nerve that I needed, and they were all itching to get back at these things that had stolen their livelihood."

I glanced around at the men and woman following him. They were a mix of all races, Blacks, Asians, Hispanics, and Whites, and there was only one other woman in the mix. But they all had one thing in common: that hard edge I remembered from the street kids I had run into on the subways. I used to try to avoid being in the same subway car as gang members because the likelihood of a White Upper West Side girl walking out unscathed was higher than being left alone by gang members.

"These are the best and the brightest in the city. I didn't just take anyone from the gang pool. They had to meet *my* standards and pass my boot camp to make the team. And everyone who made the cut had to bring their gang's armory to the table. All that firepower is what sustained us. Gangs were the only entities that still had semi-automatic weapons and an arsenal of bullets that would make the military proud."

I blinked and looked closer at the weapons they held. They weren't the normal rifles or handguns I was accustomed to. The fact they carried that kind of firepower actually gave me more hope that we'd make it to Mikhail's—as long as they still had ammunition.

He glanced around at what was left of his team. Pride filled his eyes and made his chest puff out. When his gaze returned to mine, it was icy with resolve. "These soldiers are my only surviving family. You have no place in making decisions for us."

Well, shit. How could I argue with him now?

"I don't care what your credentials are. The only one *I* take orders from is Holly," Mikhail said, cutting through whatever standoff might occur. "And without the dragon on your side, you have no hope of winning this war."

"Shut up," I snapped at Mikhail. I didn't need him throwing his testosterone into the pot. It was already boiling over with Troy. And although Troy's former Delta Force status impressed me, I still didn't like being the one subservient to a leader when I had no knowledge of track records beyond what he just spewed out.

"And how many have died because of shoddy leadership?" I asked.

"None of my trained soldiers have died. I can't say the same for those who were sent by other platoons to help round out my team, though." This time his smile turned almost feral. "They didn't particularly like my style of leadership."

I stepped closer, puffing my chest as if I were taller than this Delta Force guy, but I could only get within a head's height of him. Looking up into his hard eyes, I knew I failed at my intimidation tactic. At this very moment, Troy reminded me of the way Mikhail was when we had first been at his apartment in lower Manhattan. All business, with the force behind him.

Troy glared down at me as if I were just an annoying gnat.

"Troy, stop being a dick." Jenny brushed a piece of her dark hair out of her face. She slipped a piece of peppermint gum between her teeth. "I heard she got fried by a dragon and lived. She's not one of those prissy little girls from Brooklyn who cries if her nail breaks."

I didn't break my stare, but I appreciated what the little Hispanic girl said. She was compact and muscular, like that chick in those old fast car movies. I bet she was just as fierce.

Especially considering Troy's left eye twitched just enough for me to catch his displeasure about being questioned in a public forum.

"Is she right?" he asked.

"Yes, I did get burned by a dragon, but it wasn't from running away." Because my platoon and nearly all the others fighting for our survival had been decimated, I owed it to these soldiers to come clean. "I wasn't exactly forthcoming with my superior officers, because they had no idea that Mikhail was a dragon." I stepped back out of Troy's personal space. "For some reason, Mikhail put his trust in me and got me out of Grand Central under false pretenses." I glanced at the mini-dragon. "He wanted to know our secret. How we were actually taking down the leviathans."

"And you told him?" Troy crossed his arms.

"Oh hell no. Not at first. I wanted to get back to my platoon, but he wouldn't allow it. He said it was too dangerous and since a body was dropped with a note declaring that I had screwed up the negotiations, he didn't think I'd be welcomed without some serious fabricating of stories." I glanced at Mikhail.

"So, the dragon offered to burn you." Troy sneered at Mikhail.

"No. That was my plan."

Troy's gaze snapped to mine. "Excuse me?"

"It seemed logical at the time, but on retrospect, my commander was going to sacrifice me to the monsters no matter what story I concocted. I could have walked in the door with the dragon on a leash and he still would have court-martialed me." I shrugged and turned, pulling up the hem of my shirt so they all could see my back.

"I advised against her plan," Mikhail piped in from enough of a distance away to avoid a swat or a kick from me.

"So, you lied to your commander," Troy said.

I turned and nodded. "Yes. They would have shot him on sight had he been in dragon form, and still put me out for the monsters to tear to pieces. But Mikhail has the technology to make that bleach bomb. He can decimate their army and give us half a chance. I put my money on him for our survival." I glared sideways at the fiend. "And I still am, despite my misgivings."

Troy's sharp gaze fell on the dragon. "How did you care for wounds that grave?" He waved at me.

"I have the means and materials. I was married to a human woman who raised my children," he said, as if that made any difference. "Accidents happened."

"You have a wife and kids?" Jenny asked.

Mikhail slowly shook his head. "They made me watch as they tore them limb from limb." His chest glowed as his voice turned feral. "That was after they decimated the rest of the dragons."

"They killed a dragon after the last body drop," Troy said.

"Yes. Ricky, the only one who truly believed in their cause to wipe out the stain of humanity from the earth."

"And why did they not kill you?" Karl stepped into the field of light.

"Because I was still useful. I'm the only one who could shift, and they wanted me to infiltrate your ranks, locate your platoons, and destroy them."

"Well, you certainly did that with your path of fire," I interjected, wondering whether he was still following the monsters' orders in some way.

"That was not my intention," Mikhail snapped at me. "I had coffee because I could feel the animosity in that place. Your life was as good as over the minute we stepped in that building. I thought they'd put us in front of a firing line, not out on the street as bait for leviathans." His wings fluttered with the snarl coming from his snout. "I had a coffee, knowing that I would need enough fire power to melt bullets before they got to you. So, fucking sue me." He sauntered off in the direction of the platform to Penn Station.

Troy traded a glance with Jenny, and she smirked.

"Seems the dragon is a bit smitten with you," she said, sounding quite the opposite of a gang kid.

Maybe Troy was the type of leader who could drive the gang mentality right out of kids and replace it with a fierce loyalty that my troops seemed to have for me. Even so, her statement was off the mark by miles.

"The fuck you say?" I cocked an eyebrow at her.

This time Troy let out a laugh. "You really don't see it." He hooked his thumb toward the dragon.

"Mikhail tolerates me," I said. "That's the extent of it." I glanced after the stomping mini-dragon. He looked like a child who had just been told to go to his room. But he was headed in the direction we told him he couldn't go alone. I started after him, followed by the rest of the snickering soldiers.

I spun around and pointed at them collectively. "Stop that," I hissed and then turned to continue after my dragon, wondering whether they were right and just how I would take that after everything we had been through. His actions in the garage came to the forefront of my mind. He hadn't even looked at me that night with anything remotely like attraction or affection.

That little voice in the back of my mind piped up. *Yes, but he had just retrieved the heads of his family from Grand Central. You wouldn't be frisky either if the tables were turned.*

It always burned at the pit of my stomach when that voice was right.

Dragon Storm
Chapter 7

MIKHAIL LED US UP to the ground floor of the station and signaled for us to stay low and stay quiet. I pointed back to the underground floor we just traversed. And he shook his head.

"No storage rooms," he whispered.

The one we found at Grand Central was on the platform level, but Penn Station didn't seem to have any gradually rising platforms into the heart of the station like Grand Central had on the main lines. Here it was all stairs or narrow pathways. Understanding clicked, but I still didn't like the exposure. Some of the glass ceiling panels had already been destroyed and each step we took ground crushed glass under our feet.

He led us in the direction of one of the bigger department stores, and when we got to the metal gate, he waved us back with his wing. Mikhail crawled up the gate until his front paws were high enough to match the tallest soldier and he spread his paws three feet wide. His lower legs stretched out in the same pattern but only reached about halfway down the gate. It didn't take long for the metal to turn red between his four paws. He yanked backward and fell onto his back in front of us.

"What the—" Troy said.

"Shush." Mikhail cut him off and then rolled to his side and gently placed the grid on the ground. He repeated with the lower half and then walked through the opening as quietly as possible.

We all followed.

He pointed to the row of neatly stacked carts with the store's logo on it as we passed. A couple of soldiers grabbed carts and followed. Thankfully, they didn't grab any with squeaky wheels. That would have doomed us. When we passed the household cleaner section, Mikhail raised a wing and halted. The soldiers with the carts marched down the aisle and picked up the few bleach bottles still nestled on the shelf.

Mikhail then led us to the back where a locked door stood between us and the back office and storage area of the store. When he raised up to put his paws on the locking mechanism, I cleared my throat.

"Look, if there's a stash back there that's bigger than what we found at Grand Central, I don't want to fry the only lock that will keep it safe. Give me a second." I put up a finger. I went to the cooking utensil section and found some slim fondue pokers. When I returned, I received quite a few raised eyebrows. "I wasn't exactly an angel in my youth," I whispered.

My misspent youth had involved some level of breaking and entering. Thus, my skills at opening locks. Just because my family had come from Uptown, didn't mean I didn't dance along the line of the law. Thankfully, this wasn't one with a keypad. Otherwise, I would have let Mikhail melt the door because a keypad needs electricity to work. The light from the glass front of the store didn't reach this far back and I had to have Jenny point her flashlight at the hole. With three kebab sticks in place, I turned the set to the left as one unit.

I was rewarded with a click and then I reached down and pulled on the door handle. The door swished open, and I smiled, waving the soldiers inside. I glanced down at Mikhail, waving him along, too.

The door swung closed behind me, silently drenching us in darkness. The flashlight Jenny had didn't penetrate much. All I could see were shadows of shelving. The rest of the flashlights came to life, illuminating aisles and aisles of packed shelving, as if the store got a new shipment right before all hell broke loose in Manhattan. Fortunately for us, the store didn't have frozen foods. Otherwise, this place would stink of rot enough to make me want to barf.

We had raided some of the closed grocery stores once or twice in the beginning and those places were gag-worthy. It took at least a week to get that stench out of our clothes and it seemed to linger in our nostrils for much longer.

Still, the sight of fully stocked shelves stopped us all in our tracks. This place had not been raided, and I wondered what kind of locks they had to the outside world beyond the iron gate at the entrance that was immovable when locked tight. I had had some experience trying to break into those things. Most were locked forever without electricity to run the keypads controlling them.

The door protecting this little gold mine wasn't one that could be knocked in, either. So, with Mikhail's help, we had hit the motherload— as long as the rats hadn't gotten in here first. The only sound was of the two carts rolling on the floor as we slowly walked through the warehouse. All I could think was the carts we had would not be big enough. If I had my way, I'd bring the industrial-size cases of cereal and chips with us, but I knew better, especially considering Mikhail just kept walking and scanning the aisles. His nails clacked on the concrete floor, mixing with the rolling wheels, and it seemed like a lot more noise than it had through the store. Perhaps it was the darkness bearing down on all of us from all sides of this storeroom.

He stopped and flicked his wing down one of the rows ahead. I'd say he was grinning, but the shadows were too unpredictable. When I rounded the corner and flashlights hit the shelving, I inhaled sharply.

I thought the stash in the supply closet at Grand Central was big, but this dwarfed that stash by a multiplier of seven or eight times the number of bleach bottles.

"We might need a few more carts," he said softly, with eyes that were possibly wider than mine.

"Spread out," Troy whispered. "See what we can find in here to transport this stuff with minimal noise." The soldiers dispersed and returned a few minutes later with laundry carts, yard carts, and wheelbarrows.

We filled every container, including the shopping carts, until we could pack no more in without fear of containers falling during our trek back through Penn Station. We had five containers and some of them would require multiple trips up and down the staircases to the lower levels due to the sheer volume and weight, but it would be worth it if we could get all these packages to Mikhail's apartment building.

"Grab as many backpacks as they have and pack them with whatever food fits. We can double up packs, if need be, but we can't pass up on this opportunity," Troy ordered. "And if they have any super soakers in the toy section, grab those and we can fill up with what's still on the shelves before we go."

I traded a glance with Mikhail and then went to grab some of the cereal boxes I saw. Milk or no milk, having my pick of cereals was like stepping into heaven. I was still amazed this place hadn't been picked over at all, but I was beyond thankful for the stock that was still here.

Once everyone gathered at the storage room door, we each took an extra backpack filled with food, and ripped into the super soaker packages. There were enough for every soldier to have at least one mega soaker and one smaller one. We filled every one of the toy weapons with bleach, getting ready for the perilous trek back to the subway floor.

"Be alert," Troy said as we filtered out of the storage room as quietly as we could with our overloaded packs and carts.

I paused at the door and finagled the skewers in the lock, clicking it back into place before I pocketed my new lockpick fondue set. I wanted to make sure what was in this storeroom was kept secure in case we needed to make the trip back for any reason.

I received a nod from both Troy and Mikhail as if they had the same thing on their mind.

We made our way through the store to the opening in the security gate and filtered through. Even at our quietest, the carts still crunched the glass under the wheels loud enough for me to shiver. In the tunnels, it would be louder which meant the baby leviathans would find us quicker.

I recited a silent prayer for God to thank him for letting us find such a stash and asked for the Holy Spirit to be with us on this trek, because we needed a miracle for all of us to get to our destination alive.

Dragon Storm
Chapter 8

MIKHAIL LED US TO an internal ramp that traversed back and forth down to the lower level, where we should be safer. I never knew this wheelchair ramp existed. I just thought the handicapped people took the elevators, but this suited our purpose better than the labor-intensive climb down the stairs would have been considering the elevators were all defunct without power.

He led us to the southern-most ramp to the Seventh Avenue express line and then put his wings up, halting all of us. "Soak the ramp," he hissed.

We rapidly pumped our guns and let loose on the darkness below. The screams of burning monsters filled the space, followed by a plume of fire that lit up the tracks below, along with at least a dozen baby leviathans.

We marched forward, with our soakers aimed into the tunnel, but there seemed to be no more. Soldiers took turns covering while we got all the carts down onto the tracks. With our stash secured between us, we started a full jog, pushing carts of bleach along with us.

"Hold up," Mikhail said as he stopped.

"What is it?" I tried to make out anything in the dark in front of me. I heard an inhale and passed the procured flashlight over the area in front of us. The light passed over the hunched dragon. He was bigger than the little turkey-sized beast he had been since we fled Times Square. His eyes flashed in my direction in warning. I turned the flashlight farther down the tunnel while pumping my super soaker. The rest of the soldiers followed suit. The hiss of pressure building in the toys filled the small space but none of us saw what had made Mikhail stop.

Bleach dripped on my hands. The sharp stench drifted to my nose. We were all ready to take out monsters, but none came. "Mik?" I whispered.

"Just another minute," he said with a voice so strained that my flashlight moved to where he had been.

All I saw were human legs. Bare human legs. I stared. The last time I saw him shift from dragon to human, he was clothed, not naked and sweaty like he was now. His eyes flashed at me.

"Do you mind," he growled with teeth that were still dragon-like. Fabric still webbed between his arms and his torso.

I turned away and stared at Troy's shocked expression.

"This wasn't what it was like when he shifted before," I said. "At Grand Central, his shift was instantaneous. One moment, he was a dragon; the next, he was human. And he had clothes on."

Troy turned his gaze to me, cocking an eyebrow at me as if he didn't believe me.

"It's a little harder to shift when I'm injured." Mikhail's voice carried in the dark. "I threw a pair of jogging pants and a shirt on the top of one of the bins. Can someone bring that to me?"

Shuffling and then one of the soldiers shoved the clothes at me as if he were afraid of approaching the dragon now that he was in human form. Of course, the mini-dragon wasn't as intimidating as Mikhail St. Clare in human form. He was a monster of a man. Over six five and built like a Mack truck.

I stepped forward with the light pointed at the ground and reached the clothing out to him. I guess he expected one of the men to bring him clothing, not me.

Even so, he took them and slowly put the shirt over his head with a wince. He got one leg in the pants and then glanced at me. "Turn."

I did, and then his hand landed on my shoulder. But it wasn't steady as he balanced on one leg to fit his other into the free pant leg. His warmth penetrated my body like a welcoming embrace. Having his hand on me unearthed the feelings I had buried under my anger at his fiery actions.

"Why did you shift?" I whispered over my shoulder, trying to sweep these unwanted desires away like last month's trash.

"We need to move faster. I was slowing us down."

I hadn't noticed, but then again, I was still in marginal shape after all I was healing from, and the run had been sucking the energy from me. I couldn't imagine going faster. When his hand came off my shoulder, I turned and raised the light to his face. His rugged features were paler than I remembered and although his eyes blazed in an inferno of indignation, I could see the apology written deep in his irises.

"You good now?" I asked without dwelling on his sickly features.

"I am if you are." He glanced at my wrists. "Have you had a chance to redress those?"

"No. And I'm not going to get the chance until we are in your building." I did not want to waste time caring for any of my wounds. If I sat, it would be awhile before I got up again. It looked as though Mikhail might be in the same condition.

"Is there an extra super soaker that I could use?"

I glanced at Troy and received a nod. Someone in the back handed off one to Troy, and he in turn passed it to Mikhail. Although his jaw was tighter than usual and his gaze blazed as he looked at Mikhail. The soldier's dislike of Mikhail now that he had donned his human form was palpable in the air.

"How many of our secrets did you pass to the rest of the monsters?" he asked with a voice that carried a very sharp edge.

Mikhail looked at the child's toy in his hands. "One. The location of her platoon. But only after I destroyed it, and they captured me." He met Troy's gaze. "The rest were always off the mark enough so that the core bases were not harmed."

Troy's gaze narrowed. "But you did participate in killing humans, correct?"

Mikhail nodded. "But you already knew we were responsible for wiping out the military response worldwide." At least he didn't say it with a smile.

It almost sounded as if there were a trace of regret in his words and it took me by surprise.

Troy's hands curled into fists.

"She is the only one who can get away with throwing a punch at me," Mikhail warned and nodded toward me.

Jenny stepped forward. "So, if I decided to kick your ass?" Her voice carried the anger radiating from Troy.

"You would not live to explain your level of stupidity." Mikhail's hard tone was accompanied by a thin trail of smoke drifting from his nostrils.

Jenny's eyebrows drew together as she looked at me and then back at Mikhail. "Why does she get a pass?"

"Because she nearly burned alive and bled for your cause. She earned my respect." His voice was quiet, but his eyes had transformed into that inferno that I now recognized. He was on edge and that meant unpredictability from the dragon.

If he torched the soldiers, he'd torch the bleach. I needed to step in, otherwise, I would shoot him and right now, my heart contracted at the thought.

"When all this is over and we've won this fight, I'll make sure you each get your swipe at him," I said, which earned me a cocked eyebrow from everyone, including Mikhail. "Seriously, if they still are angry enough to throw a punch when this is over, Mikhail is going to *let* each of you punch him." I pointed my finger at Mikhail. "I'll likely be in that line, too."

"I never agreed to that." He turned back to the nearest cart and started away from us. "But *we* don't have time to argue about it. It's time to haul ass."

Dragon Storm
Chapter 9

MIKHAIL HADN'T BEEN KIDDING, but at least he was jogging at the same pace as the rest of the soldiers. I started out just behind him with Troy on one side and Jenny on the other, but soon I found the pacing a little too much. I fell back into the center of the pack as my body screamed at the exertion.

The pace slowed to a crawl and then stopped. I went to move forward but one of the soldiers put his arm out, stopping me.

"Side. Now!" Mikhail's voice hissed from the front and the scraping of the carts followed as I was pushed to the side wall.

The soldiers hoisted the carts up on the walking path on the side, as we all hugged the wall. The distinct sound of guns pumping filled the darkness and with my back to the concrete tiled wall, the tremors reached into my bones.

"Spray yourselves and the ground in front of us," Mikhail said. "And then remain quiet and very still."

I did as he said, getting my pants and boots wet before creating a line on the floor in front of me. My nose burned from the burst of bleach in the space and my eyes watered. I didn't dare wipe them as I was sure some liquid dripped onto my hands and bleach in the eye was dangerous and painful as hell.

The vibrations in the walls increased until the very ground we stood on felt as if it were going to give at any moment. Even the carts rattled enough for me to shift. A few of the ceiling tiles fell as the stampede got closer. My heart beat as hard and as fast as the vibrations in the wall behind me.

I expected a stampede of baby leviathans. What I didn't expect was light to burst through the ceiling of the tunnel, followed by a grown leviathan's foot. If we had been on the tracks, at least half of us would have been squashed. Another foot slammed through the tunnel a few yards north. The fact the beasts could break through to the tunnels wasn't something that happened often. A few of the shallower passes had been breached this way, but none of the main lines that were deeper set under the surface.

No wonder the world shook violently. The beasts were probably jumping to get the right amount of force to break through. The roadways above would be a god-awful mess and nearly impossible to navigate with the craters this had to be causing to roads without paths underneath. Another foot broke through, near enough to make me shudder.

I glanced at Mikhail, and he slowly shook his head and waved me back against the wall. The rest of the soldiers stood with wide eyes, staring at the destruction of the tunnels. We had a small edge that we were perched on. For some reason, that seemed to be enough to keep us and our treasure out of the destruction zone. If these tunnels had live trains, we would be in dire straits. The subway clearance to the walls was bare inches, and unless you stood in one of the alcoves, you were as dead as if you jumped in front of a moving train.

But it was wide enough for two of the four wheels of each cart to perch on. For the long haul, it would be difficult to balance and move at any fast pace and dropping them onto the tracks would mean that cart was a lost cause, which meant we'd have to carry the heavy containers full of bleach. And if I had read one of the posts right, we still had a distance to travel ahead of us and then we had to cross from the west side to the east side near Brooklyn Bridge. Hell, we hadn't even reached Canal Street.

How much of the subway system had been breached by the leviathans? And were there some areas that were now impenetrable?

My heart dropped, and I glanced back at Mikhail. The deep crevasse between his eyes showed his concentration. The beasts were moving north, not south, but that didn't mean we wouldn't have an ambush down the line.

We needed to find a path that branched out under the buildings and not the streets. All I could think about was the line that went under the site that once held the World Trade Center. It ran under buildings, not streets. At least a portion of it did. There was no way to get there from here without going down the Seventh Avenue express that we were on.

When the wall vibrations lowered, Mikhail cleared his throat, capturing our attention. He picked up his cart, making the muscles in his arms bulge. He nodded toward the rest of the heavy wagons. The soldiers on either side of the containers hoisted theirs and sweat popped out on their brows despite the cool air filtering down into our limited space.

With a silent side shuffle of feet, we moved down the thin path that somehow had saved us from destruction.

"How far?" Troy whispered with a voice full of strain.

"Eighteen blocks and two avenues. Assuming there isn't a section of the tunnel that isn't totally destroyed," Mikhail said in a low hush.

"Fuck."

That was the unanimous response, hissed between strained lips. Those of us not holding a

side of a cart had a super soaker at the ready as
we shimmied sideways a step at a time, waiting
for the next foot to come through the ceiling.

Dragon Storm
Chapter 10

OUR PROGRESS WAS SLOW, but we made it to the interchange that would lead us more toward City Hall and the east side rather than continue down the Seventh Avenue path, which had been trashed by the leviathans because it ran directly under the street. Luckily, when we reached the split, it was passable to get from one side of the tracks to the other.

The only problem with the City Hall track: it was a dead end. There was no exit except into City Hall itself. But from the looks of the group,

Mikhail included, we all could use a break, and this seemed like a more secure place to get some rest. One way in, and one way out. We just had to be sure to position ourselves under the remains of City Hall and not under the park, where it would be easy for the monsters to crush the tunnel—and us with it.

We still carried the carts, opting for as stealthy an approach as we could. After we got into the safety of the City Hall line, Mikhail stopped and took a bottle of bleach. He drew a line from one side of the entrance to the other, emptying the entire bottle in the process. He set the bottle down at the far side and trotted back to us.

I opened my mouth, and he shook his head, putting his finger on his lips. He pointed topside and twirled his finger. They were close enough for him to sense them. He picked up his cart and continued on until we reached the old entrance to City Hall itself. The small ramp went up into the darkness, but Mikhail led us to the far corner to a door.

He gave a quick glance at the patch of ceiling that let some colored light in and then pointed to me and then to the lock. Just the look to the stained glass above had everyone on edge.

I slid to the door and squinted at the lock as I rummaged in my pocket for the kebabs that I took from the store in Penn Station. This wasn't as easy as the single deadbolt. This had both the handle lock, which was the easy one, but the other lock was much more difficult, especially without a light shining on the lock. But after four tries, I was rewarded with a click.

Mikhail opened the door and waved us all inside the room. Our bodies and carts barely made it, and when Mikhail closed the door, I heard him let out an exhale like we had passed through the bowels of hell and made it out alive. A small light illuminated his hand and he turned, giving us our first look at our current resting space.

It wasn't much. Just a ten-by-ten empty storage room. But with the carts, it left very little room for anyone to move, much less sit down.

"Push the carts against the far wall," Mikhail said softly. "I'll see what I can do to stack them so we can at least take turns getting some rest."

"We've had worse accommodations," Troy said, but he did as Mikhail asked and maneuvered the five carts to the far wall and a couple of folks turned on their flashlights.

With everything stored in one corner, we had a little more room, but Mikhail lifted a couple of the smaller carts onto the larger ones, balancing them so they leaned against the wall. They made sure the wheels were locked on the lower carriages and now we all had the room to find a seat on the ground.

He glanced at me and pointed at my hands. "We need to redress those wounds." He crossed to me. "Did you happen to pack any of those wipes and bandages from your apartment?" He met my gaze.

All eyes were on us standing in the center of the room. I shifted under their stares and nodded as I unclipped my backpack. Now that we weren't moving, every muscle in my body cried out in protest. Everything hurt as I removed the backpacks I carried, and I lowered to a sitting position, handing him the backpack from my apartment. I was too tired to dig through it for the materials he wanted.

I glanced at his wrist as he reached across me. It was healed of the damage the iron spikes had done. Unlike mine. Now that he was focusing on my wrists, the pain flared, reminding me that I was not at my best.

The flame dancing on his fingertips doused as he reached into my pack. A half dozen more flashlights came to life, illuminating the enclosed room.

"Thanks." He pulled out the wipes and liquid bandage tube, along with Band-Aids. He looked at my left wrist first, wiping off the dirt and grime that had built up on my run. He inspected the wound and reapplied the liquid bandage on both sides before covering the hole with crisscrossed Band-Aids. At least the wipes weren't bloody like the last time.

I needed to take off my leather jacket for him to unwrap the bandage that stabilized my right wrist. As he peeled away the wrap, the layers went from damp to reddened on the inside of my wrist. He grimaced and focused on the back of my wrist first. That seemed to be doing as well as my left hand, which I was thankful for.

When he turned my wrist over, I winced at the motion. The blood drained from my face, leaving my skin cold. The room started to spin. He pressed a cool wipe onto my wrist, holding it tight in the same manner he had in my apartment.

"Breathe, Woods," he said, sternly enough to allow me to shake off the sudden wooziness.

I met his gaze, and my chin quivered. "You're not going to cauterize it again, are you?" God, how I hated that pathetic lilt to my voice and the fear that gripped my throat.

He shook his head. "No, you're not hemorrhaging like you were when I first took the shackles out. But I do need to clean the area in order to get another layer of liquid bandage on." He released the pressure on my wrist and started cleaning out the dirt that had found its way between the folds of the Ace bandage.

Relief washed over me, and I swallowed a thin line of bile that had crawled up the back of my throat. I didn't know whether I would remain conscious if he had to cauterize it again. I still don't know how I remained awake and aware last time. Although, his gentle wipes across the puncture wound sent pain spiraling through my bones.

He smiled and shook his head as he continued to clean my wound. "You pointed that gun at me like this hand wasn't as bad off as it is."

"And successfully picked two locks." I forced a smile.

Once he seemed satisfied that the dirt was gone, he put liquid bandage over the wound and let it set before putting on another pair of crisscrossed Band-Aides. He rummaged around in the backpack again and then sighed.

He glanced at me. "You didn't bring the other Ace bandages?"

"No. I had to make a choice, and chocolates won out." I met his gaze and narrowed my eyes at him. If he had been with me when I left my apartment, we would have all the medical supplies he needed to patch me up and then some. He got the message and went back to staring at my broken wrist.

"You have chocolates?" Jenny asked, perking up from her nap.

I reached beyond Mikhail and pulled out the chocolates, tore open the cellophane with my teeth, and opened the box, picking one of my favorites before I handed it to Jenny. There was enough for everyone to have a piece, with a few to spare.

Mikhail added an extra Band-Aid to each side of my wrist and then rebandaged my hand with the soiled wrap so I could function with my right hand as much as I could with my left. Then he straightened one leg and wrapped his arms around his knee, leaning his head down on his elbow.

"You okay?" I asked. His body language screamed exhaustion as much as my muscles did.

He nodded but didn't lift his head. "Sleep." He patted his thigh with his free hand. "You, too."

One by one, the lights turned off, drenching us in darkness. Teeth chattered in the dark as the chill penetrated the room despite the body heat. I wouldn't be surprised if it was snowing on the surface with the arctic blast that seemed to seep through underneath the door.

I would have preferred leaning back-to-back with Mikhail, but he reached out and guided my head down onto his leg. It wasn't as hard as I expected. His muscles were defined but it wasn't like lying on a rock. It was more like lying on a stiff pillow. And he radiated enough heat to take the chill out of the air, but not enough for me to get overheated.

Mikhail's fingers ran through the hair at my temple. The slow drag of it lulled me into a stupor.

Amid the soft snores, I heard the softest of sighs.

"I'm sorry I hurt you," Mikhail whispered and continued his light combing of my hair.

I turned, looking up at where I thought his face would be, and the soft glow of his citrine eyes met mine. I wanted to forgive him but that little voice that has kept me alive all these years wouldn't let me. Not until we were all safe and he was working on that bomb.

"Don't do it again." I turned back and adjusted to get comfortable.

He continued to run his fingers through my hair until his hand came to rest on his thigh and the glow went out. His soft snore added to the sounds filling the room, and I allowed myself to drift off into a restless sleep.

Dragon Storm
Chapter 11

I WOKE SUCKING DROOL back into my mouth, disoriented and stiff in the darkness. A moan escaped my lips as I tried to move, but a weight on top of me kept me in place. My heart leaped into my throat, pounding as quick as my pulse. It wasn't until the block holding me down groaned that my memory flooded back. The weight lifted off me and a small flame lit the space.

"Sorry about that," Mikhail whispered and rubbed his face with his free hand.

The rest of the soldiers started stirring at the presence of light in the dark room. The heat of Mikhail along with all our bodies had turned the little space into the equivalent of a hothouse. I sat up and pulled my shirt from my sweaty skin and then wiped my face with my bandaged hand, mopping up the moisture before I hand-combed my hair and stretched. I so wished for Mikhail's shower. Perhaps we would reach his apartment building today without incident.

But I knew better. My stomach clenched as I looked around. Today was the day we'd lose some people. The streets were loaded with leviathans. The subway tunnels had been smashed by their massive feet and they were hunting us with a vengeance. After all, we took their mangled dragon instead of killing him.

I had a feeling what was left of the subway system would be swarmed with baby leviathans and now that the tunnels had massive holes in them, I was sure their screams would be heard for miles.

"What's the plan?" I asked, not really aiming it at any one in particular, but my gaze traveled from Mikhail to Troy and back, searching for an answer.

Mikhail bit his lip and glanced at our piled stash. "Douse ourselves in bleach and make a run for it. We're only a few blocks northwest of the apartment. While I would have liked to get to the closest subway station, that isn't in the cards. This is the safest location right now since we are under a building. The only other station that we'd have a prayer in would be the Trade Center, but even that could have been compromised." He looked up at the ceiling. "I don't know how bad City Hall is up there, so we may end up with a wall of debris and have to make our way out via the tracks anyway."

"We'll still have to carry the carts," Troy said, and the sigh in his voice was clear.

I couldn't imagine their fatigue. I hadn't been one of the ones carrying the wagons along with double backpacks. I was exhausted with just my doubling of packs, and mine weren't all that heavy. The carts had to weigh at least a hundred pounds each. Although that didn't seem unsurmountable, carrying it for blocks while trying to keep an eye out for monsters was enough to make my mouth dry.

Mikhail nodded. "Rolling them on the pavement would be a recipe for disaster. Those mothers can hear anything out of the ordinary. And that's not a usual sound these days. Besides, we shouldn't try to make a run for it until it's dark. That way we will have the night in our favor."

"Can't they see at night?" Troy asked.

"Dragons can but I'm the last one left, so there's no danger in being seen anymore. Leviathans are nearly blind in the dark, but they can sniff you out from miles away. In our case, they'll be blocks away at best, so the deep shadows and narrow alleys are our best bet, even though that means it's also hard for you to see. The only thing we really have to worry about is if the leviathans get a whiff of us. If they do, it's over. Their smell receptors are scary accurate, and the only thing they actively avoid is bleach. The smell burns their noses just as badly as it burns their skin when you spray them. So, dousing in bleach is our only chance at this." He glanced at me and then my bandaged wrist. "That has to go. The smell of blood on the air will override the bleach."

I glanced down at my wrist and licked my lips. It hadn't been clean last night when he unwrapped it and I had no idea what shape it was in now. "What if I bleed through the Band-Aids?"

"We'll have to have a standoff because I can't compromise my building." He nearly winced saying the words, as if it pained him. "Let's reapply some liquid bandage and see if we can at least have enough of a buffer to keep it from seeping through."

Mikhail unwrapped my wrist and dropped the soiled bandage on the floor. Luckily, the Band-Aids seemed dry, but he still peeled them off and put a heavy amount of liquid bandage over my cuts, blowing on it until it had dried before he reapplied new Band-Aids. This time he put four on each, so it looked like I had a star patter on both the top and bottom of my wrist. Just for good measure, he added another couple on the one on the inside of my wrist and then took a step back. When he finally met my gaze, he still held that worried brow.

He took a deep breath and looked around the room. "Does anyone else have any cuts, scrapes, blisters, anything that could seep?"

Troy glanced around the room and received head shakes in response. "No," Troy said. "I'm pretty adamant about patching my team up for that same reason."

We all had seen the reaction of those things when there was fresh blood. Mikhail and I were lucky there weren't any leviathans within a few blocks of the park when we were chained to the statue by my former commander. If there had been, we both wouldn't be standing here in the midst of these soldiers.

I shook the morbid thoughts of what could have happened. Dwelling on that and not paying attention to the current crisis would likely get someone killed. We all had to be alert and cautious.

Troy maneuvered to the door and slowly opened it to the brightly lit tunnel beyond. Frigid air flowed in through the crack. He closed it as gently as possible. "We have a few hours to kill."

Jenny stood and stretched and started toward the door.

"What are you doing?" Troy asked as she reached for the knob.

"Nature calls," she said. "And this place is too small to cop a squat in the corner."

"No one goes alone." He reached for the nearest super soaker.

"I'll go with her." My bladder was feeling a bit heavy. I could use a little relief as well.

Troy hesitated before he handed me the loaded toy and then he stepped aside.

"Let the ladies have some privacy," Troy said, and I turned to see Mikhail on my heel and Troy's hand on his chest.

Mikhail's gaze snapped to Troy, and his eyes narrowed. Before he could launch into any argument, I said, "I'll be fine with Jenny."

I closed the door on his arched eyebrows. He looked like a hurt puppy.

Jenny slid around the corner and jumped down onto the track. A moment later, the sound of relief flooded the ground. When she was through, she nodded for me to do the same.

I climbed down, and almost landed in her water. I took a step to the side and lowered my pants, doing the same. It was harder to bend and balance with the healing burns on my back, but I managed not to pee on myself, so that was a win.

I finished and crawled up onto the platform. Jenny offered me a hand to help me to my feet and when we were standing close to each other, she leaned into my ear.

"The dragon cares about you a great deal," she whispered.

I frowned at her and shook my head. I was used to his nursemaid routine and although he doted on me, it was all a show. There were no feelings behind it. It was a means to an end for him.

She raised an eyebrow.

"He's a good actor," I whispered in her ear.

"If you don't want him, I'll gladly take a ride." Jenny grinned.

I blinked at her, and my mouth dropped open as an unwanted possessiveness spread through my blood. The thought of him with anyone else grated on my nerves like fingernails on a chalkboard.

Her grin remained. "Well, if you change your mind, let me know. He is a looker, and I wouldn't mind a taste." She took my hand and led me back to the room like a mother would lead a child.

Her comments threw me more than I admitted. Mikhail wasn't human. He only paired with me because I had a secret that he wanted. Once I told him what it was, he bided his time in order to destroy my platoon. If he cared about me, he never would have razed the museum. He would have found another way to neutralize my former commander.

That stubborn denial straightened my back. We slipped into the room and two other soldiers headed out to do the same. Two by two, the entire room came and went until we all looked a bit more relaxed.

I took a seat in the center where Mikhail and I had slept and rummaged through the bag I packed in the Penn Station store. I pulled out the box of sugary cereal I had confiscated. Others did the same with whatever their secret stash had been, and the quiet crunching of different dried foods filled the room. Mikhail sat down next to me. He had still been in dragon form at the time we were in that store. He picked at a hangnail on his thumb.

"Don't do that. You're likely to draw blood." I tipped the open package towards him.

He scrunched his nose at the sweet scent. "That's pure sugar."

"Fine. Starve." I went to pull the box back, but he shot his hand inside and pulled out a healthy handful, which, for his size, was nearly half the damn contents. I looked inside and then at him, both amused and irritated at the portion he took.

He gave me a crooked smile and shrugged. "Thanks," he muttered and dropped a few pieces into his mouth. He didn't grimace as he ate. As a matter of fact, he seemed to come alive with each small portion he took. When he finished, he said, "That wasn't half bad."

"You mean to tell me you've never had Crunch Berries?" They were my favorites growing up and eating them gave me a bit of nostalgia for the carefree days of just running to the store and grabbing these as a snack instead of breakfast. Although, truthfully, I could eat these for all three meals a day.

He let out a soft chuckle. "No. Meat eater. Remember?" He slid a sideways gaze in my direction that was full of humor.

"You two need to get a room," Marvin, one of the quieter soldiers, blurted.

A few others laughed at the remark and my cheeks heated. I focused on my cereal and didn't dare glance up.

"He had plenty of opportunity, but passed every time," I muttered with my mouth full. The bitterness of his rebuttal in the garage surfaced, but he had an excuse then. He had just retrieved what was left of his dead wife and kids.

"You were injured," he snapped, as if my comment hit a nerve.

I caught the glare he sent in my direction before he focused on his hands. I looked beyond him at Jenny. She waved her hand, as if saying I told you so.

His nostrils flared and he forced himself to meet my gaze. Fire burned in his irises, but it wasn't an inferno like his eyes had reflected back at the apartment just before he bolted away and shifted into dragon form. This was a slow burn.

"It's called transference." I rolled up the interior cereal bag so what was left wouldn't go stale and stuffed the bag back into my backpack.

"I'm not so sure," he said under his breath, stood up, and headed to the door. He cracked it and scanned the tunnel before closing it. He shuffled his feet and glanced around the room.

Everyone had smirks that I wanted to wipe from their faces. From the look on Mikhail's face, he shared my unhappiness in their demeanor.

"Give it a rest. We have more important things to focus on right now," Troy said from near the back. His gaze pierced through me as if he were trying to figure me out. "Where are we headed exactly, in case we get separated?"

"Water Street. Near Fulton."

Mikhail surprised me by answering the question. But he did not expand with a number or an exact location.

"If we get separated, I will circle back to find you," Mikhail added.

"We'll carry the bleach," Troy said, reading into the unsaid statement in the same way I had. Mikhail was all about self-preservation and if that meant he had to desert us, he would.

"I'll carry her." He pointed at me as if I were as precious a cargo as the bins of bleach.

"I can walk on my own," I snapped. I was not a bargaining chip or something to be claimed. And I certainly was not Mikhail's pawn.

"Fine," Mikhail said in a way that was anything but fine. Aggravation lines framed the sides of his lips as he glared at me as if I had ruined some underlying agenda.

We weren't alone, so I couldn't just blurt out *what the fuck is wrong with you* in front of all these relative strangers. But I did my best to convey it with my expression. Although I knew it was a long shot, I wanted everyone here to make it to Mikhail's place without harm.

"You can carry me if you'd like," Jenny offered, pulling Mikhail's sharp gaze in her direction.

"Are you injured?" he asked.

"No," Jenny answered. "But the idea of being carried by someone so..." She fanned herself with her hand.

"She is still healing from the burns and from the spikes that were shoved into her wrists. If she gets into a high-stress situation, her blood pressure will rise, and those bandages may not hold back her blood." His gaze swung back to me. "I wasn't offering to carry you out of some sense of misplaced machoism. I was offering to carry you to spare all of us the possibility of being detected."

I blinked at his venomous outburst. "Oh." I didn't quite know what else to say. I did not wish to be carried like an invalid, but he had a point. "I guess if that's your reasoning, I'm not as offended by the offer." I stumbled on my words.

"You can walk until it becomes dangerous," he said. "Then I'm hauling you over my shoulder and getting you somewhere that they cannot sense you. Understand? If I smell blood, they can smell blood, and that puts all of us in danger.”

The realization I could put the team in jeopardy slid over my skin like a dead fish. “Then why don’t you leave me here? If I’m going to put the mission in danger, I shouldn’t go.”

This time he balked at me, as if that wasn’t even an option. “You’ve never left anyone behind. Why the hell should I?”

“I agree with the dragon,” Troy said. “We do not leave people behind. Ever.”

It was my turn to use that dreaded word that means things are not copasetic. “Fine.” I put my hands up in surrender and then turned away from the men making the decisions for the rest of us. I caught Jenny’s gaze and gave her a raised eyebrow, communicating that I told her so. He wasn’t into me. He was only into safeguarding his own ass.

Dragon Storm
Chapter 12

NIGHTFALL COULDN'T COME FAST enough. All of us were getting antsy and short in the small confines of the room. Sunset couldn't have come at a better time. And now that the tunnel was painted in darkness, we used the spray bottle on mist and sprayed each one of us down from crown to toe with it. It took two whole bottles to mist us into leviathan invisibility, and even my nose was burning from being in the small space full of bleach fumes.

We filed out with the bins of bleach, shuffling along the ramp as if any noise would bring a swarm of deadly monsters. I held my super soaker at the ready, even though all I could see were shadows. Mikhail's heat swathed over me like a security blanket, and he might as well have his hand on my back, leading me through the maze that led to City Hall. I wanted to shuffle faster, put more distance between us right now, but we were leading the pack and if I didn't keep up, he'd just haul me over his shoulder.

At least he had my back. But did he have everyone else's?

That thought burrowed under my skin and I tried to shake it. I needed to focus on what lay ahead even though on first look, all that enveloped us was blackness of a building that hadn't had running electricity for years and possibly had been crushed by leviathan feet or burned out by dragon flame. As soon as we reached the top of the ramp, there wasn't a clear pathway to follow.

Mikhail sparked flames from his fingers to get our bearings. The brightness of the light made me squint. We were in a small vestibule, barely as big as the storeroom we had rested in. A door with a stairway sign on it stood at the far side of the room and a separate door stood in front of us.

"Why'd you stop?" I whispered.

"I think this brings us into the lobby and the stairs bring us to the upper floors, but I don't remember." Mikhail glanced between the two doors. "We don't want to go to the upper floors, and we certainly don't want to go out the main entrance with that tall staircase that will leave us utterly exposed. We want a street exit, preferably in back."

"And we don't want to go up the wrong staircase that opens to that little building on the east side of the little park," Troy said from behind us.

"That would actually be better than the front stairwell. At least there we wouldn't be easily seen. Dark figures on the white stairs are easy to spot, even with crappy vision."

"Make a choice. These bins aren't getting any lighter." Troy's voice carried some of the strain visible in his arms and neck.

Mikhail glanced at the far door with the stairwell icon tattooed into the steel and turned back to the door in front of him. He twisted the knob and pulled. Nothing happened. The door did not budge. He used a little more force and it groaned in protest.

"Is it unlocked?" I asked as my brain seized the fact that Mikhail's strength wasn't enough to move the door. Even with it swinging out as opposed to in.

"The knob moves easily, but..." He put both hands on the doorknob.

"Back away," I said as silent alarms went off in my head. I pulled his hands away from the handle and pushed him back as my mind raced.

"What is your issue?" He tried to get around me.

"I think it's booby-trapped precisely for someone like you." I turned and met Troy's gaze. "Shit. This is exactly the kind of place Yoman spoke of. Did you ever meet Yoman? I don't know which platoon he was with, but he bragged one night about setting up the monsters if they ever did get into the tunnels."

"Yoman was a drunk," one of the soldiers toward the back said.

"Yes, but he was brilliant with explosives." I had seen him take down a couple of buildings trying to take out leviathans. Of course, this was before we found out bleach made them vulnerable. He got away in the dust the rubble kicked up, but all it had done was aggravate the leviathans.

"You mean psychotic," Troy said. "He was certifiable. Blew himself up to try to take out a group of leviathans. This was before we knew about bleach." He looked around at both doors. "Damn it." He closed his eyes tight as if he were trying to pull out a memory, but he just shook his head.

I had wondered what had happened to him, but Troy was not wrong. Yoman was certifiable near the end.

"I remember that fool." Mikhail spoke softly as he eyed the door. "If Holly is right, a blast like what he created when he died will take down this building." He doused the fire in his hand, plunging us into the dark. "Fuck."

The way he drew out the word sent a rash of gooseflesh over my skin and made me wish that he would whisper that in my ear, but under vastly different circumstances. I dismissed the thought with a wave of my hand.

He's a dragon. I'm human. Nothing we do would work, regardless of the fact he had a human wife before.

Man, I needed to get laid so this string of thoughts would fade away. It had been forever since I had been with someone and that was probably why my mind kept wandering into the gutter instead of focusing on the danger surrounding us.

"It looks like we have no choice but to find our way out through the tracks," Troy said with a heavy sigh.

"Fuck that. Why don't we try the stairwell? We can always circle back down from the second floor," one of the male soldier's said. And their voice got farther away as he spoke, along with the squeak of wheels rolling across the floor.

Mikhail lit his fingers again just as Diego reached for the door.

"No!" I called louder than I meant to, and Mikhail spread his arms and pushed the rest of us back down the ramp with four of the five carts. He shifted into dragon form to move all of us and our shopping carts down and onto the subway tracks.

The explosion rocked the building, dropping dust on top of us. Mikhail didn't stop at the entry, but pushed us back as far as our bleach line. Protecting us from the initial explosion. He shifted back to human and hauled me over his shoulder.

"Run!" he ordered and jogged away from the station.

We were only what would have been less than a block away from the building when the secondary explosion triggered. This one not only dropped tiles onto us, but the already compromised tunnel seemed to collapse all around us.

The soldiers pushed the carts instead of carrying them as they ran. We got to a platform and stopped for a moment to collect our breaths. This was the Broadway City Hall platform. And I did not want to be this close to the destruction.

"Lower tracks," I hissed.

Mikhail slowed for a moment and hopped up on the platform, helping the others. He seemed to understand my request, and led the group down into the bowels of the tunnels. This area had a lower level that had been meant for the express trains, but it was unfinished. The gate to the lower level was locked, but one kick from Mikhail, and the metal gave. He caught it before it crashed into the stairway and then stepped aside so the team could bring our stash down. Then he pushed the door closed again, attempting to reengage whatever had kept it closed before.

The sounds of a super soaker dousing the entry filled my ears and then Mikhail lit his fingers, letting a soft glow lead the way. He took the southwest tunnel, making his way slowly and carefully as the team followed. Now that we weren't running, the soldiers carried the carts.

"You can put me down now," I said as I bounced on Mikhail's shoulder, making each word come out in a huff of air.

"Oh. Right." He gently set me on my feet. "I don't' know if we can get out of here with our carts. We might need to leave them somewhere and only bring what we can carry. Then, once we figure out their patrol patterns, we can do a couple retrieval missions to get the rest."

He wiped his face with his free hand.

I didn't like the sound of his plan, but before I could speak, Troy chimed in.

"That's the only path in, isn't it?" Troy hooked his thumb back the way we came. Troy's face was pale and his eyes held a haunted quality, like he was just coming to terms with what happened.

I did a quick head count. We were short more than just Diego.

"Where's Jenny?" I liked having another female on the team, even if she did have the hots for Mikhail.

"She and Karl went after Diego just before your boy swept us down to the tunnel with his wings."

"Why?" I couldn't help the question. My brain had stalled when I saw Diego heading for what I had already deemed the danger zone.

He shrugged. "I would have gone after him myself, but I didn't get the chance." This time he leveled a glare at Mikhail, as though he had been the one to trigger the bomb that killed three of his soldiers. He put the bin down and stepped forward, fisting his hands.

I stepped between them, putting my palms on Troy's chest to keep him from doing something that would result in Mikhail losing his temper. I had seen what a single punch from an angry dragon could do. Troy's heart hammered against my splayed fingers.

"He was trying to protect us." I used the softest voice I could to try to defuse whatever he had in mind. Based on the beat of his heart and the glare in his eyes, he wanted to deliver a big dose of whoop-ass. But right now, that would further delay us from safety.

Troy looked down at me and then my hands on his chest.

"I don't need you stepping in," he snarled and grabbed my wrists, forcibly removing them from his body.

I hissed as he squeezed my injuries. Before I could react, Mikhail's hand shot out and closed around Troy's throat. Troy released me and his eyes widened at Mikhail.

"You dare hurt her?" Mikhail growled in a way that promised death.

"Let him go, Mikhail. He's just lost three of his own people. He did not intend to hurt me," I snapped as I spun to face him. The look in his eyes told me reason was not going to work in this instance. "Stop this bullshit," I ordered in a snarl. "Both of you. Otherwise, we will not make it out of here alive."

I wasn't sure whether it was my tone or my words, but Mikhail slowly released Troy's neck. "I am sorry you lost some of your people." He stepped back. "But if you harm Sergeant Woods ever again, it will be the last thing you do."

Troy held the glare for a moment longer and then looked down at me. "I did not intend to hurt you."

I couldn't tell whether he was sincere or not, but it didn't matter. I just wanted the safety of

Mikhail's building right now and not the bullshit of high emotions that we were all experiencing.

"I know. Now can we please move on?" I waved in the direction we were headed before Mikhail had put me down. Instead of waiting for a response, I took it upon myself to lead this not-so-merry little band of ours and marched ahead.

"She sure is a pistol," Troy mumbled, loud enough for me to hear.

"You have no idea," Mikhail replied, and then their footfalls began.

I didn't bother looking over my shoulder until I came to a fork in the unfinished tunnel. Both avenues were dark and neither gave me any indication of direction. Mikhail stepped to one side and Troy the other, both with the same perplexed expression I was sure I sported.

"Which way?" I asked, trying to remember all I had read about these old, unfinished tunnels.

"One leads to a dead end, the other will gradually narrow down to nothing," Mikhail said.

"So, both are dead ends," Troy said.

"That's what it sounds like to me." I glanced at Mikhail. "Which way?"

"We want the dead end because there's an exit that goes up to the street level. I don't think there's any exits in the one that narrows down to nothing because it's under the current tunnel." He studied both openings and shook his head. "You choose."

I sighed and did a silent eenie, meeny, miny, moe and ended up choosing the left tunnel despite ending on the right side. I always went against the grain, and it had worked out for me for the most part.

It wasn't until we went the equivalent of a few city blocks that the ceiling felt as if it were sinking closer to us. I slowed and glanced at it and then over at Mikhail.

We went another block and the slope in the ceiling became evident. I chose the wrong path. I slowed to a stop; so did the men following with the carts in their grasp.

"We need to go back and take the other path," I said, owning the mistake.

A few groaned, but they let us move to the back of the line and lead the way. I wondered just how much their arms and backs would be hurting once we got somewhere we all could rest without the fear of what was around the next corner. Guilt bit at the edges of my mind. The only saving grace for us was there were no baby leviathans on this level as the only entry was the one we came down and none of it had our signatures on it. Plus, the bleach Mikhail had sprayed would deter them from climbing down the stairs.

We made quick work of backtracking and once headed in the right direction, we made our way until the tunnel just ended. The men put down their loads and leaned against the walls, stretching their arms.

Mikhail grabbed a bottle of bleach out of a cart and walked a few paces back, laying down a line of the liquid across the tunnel. He emptied the bottle in the process and then set it down on the other side of the line before he came back to us.

"What's that for?" Troy asked.

"Protection." Mikhail glanced around the tunnel and sighed. There wasn't a formal exit like we had seen in several places between stations on our journey. Instead, there only seemed to be dirt-caked walls. Mikhail started at one end and walked, with his fingers dragging on the wall. He stopped at one point and then wiped his hand across the wall, wiping dirt off a dark metal door. There was no doorknob but his slow progress of clearing the dirt away revealed a hole where a knob should be. He lightly clapped his hands to rid them of the dirt and grime he had cleared and then he reached into the hole. With the meat of his palm on the door, he slowly pushed.

The hinges creaked loud enough for me to understand his preparation with the line of bleach. If any baby leviathans were loose in the tunnels, that high-pitched whine would bring them forth despite the bleach barriers. Once Mikhail had the door wide, he waved the crew inside the cramped space. A metal staircase looped back and forth up at least three stories.

Once we were all squished inside, he closed the door. That loud squeak radiated through the concrete room we stood in, and everyone froze in place.

"Take a load off for a bit," Mikhail whispered. The men pushed the carts into the corner under the stairs and found places to sit on the steps. Mikhail climbed the stairs and I followed, with Troy at my heels.

"I hope the doors up top don't make a ruckus like the door below," Mikhail said softly. "Otherwise, we are dead."

"We should probably catch some rest here before we try to carry those carts up these stairs," Troy said as we continued our ascent in the stuffy stairwell.

We passed by another landing with an exterior door. This one had a doorknob and a designated railway path for the 2 and 3 lines. Mikhail pressed his finger to his lips, and we slid by the entrance of the subway tunnel. The higher we reached, the more natural light bathed the stairwell. We rounded the last corner and paused. Mikhail closed his fist, dousing the fire that had led us up most of the stairs.

The exit was warped and indented, but it didn't look like it was done by a leviathan foot. No, this looked more like a building toppled onto the exit. However, light still filtered through the crack.

Mikhail ran his hand through his hair and took a seat on the stairs in a defeated posture. I opened my mouth, but he shook his head and put his finger to his lips again. He pointed down the stairs more emphatically, but as we started down, he didn't follow.

I hesitated and then waved Troy down and climbed back up. Mikhail had his head down, his elbows on his knees and his palms propping his head up. He didn't look up at me when I stepped into his field of view.

"I've failed you," he whispered, and my heart nearly stopped.

I knelt and pulled his hands away from his face until he met my gaze. I couldn't have him thinking he failed me—or humanity, for that matter. I searched his defeated gaze and shook my head.

"I can't open that. If I do, we're likely to be smothered by debris." He pointed above him.

I glanced up and weighed his words. "But there is light coming through." I brought my gaze to his. "So, there is a path out, however harrowing it may be."

He reached out and cupped my cheek, running his thumb along my skin. It was something a lover would do, and it created a web of sensations through me that spread like a warm blanket. But the four words that fell from his lips chilled me to the core.

"It will make noise."

My heart sank. Noise meant the monsters would come in droves.

Dragon Storm
Chapter 13

WE GATHERED ON THE ground floor. Mikhail stared at the ground without making eye contact with anyone. It was as if he were trying to pull the right words to explain our situation. Instead of letting him struggle through it, I cleared my throat.

"It seems that there is building debris on the exit," I said quietly.

Faces fell, so did whatever hope reflected in their eyes.

"But there is light coming through," Troy said as he waved up the stairwell, as if that would change the truth.

"Yes. But opening those doors will make a lot of noise and I don't know how much of it will fall into the stairwell." Mikhail met Troy's gaze.

Troy bit his lower lip. "Aren't buildings collapsing here and there anyway from the damage you did?" He cocked his head in a challenge.

Mikhail stared at him and nodded, but didn't react to the dig. He traded a glance with me before he asked, "Are you willing to risk being buried alive?"

Troy studied the ground with his lower lip sucked between his teeth and his brow creased in thought. It took him a good five minutes of internal debate before he spoke. "The alternative is going back through the subway system, and we all know that's been compromised. The likelihood of us reaching our destination going that route is slim." He took a breath and then met Mikhail's gaze head on. "So, yes. I think we'd rather risk being buried alive if it means we have a chance of defeating them in the end. Pour bleach all over the landing up there and then open it up. Let them come investigate. We will wait it out down here and when night falls, we'll attempt to climb out. If we can't, then we'll be forced to backtrack."

The rest of the soldiers nodded. "We agree," a few of them piped in softly.

Mikhail glanced at me and licked his lips. "It's dangerous for everyone here, including me." He stared into my eyes, trying to transmit his thoughts on the matter visually. "But I'll attempt it if you agree it's the right course of action."

The fact he didn't frame it as a question made me shift my weight. I knew he wasn't convinced this was the right route to take just by his non-question, but I couldn't see any other way out. And if anyone could survive having a building fall on him, it was Mikhail. No one else in this stairwell had the strength to open the door. I slowly nodded. "I'd not only douse that landing, but the stairs leading down to deter any sort of investigation. But other than that, I agree that it is our best chance," I answered. "Just don't get cut," I added and squeezed his hand.

Mikhail gave me an uneasy smile. "I'll try not to." He glanced around and sighed. "Just stay put." He grabbed a couple of bottles of bleach and headed up the stairs.

We piled back under the stairwell next to the door to the subway tunnel and waited. The stench of bleach filled the space and then the ripping of metal echoed off the walls, followed by such a racket that we covered our ears. Dust mingled with bleach fumes.

My heart thundered as silence settled. Mikhail didn't come down the stairs like I thought he would. The ground around us shook. The need to run up to make sure he was all right gripped me, and I moved toward the stairs.

Troy grabbed my arm and shook his head, as if he read my thoughts. He put his finger to his lips as well and pulled me deeper into the alcove with the rest of the soldiers and our bins of bleach.

Of course, Troy was right. If I went running blind up the stairs, I'd compromise everyone, including Mikhail if he was okay. If he wasn't, we'd eventually dig him out and get him to his apartment building. I just hoped he was alive and stayed that way.

Even so, Troy kept his grip on me, as if he didn't trust me to make the right decision. I tried to shake his hand off, but he kept it solid as he glanced up at the ceiling above us. The concrete held. Even with our flashlights out, I could see the fear in his eyes.

"Another building collapse?" the gravelly voice of the Serpent King echoed from the street level.

"Looks that way," another said in a ghastly voice that I never heard before. I had to assume that was a leviathan speaking, although they had never spoken English before. I'd only heard the hideous hissing noises from them. But then again, they were usually doused with bleach.

"Can you detect any traces of blood like the other collapses?"

Sniffing, followed by a cough. "No, sir," the pained voice said. "No blood, but that stench that burns my nose is present."

Silence followed, as if the monsters were considering the presence of bleach as a sign of some sort. And then the Serpent King's voice asked, "Have you ever smelled that with other collapses?"

"Yes, sir. In some buildings, but not others."

"And the buildings that you have smelled it, have you also smelled blood?"

I raised an eyebrow and met Troy's gaze. He just shrugged. But at least there was no smell of blood, which meant Mikhail was not bleeding at all. Or if he was, it wasn't significant enough to overpower the bleach. Yet.

"Some yes, some no. There's no discernable pattern."

More silence as the rubble shifted and more bricks tumbled down the stairs.

"I want a few of you to watch the building. If anything tries to escape, crush it." The order came through loud and clear.

We would have to wait out their watch, which meant we wouldn't be able to get to Mikhail any time soon. I didn't know what shape the rest of the stairwell was in or what the debris above ground looked like either. Thankfully, we had food and water to last at least another day before we'd have to figure out something more permanent.

The presence of leviathans also meant no light that might bleed out from the rubble, and no speaking until we had a chance to escape this deathtrap.

After a few minutes of quiet shuffling above, it seemed the sentries found their guard spots. I peeled Troy's hand off my arm and signed to him that I was going to check the stairs. He glanced at his men and then nodded with a signal for me to be very, very quiet.

I did not climb to my feet. Using my hands and knees made only a whisper of noise on the steps versus the footfalls that my boots would have made no matter how quiet I wanted to be. Two flights went without a piece of the building above visible despite the dust hanging on the air like an unwanted fog.

It tickled my nose, and I clamped down on both my nose and my mouth, stopping the need to sneeze. As the tingle abated, I blinked back the latent tears leftover from the close call. Light filtered in much more readily as I climbed the steps to the third-floor landing. There was enough brick and glass to slow my ascent. I didn't need to cut my hands or knees on what was strewn all over the ground. I moved far enough to take a glance around the corner and up the stairwell.

My throat tightened. Mikhail was partly lying out of the rubble down the steps. The metal door covered him from the brunt of the ruins, but he now seemed trapped under that same sheet of metal and he was not conscious. A large bump marred his forehead, as if the metal jarred into him and knocked him out. He was lucky it didn't split his head open. I gently brushed the scraps of glass away from the path in front of me and slowly moved toward him, mindful of the dangers above.

As I climbed closer, his eyes blinked open, darting around as if he had no idea what had happened. At least he had the wherewithal to not make noise. When his gaze landed on me, his eyes widened. I put my finger to my lips, using the same silence gesture he had, and then pointed above and made claws out of both hands to signify monsters were up there.

His brow knit and his lips thinned, and he jabbed his jaw in the direction of the stairs. He was trying to tell me to get out of there, but I took another step closer, ultra-aware that around the corner there was a pile of building wreckage blocking the stairwell and beyond that, some leviathans waited for any sign of life.

I shook my head. I was not leaving him.

"Go," he mouthed.

"No one left behind," I mouthed slowly, making my point without words.

He closed his eyes and shook his head before he laid it back on the concrete. Wincing, he pulled his arm out from behind the rubble and pointed down the stairs. When his eyes opened, they were in his inferno mode, which meant I needed to heed his warning.

I slowly traced my way back down to the landing. But I really didn't want to slip around the corner. I wanted him within view. Something inside me balked when he pointed again, especially because it came with another grimace. But I had to trust him, trust that he was not mortally wounded and wouldn't slip away while we waited the monsters out. I moved slowly out of his view and then leaned on the wall with a frustrated exhale.

I stood in place for roughly ten minutes and then peeked around the corner. Mikhail was attempting to pull himself out from under the rubble without shifting the debris. Sweat dripped from his face onto the stair. At least I thought it was sweat, until he happened to glance in my direction.

My jaw slackened. It wasn't sweat but tears. His face was as red as a tomato. Ignoring his silent plea, I nearly ran up the stairs despite the shake of his head. I swept the glass aside with my boot and knelt, cradling his head in my lap.

His hand shook as he signed for me to leave.

"No," I whispered in his ear. "What can I do?"

He shook his head and used his hand to communicate letters slowly. "I am broken," he signed.

I blinked and my gaze met his; I repeated the letters representing broken to make sure I understood what the hell he was saying.

He nodded. "Can not feel legs," he signed.

I slumped against the wall and wiped my face. "We'll figure it out," I signed. "We have enough carts to carry you."

He shook his head. "Leave me."

"We need you. You have the knowledge to build the bomb and the fire to destroy the leviathan's once the bomb goes off," I signed slowly.

He closed his eyes. "I don't think I'll be able to fly, which is the most efficient way of destroying them."

"Then we figure out another way. Hell, I can push you through the masses while you torch those fuckers if I have to."

That earned me a tilted smile. I took his free hand in mine and ran my fingers through his hair while I stretched out on the stair below him. We couldn't attempt to move the metal pinning him yet. I also didn't want to try to pull him out and break open skin. The smell of dragon blood would be our demise, even more than human blood.

A small noise below made me turn my head. Troy was at the base of the stairs. I gave him a shrug and signed, "Mikhail is hurt."

His gaze went to the head buried in my lap and then met mine. "How bad?"

"He can't feel his legs," I signed.

Troy closed his eyes and then started up the stairs.

Mikhail lifted his head and put his hand out in a stop signal.

Troy obeyed.

"Not yet. Wait until dark. Otherwise, they will attack," Mikhail signed. "They may still attack in the dark, but at least they won't have clear targets."

Troy nodded. He pulled out a bottle of water and offered it to me. I reached out and he came far enough to hand it to me, his steps only a whisper that couldn't be heard above the creaking of some of the debris. He also put a spray bottle on the stair below me.

"Thank you," I signed.

"Any time," he replied with his hands. "See you at dusk."

I gave him a thumbs-up and then opened the water, taking a small sip before offering Mikhail the bottle. He took a small sip, but some of it landed on my pants below him. He capped the bottle and handed it to me before laying his head on his arm across my legs.

I resumed hand-combing his hair gently. It was as silky as I thought it would be, and the slow motion lulled him into the even breathing of sleep. As I stared down at his profile, I let my mind flow over everything that had happened between us. It wasn't transference that tightened my throat.

This was truly the first time I had to reflect on this pressure in my chest. To examine my feelings and identify them as true. Despair raked

through me as I realized I was falling in love with
one of the monsters that had declared war on
the human race.

Dragon Storm
Chapter 14

AS THE LIGHT BEGAN to fade, those horrid voices came from above, making me stiffen in place.

"Has there been any sign of life?"

"None. Not even rodents fleeing the rubble. There have been shifts in the debris, so don't get too close."

"We'll stay clear. You're relieved for the night."

"Try not to fall asleep from boredom."

A snicker followed and then feet pounded away. It wasn't too long before we heard snoring from above. The idiots fell asleep.

I glanced down at Mikhail. At least he hadn't snored in his fitful sleep. I glanced at the shadows in the stairwell below and as if I had called out loud, Troy slid into view with a couple of soldiers behind him. They made their way carefully up the stairs. In the darkening space, they inspected the metal holding Mikhail pinned on the landing.

Mikhail jerked awake, and I palmed his cheek as I slid out from under him. I sprayed us all down with the bleach and sprayed the debris above Mikhail as well. Whatever they were planning to do would shift things and I didn't want the monsters deciding to put a foot into the hole and effectively crushing us. Any shift would send a plume of bleach scent upward and hopefully that would be enough of a deterrent.

Troy tapped me on the shoulder and mimed me pulling. He snapped his finger and Adam, another one of Troy's soldiers, came up the stairs behind me, just in case Mikhail came out faster than we anticipated. It wouldn't do for us to tumble down the steps, so Adam stood behind me with his palms bracing my lower back.

I maneuvered enough to get my hands under Mikhail's arms. He laid his head on my shoulder and grit his teeth. He wrapped his arms over mine, understanding that he wasn't going to be able to stop this rescue operation.

I glanced at him, and he gave me a small nod, although he looked much paler than he had when I first saw him. I, in turn, nodded at Troy.

Troy counted down with his fingers and then the three lifted the metal door from the end closest to the stairs. They tried to keep it level, too. A feat that I marveled at until Troy nodded at me.

I pulled Mikhail. He shifted more out of the debris but then it seemed as if he caught on something. He arched and hissed between closed lips. I saw what was preventing me from pulling him out and put him on the stairs and pointed at Adam behind me, silently instructing him to take my place.

He did, without hesitation.

I crawled into the space over Mikhail, praying that Troy and the other two could sustain holding the door. If not, I'd be crushed under the weight. Even so, I braced my back against the metal and gripped the concrete cylinder that had Mikhail's right leg pinned. I barely moved it the first try. If I could make noise, it would have been better, but the next try, I got it high enough to see the damage.

Mikhail would probably never walk again, but what was more concerning was the fact his calf was not a bloody pulp. Instead, it looked like a mass of purple, as though his skin was all that held in the crushed bone and mangled blood vessels.

Adam pulled and Mikhail's leg released. I crawled backward as fast as Adam dragged Mikhail free, and then Troy and the other two lowered the metal door as gracefully as possible. The debris groaned and shifted again, sending a few bricks crumbling down the steps as we carried Mikhail into the safety of the darkness below.

When we reached the bottom of the stairs, we passed through a heavy blanket that had been hung, blocking out light and dust from above. It also made the space below as dark as a cloudless night in the sticks. When the flashlights went on, we all squinted.

My eyes adjusted fairly quickly, and when the soldiers set Mikhail on his side, I winced. Just one good look at his leg was enough.

"His leg needs to be amputated," Troy said, softly enough for me to almost miss it.

I could not fathom cutting him open here in this stairwell.

Mikhail was already shaking his head.

"They'll smell dragon blood, even through the bleach," I said quietly. "We have to get him to his apartment building. Then we can do whatever surgery is necessary."

Mikhail pointed at me and nodded, and then his eyes slipped closed. Tears leaked out of the side of his eyes and his teeth grit together as sweat formed on his forehead. His nails began to form the familiar claws. Mikhail was shifting.

I pushed people aside because I did not know whether he could contain his form or whether a full-fledged dragon was going to transform in front of us or whether he was just shifting into the mini-dragon he had been throughout most of this little band's travels.

A full dragon in this cramped space would crush us all to death.

Mikhail's eyes flashed open with a citrine glow and that reptilian shape. His teeth elongated and he met my gaze. Concern flashed across his features just before they morphed. Somehow, he contained his agony as bones popped out of place and then rearranged. Iridescent scales seemed to pop out of his skin, covering every inch of his form, including his mangled leg.

He remained in his human size, but even with the transformation, he didn't seem to be able to move from his spot on the ground. Without prompting from anyone, he closed his eyes again. This time, he shrank his form smaller than before, arching in torment until he finally collapsed in a heap on the floor. His breathing sounded labored, and I leaned over, scooping him into my arms.

He released a small hiss but then settled into my arms, wrapping his wings around himself as if he were a tiny child in need of comfort. I glanced at Troy and Adam and the others who had witnessed this insanity.

"We need to take only what we can carry. If he was right on the location, I can get us to the apartment building. Just make sure you have those super soakers loaded up and at the ready. If we run into trouble, then we'll have to start shooting because I don't know if Mik has enough energy to spare us a fire." I was glad my voice remained calm, without any of the panic pounding my muscles straight to the bone.

"Will he heal like that?" Troy whispered and pointed.

I couldn't tell whether the lilt in his voice was wishful thinking or something else. I didn't bother clarifying because I didn't have a concrete answer for him. I just shrugged. Mikhail's chest already rose and fell in that even cadence of sleep. He needed rest if he had any hope of healing. But I didn't know whether sleep would be enough. Not with his declaration that he was broken and didn't think he'd be able to fly. His wings seemed fine to me, but then again, I'd never been a dragon, so I didn't know about the complexities of his spinal structure.

As the six soldiers packed what bleach they could carry in their backpacks, I kept Mikhail safely tucked in my arms.

Troy turned with a fully loaded backpack, and he helped me slide it on without jostling Mikhail. He clipped it around my waist and above my chest and then tightened it.

I winced but kept Mikhail as still as possible despite the weight pulling me backward. I adjusted my stance, so I was more hunched over Mikhail and the pack settled easier on my back.

I made sure Mikhail was protected by my arms, and I'd keep him nestled as comfortably as I could until we reached his door.

If we reached the building.

All I knew is we had to try, especially since Bozo One and Bozo Two up top were sleeping. That could allow us to sneak away into the dark without being seen. And once we were in Mikhail's apartment building, we'd have to assess whether what we had was enough to do sustainable damage to the leviathans.

If it wasn't enough, then we'd have to figure out a viable recovery mission for the rest of our resources left in this stairwell.

Dragon Storm
Chapter 15

W E TRADED THE FOOD, water, and clothes in our backpacks with bottles of bleach. Between the remaining seven of us, we were able to get a little more than one of the biggest carts of bleach packed away and still be nimble on our feet. Once we finished, all lights were extinguished. One by one, we made our way beyond the blanket. The stairwell had gone from having ambient light to pitch dark as we climbed, with Troy in the front and me right behind him.

I held his belt loop and in turn, Adam held mine, and so on down the line. I was the only one not equipped with a super soaker at the ready. Mine hung on my back because with Mikhail nestled in my arm, I had no way to wield the gun.

Without the aid of lights, climbing the mountain of rubble was challenging to say the least. Each step needed to be tested to make sure it could bear our weight. So, the trek was slow as each of us followed Troy as best we could in the dark. When we broke through the surface, a sliver of a moon gave us enough visibility to see the sleeping leviathans. They had taken up residence in the street, blocking both the north and south exits. We wanted to go east, so we shuffled along the edge of the buildings until we came to the alley between them.

Our visibility was fleeting as clouds moved over the only light in the sky, hiding the moon behind them.

We did not know whether we were going down a dead end, or whether it would open up on the next avenue, but we had to take the only immediate path available to us and pray it would work.

One of the leviathans huffed and we all froze, holding our breaths while pointing the soakers at the alley entrance. When the snores resumed, we collectively let the air out of our lungs and continued our slow progression deeper into the darkness.

My arms ached from the weight of Mikhail. Even in this little package he surrendered to, he was not a light load to carry. Twenty pounds of dead weight felt like concrete in my arms. I couldn't imagine trying to carry his two-hundred-pound human form. As it was, we were slower with the bleach load we carried, and I wasn't sure we would have made it out of that stairwell with Mikhail over someone's shoulder.

Troy stopped in front of me, and my wandering mind snapped back to the present. I put my hand back to stop Adam from plowing into both of us. He did the same until the end of the line.

"Fuck."

The muttered swear was loud enough for me to pick it up and I prayed it didn't echo down the alley to where the sleeping monsters would hear.

Mikhail didn't stir.

Troy moved to the right slowly, as if feeling his way along whatever barrier he had encountered.

I tilted my head back and I saw nothing. No stars, no moon. Nothing, which meant either we were under some sort of overhang, or tonight's cloud cover had thickened.

Rain would be our worst enemy. It would dilute the bleach and reveal our scent. My heart jumped into my throat at that thought. Especially if we had indeed hit a dead end. There was no place to hide once that happened. Our bleach would be ineffective, and we had too many streets to cross to get to the apartment.

As if God thought it was great fun to challenge us in such a way, a drop hit my forehead. But no others followed. However, the sticky, heavy air of a foggy mist wrapped around us. It was still dangerous, but at least it wasn't a soaking rain. But still, prolonged exposure to this mist would eventually render the bleach we sprayed on ourselves useless.

Troy understood the dangers as well. He moved quicker, trying to find a viable way out. When he hit another barricade to the right, his muttered curse wasn't as audible. He backtracked and the team followed like a centipede turning on its axis.

This time he found a passage on the left side, and after a few steps, it jogged to the right. When it jogged left again, my senses flared. I was sure this was taking us away from where we needed to be. When we veered right again, I began to think the labyrinth we were in was a twisted maze meant to disorient.

It wasn't until we stepped out onto a street that we halted. The white letters on the sign nearly made me cry with relief. We were on Pearl Street, which meant the apartment wasn't as far as I had anticipated. But without seeing the nearest cross street, I wasn't sure which direction to take.

Our eyes adjusted to the more open lane before us, and I took Troy's hand, spelling out the most pressing question.

"What's the nearest cross street?"

He pushed me back into the alley, along with the rest of the soldier train and then spelled out "Wait here" with his fingers.

I patted Adam's hand holding my belt twice, which meant to hold tight. I breathed slowly in through my nose and out through my mouth, calming my pounding heart.

When Troy blocked the exit, I jerked. Thankfully, I did not yelp. He took my free hand and signed, "Maiden to our left."

I nodded and mentally pictured the map of downtown in my head. If I calculated right, we only had two short blocks before we got to Mikhail's building. There had to be multiple ways to enter but I only knew of the Water Street entrance.

"Any signs of patrols?"

"No."

I needed to wake Mikhail before we made a run for it. He was the only one with the building code to get us inside, and I could not chance waking him up at the last minute. I stepped back, giving Troy a chance to squeeze back into the narrow walkway we stood in.

I leaned close to the dragon's ear. "Mikhail," I whispered and gently jostled him in my arms. Nothing happened. No startle. No eyes suddenly glowing in the dark. No reaction from the dragon in my arms. My heart thundered at the lack of response, and I held his chest to my ear, holding my breath.

His heart was still beating, and I closed my eyes as a wave of relief nearly cut me off at the knees.

"Mikhail," I said a little louder and shook him a little more vigorously.

I bit my lip. Instead of repeating my actions, I pressed my lips to his cheek and whispered his name in his ear like a lover would. I kept the mounting panic from my voice, but if he had any level of consciousness, he'd feel my runaway pulse. The smallest of citrine light flashed before it fell into dark again.

"Wake up," I whispered in the same seductively sly way I imagined men liked. That drummed up a sigh from his form. "I need you," I continued, whispering in his ear low enough so no one else but him could hear.

This time when his eyes fluttered open, they stayed open and focused on me as if I were a stranger. He blinked a few times and then tried to move, and his eyes squeezed closed as his teeth gnashed for a moment.

"Woods?" he said just as softly, as though he sensed the danger around us.

"Yes," I whispered in his ear. "We are a block away from the northwest side of your building. Is there an entrance on this side?"

He shook his head slowly. "Three-five-two-seven-six-one," he whispered and closed his eyes. "And wait until the patrol goes by before making a break for the door. That will give you a ten-minute window."

I nodded and cataloged the number sequence he just gave me, wondering what the significance of the numbers were. I would bet my life that was his passcode to get into the building and they were dates that meant something to Mikhail. Without the passcode, the only other way into the building was with Mikhail's human fingerprints. Shifting back was not in the cards. Besides, he had gone limp in my arms again.

I took Troy's hand and relayed the message of waiting until the patrol passed. We had been in this spot for almost a full ten minutes between his run to see where we were and now, so there had to be a leviathan in the vicinity. And with the mist, the bleach scent was not as pronounced.

I took the spray bottle and pushed Troy aside, spraying the entrance to the alley before I took a step back, pulling him along with me. I hoped like hell that was enough to deter a heftier sniff of this alley, especially considering the mist had turned to a steady drizzle.

It didn't take long before the ground trembled at approaching feet. Large feet. The kind that belonged to a Godzilla-sized reptilian monster. The beast slowed to a stop near the alley, took a sniff of the air and then immediately sneezed.

"Damn building," it muttered and marched off.

We waited until the trembling lessened and then I tapped Troy. He turned and I tapped Adam behind me before grabbing onto Troy's belt. Adam's hand gripped my belt and our little caravan started on the last leg of our deadly adventure.

Dragon Storm
Chapter 16

WE KEPT CLOSE TO the buildings as we slid down Pearl Street, in the direction of Fulton Street. When we passed the sign for John Street, I yanked on Troy's belt, trying to steer him across the street where the northwestern-most corner of Mikhail's apartment building stood.

Even in the near blackness surrounding us, I could make out the perceived destruction of the building, which was why I was sure Troy hesitated. Mikhail's building glamour still amazed me. All that ruse with silkscreens and decals, but it worked, and if we didn't want to get caught by the next patrol, we had to haul ass.

He glanced over his shoulder at me, and I nodded toward the building across the empty street and pushed him forward. He followed orders just as effectively as he issued them. Halfway across the street, the ground shook and we broke out in a run.

I had no idea whether we were running toward a leviathan or away, but we needed to get to the opposite side of the building so I could get us inside the lobby and out of danger. And now that we were on the move, I mentally repeated the sequence Mikhail had given me.

Three-five two-seven six-one. Three-five two-seven six-one. Over and over, with each step, the numbers flashed in my head. I prayed I'd get this right because I didn't think we'd get more than one shot at cracking the security system. If I entered it wrong, I feared the building would lock us out until Mikhail's hand could be scanned.

Of course, if that happened, we had better find another tight spot to hide. Otherwise, we would be easy pickings for the leviathans, especially if they swarmed. And if they all converged on us, we did not have enough bleach or firepower to take them down.

When we got close, I let go of Troy's belt and grabbed Adam's hand, pulling him into my place. I put on the speed, passing Troy. At the corner, I stopped and put my free hand up, stopping the procession. I glanced around the corner. Nothing moved in the darkness, and I exhaled, hoping that I wasn't missing anything in the direction of the door. The opposite way was just as clear, giving me the go-ahead to slip around the bend. The door was only a quarter of the way down the length of the building, and I ran my hand along the building's side next to the door, getting frustrated by the second, especially because that familiar tremor had started in the ground.

Somehow, I triggered the panel and the keypad appeared. I blinked at it and closed my eyes, inspecting my memory because I had totally blanked on the sequence during my search for the damn pad. I rubbed my fingers together and opened my eyes. Without overthinking it, I hit the numbers. Three, five, two, seven, six, and then the one. The panel closed and an almost imperceptible click sounded. I yanked the door open, and Troy held it, waving all of us inside the lobby.

He closed the door as quietly as he could and then stepped back, staring out at the street as the tremor turned to a rumble of feet. I sprayed the base of the door and backed up slowly, along with the rest of the men. This time, a group of young leviathans ran by the window without stopping. Like they smelled something that was worthy of attack. I glanced over my shoulder and mentally counted the group. There should have been seven of us. The caboose was missing.

My gaze met Troy's in the darkness and then a howl tore through the street. All our gazes swiveled toward the noise and then squeals followed. But the screaming did not stop, despite the painful wails of the leviathan. Troy stepped toward the door, and I grabbed his arm.

"Going out there now is suicide," I whispered. As if making my point, the pounding of adult leviathan feet shook the room and then at least a half-dozen pair of bone-crushing feet ran by.

We stood, helpless, as the human scream cut off.

I closed my eyes and took a breath. We had to put as much distance between us and the street level as possible. I crossed in the dark to the stairwell and opened the door, waiting until everyone was inside, including Troy. His pain was palpable on the air. But as soon as I shut the door on the lobby, drenching us in the complete blackness of an interior stairwell, I felt the wall for what I needed and hoped like hell Mikhail's grid was still operating and it extended through to the ground floor like it had throughout his apartment.

With the flip of a switch, the dull stairwell lights flicked on. Silence blanketed the small band of soldiers. Even with the death of one of their comrades, the presence of electricity made everyone's eyes widen. Troy blinked and then snapped his gaze to mine.

"Go," I whispered and pointed up the stairs. "I'll explain as soon as we put some distance between us and the ground floor."

Mikhail's eyes fluttered open. "Floor fifteen," Mikhail croaked from the crook of my arm. "Same code."

"You heard the dragon." I shooed them ahead and we climbed as silently as possible. I was certain Mikhail's penthouse was much higher than fifteen floors, but I wasn't going to argue with him in front of the troops. Not with having just lost another one of our own.

I would need to go searching through the building at some point to see what the floors held. Beyond the penthouse, I only was aware of the steel panic rooms that he had used to do my bidding. I still couldn't believe my stupidity. I nearly died from him blowing his flame at me.

Between the medical equipment he brought back to the penthouse, along with the fresh food, I was sure there was a meat freezer somewhere, along with a greenhouse. But what other surprises this building held would have to wait until we got to safety.

At floor fifteen stood another keypad. I hadn't noticed any others on the floors we passed, either. I stepped forward and pressed the same sequence in again. The door clicked and I pulled it open, waiting on the landing until everyone passed. As I stepped inside, I turned off the lights in the stairwell.

The first thing I noticed about this space: there were no windows. When I closed the stairwell door, it clicked again, locking us in the dark. I felt along the wall until I found another switch. A single bank of lights clicked on. It was enough to illuminate the entire open floor. A dozen cots lined one side, along with shelving that held clothing meant for a lab or a hospital. Towels and linens sat neatly folded next to the clothes. In the far-left corner stood an equally large double cabinet labeled First Aid. An industrial-style kitchen lined the other side, along with a half-dozen round cafeteria-style tables. The back wall had a men's restroom and women's restroom on either side. Immediately to our left before the line of cots, was a couple of industrial sized washers and dryers.

"What the hell?" Troy turned to me.

"My lab employees stayed here during highly focused testing," Mikhail said. "Showers are available and there should be enough frozen and dry goods to keep you until we can make that bomb. Just make sure you don't trash the place. If you use it, clean it."

Troy's head cocked like a puppy's would. "Showers?" His eyes lit up. I'm sure I looked the exact same way he did when I found out. "You have running water?"

"Yes. If you need me, use the call button." He nodded his head to the wall, where an intercom system sat.

"And where are you going?" Troy's eyebrows lowered into a suspicious glower.

"I need Woods to bring me to the medical ward."

Troy hooked his thumb toward the first-aid cabinets.

"I need more than what those cabinets hold," he said.

Troy glanced back at his team, who all were looking longingly at the rest rooms across the way. "Go clean up," he ordered. "I'm going with Woods and the dragon."

No one made any sort of stink at them being separated. In fact, they dropped all their equipment where they stood and made a beeline to the shelves, pilfering scrubs and towels before disappearing into the men's room.

"I just need Woods," Mikhail said.

"And I'm her superior, so either I'm taking you alone, or you can deal with both of us."

Mikhail grumbled but nodded, and I had to use the keypad to unlatch the door again. Troy stood over my shoulder, I'm sure to learn the code, but I typed it in too fast.

"What's the code?" he asked as the door closed behind us and I flicked the switch to illuminate the stairwell again.

I opened my mouth to tell him, but Mikhail interrupted. "Three-five-two-seven-six-one. Same as the building entry code."

He surprised me. I didn't think he'd give up his precious building codes so easily.

"Now that you have the code, you can run recovery patrols whenever you can without having Woods with you and your team."

Troy grunted and sent Mikhail a sideways glare.

"Would you prefer being my nursemaid while I heal?" Mikhail growled, his voice full of venom and anger.

I raised an eyebrow. "I'd actually prefer going on the mission," I mumbled.

"I'm not cut out for caretaking," Troy said, walking straight into the trap that Mikhail laid out for him. "I'll let Woods nurse you back to health, but you need to give me all the codes for all the rooms in this building. I don't want to be locked out, or locked in anywhere, understand?"

Mikhail glanced at me and then at Troy. "I'll give you access to everything except the penthouse. That is my domain and my domain only. As for the rest of the building, respect what you find, and don't fuck with the things in the lab. Understand?"

Troy's lips thinned. "Does she get the code to the penthouse?"

Mikhail exhaled through his nose and some smoke came with it. "No. It's my domain. No one gets that code."

We hit the landing for the twentieth floor and before I could berate him for his lack of trust, he interjected. "This is the floor. The code is three-five-one."

I punched in the numbers, and we entered. I did the same turn off the stairway lights, turn on the floor lights and turned, taking in the sterilization corridor we were in. The room beyond it held an operating table in the center and all the medical equipment that you would see in an operating room.

"When we get inside, I need you to put me on the table and then go clean up and get into sterilized scrubs because you will have to amputate my leg at the knee, and I would prefer not to get any more of an infection than I already have." He glanced at Troy. "You stay in here, please."

His voice carried such exhaustion, but I could not fathom doing what he was saying without help. "How?" I asked as the door whisked open.

"I can do it," Troy said. "I had field medical training overseas."

Mikhail glanced at him and nodded. "You both have to clean up, though."

Troy nodded, and I glanced at him and then Mikhail as we walked into the sterile room. I set him on the table and headed into the far room that had showers and sinks for sterilization before surgery and cleaning up after. My stomach knotted, but Troy was already stripping his clothing and heading toward the shower stall.

I didn't know where to look, but understood the need for expedience, especially because when I glanced through the window Mikhail was shifting back to human form and this time he cried out in pain. Thankfully, he kept his fire in check; otherwise, the entire medical suite would be compromised.

I stripped and stepped into the shower, taking the opposite spigot from Troy. I used the antibacterial soap on my entire form, including my hair, and then stepped out, taking a towel and drying off. I avoided eye contact with Troy as I dressed in the scrubs and the little paper shoes. Squeezing out the water from my hair, I curled it up into a messy bun and slipped a hair net over it. Before I walked into the surgical room, Troy handed me gloves and a mask.

"He did that to you?" he asked as he paused at the door.

I met his questioning gaze, knowing the burn scars on my back and legs were significant. "He did not want to, but I insisted it was the only way." I let out a laugh and looked through the window as the groans silenced. "In the end, he was right, and I should have listened to him and figured out a better story line." I shrugged and met Troy's gaze. "He nursed me back to health, so I have an obligation to do the same."

"Obligation," he huffed and opened the door, waving me inside without another comment.

Mikhail lay stretched out on the metal table, covered in sweat. He turned his head toward us and nodded toward the IV machine. "There are IV bags in the medical cabinet over there, along with a healthy supply of penicillin. I will need a bottle."

"That will kill you," Troy said.

Mikhail's lips tilted into a smile. "A dragon's metabolism burns through it much faster than a human's does. Besides, the infection is already hitting my bloodstream, so..."

I crossed to the cabinet and opened it. He wasn't kidding. There was an entire shelf of antibiotics, along with another full of morphine and other drugs all kept chilled in the refrigeration unit, including piles of IV bags and a few liters of blood. Mikhail was instructing Troy where the tools were and when I stepped back next to him, my face chilled at the array of things Troy had on a table next to the operating gurney. My gaze locked on the bone saw and I swallowed hard.

Troy was in the process of cutting off Mikhail's pants.

"Woods," Mikhail snapped, pulling my attention to him.

I put the bottle on the table and hung the IV bag from the T-bar near Mikhail's head. He pointed at a needle in a plastic package. I picked it up.

"Give me that and the penicillin, and help me sit up."

I opened the package and handed him both items. I watched in fascination as he filled the entire length of the barrel with the contents of the bottle and then looked at me.

I stepped close and helped him sit up. Troy was smearing his right thigh and knee with iodine, and Mikhail took my hand and put it on his inner thigh.

"Find a vein for me," he said.

I glanced at his thigh, seeing exactly what was wrong. Too many red lines traversed from his knee.

"You don't want to hit the artery," Troy said. "That'll pump the medicine right out of him. You sure you don't want it in the arm?"

"Closer to the point of infection is better," Mikhail said.

Troy took the needle from him and ran his finger on the inside of Mikhail's knee, just above the damage. Next thing either of us knew, he plunged the needle in and slowly depressed the plunger until the plunge flange was flush with the barrel.

He then helped Mikhail lay back and took the IV and set it up in Mikhail's arm. "Grab me some of that morphine," he said as he set up a tourniquet around Mikhail's thigh.

"No," Mikhail said. "I don't want to be sedated, especially not with morphine. That shit will kill me."

Troy's eyebrows rose. "You really will need something."

Mikhail shook his head. "No. There's no time. Just cut it off before more poison gets into my bloodstream."

I went to take Mikhail's hand, but he shook his head.

"I'll crush it," he said and the flash of trepidation that crossed his eyes made me swallow hard. "Besides, he may need you to hand him things."

He took hold of the rails on the side of the table and looked at the ceiling. The sound of a bone saw yanked my gaze to Troy. He flipped his PPE over his face and focused on Mikhail's knee.

"Shouldn't you, like, use a scalpel or something first?" Heat enveloped me, and I recognized the panic seizing my muscles. But I was helpless to control it. Even deep breaths didn't help.

"There is no time. Tighten the tourniquet." Troy nodded to the strap around Mikhail's thigh. He didn't wait for me to follow through on the order. He just lowered the blade.

I scrambled to tighten the strap and I held it in place with all my strength. The belt dug into Mikhail's skin, leaving the area below an almost purple color. My stomach wanted to purge itself, but I swallowed back the bile. Maybe later I would let myself vomit, but for now, I needed to do everything Troy told me to so Mikhail wouldn't bleed out.

Mikhail stared at the ceiling without so much as a wince as the saw dug into the skin just below his knee. His forehead broke out into a sweat and the IV bag lowered faster than just a slow drip.

Blood splattered over both Troy and me as he cut through Mikhail's flesh.

But Mikhail didn't react until Troy hit bone. A low groan escaped through his tight lips, and he squeezed his eyes shut. His hands gripped the bars tight enough for the metal to creak from his hold.

A few moments later, Troy finished the dismembering of Mikhail's crushed appendage from the rest of his leg. He swept it away and grabbed clamps from his utility table and took the arteries in Mikhail's leg, clamping them shut before he quickly sutured them. He repeated the process with the veins as well until it seemed like the flow of blood slowed to a trickle.

"Let up on the pressure," Troy ordered.

I eased up as Troy stared at the oozing open stump. I had no idea what he was looking for, but when he held his hand up, I stopped loosening the tourniquet. He removed the clamps and then waited a moment; then he gave me a nod. I continued loosening the belt until there was no more pressure holding back Mikhail's blood. The stitches Troy had done held.

He picked up another tool that looked like a saw, but he held the flat end on the bones and turned it on, grinding the edges of Mikhail's tibia until it was smooth and flush with the muscle. He took bone cutters and extracted the small amount of the fibula that was left; then, he took the flap of skin he had left on the back of Mikhail's leg and pulled it over the amputated end and started stitching Mikhail back together.

It wasn't quite as much of a hack job as I had expected. I had a new respect for Troy's abilities despite his disgusted scowl that persisted throughout the surgery. I wasn't sure whether it was just doing the operation that painted that expression on his face or something deeper and darker.

But as he finished and stepped back, his gaze met mine and that scowl became unreadable.

Dragon Storm
Chapter 17

TROY AND I LEANED against the wall in clean scrubs, sipping on bottled water we found in one of the cabinets, waiting for Mikhail to regain consciousness. He passed out at some point while Troy was mending his stump.

When he was finished with Mikhail, neither of us could leave the room in such disarray. It wasn't sanitary. We scrubbed the floor and the table, gathering all the waste, including Mikhail's leg, and bagged it up, along with all the bloody gauze pads and rags.

We even stripped Mikhail, cleaned him up, and put a johnny on him so he wouldn't freeze before we each took turns washing ourselves of all the mess in the shower.

With clean scrubs on, we checked on Mikhail again, but he remained unconscious. At least his breathing was regular, and he was not nearly as pale as he was when we came in. Even the lines in his leg had faded. Even so, Troy gave him another dose of penicillin just to be sure any chance of infection was knocked out of him. Then he replaced the intravenous bag and sauntered over to the other side of the room and took a seat on the floor, looking every bit as tired as I felt.

I crossed and took a seat next to him and let the last few hours sink in. The shakes started, but at least my stomach gave me a reprieve. I didn't throw up and I kept my hands clasped around my knees so Troy wouldn't see me shaking.

"Your surgery skills are impressive," I said when I felt my voice would not hold the tremors still accosting me. He had done an amazing job without so much as a flinch.

"The fact you didn't hurl or pass out impressed me." He glanced at me and then at the pristine room.

"I almost did," I admitted, and heat rose in my cheeks. I reached for my water, and he intercepted my hand.

"Look, even though you turned twelve different shades of green, you kept it down. Most wouldn't have been able to do that."

I stared at his hand holding mine, digesting his words and the way he gripped me. It wasn't gentle, and nowhere in the same vicinity as holding Mikhail's hand, but it still warmed me in a way I wasn't sure I liked. I glanced up at him.

"You're a good leader." I didn't know what else to say as I pulled my hand out of his grip and picked up the water. Uncapping the bottle and taking a sip gave me the precious seconds to figure out what else to say to the sudden awkwardness that crawled between us.

"I should check on the guys." He stood and glanced at Mikhail and then the floor before he looked at me. "He's it for you?" He hooked his thumb toward Mikhail.

I blinked at his blatant question and looked at the table where Mikhail's chest rose and fell in an even rhythm. When I met Troy's questioning gaze, he let out a small laugh and shook his head as his expression morphed from the cocked eyebrow to a scowl. Without another word, he headed toward the door. I remained seated, watching him go.

That little voice inside me said to stop him because I thought he had just opened a door that I hadn't even considered. And as flattered as I was, my heart belonged to the dragon on the table, even though that future was as doomed as we were.

I had a moment to wonder whether I would regret my silent inaction. But then the door to the operating room closed. The sound echoed in the sterile room like a tomb shutting forever.

"Should have stopped him." Mikhail's hoarse voice broke through the ringing in my ears.

I got to my feet and crossed to him as a hot flush of aggravation scraped my sterilized skin. *Why the hell was he pushing me away?* "Why?"

"I'm broken," he said, as if his physical state mattered to me at all. "He isn't."

I cocked my head and stared at him. That wasn't a valid reason to suggest I start something with someone else. "We all are broken, Mikhail." I sighed. "If you haven't figured that out yet, you're not as smart as I gave you credit for."

His lips cocked into a partial smile. "You aren't."

His comment pulled a laugh from my chest. He had no idea who I was if he didn't think I was marked by this war. In some ways, I was far more broken than he could ever be. "I'm just as broken as you are, so don't kid yourself." I handed him my water bottle. "What makes you think Troy is even interested, anyway?"

Mikhail took it without reservation and propped himself up with his left arm that wasn't hooked up to the intravenous liquid. He drained the bottle and then wiped his mouth with the back of his hand. "Thanks." He handed me the empty before lying back down on the steel table. "I've caught him glancing at you a couple times."

"So?"

"He's human. I'm not. I just thought it might be..." Mikhail trailed off and looked away as his eyes blazed in a way I'd never seen before. They flared almost green. "I need my bed." He blinked away the flames in his irises.

"Did I just detect... jealousy?" I asked, amused by his reaction.

"No. I just need some rest. And I need you to help me to my bed in the penthouse." He avoided my gaze.

"And how do you suggest we get you there?"

"It's only ten more flights." He methodically removed the lines from his arm and handed them to me, busying himself with anything that seemed to keep him from meeting my gaze. "You can dump all the trash in the incinerator over there." He pointed to a metal door in the opposite wall. "It fires up when it's full."

"Ah." I couldn't think of anything witty to say to him. Not with the conflict written in his body language. It was as if truly admitting he felt something other than being my caretaker wasn't in his makeup. I took the line and the empty bag off the T-bar and crossed, opened the metal chute and dumped the line and bag, because I needed the time for my own self-reflection.

Troy was a handsome man, but with the interest he showed today, there seemed to be an underlying hostility and I really didn't want to try to crack that nut. Not when my heart belonged to the damn dragon, despite how much that made me feel like a traitor to my own kind.

I dumped the garbage bag that we had packed with all the rags and leftovers from surgery down the incinerator path as well and then finally turned my attention back to Mikhail. But he was no longer in human form. I had been too deep in thought to hear his transition.

A little one-legged dragon met my gaze.

"Bring a couple doses of penicillin and a couple of needles." He gruffly barked the order, as if he were just as annoyed with me as I was with him.

His tone crawled across my skin, and I tightened my jaw, grinding my teeth.

Why couldn't we both just be honest with each other for a second?

I turned and grabbed a plastic box off the shelf and put two bottles of antibiotics and needles into the container, along with a tube of topical antibiotics and a couple sets of bandages. His leg dressings would need to be changed whether he was in dragon form or human form, and I didn't want to be running up and down ten flights of stairs multiple times a day.

"Can you also grab one of those containers of green gel?" He pointed to the lower shelf that had four canisters of what he asked for.

I had no clue what it was, but maybe it was some antibiotic gel that could be spread on his leg easier than the paste-like topical ointment. "Anything else?"

"As many towels as you can grab. A scalpel, a needle, and some suture string," he added to my growing list.

I stared at him as the items sunk into my tired brain. "What the hell do we need a scalpel for?"

"If I have a prayer of ever walking again, I need you to put that green gel directly on the break in my spine."

What did he just say? "What the fuck? Why didn't you have Troy do that while he was here?"

If a dragon could press his lips into an invisible line, that's what Mikhail's expression was, but he finally opened his mouth after a few heartbeats. "Because that's dragon blood and it is very rare. I didn't want him to know it existed and that it has healing properties that seem miraculous." He met my gaze. "Besides, once you do what I ask, I cannot move until it does its thing, and the only place I'll be in a comfortable position is on my bed."

"I've seen you bleed, and it doesn't look like this." I shook the container.

"That's because I'm not a full-blooded dragon. I'm a half-breed. Remember?" Even his tone challenged me, like anything I said would be the wrong thing.

My brain just caught up to what he said about the contents. "Miraculous how? And exactly how long do you have to remain still?"

"It has healing properties. And as far as how long I'll be laid up, it could be hours or days. It depends on how damaged my back is. If the nerve is severed, I'm not sure it will work, but if it is just pinched or even nicked, I have a chance."

Healing properties. "Could you have used this on my back?"

"No. Not without risking your life further." He met my gaze. "I thought of it, but sometimes humans have a deadly reaction to it and I did not want to take that chance."

"Oh." Right, because if he had and it killed me, he never would have known my secret about bleach. I looked at the green goop and then put the container in the box. Before I closed it, I added a second canister of dragon blood just in case, and then dumped the items he listed off in and snapped the lid, turning back toward the diminutive dragon lying prone on the table.

I studied him. He was such the opposite of that big bad dragon that I encountered in Grand Central, and it had nothing to do with his injuries. That fire in his gaze had dulled and he seemed... softer. Less menacing.

I wondered whether it was just the exhaustion playing tricks on me. "Before I do any sort of surgery on you, I need a nap."

His stare hardened. "It has to be as soon as we step inside. I've gone longer than I should have and if we wait, there will be no chance of recovery."

Great. Now his entire future was in my lap.

"What if I screw up because I'm so tired? What if I sever your spinal cord trying to open you up?" I snarled as I stalked toward him.

"We will deal with it if that happens." His eyes closed. "Look, Holly, I need you to carry me upstairs and then cover the bed with those towels and put me on them. I'll shift and then I'll direct you as to what to do. I trust you." His eyes opened to that shimmering citrine that I had gotten used to.

"Fine." I dropped the container into a bag with a dozen towels and hauled it over my shoulder before I picked him up in my arms. "I swear, you just like to nuzzle up to my breast," I muttered as we crossed and stepped out through the sterilizing air lock.

He let out a soft chuckle. "Would that really be so bad?"

I rolled my eyes and started the ten-story trek with Mikhail nestled against me.

Dragon Storm
Chapter 18

TEN FLOORS WITH LEGS that already felt like spaghetti was not a picnic, especially carrying Mikhail and the bag of medical supplies, along with a load of towels slung over my shoulder. By the time I got to the landing for the penthouse, I was out of breath, and I had to put the package down before I focused on the keypad because he obviously didn't have keys on him this time.

"Two, four, six, eight, zero, five, pound, star," Mikhail said.

I glanced at him. "Any significance?" I asked as I typed the simple passcode.

"None. Just easy to remember," he said as I swung the door open to a sun-drenched apartment and shuffled the bag inside with my foot before we followed. No wonder I was so tired. His leg surgery and the cleanup took all night. The last time I had slept was at least twenty-four hours ago, when we had the entire crew with us. Now we were down by four, with a severely injured dragon.

I shook the exhaustion away and punched the code in again, reengaging the lock. "And you really thought I wouldn't have been able to figure that out?"

The little dragon grinned, and I had to stop the urge to just drop him and let him fend for himself. Only this being could swing my moods as wide as a pendulum.

"You would have put way too much thought into it," he answered.

I snorted a laugh at his comment, swinging the emotions back to humor. He was right; I would never have guessed as easy a combination as what he had for this place. "And the front door. What significance is that code?"

"That was mine and my wife's and kids' birthdays."

His answer silenced me.

I had guessed that might be the representation, but I hadn't been sure. *He did have some sentimental bones in his body. Although we may have just removed the only one left.* The last thought nearly sent me into another fit of laughter. I was way too tired to do surgery on Mikhail. *What the hell was he thinking?*

"When's your birthday?" I asked, trying to focus my mind on something other than what he had asked of me.

"June first."

Even as my mind wandered to spring and started making plans for a birthday that I had no idea whether either of us would reach, I crossed into the bedroom and set him down on the chair. Once the bed was covered in the multiple layers of towels, I hoped it was enough. If not, his mattress would be ruined. My brain kept swirling, kept trying to avoid the inevitable, and I turned, moving him from the chair and onto my towel mound. I placed him gently on his stomach and stepped back.

Transforming from dragon to human was slower this time, unlike that first time in Grand Central where it was within a blink. And it wasn't nearly as fast as his shift in the tunnels either. Maybe that was a true indication of just how broken he really was. When he finished, a sheen of sweat glistened on his bare back.

The johnny he wore lay open, giving me a full view of his perfectly shaped ass and thighs. The bandages on the stump of his leg were soaked through and would need changing as well. I pulled the chair close to the bed as he turned his face toward me.

"Can you get a damp cloth from the bathroom and wipe off my back?" His tired eyes met mine like dull mirrors into his pain.

The soft question was not in any way demanding and I gave him a smile. "Sure." I got a hand towel out of the cabinet and wet it, making sure it wasn't too cold. When I came back into the bedroom, I took a seat on the edge of the bed and gently ran the towel over his backside, cleaning him off before I reached for the bandages on his leg.

"That can wait until after," he said.

I swallowed and nodded as fear coiled like lead in my belly. "You'll have to talk me through this," I said, silently wishing that Troy was here to do the surgery part. The idea of slicing Mikhail's skin made my stomach tighten in the most uncomfortable way. But I had to just suck it up.

He grabbed his pillow and hugged it with his face toward me. "The break is in the lumbar area. My upper thighs and hips feel like pins and needles, but from the middle of my thigh down, I feel nothing."

I looked at his lower back, specifically at the bruise above his fine ass. "You have a bruise."

"Can you run your finger down my spine and see if you can feel the damage? Start in the middle of my back and don't stop until you feel the normal spine again, okay?"

I did as he suggested, running my fingers down, feeling each disc and the strong cords of muscles on either side. When I got to the top of the bruise, it changed under my fingers, bulging out in a weird jut. His breath sucked in for a moment. Below the jut, his spine seemed to disappear for about an inch before the natural bumps like the spine above the bruise resurfaced.

"I know where the damage is," I said. "It's about two inches in total right after the start of the bruise."

"You're going to need to cut a little above and end a little below that area."

"I really don't know if I can do this," I said staring at my shaking hands. "I could go get Troy."

Mikhail closed his eyes. "You are the strongest woman I have ever met. I need *you* to do this, now. Besides, I do not trust Troy. And waiting for you to run down the stairs and back is not an option."

"Damn it, Mikhail, what if I fuck up?"

He met my gaze. "Then I remain paralyzed."

I sucked in a loud inhale and searched his eyes. His cross expression softened and his brow smoothed out as he seemed to push down whatever aggravation had bled into his voice.

"Holly, you have the opportunity to possibly fix that. It's no guarantee, but every second you waffle is a step toward this being permanent," he said with a softness to his voice that belied the urgency in his eyes.

"Shit. Way to put the pressure on." As much as I did not want to do this, his argument was compelling enough for me to at least attempt this insanity. "Are you sure I'm the one with a death wish?"

His half tilt of a grin and shoulder shrug made me want to slap his ass good and hard, but I refrained. Instead, I set the medical supplies out on the towel next to him and picked up the scalpel.

"Where do I cut?" I asked before I chickened out.

"Right over the spine. Just give me a minute." He pushed the pillow away and set his forehead down on his folded arms so I couldn't see his face. But the muscles in his jaw tightened. "You'll need to do a T cross at the top and bottom after you do the initial incision and then peel back the skin so you can see the bone underneath. Once you do that, you'll have to spread the contents of one of the jars down the length of the bone that's visible. From the good section, through the bad and back to the good. Then you can close the skin and stitch it up."

"Why didn't we do this with your leg?" The question bubbled up from my need to stall. His directions haunted me, and I couldn't fathom why, if this dragon blood was such a healing elixir, he didn't take this route with his crushed leg.

"My leg was crushed beyond repair, my back..." He sighed and glanced at me. "I still have a chance as slight as it is, it's still worth the attempt."

I nodded, took a breath to settle all the doubts building in my mind, and steadied my hand with the scalpel to the spot just over the bruise and then recentered it a few centimeters higher. "Tell me when you're ready."

A few deep breaths and then I saw the muscles actually relax throughout his back. It was as if someone gave him a strong sedative.

"Go," he said.

I lowered the scalpel and paused right before I touched his skin. I couldn't go through the spine and cause more damage, but I had to go deep enough to actually reach the bone. I almost chickened out, but his words propelled me forward. This was an attempt to fix what may have already been done. If I didn't try, he definitely wouldn't walk again. He might never fly again, either, from what he had said, and we needed him to fly in order to deliver the bleach bomb we had yet to build.

I let my mind mull over things, but my hand sliced through skin until the blade hit bone, and then I dragged it lower at the same depth, over and through the area that was damaged. Mikhail groaned, but did not move. I finished the first cut and then did a couple of T cuts at the top and bottom of my incision.

Blood seeped down his sides as I peeled back the skin, and I ignored the flip of my stomach at the clear view of his mangled spine. I wasn't sure this would work, but I quickly took the cap off the green goop and spread the dragon blood over the visible damage, doing exactly as directed. One jar was more than enough, and I used every last ounce of that thick blood before I folded the skin back together. I dried my hands with the hand towel before I took the silk and threaded the suture needle.

I took my time trying to stitch him up as neatly as I could, but I was not as skilled with sutures as Troy. When I finished, I spread antibiotic ointment over the crude capital "I" carved in his back and covered it with gauze.

I got a clean towel and wiped up his sides before I went into the bathroom and dumped the soiled cloth into the hamper. When I finished cleaning off his blood from my arms and from under my nails, I turned and fell on my knees before the toilet, vomiting a hot stream of bile that had coated my throat through most of the hack job I did on his back.

With a shaky hand, I flushed the toilet, and then crossed to the sink and splashed cold water over my face and brushed the vile taste from my mouth. I couldn't wipe out the dirty feeling and stripped out of the soiled scrubs. The shower felt heavenly and the need to feel clean ebbed away with the sweet scent of soap that filled the steam. I closed my eyes, letting the water wash the stress from my body. When I finished, my fingers had pruned up and I dried off before combing out the knots from my hair.

I had no idea how long I had been in the shower, but I needed it as badly as Mikhail needed me to cut his back open. Without a stitch of clothing on, I crossed to the closet and perused his wife's clothing until I found a similar dress to the crushed velvet one Mikhail had insisted I bring with us last time.

This was cotton with short sleeves, but it was just as comfortable on my tired skin as that crushed velvet had been. A part of me wished I still had that with me, despite it being soiled with my own blood.

I turned and Mikhail stared at me with a cocked eyebrow. The glow from his eyes was duller than usual.

"I needed something clean," I explained and smoothed the dress.

He pulled the pillow back under his head with a nod, and his eyes closed. "I think I might need another dose of penicillin," he said with a slurred voice. He straightened his arm out to the side.

I didn't hesitate and without direction, I filled the canister of the needle with the entire contents of the drug vial, plucked the needle with my finger to get any air bubbles out, and then turned his arm. His veins already stood out against his skin, and I slid the needle into one and depressed the plunger, sending medicine he needed into him.

"Thank you," he whispered after I took the needle out. He pulled his arm back under the pillow.

"Is there anything else I can get you?"

"No. You can lay down and get some sleep, though. You look like you need it." He looked at me with one eye and then that fluttered closed.

I didn't think I'd be able to sleep. Not after the last two surgeries I participated in. But the exhaustion pounding in my temple said otherwise. I crawled onto the far side of the bed, pushing the edges of the soiled towels closer to Mikhail and stretched out, facing him.

I studied his profile and then let my gaze drift over his strong arms and his upper back. I glanced back at his face before I got to the patch job I did, and his citrine eyes studied me with open adoration.

"Don't look at me like that," I said even though I could live the rest of my life under the light of that stare. It warmed my soul the way no other ever had.

"Like what?"

"Like I am special to you." I rolled onto my back and chose to stare at the ceiling as silence pervaded the room.

"You are."

I turned my gaze to him. "It's just transference." I repeated what he had spouted to me in that concrete garage we found ourselves in after leaving this place to make our way back to my platoon. That had only been days ago, yet it felt like weeks.

"No, Holly. It's a little deeper than that," he said, jarring me.

He chose now to declare his feelings? Now, when all I can see is his blood spilling on the floor? I backed right into denial. "No, Mik. It's not." I returned my gaze to the ceiling. "It is impossible."

He let out a huff of a laugh. "Apparently nothing is impossible with you."

"You are a sappy fuck when you're injured." I glanced back at him and damn him, he flashed that endearing smile that made my knees weak. Thankfully, I was already lying down.

His smile faded as his eyes fluttered closed. A heavy sigh followed and then the cadence of his breathing when sleep gripped him filled the room.

I turned my gaze back to the ceiling, wondering yet again how the hell I was going to get my heart out of his grip. He was a dragon, after all, and as much as I was enthralled by him right now, it would never work. Especially if we failed at our attempt to stop this war.

Dragon Storm
Chapter 19

SLEEP YANKED ME DEEP into the abyss and with it came nightmares.

Nightmares of leviathans shredding Mikhail to pieces while the Serpent King laughed, and I watched, unable to save him.

A hand touched my face, and I jerked with a gasp. Troy's blue eyes stared at me from the spot where Mikhail should have been. "You've been sleeping for two days," he said.

I blinked and sat up.

My gaze took in the darkened bedroom. When I looked back at the figure next to me, Mikhail was there and snoring in that light way of his that sounded like a chair scraping in the distance. I reached over, but it seemed like the distance was impossibly far. Stretching even more than humanly possible, my fingers finally grazed the edge of the bandage. I pulled it back away from Mikhail's skin but there was no ugly incision on his back, just a bulge in his spine that seemed to be pulsing. I quickly covered it up again, confused.

I had done what he asked, hadn't I? Doubt as thick as the low-lying fog that rolled through the room scratched at my mind.

He turned toward me. "My lower right leg has been hurting for hours." His voice was groggy and off. Like it wasn't Mikhail speaking. It actually reminded me of the Serpent King's awful voice, and I shivered.

"You don't have anything below your right knee anymore." When I glanced at his leg, it was shredded to bits, with strings of flesh hanging from his knee; bits of bone scattered on the towels and blood poured from his stump. Much more blood than I had ever seen. It soaked the bed, spreading toward me like the breaching of a flood plain. I pulled my legs up higher, away from the advancing mess, and my chest hurt with the thunder of my heart.

I dumped the container of dragon blood in a line around me, hoping it would stop the blood from reaching me like bleach stops leviathans. When Mikhail's blood hit the green line, it burst into flame, driving me off the bed and sending me running to find help.

"Dragons run hot," Mikhail called from the bedroom and then broke out in a laugh that nearly scared the piss out of me. But then he added, "When you come back, bring a set of crutches."

The stairway elongated as his laughter followed me down. It seemed to take forever to get to the floor that the soldiers were on. I stared at the keypad and blinked.

The outside street surrounded me, and I held a dragon egg. Jenny stood beside me, but half her body was blackened from the blast. "Beware of Troy. He has ulterior motives."

When I turned to face her, something yanked her into the shadows. I turned back to the door, trying to keep the egg nestled in my arm. But Troy was there, with a mouthful of sharp teeth like a shark.

He swung his fist down, smashing the dragon egg in my arms. My stomach dropped, and I turned away to be standing in the soldier's room with a biting need to have Troy come tend to Mikhail.

Troy sat at one of the tables with a coffee, with everything perfectly in place and a smile that made me pause. His teeth were normal, and he had never truly smiled at me. More like glowered, but here he was beaming.

Suspicion flowed through my blood like hot syrup as I crossed to the table. My bare feet padded across the cool industrial floor. Each step sent a jolt through my bones until I stood opposite Troy. "I need you to look at Mik. I don't think he's okay."

Of course he wasn't. Fire probably had taken him and everything else in the apartment. My heart jumped and the urgency increased.

Troy's eyes sharpened. "So, you're going to let me into his private quarters?" he asked with a smile toying on his lips like it was something taboo.

Everything about Troy seemed taboo at this point and Jenny's strange warning surfaced, but I rolled my eyes at him.

I did not have time for this. We needed to get back to Mikhail. "We need to stop on twenty so I can grab crutches for Mikhail." This seemed to be more important right now than checking on Mikhail, and I couldn't fathom why.

A strange need pulled me right into the operating room and I turned, blinking at the surroundings. The walls and floor were painted with blood, except it wasn't red; it was green. I gasped as red blood pooled on the operating table. If it fell, the room would burst into flame.

I spun around, and Troy stared down at me. "I find myself very bothered by the idea of you and the dragon... together." His piercing blue eyes stared down at me as if I were his prey.

My heart sped up. What was between Mikhail and me was none of his business. I went to speak, to tell him just that, but he advanced with a feral hunger written on his face, pulling his lips into a knowing smile. His eyes carried such intensity that I swallowed hard.

"What if we are the last ones alive?" he asked as he cornered me.

I cocked my head, as my mouth dried up. My glance went to the operating table and the red blood slowly creeping toward the sides.

"The only humans left on Earth?" he clarified

His question crawled under my skin like a tick, festering, separating the need to get out to include the need to look at Troy. He kept my gaze, but there was something underneath all these questions and it went back to his first statement.

"Is this all about humanity or is this about you?" I narrowed my gaze at him. "Are you jealous of Mikhail?"

"I'm human. He's not."

Weren't those the same words Mikhail had used last night?

He started to turn away and I went to grab his arm. He moved like lightning, grabbing my wrist and slamming me against the wall. His chest rose and fell like he was trying to control a wild beast inside him. Instead of answering me, he crushed his lips down on mine.

My mouth popped open in surprise, and he took the opportunity to explore my mouth with his tongue. The low groan that came from the back of his throat both chilled me and sent a thrill through my entire form. I had not been with anyone for a very long time, and Troy knew what he was doing.

I found myself sinking into the kiss, my heart pounding hard enough to remind me of how alive I was. My free hand pressed against his chest, feeling the same heightened pulse from him. His hand descended my arm, finding my breast, and his soft caress belied the demanding kiss.

God, I needed this. But what would Mikhail do if he found out?

God knows my body was screaming at me to ravage him, but the blood on the table had just breached the edge. We had to move or we would die in here. I pushed Troy's chest, moving him away. "Mikhail will kill you."

The way he grinned sent chills through me, and a panicked sweat broke out on the back of my neck. It was as if he didn't want to leave this room. It was as if he wanted us to go up in flames.

"Not if I kill him first," he said and was gone.

My heart thundered and I grabbed the crutches. The route to the stairwell elongated like one of those funhouse mirrors, and my sprint became sluggish, like I couldn't stop the inevitable. I burst through the door to the stairs just as the operating room flashed into hot flames.

The next door I flew through was the one for the penthouse. Troy's gait through the living room slowed, as if I had never lost sight of him.

He spun around and glared at me. "I guess money does buy everything," he snarled at me. "Including your alliance." He turned and looked down at the street below and his shoulders tensed.

I was not in the mood for his anger or the accusations flashing over his face. "Stop acting like a damn teenager."

As I stood next to him at the window, the world below changed into a landscape of writhing leviathans crawling onto the shore. Thousands of them poured onto the street like ants fleeing a drowning ant hill. My skin seemed to shrink, pulling me into myself.

He glanced sideways at me. "Those things are multiplying by the minute."

"Your point?"

He looked at the leviathans below, his anger bleeding away and his expression growing serious. "Can he do what he says he can?" he asked without looking at me. Doubt pervaded his tone.

"Yes. It doesn't matter if he can walk or not; his mind is still sharp. Just look at this building. He's made it functional on its own grid and disguised it to the outside world. Both human and monster from the street level think this is one of the destroyed buildings. If he can do that, a bomb ought to be a snap." I had faith in Mikhail's abilities.

I turned toward the bedroom. "Time to check his leg."

He grabbed my hand and pulled me into his arms. "I want a chance."

"A chance for what?" I asked, but I already knew, and it really was hopeless. As hopeless as Mikhail and I having any future. But if I was putting my bets on one of them, it was the one who had already captured my heart whether I liked it or not.

"A chance for you to see someone other than a dragon." He glanced toward the bedroom and then met my gaze. "Please."

Fuck. I knew his intentions. I knew he wanted a physical relationship with me, which was more interest than Mikhail had shown. Hell, I needed to scratch my own itch in a very bad way. I hated this precarious position. Plus, his question had burrowed under my skin as well.

What if we were all that was left of the human race?

That meant I was the only one able to carry children and perpetuate the species. Double fuck.

And he said please. Triple fuck.

I was in one hell of a corner with only one way out. I nodded and a growl from the bedroom made us both turn.

Mikhail stood on one leg, hugging the doorjamb with the johnny skewed off one shoulder. He had such an angry glare that I attempted to pull my hand from Troy's grip, but it was impossible.

My heart thundered. "You shouldn't be up."

He huffed, like it didn't matter. "I'll be fine," he growled.

I finally yanked my hand free and started across the room. He put his hand up and shook his head, as if I had somehow betrayed him.

"Go." He pointed at the door.

"The fuck I am," I snarled back, suddenly more furious than I had been in a very long time. "What is it with you?" I yelled. "Thinking I'm a fucking possession of yours. You don't own me. So, this crap stops now." I pointed at Mikhail. "You and I have some shit to work through before you have the right to give me any rage on whatever choices I make."

I stomped into Mikhail's office and slammed the door. The walls shook with the force. I didn't want to deal with the emotional and physical pull between dragon and human right now. Not when we had armies marching up from the deep in numbers that scared the shit out of me.

I turned, and Mikhail stood inside the door on both legs, like he had so many weeks ago when I had found solace in the library. I hadn't even heard the door open.

He crossed the distance gracefully, as though he had never been injured. "I'm in love with you."

His simple statement nearly took me out at the knees. "Then why the fuck did you tell me I should have gone after him last night? Why the mixed signals?"

"He's human and not broken like I am."

"We are all fucking broken!"

He grabbed my face and kissed me so gently that it silenced me. "I'm sorry," he whispered after his lips left mine. "I was not thinking clearly, and obviously my pushing you toward Harrington wasn't well thought out." He took a deep breath and met my gaze.

"Mikhail," I said softly, pressing my cheek into his palm.

"He wants to fuck you. But I want a life with you. I don't care if it's a day or a thousand years, either."

"I need sex," I blurted and my cheeks immediately heated. I couldn't see being with someone without consummating the relationship in any way.

Mikhail chuckled. "I am a man. I probably need it more than you do."

I blinked at him. "But you never showed any real interest in me."

He rubbed his thumb across my cheek. "You were injured and the one time you got all uppity about it had been after I collected my family's heads. I wasn't anywhere near the right frame of mind after that ordeal. But that wasn't because you are not desirable." His eyes moved from mine, down the front of my dress and back. "I am not so different from Troy in my wants either, but I know there is a time and place for intimacy, and we have not been given the chance for that yet."

Holy fuck. I stared at him, melting from his words. Instead of speaking, I pulled him to my lips and this time the kiss was not a chaste brushing. This time, I demanded more. Oh, and he delivered in spades.

Mikhail St. Clare knew how to kiss. His tongue gently explored my mouth and he pulled me into his arms, deepening the experience. His gentle expertise slipped to more aggressive, as if he just gave in to all his feelings. It was magical, until he pulled away.

He stared into my eyes. "I need to know how you feel," he said with a raspy voice filled with the same need coursing through my veins.

"There are times I hate you, like when you haul me over your shoulder as if I'm a useless human."

His lips twitched into a smile. "And other times?"

"Other times I could just throttle you for being so damn blind."

His smile faded. "I was not blind. I was in denial. Because, seriously, how could you love me after all that I've done to your kind?"

I blinked at his words. They seemed more like my thoughts than anything that would come from Mikhail. "I care a great deal, but I need to get laid so I can think straight again."

He snorted laughter. "I stopped fucking for fuck's sake a long time ago."

"Maybe you should start again."

"Maybe I will, but the bed is a god-awful mess. And you, my dear, are ovulating, so today is not the day for fucking."

I balked and he pushed me back in the seat.

"But that doesn't mean I can't give you a preview of what life with me would mean for you."

He tore my dress in half, straight up the middle, with no effort at all. I gasped as he pushed my legs apart and lowered his mouth to my core.

Dragon Storm
Chapter 20

SHAKING. SOMEONE WAS SHAKING me. My eyes flew open to the darkness of the bedroom. Mikhail trying to shake me awake.

"Holly. I need more penicillin," he said with a groggy voice.

I blinked at the blackness surrounding us and then at the vividness of what felt like moments ago. Jesus, it must have been a dream. "What time is it?" I reached for the light on the nightstand and flipped it on.

"I don't know."

I turned back to him and gasped. He was bathed in sweat and both bandages had been soaked through. And not by perspiration. His eyes were bloodshot, and he was as pale as I'd ever seen him. My strange dream evaporated.

Fear enveloped me. Mikhail needed help.

"Oh, fuck," I whispered. My hands shook as I opened the container that held the last dose of medicine and the needle. I stripped the sterile packaging off the needle and unscrewed the medicine, stuck it inside and pulled the contents into the canister. I tapped the needle to get out any air and then took a slow and steadying breath.

"Easy," he whispered and held out his arm.

I closed my eyes and breathed a few more times to shake my complete disorientation out of my head. "When I'm done, I need to go get Troy." My voice cracked.

He didn't argue. He just watched me with a perplexing gaze. After I finished, he said, "Thank you."

"I need to go get Troy, okay?"

He nodded. "You talk in your sleep."

Beyond the pain, I saw some humor in his eyes.

My heart hammered and I wasn't sure whether it was because of his state or what he may or may not have heard. It was becoming more and more fuzzy to me by the minute. He just smiled in a way that made me shift.

"We can talk about it when I'm not in such a sorry state," he said. "I need soldier boy to make sure..." He looked away like he didn't want to say the words. "To make sure I'm not dying." His eyes found mine.

My heart jumped in my throat, and I bolted. My hand still shook as I punched in the code. I barely remembered the stairwell light and then I was running down the stairs at a pace that if I tripped would kill me. But the way Mikhail said what he did set my heart on triple beat.

I punched in the code for the room on fifteen and raced in, throwing the light switch. My gaze flew over the cots until I zeroed in on Troy, ignoring the growling and grumbling to turn off the lights. I crossed and grabbed his hand, pulling him out of the cot and toward the door. I didn't care that he was only in a wifebeater and skivvies, either.

"Something's wrong," I said.

That seemed to wake him up in full. He swiped the lights off as we exited and took the stairs two by two, stopping at the twentieth floor. He started punching in the code and I grabbed his hand, pulling him up the stairs.

"He's in the penthouse," I said and without further explanation, we catapulted up the remaining ten flights. The door was still cracked from my run. I closed it and flipped on the lights, pointing toward the bedroom.

Troy gave me a cursory look and headed that way as I leaned back against the door, trying to catch my breath.

"Christ, what the hell did you do to his back?"

I stumbled into the bedroom. Troy held the bandage in his hand. The ugly I stood out against his back but now there were red lines coming from the sutured skin. He looked around, then headed into the bathroom and came out a few moments later with a bottle of peroxide. He poured it over the wound.

Mikhail hissed as his eyes popped open.

"Seriously, Woods, what the fuck did you do?" he asked again as he tossed the now empty bottle into the garbage.

"She did what I asked," Mikhail said.

"Well, whatever she did, your body is rejecting it."

"My left foot is tingling."

"The lines coming from her crude incision tell me whatever you had her do, it's poisoning you. You are burning up."

"Dragons run hot," both Mikhail and I said at the same time.

Troy sent me a glare. "Go get more antibiotics and some iodine from downstairs. Along with a clean scalpel. I'm going to try to fix this."

I stopped. "Your left leg?" I asked, turning back.

"I still can't move it to bang out the pins and needles."

"It's working then."

I just got a shoulder raise in response.

Troy pointed. "Please get me what I asked for so we can remove the infected skin." His voice was a little softer this time. "I'll look at his leg too, but I don't see any evidence of blood poisoning."

I nodded.

As I was leaving, he scolded Mikhail for having a rookie do a surgery like that. The admonishment was received with a grumbled apology from the patient.

I grabbed the bag that I had used to bring things upstairs last time and went down the ten floors to the medical unit. I filled the bag with both topical and intravenous antibiotics, needles and a scalpel, and grabbed a couple bottles of iodine, along with nearly all the bandages. On the bottom shelf next to the dragon blood was a vial, and I picked it up. I stared at one of the vials of morphine and added it to the mix along with an alternative, oxycodone, just in case whatever Troy was going to do to him was more painful. As I was walking out, I grabbed a pair of crutches on impulse.

I was out of breath when I got back to the apartment and this time, I engaged the keypad to lock up. The type of exhaustion that made my stomach do a slow roll gripped me as I crossed to the bedroom.

Mikhail's leg was wrapped in clean bandages and the old ones had been stuffed in the garbage. Troy extended his hand, and I put the iodine, scalpel, and painkillers in his hand along with a wrapped needle, careful not to stab him with the sharps.

"I didn't have nearly enough sleep." He wiped his face with his free hand. "Are there better lights in here?"

"There's a light stand in the library," Mikhail said, looking over at me.

His voice slurred in a way that concerned me.

I went and found the light, unplugging it and carrying it into the bedroom. I plugged it in and turned it on high right next to where Troy stood, careful not to blind him with the lights. It truly illuminated his back.

How could I have thought the dragon blood would be a miracle cure? Right now, it looked like a child carved him up, and my stomach tightened.

How could I have thought that dream was real?

I looked at the two central figures who had starred in my dream and wondered how I would really react if the same situations presented themselves. Would I shun Troy for Mikhail? Did the dragon truly own my heart? The only thing real about the dream was I indeed needed this horny itch scratched. But right now, all I wanted was for Mikhail to be okay.

"Morphine or oxycodone?" Troy asked.

"Oxy. I'm allergic to morphine," Mikhail said.

"Keep him entertained," Troy said to me and pointed to the spot next to his head. "This is not going to be pleasant." He sent me a grimace and only loaded the needle with a small dose of oxycodone and waited until I was seated with my back to the headboard before he shot it into Mikhail's ass.

Mikhail's brow furrowed, and I ran my hand through his hair like I had done on the stairs. He tilted his head so he could see me and put his hand out. I put mine in his without thinking and held on, even when he squeezed his eyes closed. He didn't squeeze any tighter, like he was still mindful of my frailty even in the midst of his agony.

I kept stroking his temple as worry ran through my bones like a contagion.

"I think we should talk about your dream." He opened his glossy eyes and winked at me, which made me second-guess grabbing the drugs.

Troy glanced up for a moment, and then back down as his jaw tightened. The nuance of aggravation flushed his features and then he shook it away and refocused on what he was doing.

"I dreamed they were multiplying in the thousands and flooding the streets." I swallowed. "And we were the last ones left on Earth."

"Sometimes I think we are," Troy said as he worked.

"There are more of you hiding in places they can't discern," Mikhail said. "As long as no one cuts themselves, they are safe."

My gaze snapped to his back. Human blood was one thing; dragon blood was another. Those beasts could home in on dragon blood from miles away. "Your blood," I whispered.

"Air is filtered." Mikhail met my gaze. "The only place it isn't is the lobby."

"So don't bleed in the lobby," Troy said with a nod, like he needed something else to concentrate on too.

"Boy picks up fast." Mikhail gave me a lopsided grin. "But that really wasn't what you were talking about in your sleep."

"How much oxy did you give him?" I asked Troy.

"Just enough to take the edge off while I do this," he said, still cutting away the inflamed and rotting flesh, along with scraping away as much pus as he could. He shook his head as he worked, silently moving his lips in what looked like a stream of swears. He poured more iodine over the wound and then looked up at me. "You don't still happen to have some of that liquid bandage, do you?"

"No. I think it's with the rest of our stuff down with the bleach."

"Do you have butterfly bandages?" he asked Mikhail.

"In the bathroom. Under the sink, behind the towels, there's all sorts of stuff," Mikhail muttered.

Troy pointed his chin toward the bathroom. I peeled my hand out of Mikhail's and went to look for whatever he had stowed away in the cabinet. He had quite a few first-aid kits and boxes of bandages of all sizes. Even one still in a sterile package that was big enough to cover the entire mess on his back. I brought everything to the bedside and dumped them on the end of the bed.

In the third kit, I found a tube of liquid bandage and handed it to Troy. He had taken out all the rough sutures I put in. He snatched the tube and opened it, tracing the I with the skin glue. He waited a few moments for the glue to dry and then he took the bandage in the sterile package and opened it. Only the edges were sticky and he gently covered the wound so none of the sides touched the cut.

The garbage bucket next to him was full of the kind of waste that would stink in a few hours. I would need to throw it in the incinerator as soon as we were done here. He set out three containers of antibiotics, with three needles, on the nightstand next to me.

"Every three hours." He pointed and then headed into the bathroom to wash up his hands.

I nodded and straightened up the bed. Mikhail watched me.

"I'm going to throw this stuff down the incinerator downstairs. I'll be back."

"Then we can talk," he said with a goofy smile.

"You're high."

"Mhmmm."

"I can take that stuff down," Troy said as he came out of the bathroom.

"He can take that stuff down," Mikhail mimicked.

"I appreciate the offer. But I need to grab my clothes from down there anyway and get them in the washing machine, so I don't have to trounce around in a dress."

"I'm going to try to get a little more sleep until daybreak at least," Troy said. "Then we need to start putting together a strategy for transporting the rest of that bleach."

"I'll be down."

"You need to administer his medicine." He pointed at the neatly lined up row of medicine. "We can talk strategies later."

"Okay." I picked up the garbage can. "I'll be right back," I said to Mikhail as we left the room together.

I punched in the code without caring whether Troy saw it or not. I was tired and frazzled and really, I was avoiding Mikhail. I wasn't ready to talk about my dream. Not with all the ramifications.

Troy walked silently next to me, and he was the one who opened the door to the operating room, holding it open for me. I dumped the contents of the garbage can down the incinerator shoot and went to the scrub room to find my clothes.

I pulled them off the hooks and turned to leave. Troy leaned against the door, blocking my way out.

"Can I be blunt?"

My throat closed, forcing my voice to squeak out an answer. The dream surfaced and I couldn't stop the shiver that started at the base of my spine. "Sure."

"What is your relationship with the dragon?"

I stepped back and bit down on the instinctive "None of your business" that wanted to tumble from my lips. "Why?"

"I'm just trying to figure it out."

"He's my... friend." That much I knew. After all we had been through, he was the one I could count on to have my back.

"Just friends?"

The dream flashed in my mind and the way my heart had soared when Mikhail kissed me. I focused on Troy. "He's a dragon. I'm not," I finally said. It wasn't really an answer either, and my stomach squeezed.

Half of his lips formed a smile. "Go tend to your friend. I'll come up in the morning after I get a few more hours of sleep." He turned and sauntered to the door, giving me a full view of his backside clad in tight boxers and what I could be missing.

On the way out of the scrub room, I grabbed a pair of crutches on impulse.

Troy held the door open and turned off the lights before latching the lock behind us. "Don't forget to turn out the lights in the stairwell when you get up there." He headed down as I turned away from the pleasant view and headed up to my naked dragon.

Dragon Storm
Chapter 21

MIKHAIL'S EYES WERE CLOSED when I checked in on him. Instead of just dropping my clothing on the ground and crawling into the bed like I wanted to, I headed to the laundry room and dropped my clothing in the washing machine before I turned out the lights and made my way back to the bedroom.

The light from the library was still in place by the bed, and I was tempted just to leave it, but with my luck I'd trip on it in the middle of the night while I tried to get to the bathroom, so I unplugged it and moved it to the far side of the room. I didn't want to do something that would startle Mikhail into moving when he shouldn't.

I set the bedside alarm for three hours and turned out the light. When I finally settled, facing Mikhail, I glanced at him.

His eyes were open and still held that glossy drugged quality. "Holly?"

There was so much in the way he said my name that the walls slammed into place. I didn't want to be harassed about a dream. A dream I wanted so badly to be true, no less. "Not tonight, Mikhail."

"Yes. Tonight. Because I'm drugged up enough to speak my mind and possibly not remember in the morning."

I sighed and met his serious gaze. "I'm not in the mood for your razzing."

"As tempting as that may be, I'm not going to razz you, but I do have questions. Were you dreaming about me?"

"You already know the answer to that." I went to roll away, but his hand landed on my arm in a soft, but insistent grip.

He smiled timidly, like what he had to say was concerning and yet he had to say it. "Then you are experiencing the same... emotions I am?"

"And what are you experiencing, Mikhail?" I did not want to play this game and my voice held every ounce of exasperation pummeling my muscles.

He gave me a heavy sigh. "At first I thought it was just pure lust. If I hadn't burned you, I probably would have coerced you into bed before we left this apartment." His grip on my arm changed to a soft caress.

His admission caught my full attention. "So, you *did* want to know me in the biblical sense."

"I want to know you in *every* sense. Yes."

I scrunched my eyebrows together as I studied the openness in his gaze. "Then what the hell is with the mixed messages? Why push me toward Troy?"

He huffed. "You asked me that in your dream." He closed his eyes. "I'm toxic, Holly. As much as I want the dream—" He opened his eyes again. "My dream, not yours—I know I'll screw up."

I wasn't quite sure what to do with that confession, so I focused on his earlier words while I digested this new one. "You said at first it was lust. What is it now?"

His hand moved to my cheek. "You really have to ask?" He searched my eyes like he was looking for the answer instead of giving it to me.

"No games. I really need to hear it from you."

"It's more. Respect, adoration… all the things I promised myself I'd never let enter my life again, because the loss that is inevitable will crush me this time."

"It's not inevitable." I put my hand over his. The warmth of him in contrast to the feeling he was pulling away now that he had said his piece made me want to hang onto this puddle he created in my chest.

"You are not immortal. Death is inevitable. It's just a matter of decades at best, hours at worst."

My skin broke out in gooseflesh, and I thought I understood his dilemma. My lips pulled down at the edges, and I pressed them together at the sudden drop of my stomach.

"Love can't overcome death." He rubbed his thumb over my bottom lip. "And if I'm not careful, I could be the cause of your death. I cannot live with that."

A chill skittered up my spine. "What the hell are you talking about? You were married to a human before. What makes *me* so different?"

"*You* can still have children."

My brain raced back to our conversations in the dark subway system after he broke me out of Grand Central. If he got me pregnant, I would die in childbirth. Dragons ate their way out of the egg. And in a human, the egg was the womb. I closed my eyes as sharp pain gripped my chest.

"So, because of that, you chose not to love me?"

"No. In spite of the danger, in spite of trying to deny it to myself, I've still fallen in love with you." His eyes shone brighter, giving me a view of his sad smile. "And as much as I want you—as much as I love you—I cannot sentence you to such a horrifying death."

I rolled away from him so he wouldn't see the tears that sprouted in my eyes. "Troy asked what you were to me." My voice shook with silent tears.

"And what did you say?" His fingers gently ran through my hair like I had done to him earlier.

"I lied. I told him you were my friend." I closed my mouth on the sob that wanted to escape.

"I am your friend," Mikhail whispered and ran his fingers down my back.

"No, Mik, you're far more than that to me, too. And I can't keep ignoring it."

"Maybe if you get laid, it will clear your head," he said with a lilt in his voice that made me want to smack him.

I turned enough to glare at him.

"Your words, not mine." He grinned like an adolescent fool.

I couldn't believe this ancient being could carry so much wisdom at the same time as so much bullshit. "You're such an evil shit sometimes." I sniffled.

"I am. Especially since I won't remember this, and you will." His eyes sparkled with mischief.

"Evil son of a bitch," I repeated and settled in with my back to him.

A few minutes later, his hand fell onto the bed, and his snore started almost immediately.

I stared at the clock. Tears blurred the numbers and I let them fall as my heart broke. Mikhail would never give in to his feelings. Not if it put me in danger. And damn him, now that I knew what was in his heart, I would never leave his side.

Talk about an impossible situation. We had more chance of taking out all the monsters without an injury than acting on this ache in our chests.

Dragon Storm
Chapter 22

THE ALARM WENT OFF every three hours, waking both of us. I administered his antibiotic just as Troy had prescribed. The first two times, Mikhail was still in a drugged stupor, and he just laid his arm out for me to do my thing. Then he folded it back under the pillow and started to snore immediately.

The third time, sunlight brushed the room. And I stretched. All in all, I probably scored ten hours of solid sleep. I needed something to eat after I gave Mikhail his meds. I turned to him, and he stared at me with a creased forehead.

"I hurt everywhere." He lowered his arms to his side.

I gave him his morning dose of penicillin. "You've been in the same position for a little more than a day. I'd imagine you'd be stiff."

"Troy didn't give me morphine, did he?" he asked with his brow creased.

"No. He gave you oxycodone."

Relief washed over Mikhail's face, and he closed his eyes. "Morphine can kill me. Kind of like penicillin can kill you."

I froze in place with the empty needle in my hand. "You're allergic to it?"

"Yes. I told you that last night. At least I think I did. It might have been in the operating room." He rubbed his face. "It fucks with our ability to breathe."

"You should have been clearer about that," I snapped as my heart pounded in my chest. I could have killed him last night had I not thought to grab something else besides the morphine. I took the full vial on my nightstand and tossed it into the trash because I did not want any mistakes, especially because the vials didn't look any different between the penicillin and the morphine. Same size, same shape, and same white label with faded black lettering.

I swallowed hard and tossed the empty needle in the garbage as well. Before I left the bedroom, I ran my finger down the length of his foot.

He jerked it away and looked down at me with irritation in his eyes. "Hey. That tickles."

I stared at him as hope filled my chest. I slowly ran my hand up his calf, massaging as I went.

"That feels good." He closed his eyes.

I don't know what possessed me, but I didn't stop at his knee. I went higher and received a rumble of satisfaction in his throat as I massaged both thighs now.

He feels my hands on him. The thought galloped through me as fast as my heart clanged in my chest. I wasn't sure why I was compelled to continue. Maybe it was that satisfied rumble coming from him or the conversation last night or I don't know what, but I couldn't stop. His warm skin felt like silk under my fingers. His muscles pulled taut and then relaxed as I worked out the kinks.

Even his ass was a wonder to knead. Hell, if he had been on his back, I think his cock would have been as hard as a rock and waiting for satisfaction. I skipped over his lower back for fear that rubbing near the incision would irritate it and set him back again, but his middle back and shoulders were just as much of a playground as the rest of him.

His breathing was low and relaxed, and I stopped after massaging each arm. He turned to look at me, meeting my gaze. The sleepiness slowly cleared, and he looked over his shoulder and bent his left leg and then rolled his ankle around.

"It worked," I barely whispered. "This isn't a dream, is it?"

His gaze popped back to mine. He reached out and pinched my arm.

"Ouch." I swatted him away. I retaliated and he sucked air through his teeth.

"Not dreaming." His gaze lingered on me. "Did you by chance bring me anything to walk with?"

"Crutches." I pointed to the wall near my side of the bed.

"Think you can bring them to me?"

"Should you really be moving?"

He bit his lip and lifted both legs, one at a time and then shrugged. "If I don't, I'm going to soil this bed," he said. "And I don't think I've done that yet."

I got the crutches from where I left them and stepped away as he slowly shifted to push himself into a sitting position. Then he hauled himself up using the crutches and used them like he was an old pro.

The bathroom door shut against my lingering stare.

"No showering yet," I called through the door and then collected all the bloody towels, throwing them into the garbage. I also stripped the comforter and took that to wash, transferring my clothes to the dryer before I shoved the comforter into the washing machine and started it on a large load.

When I came back into the bedroom, Mikhail had already slipped on a pair of sweatpants and sat on the side of the bed. Thankfully, none of the mess slipped through the towels to stain the sheets. I didn't think it made it to the comforter either, but I wanted it clean just in case.

I used the moment to slip into the bathroom, relieve myself, and polish my teeth and to avoid the overwhelming feelings tightening my stomach.

His brow was creased, and he hadn't moved from where he sat when I came back into the room.

"We talked, didn't we." It wasn't really framed as a question and his eyes searched out mine.

I stayed just out of arm's reach and nodded.

His eyes narrowed as he stared at the wood floor under my feet. "It's all... fuzzy."

I couldn't do this. I couldn't pretend I didn't want him, and he didn't want me. I started out of the room, and he had enough of a reach to grab my wrist and pull me to the spot in front of him.

"What did I say?" His eyes searched mine and then they closed.

"I'll get out of your hair." I broke his grip on my wrist, turned, and walked out of the bedroom, straight to the door. I couldn't be by his side in the light of day. Not knowing that he was purposely ignoring his feelings.

The squeak of the crutches followed and before I could get the entire code in, he pushed me against the door, his breath heaving from the exertion of moving that fast.

"Don't..."

"Don't what?" I spun, facing him. He was close enough to smell the sweet freshness of his clean breath.

"I—" He stopped and dropped his head. "Don't go."

"Why should I stay if you are going to deny both of us the possibility of real joy? Do you know how rare that is?"

He growled, actually growled at me, and then both crutches fell to the floor. He took my face in his hands and crushed my lips with his. It wasn't the sweet kiss from the dream, but it was a damn fine start.

I pinched him again.

"Ouch. What was that for?" He pulled away to look me in the eye.

"Just making sure."

A slow smile appeared. "That dream really fucked with your head, didn't it?" He pinched me, and then resumed the kiss despite my whine. "This is real," he whispered against my lips. "And it will be the death of me," he added. And then his mouth demanded more, his tongue searched, teased, played with mine until he nearly lost his balance, reminding both of us of his less-than-optimal health.

I slowly pushed him away and reached down, picking up one crutch and the next before I stood up. "You need these. Otherwise, we're going to end up on the floor."

"Maybe that was my intention." His eyes sparkled bright.

As much as I wanted that, I knew it would strip him of all his strength and could do some damage to whatever healing had already taken place. "Nourishment before we deplete you of all your reserves." I slid out of the space between him and the door and headed into the kitchen.

He took a seat on the other side of the counter, watching my every move.

"Stop staring. You're making me self-conscious."

His smile slowly faded. "Holly?"

I looked up at him.

"We can't take our focus off the goal," he said softly, like it was going to set me off.

I sighed and met his gaze. "No. I suppose we can't do that. This..." I waved my finger between the two of us. "This will have to wait until we've done our job."

He bit his lower lip for a few minutes while I cracked eggs into a bowl. "It is something to look forward to." He met my gaze. Then a smile formed again, like a ray of sun breaking through storm clouds.

God, he was a gorgeous man when he smiled like that. His citrine eyes lit up like fireworks when his smile reached them. I couldn't think of a better way to reward ourselves if we were successful. "Another driving motivation for both of us." I grinned back.

He sighed and shifted on the chair as his gaze traveled over me like a soft caress. The gentleman in him wouldn't say what was behind that look.

"Until then, I'll just rely on my dreams," I said with a wicked smile.

His cheeks turned a pleasant shade of pink. "I can assure you, I'm much better in real life than a dream."

Before I was able to form any sort of verbal reply, a knock on the door interrupted our teasing.

"Troy," we both said at the same time as reality yet again crashed into us.

I set the bowl of eggs I had been whipping down on the counter and crossed to the door, swinging it open.

Troy carried two cups of coffee in his hands, and he stepped inside, handing me a cup. "I didn't see a coffee machine when I was here earlier and figured you might need one." His glance landed on Mikhail sitting at the counter and his eyebrow cocked. "You're looking better than the last time I saw you."

"Yes. The antibiotics every three hours was a smart call. It helped a great deal."

I pointed at Mikhail. "You still need one more dose." Then I glanced at Troy. "Do you want some scrambled eggs?" I pointed at the mixture in process.

"Thanks, but I ate with the guys. They are enjoying the accommodations, but we can't let ourselves become too complacent." He glanced at Mikhail. "I can grab you a coffee if you'd like." He pointed toward the door.

Mikhail took a sip of his orange juice and shrugged. "I don't drink coffee, but thanks for the offer."

"Did you talk strategy?" I asked as I poured the eggs into the pan. The sizzle filled the space.

"Not yet. We need to be in top shape before we go out. Tiredness breeds mistakes. Another good night of rest and a day of nutrition, and we'll be ready to go."

That made perfect sense to me, and I focused on not burning our breakfast.

"I should check your bandages," he said to Mikhail and waved toward the bedroom.

They left me to finish cooking the meal. A dangerous endeavor in itself, but I managed not to burn the eggs and the toast came out golden brown. Not one error in the breakfast department. I buttered the toast and set them on each of the plates. I put salt and pepper on the counter and a couple of forks.

They still hadn't come out yet. I placed the plates on the counter and crossed to the bedroom as worry replaced the growl in my stomach.

"Breakfast is going to get cold." I pushed the door wide open.

Mikhail hiked up his sweatpants and glanced at me over his shoulder.

His eyes conveyed more than Troy's, and Troy's held enough concern for me to swallow hard.

"What's wrong?"

"His leg looks better, but there are still signs of infection with his back. So, I want another twenty-four hours of antibiotics. One vial every three hours."

"I... um. I don't know if there is that much left."

Troy met my gaze and then seemed to digest my words. "After you eat, we can go check to see how many there are. If there isn't enough, I'll figure out the dosage you need to spread it out over that period."

With a clean patch on his back, Mikhail crutched into the living room and took a seat in front of his plate.

"Are you sure?" I asked Troy before we followed.

"The red lines have diminished, but they are not all gone."

I took a deep breath and nodded. I needed food before I ventured back down to the medical facilities.

"There isn't anywhere else you keep medicine like that, is there?" I asked and then took a bite of my breakfast.

"No. I thought I had enough stocked away. I guess I never entertained the thought it would be for me." Mikhail dug into his food without saying more until he cleared his plate. "I can go down with you."

"No. You need to rest. I don't want you exerting yourself. Especially if there isn't enough antibiotics. Overexertion will set you back." Troy didn't give any leeway in his answer.

"Yes, sir," Mikhail said, although he was not happy about it.

I started to do the dishes.

"I can do that. You go with the sergeant to see what's left." He crutched around into the kitchen and moved aside so I could slip out. He didn't offer me any assurances either, and I couldn't help but think maybe we were doomed.

Doomed by our situation.

Doomed by the monsters.

Doomed by fate.

I gave Mikhail one last glance and headed down the stairwell for the umpteenth time in the last twenty-four hours.

Dragon Storm
Chapter 23

WHEN WE STEPPED INTO the operating room, Troy took my arm and turned me to him. "Can he do what you say he can do?"

Another dream déjà vu. I blinked up at him and practically recited word for word what I had in the dream. "Yes. Just look at this building. He's made it functional on its own grid and disguised it to the outside world. Both human and monster from the street level think this is one of the destroyed buildings. If he can do that, a bomb ought to be a snap."

Troy kept his hand around my upper arm. "I don't doubt that he can build it. I think any of us in this building right now has the capability of doing that. It's the delivery of it that has me concerned." He took a breath. "If it's not done at the precise height and velocity, it will only injure a fraction of their army. And how do we get them all in one place to begin with?"

Damn, he was sharp. I stared up into his blue eyes. "We hadn't gotten that far in the plan." I knew Mikhail pondered the delivery system, but I don't think he got far enough to have a detailed plan of attack. Or if he did, he hadn't shared it with me yet.

"What else is in this building?"

Neither of us had had time to explore. "Labs. At least that is what he hinted at before. But I don't know." I glanced at his grip on my arm. His hand was warm and solid, and it unnerved me. "We need to find out how many vials of antibiotics are left." I reminded him of our initial purpose for visiting this room again.

He looked at his hand still gripping me. "Oh. Sorry." He let go before he stepped back giving me some room.

I started toward the medicine closet.

"What if he's just bullshitting us?" he asked. "What if all this is part of the game?"

I paused with my hand on the cabinet and glanced at him. He stood with his hands on his hips and his head bent so he was studying the floor. His concerns were ones I had been working my way through since I was dragged out of Grand Central weeks ago.

I crossed back to him and tilted his chin up so he would meet my gaze. "I went through the same thought process as you are going through. I doubted his motives. If he truly wanted to do us harm, he would have let us perish in that bomb at City Hall. He didn't have to save any of us."

"He did it to save you." He pressed his finger against the bare skin above my breasts and he didn't remove it right away.

Silence settled between us, his gaze intense and sharp. His hand settled onto my skin, right over my heart.

My heart that was beating like a sparrow caught in a trap. His eyes dropped to the connection of our skin. Then he licked his lips and slowly pulled his hand away as if he just crossed a line he knew he shouldn't have.

My libido balked, but my heart sighed with relief. Too much of the dream had already been laid bare in real life and I couldn't fathom the ramifications if he were to go further.

I turned back toward the medical cabinet when Troy muttered, "Fuck it."

He spun me around and planted a kiss, pushing me against the medicine cabinet. One of his hands landed between my legs and the other on my breast as his tongue swiped across my lips. And damned if he knew the spots to rub just right.

I opened my mouth, and instead of arguing, I let my tongue play with his as his hands worked a physical magic that set my body tingling. When he started pulling my dress up, I pushed him back.

"We... um..." I wiped my face, trying to put my thoughts together, but the bulge in the front of his pants made that difficult. It had literally been over a year since I'd had the opportunity to get laid. And although my heart was all in with Mikhail, I really needed this to be able to focus on what we needed to do. But I was sure if Mikhail found out, he'd have one hell of a hissy fit.

"Don't read too much into it, Woods. I just..."

I stared at his hungry blue eyes. "Need to get laid," I finished his sentence as the need took over my entire being. I moved toward him.

Before I could blink, he had me in his arms and kissed me hard enough to yank the air from my lungs. My hands found his belt and fumbled with it as he moved me to the tabletop and pushed my dress up around my waist. In the next instant, his entire length was inside me.

We moved like frantic teenagers. His mouth on mine, plundering as his hands gripped my thighs, moving me with such force my breath exhaled hard with every thrust of his hips. It was fast and hot and when it was over, we were both panting like animals.

He held me in place as the last of the tremors gripped him. I dropped back on the table trying to catch my breath. Guilt bit at the edges of my mind, but my body was totally satiated. At least now I wouldn't obsess over Mikhail so much and my focus could be on killing the monsters.

Troy smiled an exhausted smile. "I'm sorry, Woods, but I've been wanting to do that for a while." He pulled out and stumbled back as he zipped himself up. He hand-combed his hair and turned back toward the medical cabinet.

"I'll be right back." I headed into the scrub room and the bathroom stall just beyond the showers. I relieved myself and then cleaned up as best I could with a wet washcloth. My cheeks were still rosy from the exertion and my hair was a mess. I tried to tame it into submission, but that wasn't working, so I dampened my hand and used water to get it in order.

I came out. Troy had four vials on the table, and he was chewing his lower lip. I wasn't sure whether it was because we were short the medicine or he was reflecting on what had just happened.

"Is that all there is?" I went to the cabinet to rifle around just in case we missed something. I slammed the cabinet closed and looked around, hell-bent on ignoring the elephant in the room.

"I already looked in the logical places while you were cleaning up." Troy met my gaze. "We might need to make a medical run."

His statement pulled the air from my lungs, and I slumped on the cabinet. Medical runs were more dangerous than the bleach recovery was. At least that had a known path, a known destination, and a known stash. Medical runs were usually a bust. Most pharmacies were barren, and hospitals were worse. They were usually crumbling structures like the one Mikhail had gone into before we got to my platoon.

I guess my face reflected the near panic that sent my heart into my throat because Troy said, "Before you get all worried about your friend and shit, let's see if this clears it up. I'll be back before nightfall to check on him."

I didn't correct his reference of Mikhail as my friend. Somehow, I knew all this would bite me. I just didn't know when.

Troy came over and put the vials in my hand, closing his around mine. "He isn't just your friend, is he?"

I blinked up at him, taking the medicine. "No. It's... complicated."

He inhaled and raised an eyebrow. "So, you'd prefer if I kept this quiet."

I stared up at him and nodded. "I needed an itch scratched," I said, almost cringing at how crude I sounded.

"That makes two of us," he said. "But when all this is over, and the monsters are gone, and the world awakens, the three of us are going to have to have a coming to Jesus on the subject."

I blinked and my mouth ran dry.

Troy looked down at my hands. "After his next full dose, give him half doses every three hours." He added eight syringes to the pile in my hand, and then led me to the door and sent me up the stairs.

My brain was still reconciling his words when I got to the penthouse door. I balanced my stack of meds and punched in the code. Mikhail was in the chair, reading a book, with his leg on the ottoman as I entered the room.

I didn't say anything. I just crossed to the bedroom before the jars in my arms fell and broke. I organized them and then looked at the clock. We still had a good half hour before his next dose.

When I stepped into the living room, Mikhail's stare pierced through me. His irises blazed and his jaw muscle jumped.

"There were only four vials," I said, but I couldn't quite meet his gaze.

He silently stared at me and slammed the book closed, making me jump. "You do know a dragon's sense of smell is at least a hundred times that of humans, right?"

I pressed my lips together, sucking my lower one between my teeth as my brain wrapped around his words. *Could he smell...* I looked up at him, at the glare in his eyes. *Oh, God. He could smell that I had sex.*

His eyes narrowed to slits. "What kind of game are you really playing?"

"I don't play games." But my words sounded meek, even to my ears.

"Bullshit!" He heaved the book across the room. "I bare my soul to you, and you fuck someone else?" Smoke curled from his nostrils.

"I didn't intend to." It sounded like such a weak argument, and I expected him to turn me to ash at any moment.

"Did he force himself on you?" He growled the words.

I looked down at my hands and back up at him, shaking my head. "No."

Hurt flashed for a moment and then his eyes turned to steel. "Why?"

"Because I cannot focus with this much sexual tension. It diminishes my ability to think. And we need to focus on what we need to do," I snapped. "Basically, you're making me crazy."

"You're blaming your lapse of judgment on me?" He stood and grabbed a crutch. "Fuck you, Woods!" He headed toward the bedroom with smoke billowing out of his nostrils.

I intercepted him, blocking his retreat despite the warning signs. He could toast me at any moment, but I didn't care. I needed to make this right. "You're the one who keeps pulling away."

He leveled a smoke-filled glare. "I wasn't the one who pulled away this morning."

I took a deep breath. "True, but then you hammered the point home. This wasn't something we could focus on right now."

"I did not say that. You did."

"You said we had to focus on the goal."

He pressed his lips together and his entire face turned red. "Own your shit, Holly. Don't put the blame on me for this one."

I blinked at his furious glare. "I'm human. I am prone to fucking up things."

"And you certainly fucked this up." He pushed past me and slammed the door.

I leaned my forehead on the door as my throat tightened. This was the polar opposite of the dream. I royally screwed myself. "Mikhail?"

Silence. But I could see his shadow against the door. I swallowed hard.

"I'm sorry. I wasn't thinking at all," I whispered. "He made a move because he assumed we were friends and I... I was selfish."

"You don't have the foggiest idea what love is," he said with a voice full of bitterness.

I sighed. "You're right. Every time I've let someone in, they've crushed me in the same callous, thoughtless way." My history with men even before the pandemic was a repeat of today, except the other way around. I bared my soul, and they fucked my best friend.

The alarm went off in the bedroom. "You need to let me in so I can give you your shot," I said, hoping he wouldn't sabotage his progress.

His shadow didn't move and the alarm shut off with a bang as if he heaved something at it. "I trusted you," he finally said.

"I know."

"With my life."

Tears blurred my eyes. I covered my mouth, but a sob escaped between my fingers. He was right. I needed to own my shit. There was no valid reason to break his trust. I slid down to the floor and put my head on my knees, letting the tears flow.

The bedroom door opened, and he took a seat next to me and leaned against the door jamb. He didn't touch me, and he didn't speak. When I finally looked up at him, his expression was unreadable.

"I knew you'd be the death of me," he whispered and ran his hands through his hair.

"I'm sorry." My voice hitched through the words.

"I will turn him to ash if he gets near you again."

I just nodded and climbed to my feet. I crossed and grabbed the last vial that I had brought from last night and one of the needles. When I came back to his side, he held out his arm and looked away. I gave him the shot and ran my finger down his arm near where I pricked him.

He yanked his arm away with a feral growl.

I opened my mouth to ask him whether he'd ever forgive me or whether I had done irreparable harm to what had actually started. But before I could form words, he interjected.

"Do not even think about asking if I'll ever forgive you. Now is not the time. And just so you understand the ramifications of your actions, it will be a cold day in hell before I touch you again." His eyes blazed. "You can sleep on the couch. And do not touch my wife's things again. Understand?"

I leaned back, accepting his vitriol. I deserved every ounce of it, and I'd take it until he was physically better. I glanced at the line of penicillin. "Where is the nearest drug store?" I brought my gaze back to him.

He blinked at me, narrowing his eyes. "What?"

"That is the last of the penicillin." I pointed at the vials. "I need to know where the nearest drug store is."

He studied my face and then looked at the four vials on the nightstand. Something flashed across his face, and he shook his head. "I'm not letting you go on a suicide mission."

"You don't have a say in the matter."

He grabbed my throat and brought me within an inch of his face. "I have the only say," he growled. Smoke drifted from his nostrils and his irises were fully engulfed in flame. "My terms are the only terms, or I will turn this entire building into ash and let the leviathans tear me to pieces."

He let me go with a shove.

I fell back on my ass and glared at him as I rubbed my throat, shocked at his behavior. It lit the stubbornness inside me as well as indignation. I stood and stripped off the dress, throwing it on his lap, and marched away before the tears started again. My clothes had long dried in the dryer and I put them on before I moved the comforter to the dryer.

I crossed into his study and slammed the door. But before I threw myself on the couch, I glanced at the clock, calculating when Mikhail's next dose would be.

I wanted to smash everything in the room.

I wanted to curse Mikhail to hell.

And I desperately wanted to turn back the clock and stop myself from making this catastrophic mistake.

Dragon Storm
Chapter 24

I EMERGED FROM THE den nearly three hours later, ignored Mikhail lounging on the couch, and used the bathroom. The comforter was dry, so I carried it to the bedroom and dumped it on the bed before grabbing his next dose of medicine. I only filled the needle halfway and then went out to the couch.

He stared at me as I tapped the needle before stabbing it in his arm and depressing the plunger. His gaze lowered to his arm and his head tilted as he looked back at me.

"Holly?" He put his hand on his chest. His breath wheezed.

I looked at the needle and my eyes widened. *What the hell had I grabbed? I threw the morphine away, hadn't I?* I dropped the syringe and bolted into the bedroom with my heart pounding and my throat tight enough to make me gasp. I flipped on the nightstand light.

I picked up the vial and my finger moved the label. Although the top one said penicillin, the bottom one had morphine stamped in that faded black lettering. "No, no, no, no." I repeated the words and looked at the next and the next and the next, pushing the fake labels away from each one. That bastard gave me morphine vials, not penicillin, knowing Mikhail was allergic.

"No!" I screamed and ran into the living room. Mikhail didn't need to turn Troy to dust when he saw him. I was going to cut out his heart with a spoon. "No, no, no. Mikhail. Please don't leave me."

His breath came in alarming hisses like he wasn't getting enough oxygen and I straddled him.

"Now's not the time," his voice labored.

"The bastard gave me morphine, not penicillin." I pulled Mikhail up and onto his feet. "Walk with me, keep moving, maybe you can burn this shit off with your dragon metabolism." I nearly dragged him from one end of the apartment to the other, alternating between panicking and seething.

"Nasal spray in medicine cabinet." His breathing was shallow now.

I didn't even doubt him. I moved with him into the bathroom and swung open the cabinet. He raised his hand, pointing to something behind his shaving cream.

I pulled it out of the cabinet.

"Bed," he whispered.

I pulled him into the bedroom and laid him down and then read the instructions. Why Mikhail had an antidote to an allergic reaction to morphine in his bathroom I didn't want to know, but I was so thankful he did. I shoved it into his nose and depressed, then followed with his other nostril.

"I'm going to kill that bastard," I whispered as I re-read the directions.

Mikhail grabbed my arm. "Again." This time his voice wasn't as labored.

I plunged the nasal spray into each nostril again. Waited a moment and then did it a third time, which emptied the rest of the antidote into his system. I lay my ear on his chest, listening to his lungs struggle.

"Please, please don't die. I'm an idiot. An idiot who is in love with your dragon ass and possibly the stupidest human who ever walked the planet. Please, please, please don't die on me. Not now." The mantra continued.

So did his heartbeat. After a while, his breathing evened out.

And after an even longer while, his arms engulfed me. I sobbed on his chest. Harder than I had at the door. Mikhail held me and kept breathing long, slow, steady pulls.

"I'm okay," he finally said with a slur.

I shook my head, not accepting his placation. "I could have killed you." My voice shook. I looked up. "I almost did." My chin trembled. "If you didn't have that in the medicine cabinet..."

"Any time I give someone morphine, I stock my cabinet." He met my gaze. "You're the reason I had it." He brushed my hair from my face. "A little bit of serendipity there."

I let out a near hysterical laugh that ended in tears again. Finally, when the well of tears dried, I sat up and wiped my face. "Do you own a handgun?"

He shook his head. "But I do have an ancient katana in the study on top of the bookshelves."

"Are you out of danger?" I did not want to leave his side if he might have a relapse.

He nodded.

I stood and swiped all the bottles off the nightstand. "He is mine." I leveled a glare and then marched out to the living room and lined up the vials on the kitchen table within view of the door, breaking all the fake label seals, and placed the needle in front of the display before I went into the den. I had missed this gem before, but that's because it wasn't displayed like it should have been. It was nearly hidden.

I climbed up the shelves and grabbed it off the top, admiring the beautifully ornate sheath. I removed the blade and marveled at the perfect steel. It was sharp enough to draw blood when I ran the edge of my thumb along the blade.

That would do. That would do just fine.

I grabbed it and then unlocked the door, cracking it before I took a seat in the corner chair in the shadows with only the light from the laundry room on, illuminating the vials on the table.

I laid the blade across my lap and waited.

I did not care what Troy's reasoning was for what he did. He was going to die tonight by my hand.

Dragon Storm
Chapter 25

ANOTHER COUPLE OF HOURS went by before the door creaked open. Troy silently closed the door behind him. His gaze landed on the vials lined up and the empty needle laid in front of the display. He reached for the door, but I had engaged the lock code so the moment it closed, the lock engaged.

"You killed him," I said, making my voice low and menacing.

He stiffened and turned, scanning the apartment until his gaze landed on me.

"Was fucking me part of the plan?" I cocked my head. He hadn't yet seen the blade in my lap. I had to be careful. He was military and despite my black belt that I earned before the world went to hell, I was sure he, as an elite soldier, had many more moves than I had. So, my best bet was a surprise attack.

"No. Blood poisoning is a painful way to die. Morphine overdose isn't."

I narrowed my eyes. "Are you telling me you were honestly trying to be humane?"

"There wasn't any more penicillin." He took a step closer.

We had gotten sidetracked before I could open the cabinet, but I had been certain there had been more the last time I grabbed some, just not certain that there were eight left. "Did you know there wasn't any left when we went down there?"

He looked at the floor and then up at me.

"You took them."

"My first priority is to my team."

My hand gripped the blade harder. "So, again, that advance was what, a diversion so you had the opportunity to poison Mikhail?"

He pressed his lips together and his open expression morphed to a glare. "He was a dragon," he hissed. "A filthy fucking dragon."

"Then why fix him up? Why amputate his leg and fix the issues with his back incision?"

He shrugged. "Medic training. And there was no way you'd let him die. But it ultimately gave me the opportunity I was looking for since we set foot in that subway tunnel."

I refrained from jumping up and charging. There were still too many steps between us. I just glared at him. "So, you used me."

"Yes. I screwed with your mind and scratched my own itch. Plus, fucking the dragon's mate—well, that was an added bonus and a big middle finger to the bastard." He stepped closer. "You didn't seem to mind, though."

I remained silent.

"Now *we* can get it on any time *we* feel the need."

"We?"

"Considering you're a traitor to the human race, my team and I have earned liberties whenever the fuck we want." He slipped something over his fingers. Brass knuckles caught in the light. "If you put up a fight, I'll knock you into tomorrow." He held up his hand to show me his new jewelry and stepped within my striking distance.

I stood and spun, aiming for his displayed wrist. It was easier than slicing butter and his hand flew into the side of the couch.

Troy blinked and stared at the stump of his arm as blood shot out of his veins. He screamed and gripped his wrist as I moved back into my next defensive form again.

"Bullshit." This time I lunged into a fencing move and plunged the tip of the blade right into his junk. With a flick of my wrist, I drove the blade across, slicing through whatever I had skewered, and then I retreated a couple of steps, with the blade dripping blood.

His scream went silent, his face turning nearly purple as he fell to his knees. Just as his breath hitched, I spun, releasing a scream of fury that drowned out his high-pitched wail. I sliced through the air with everything I had. The blade hardly caught as it sliced through skin, bone, and sinew, and the bastard's head rolled across the floor. I kicked his headless body backward and stood, huffing with the wrath shaking my entire body.

"Damn, woman."

I looked up at Mikhail in the doorway, leaning on a crutch as he watched me slice up the asshole who compromised me and nearly killed him.

I ran my hand through my hair. My breath still came in heavy pulls. I had never killed a human before. It did not satiate the wrath coiling inside me, either. I wanted to slaughter them all because those bastards on the fifteenth floor were in on this sick plot.

"Excuse me while I go slaughter some more pigs."

"There are four of them, Holly. And you won't have the element of surprise."

I glanced at him, and a new thought dawned on me. One that chilled the fury a few notches. This bastard was alone with Mikhail before we went for the medicine. I dropped the sword on the floor and crossed to him, unconcerned that I was covered in blood. I'd wash it off. I turned Mikhail around and pulled up the shirt he had put on earlier and ripped the bandage off his back.

There were lines traversing out from the incision, but it still looked better than last night. I pulled him back into the bedroom and reached into the box I had brought the other night to grab the second container of dragon blood.

"Shower, now."

"Holly—" he started to argue.

"I don't know what he put on you." I met his gaze. "I administered the antibiotics, but who the hell knows what he's done to make sure you suffer before I gave you an overdose."

I pushed him toward the bathroom. "Strip," I ordered and then turned on the shower. I followed my own orders and stepped in before he did. The water ran red, and I made sure my hands were clean before I soaped up a hand towel.

I moved Mikhail into the spray and gently washed his back from his shoulders all the way down to his ass. The liquid bandage held well enough on the cut I did to his back.

I reached into the bathroom, grabbed the small bench, and put it under the water stream. "Sit."

He did, and I washed his chest, his stomach, his privates, and his legs, ignoring the fact that I was obviously turning him on. I stopped at the bandage around his stump. I handed him the washcloth and then unwrapped the bindings. It didn't look as angry as it had last night, and I gently washed him and then turned the shower off.

"Stay." I reached for a towel and the dragon blood. I dropped to my knees in front of him and took the dry fabric and blotted his leg dry before I handed the bath towel to Mikhail. He put it over his lap, covering his reaction to me.

I took two fingers full of dragon blood and spread it over his stump. This elixir made it so he could walk again. I doubted that it was what caused the blood poisoning. That probably had to do with the non-sterile environment of his bedroom and my inexperience at wielding a scalpel.

I hated to admit that Troy had done an exemplary job at amputation. I glanced up at Mikhail and a horrifying thought dawned. "Did you really need to have this leg removed?"

He touched my cheek gently. "Yes. That would have killed me had he not done it."

"None of this makes any sense." I left the shower to retrieve more bandages for his leg, and I covered his stump in the same manner as it had been. Then I made him stand and turn again while I traced the cut with dragon blood and covered it.

He stood with his back to me, holding onto the shower walls for balance.

"I heard what he said."

"Yeah, well, I was stupid. He did such a good job on you medically, I never suspected he would double-cross you. I didn't realize how deep his hatred was. I underestimated him."

"You weren't the only one." He glanced over his shoulder at me as he wrapped the towel around his waist. "You still have blood in your hair." He hopped out of the shower on his left leg while holding onto the walls.

I moved the bench outside the shower for him and then turned the water back on. I scrubbed my skin and washed my hair three times before the water finally ran clear. When I turned the water off, he handed me a dry towel. I cleaned off and stepped out, scanning the bathroom.

Scanning the carnage.

"I made a hell of a mess of your apartment, haven't I?"

"You've made a hell of a mess of my life." Mikhail looked at the blood-streaked floor and then up at me. "But I can live with that."

"I still have to take care of the others."

"While I appreciate you going all *Kill Bill* out there, I don't want you going alone to address the problem." He pulled me in front of where he sat, and the reference pulled enough of a smile to his lips for me to sigh.

"You can't climb down fifteen flights, Mikhail."

"Yes, I can. I've got crutches."

"Like that is real stealth." I rolled my eyes at him.

"No, I suppose it isn't, but you could carry me." He gave me a smile. "The last time they saw me, I was in mini-dragon form. If you strap that sheath on your back and I play dead…"

He held both my hands in his, gently rubbing the backsides with his thumbs, and I glanced down at the embrace.

"I thought it would be a cold day in hell before you touched me?"

"I thought you had betrayed me but I don't think you really had a choice whether you realize it or not."

I started to pull my hands away, because he was wrong. The choice had actually been mine, not Troy's. I could have left it at pushing him away.

Mikhail clamped down. "He orchestrated it."

"I could have stopped it, but I didn't." I met his gaze. "I'm owning my mistake. Don't water it down."

He nodded but still kept my hands in his. "At first, when that drug hit me, I thought you had done it on purpose. Then I saw your reaction and I wondered how the hell I could have ever doubted you."

My throat tightened. "I really do love you, Mikhail. Which isn't easy for me to admit. And I don't expect you to forgive me for what I did."

He stared into the depth of my eyes. "I love that you aren't begging for forgiveness. Although having you on your knees before me in the shower..." His lips cocked into a smile. "A little groveling like that might work."

I let a small laugh escape. "I saw how much you enjoyed that," I admitted. I glanced at my bloody clothing. "I know you said I couldn't touch anything of your wife's." I started and he squeezed my hands. "Any chance you can let me borrow something to wear?" I met his gaze.

He slowly released my hands. "Grab a pair of jeans and a t-shirt." He nodded toward the bedroom.

I headed to the closet.

"And bring me a pair of sweatpants," he called from the seat in the bathroom.

I still felt as though I walked in slow motion, as if this were a dream, but I knew it wasn't. Still, I pinched my arm to be sure. Pain filtered from the point of the sharp pinch. *Not a dream.* I took a deep breath and the smell of death filtered in from the living room like a reminder of the mess I'd have to clean up later.

I glanced in that direction and the blood pooling slowly across the floor toward the kitchen. I refocused on the closet and pulled a pair of jeans from his wife's side of the closet and then moved the door, so I had Mikhail's side. I didn't want one of his wife's T-shirts constricting my movement, so that left Mikhail's. I debated on which one of his to take and opted for a gray one that seemed more worn than the others. I loved the blue and the green ones on him too much to ruin them, and I was certain that whatever I did would ruin the clothing I wore.

After all, killing was messy. And that was exactly what I intended to do.

I grabbed a pair of sweatpants off the hook on his side and headed back to the bathroom.

Mikhail looked more like himself than he had since I found him pinned under the debris. I crossed to him and stood with the pants in my hand. Contemplating killing the men downstairs somehow made me feel unclean.

Troy had been a different situation; he had actively tried to kill Mikhail and deserved death.

"I have a better idea than walking in with me in your arms. We can stop on twenty-nine and I can cut the building's power in the stairwell and on the floors below," Mikhail said slowly, as if working through an alternative plan in his mind.

"I won't be able to see anything."

"Not necessarily. I might have a night scope or two down there. And I can just walk in and toast them in one blast."

A night scope or two? Man, I needed to see what other goodies this building held. But right now, his idea bloomed too many problems in my head. I handed him the pants as I mentally poked holes in his idea and then in the original plan. Neither of them held tight.

Mikhail pulled the pants on under the towel, seeming more modest now that we had admitted our feelings to each other.

And the more I thought about dropping us all into the dark, the more it disrupted the element of surprise. "They have flashlights, and the bleach is down there, so toasting them could destroy our fuel for the weapon against the leviathan army." That itch of doubt in Mikhail cropped up, but his slow nod and scowl of understanding wiped that out of my mind. "Besides, if the power goes out, they'll know something is wrong. And they do have guns."

He took a deep breath, still nodding. "You're right. I can't just torch the floor. We need that bleach." He closed his eyes with a sigh. "What do you suggest?"

My mind flowed over everything Troy had said. There would be only one entry of mine that made sense with all the information I had been given. But Mikhail was not going to like it at all. "Rip my shirt like we were in some sort of a struggle."

Mikhail didn't question me and did as I asked. I assessed my reflection. The jeans wouldn't work if I was to pull off the plan formulating in my head.

"Are you sure there isn't any women's underwear here?" I glanced back at him as I peeled the jeans off.

Mikhail glanced at me as though I spoke Greek. His gaze dropped to my bare legs and his complexion paled a fraction, but he stood and grabbed the crutch. I followed him into the bedroom. He opened the closet and pulled down a box from the top shelf and held it out for me with dread painted in his eyes.

Inside were little lacy thongs that were definitely not my style, but it would be a hell of a lot better than fighting nude from the waist down. I grabbed a black pair and slipped them on. Again, it was scary how much his wife and I were similarly built.

"I don't like this." He eyed me with deep worry creases in his forehead.

With a deep breath, I launched into the plan formulating in my head. "You need to stay in the shadows of the dark stairwell and hold a handful of my hair while you tell them to have at me. You need to tell them you need to go get rid of the body and you'll be back to have another go."

Mikhail's gaze hardened and his shoulders went rigid. "I'd rather lose the bleach we have than lose you, and this is primed for something bad to happen."

"I will have the sword behind my back. Besides, with the way I'll be standing, they'll think my hands are tied behind my back until it's too late."

He shook his head slowly at me. "No."

"Do you trust me?" The doubt that passed over his features burned but he was right. Trusting me with what I did was a stretch for him right now. "Let me rephrase. Do you trust my abilities with that sword?" I amended, because doubt screamed in his eyes and the set of his frown.

He glanced toward the living room and then nodded despite the displeasure written in the lines around his mouth.

"I need you to try to sound like Troy and say 'Have at her. I've got a body to get rid of.'"

Mikhail repeated the words, but he still sounded like Mikhail. His voice was much deeper than Troy's and very distinct. Although the New York accent worked, the tone needed adjusting.

"You need to make your voice a couple octaves higher."

He tried it again and practically nailed it.

"That was scary perfect." I gave him a smile, but I wasn't sure it convinced him that this would work. "Now the only thing missing is the brass knuckles. If you have them on the hand holding me, where they can see them, it will complete the ruse."

We crossed into the living room, and I tiptoed around the blood, going for the severed hand by the couch. It was harder to get the brass off the stiff fingers than I thought, and I managed to get a couple drops of blood on my leg and all over my hands in the process.

It gave me an idea. I handed the metal to Mikhail and then purposely dragged my hand over the side of my face, as if Troy had clocked me with the metal knuckles. I would never *not* put up a fight and if I showed up all pristine, that would raise a warning.

But I couldn't have blood all over my hands. I picked up the sword and headed into the kitchen, washing off both my hands and the blade.

As I dried my hands with a towel, Mikhail leaned his crutch against the wall and closed his eyes.

His transformation was much quicker than the last time on the operating table. It gave me hope that the antibiotics I had given him worked. He was actually getting stronger by the minute.

With the sword carefully secured in my right hand, I scooped him up, grabbed the crutch, and punched in the code. The stairwell was still lit up and I descended toward a very uncertain future.

Dragon Storm
Chapter 26

WHEN WE REACHED THE fifteenth-floor landing, I put my ear to the door. I could hear music and talking, like they were having a party in there. I put Mikhail down. His shift back to human form was fast. Almost as fast as his original shift back at Grand Central, which gave me the courage I needed to do what must be done if they indeed were in on Troy's warped plan.

When I handed him the crutch, he looked uncertain, but I gave him a nod. If they were innocent, they would rush to my aid. If they were guilty, they would rush to take advantage of a bound and near naked woman.

Deep down, I prayed they were innocent, but I knew better.

I held the sword so it wouldn't hit me or Mikhail, and he turned the hall lights off, standing in the shadows at my side so he wouldn't get nicked by the sword, and no one would get a clear look at him.

"Ready?" he whispered in my ear, and I nodded. He gently kissed my clean cheek closest to him. "Don't get hurt."

He punched in the code and unlatched the door. With his brass-knuckled hand holding a fistful of hair, he marched me into the room with only part of his arm in view.

My heart dropped at the rigging in the center of the room. It was a mass of chains meant to hold me in whatever position they deemed suitable. My grip tightened on the sword.

"You bastard," I whispered.

"Have at her while I clean up the body."

The door closed behind me, and the four men smiled like hyenas.

"Looks like Troy had a little fun with you before he brought you down."

Juan stayed over by the chains, but Adam, Marvin, and Henry came forward eagerly. Their tented pants announced their intentions as clearly as the hungry looks on their faces.

I widened my eyes, studying them as they approached. They were all about the same height, which gave me an advantage. I had one chance and I turned enough to regrip the sword, faking like I was cowering away from them.

"Bitch isn't such a badass now."

If they actually got close enough to grab me, I was screwed. So, my timing had to be perfect. My heart thundered. When they stepped into range, I twisted, swinging the sword like a baseball bat with a complete follow-through, enough so that I had to pull back before the blade hit my backside.

Nothing happened for a moment. It was as if I had completely missed my targets, but they had stopped in their tracks. Red rings formed on their necks. All at the same height from the floor, but one was closer to the jawline and the others were right smack in the middle of their throats.

Juan stood at the chains, blinking as if he didn't quite understand what had taken place. It wasn't until I kicked Marvin in the chest that Juan's eyes widened into saucers. Marvin's head rolled across the floor toward him.

He stared at it and looked up at me as I stepped into the space the asshole had occupied a moment ago.

I held the dripping blade in front of me and smiled.

Juan turned toward the cots where their bags were located. Where their weapons were. He sprinted. Calculating distance and speed in a millisecond, I launched the sword like a javelin, thankful for the days of track and field in high school. Like my uncanny ability to hit the bull's-eye in any dart match I've ever taken part in, the sword hit Juan just above his ear, stopping when the hilt hit his head. It threw him to the side, where the sword pierced through the front of one of the cabinets.

Juan twitched a few times and then the smell of urine filled the room as his body went slack, hanging from the blade like a sick marionette.

I punched in the code as both Adam and Henry's bodies toppled over.

Mikhail opened the door and surveyed the damage. "Fuck," he said in that long, drawn-out way of his. "Remind me to never get on your bad side."

"I may not be a formally trained soldier, but I've got a black belt and some mad javelin and dart skills. So, yeah. Don't piss me off."

"The true test of your grit is cleanup."

My cockiness faded. "Is the incinerator shaft only on twenty?" I surveyed the damage before me. The thought of dropping the bodies down that dark shaft rolled my stomach.

Mikhail shook his head. "The only place without a garbage shoot is the penthouse."

My gaze landed on the chains they prepared for me. "I killed five men," I said softly and the shakes took hold.

His hand landed gently on my shoulder. "No, Holly. You killed five monsters."

Dragon Storm
Chapter 27

CLEANING UP REMINDED ME that I was a killer now. No different from Mikhail. I did what I had to do to survive, even though it made me physically ill. He helped however he could, but I didn't want him lifting anything heavy and straining his back. The last thing I wanted was to pop his liquid stitches.

Once everything was cleaned up to the point of being sterilized, I stripped in Mikhail's bathroom again and he gathered all the clothing, tossed it into the washing machine, and dumped nearly an entire bottle of bleach into the water along with detergent.

I balked at the waste, but I secretly hoped it took the blood out of my clothing, especially because that one outfit was all that was truly mine in this place.

We showered again. Diligent about cleaning every drop of blood off our skin. There was nothing sexual about it, and he was quiet and reflective as he washed my body. No words passed between us. But as soon as the drain ran clear, my teeth started to chatter, like I hit a wall of frigid ice and couldn't pull myself free.

I repeated the dragon blood regimen like before and covered his wounds before we dried off. All the while shivering as if we were in a snowstorm with no shelter.

He handed me a nightgown like the one he had lent me when I was healing, and he pulled on boxers and then held the covers up for me to crawl into the bed. I didn't balk or argue. Instead, I slipped under the covers with my back to him, praying that my chills didn't crack a tooth.

It wasn't until Mikhail pulled me against his chest and his warmth wrapped around me that my shivers subsided. Tears began to leak out of the corners of my eyes in a steady stream as the day's events hit like a thousand gnarling leviathans.

He held me as I cried, like he knew the purging of tears was necessary in the face of what amounted to murder. He let me cry without empty platitudes. He let me mourn the loss of some of my own humanity.

When my sobs stopped, he whispered in my ear, "You will be okay, Holly. You're the strongest woman I've ever known."

And yet I was not strong enough to say no to that bastard. That would haunt me for the rest of my days. But perhaps Mikhail was right; he would have coerced me somehow. Although, a part of me didn't believe him. A part of me knew I had lost my moral center over the past week.

I needed the threats to end. I needed a quiet life. And I needed Mikhail to be a part of it, even if that meant hours or days instead of a lifetime.

"Tomorrow, we'll start making bombs," he whispered in my ear just before I let the world drop into the blackness of restless nightmares.

The End

Continue Reading Book 3 on the next page.

Dragon Dawn
Season of The Dragon
Book 3

Dragon Dawn
Chapter 1

AWARENESS FLOWED IN LIKE an unwanted pest. At least if I was sleeping, I could ignore the rawness scraping my insides every time I looked at the arm draped over me like a protective blanket. I couldn't shake the certainty that I had screwed up.

Darkness still reigned over the land like an iron fist. With it came nightmares, but those were nothing like the reality we now lived in. The streets of this once bustling city remained silent, except for the trembling steps of the monsters patrolling. Hunting for those of us who remained entrenched in our hiding places.

I glanced down at the hand entwined in mine and then over my shoulder at the sleeping dragon. Mikhail St. Clare. He was a sight to behold, gorgeous to a fault with his strong chiseled features. He towered over me at six five and two hundred pounds of solid muscle. And damn him. He was the epitome of a gentleman.

A gentleman who I betrayed in the worst of ways, and yet, he still protected me as if I were an innocent child, or a cherished love.

With my mind so restless, I wasn't going to get any more sleep tonight and the escape I had hoped for in sleep was anything but. Gently, I moved his arm and grabbed the dress I had been in yesterday before the shit hit the fan.

The soft fabric hugged my form as I padded to the living room window. When I glanced down, I expected to see hordes of leviathans crawling out of the river like in my dreams. But the streets were silent, as if God knew I needed a reprieve.

My gaze moved to the back of the couch, and I sighed. Despite scrubbing, there were still blemishes in the fabric. A reminder of the first man I killed yesterday. Troy. The asshole who compromised me and used me in an attempt to murder Mikhail. I forced my gaze away from that reminder. At least the floor had been wiped clean of all traces of death.

I glanced toward Mikhail's library. He had returned the katana back there, to where it had been stored, after he removed the blood and polished the steel to a fine shine, as if it had never decapitated four men. That had been the last thing he did before we washed up and fell into the bed.

Everything had been done in silence and any time I looked at him, a crease was set between his eyes, as if he were deep in thought. I couldn't speak because if I opened my mouth, vomit would have been added to the mix of blood and gore. Cleaning up after my own murder spree had not been a catharsis for me. Instead, it slammed home my sins.

The shift in the ground tremors occurred, and my gaze jumped back to the streets. A dozen small, dark figures ran by the building, followed by two larger shadows. I sighed. Young leviathans were much like stampeding bulls when they caught the scent of blood. And the two adults were likely their parents. I turned away because I did not want to catch a glimpse of what they were chasing when they finally caught it.

My mind flowed back to the soldier who had lagged behind us when we all made a run for it. He had been caught and torn to bits by those monsters. I shuddered.

"What are you doing?"

I yelped and spun at Mikhail's sleepy voice. I covered my heart. "Don't scare me like that." His hair was disheveled, and he now had on a pair of silky black boxers. I hadn't heard a thing, which unnerved me.

He glanced down at his crutches and lifted them silently, as if to say, *These make noise.*

"I couldn't sleep." I turned back to the nightscape below.

The sound of crutches receded. I glanced over my shoulder, and he wasn't in the doorway anymore. My chest squeezed at his absence. I crossed to the doorway to see him back under the covers, with his back to me.

Instead of crawling into bed again, I went back out in the living room and scanned the cityscape from the middle of the furnishings. His lack of empathy annoyed me tonight. He could have at least come over to give me some emotional support while I grappled with being a killer.

As I stared over the broken landscape, I wondered whether he had these same regrets after he decimated thousands with his fire. For me, it was only five humans. Five humans who deserved death.

I turned away from what the monsters had done to my city and stretched out on the couch. My insides knotted with mixed emotions. I stared at the shadows on the ceiling, wondering whether I would ever get over this despair raking fine nails across every inch of my skin.

I wished for the nights before the monsters came. The constant noise assaulting my ears had been like a lullaby to me. I could sleep through a tornado or hurricane with ease, but since the silence settled, it was difficult without the white noise of the city. Especially when sporting a guilty conscience.

I didn't need more reflection time on what I had done to both Mikhail and to Troy and his soldiers. But the what-ifs kept playing in my mind like a sick game of replay your mistakes. The biggest unknown was Troy. *What if I had stuck to my initial reaction of pushing him away? Would he have forced himself on me or just waited until Mikhail was dead to rape me?*

Would he have been able to switch the labels? Or would he have to come clean on stealing the reserves? Or would he have just clocked me in the head and come up to administer the drug himself with some excuse as to why I wasn't with him, and then leave Mikhail to die alone?

Every scenario ended with Mikhail dead and me in chains, being used as their human sex toy. I could not find an alternate scenario that would have played out the way it had. Maybe if Jenny hadn't died, things would have been different. But then again, maybe it would have been worse.

Dawn broke through the dark, lightening the shadows that I had been studying all night. The toilet in the other room flushed and then the sink turned on and then off. It took a few minutes for Mikhail to come out to the living room, dressed in only his silk boxers. His hair was combed into place as opposed to the mess it had been when he checked on me in the middle of the night.

I stayed on the couch as both exhaustion and the quiet stress that filled the room gripped my muscles. Mikhail grunted at me and headed toward the kitchen, his brow still creased like it had been before we went to sleep.

He banged pans as he prepared breakfast, slamming dishes and the refrigerator, too.

I sat up. "What the hell is your issue?" I snapped. My filter didn't work when I was this tired.

He glared at me as if we hadn't fought our way through my indiscretion and then went back to preparing the food.

I laid back down with a huff.

"Don't you dare huff at me," he growled. "Especially not when you still reek of that bastard."

It was as if someone poured hot lava into my bloodstream. I nearly jumped to my feet. I pointed at him. "If you hadn't been such an asshole about things for so long..." The lame excuse came off my tongue before I could stop it.

His reaction was a feral growl, and he threw his plate of food at the wall behind him. It shattered and he took to his crutches, storming back to the bedroom without another glance at me. Then he slammed the door, but not before a litany of colorful language escaped his mouth.

Another door shut and the shower went on.

I closed my eyes and shook my head at my reaction. I should have just let him be. Let him get out his aggravation with the dishes instead of becoming snarky. I glanced at the dress I wore and reprimanded myself for being so damn stupid. I had worn this dress when Troy and I screwed around.

No wonder I set him off.

Dragon Dawn
Chapter 2

I TENTATIVELY APPROACHED THE shower stall as his anger pulsed between us as loud as the silence he treated me to. I didn't mean to fall into the blame game again, but it seemed to be my first defense lately.

He had been so supportive of me yesterday, but I murdered five men with a katana. Perhaps he just didn't want to piss me off more than I already was.

I stepped into the shower behind him and reached for him.

"Don't, Holly," he said with a voice full of warning.

I didn't listen and the moment I touched his back, he spun, grabbed my wrist, and slammed me face-first against the side wall with his body pressed against me.

"You really need to learn to fucking listen," he growled in my ear. He spread my arms wide on the wall. "Do not move."

The menace in his hissing voice kept me in place as he reached for his crutch in the corner of the shower.

"Mi—"

"Shut it." He pulled my waist away from the wall. With the crutch, he spread my legs apart as wide as my hands. "And do not move a damn muscle."

I started to lower my arms. And his hands grabbed my wrists, slamming them back in place.

The crutch fell against the wall. "I'm still pissed, so do not try my patience right now."

His grip on my wrists was tight enough to hurt, but not enough to draw a wince. My heart thundered, and I didn't dare look back at him. Not with the feral tone of his voice.

"You want to know what's going through my mind? What's been on replay against the back of my eyelids all fucking night?" His body rubbed against me as he centered himself behind me, using my arms for balance.

I shook my head because I did not want to know at the moment. His hands slid from my wrists down my arms until one hand cupped a breast and his other continued south. When his fingers found my clit and started circling, I let out a surprised moan.

"Do not move," he said again and this time he squeezed my nipple.

I blinked and stared at the wall. His hand between my legs kept circling in slow motion, heightening my arousal with each rotation, while his hand on my breasts manipulated my nipples until they were so hard I thought I'd scream.

"Did you come for him?" he whispered in my ear.

That question was like being doused with cold water. All the heat he had built up inside me fled.

"What?"

"Did. You. Come. For. Him?" He enunciated each word, as if the weight of them were too much to speak at once.

I shook my head. Troy had fucked me fast and furious, with very little foreplay. Although it had satisfied my itch, it had not satiated me the way a good orgasm did. "No," I breathed, holding myself in place because I was now afraid Mikhail would stop what he was doing if I did move.

Mikhail's fingers still rolled over my clit in that same pattern of slow seduction. "Was it fast or slow?"

I let out a laugh. I couldn't believe he was asking me to describe it to him. That earned me another nipple pinch, this one pulling a gasp from my lips. "Fast," I said with a whine, and he released my breast.

He grabbed the crutch to steady himself, and then his hand reached beneath me, spreading my opening while he guided the head of his hard cock into my pussy, just enough to create a pleasant pressure. Then the bastard paused.

My brain swirled and my muscles quivered. I wanted to lower myself onto him, feel him inside me. I wanted every last inch of him pounding me until we both fell on the shower floor in satiated bliss. But I remained in place, wondering whether this was another fucked up dream. He kissed my shoulder and squeezed my breast.

"Come for me," he whispered in a husky quality that I had never heard from him.

I wanted that tone whispered in my ear every day of my existence. It was so fucking hot. And then he slowly entered me while still playing with my clit.

"Come for me, Holly," he repeated as his lips found the nape of my neck and he began sucking his way up to my earlobe, creating a web of hot chills through me.

He stretched my core, driving me nearly insane with his slow advance. "Fuck me, Mikhail," I said.

His progression stopped, his hand on my clit stopped, and his kissing my neck stopped. I trembled in fear that he would walk away, and this would be the last time he ever touched me.

"No," he growled in my ear. Then he started the slow pace again, as if I hadn't just triggered a flare of anger. "Come for me." This time it was delivered in a demanding tone, as if I could just orgasm at the drop of a hat.

I dipped my head against the wall as his fingers played me like a practiced guitarist and his member created such a slow friction inside. Heat built up through every muscle until I was stretched taut. And yet he still kept going at a scream-worthy snail's pace.

His lips resumed on my neck; his free hand caressed my breasts with such tenderness that I moaned his name.

"I want to feel you come," he whispered and then nibbled on my earlobe.

His hand moved faster, coaxing me to that plateau that very few men had ever really gotten me to. This was beyond measure. Beyond imagination. And certainly, beyond any dream I'd had of Mikhail. The lack of our bodies touching made this surreal, almost punishing.

My body flushed. Heat enveloped me, and I let out a scream as my body obliged his demand and arched into his hand. It was so strong that my fingers attempted to dig into the rock of his shower.

His soft, drawn-out "Fuck" heightened my reaction. It did exactly what I imagined hearing that whisper in my ear with all the thick sexual connotations in it would do. I wanted him to go faster. I wanted him to slam into me with all his force, all his length, and I think I actually started begging him.

But the minute my orgasm ended, he pulled away and crutched out of the shower, leaving me to nearly collapse on the ground as the sudden emptiness enveloped me.

My legs buckled, and I slid down the wall into a puddle of confusion as the warm water beat down on my body. When I stopped quivering, I slowly climbed to my feet, turned off the water, and wrapped a towel around my body.

Mikhail lay on the bed on his back, with his foot on the floor and the bandages around his stump dripping on the carpet unchecked. He stared at the ceiling with aggravation carved around his tight lips, as though what he had just done did not accomplish what he hoped.

The towel over his waist didn't hide his member still standing at attention.

I was still in a state of disbelief. The way he left me hanging was cruel. When I stopped between his legs and reached for the towel, his gaze snapped to mine. He shook his head.

But this time, he was not in control. I snatched the towel away, hell-bent on having my way with him.

"Holly."

The warning in his voice did not deter me as I reached out and slid my hand down his shaft. His eyes flared bright as I stroked him with long, slow strokes, being just as tenaciously stubborn as he had been in the shower. It wasn't until I lowered to my knees and took him in my mouth that his eyes rolled back in his head. His hand threaded into my hair, trying to guide me, but I resisted. Going at an insanely slow pace. Just like he had.

Instead of going faster, I took him deeper and sucked harder. And then I pulled away and rolled my tongue around his tip.

Mikhail propped himself onto an elbow. "Did you..." He closed his eyes and laid back down as if he didn't want to ask that particular question.

But it still hurt. It stung deeper than the burns on my back had.

"No, Mikhail. I've never done this to any man before."

His eyes shot open, and his gaze landed on me, his mouth forming a little O of surprise.

"Now come for me," I demanded and went back to doing exactly what I wanted to do to him with my mouth. I wanted to make him groan my name as he let himself go.

I wanted Mikhail to surrender to me the way he made me surrender to him in the shower.

After all, turnabout *was* fair play.

Dragon Dawn
Chapter 3

W E LAY SIDE BY side, staring at the ceiling. Silence brushed my skin unpleasantly. I had no idea what to expect now.

"What does this mean?" I asked, almost tentatively.

"It wasn't supposed to *mean* a thing." He covered his face with his arm. "It was *supposed* to get you the hell out of my system and then you..." He shook his head. "It's like you fucking devoured my goddamn soul."

I blinked and glanced at him. "I...I, um. I'm sorry?"

He snorted a laugh and moved his arm to meet my gaze. "What the fuck are you doing now?" Mikhail never really swore before, but lately, he seemed to have adopted my dirty mouth.

"Apologizing?" I had no idea what to say. The vibes he was transmitting were all over the map, and I didn't know whether to apologize or chide him for being such a buzzkill.

He shook his head and covered his face again. "You will be the death of me." He sighed heavily and sat up, grabbing the towel and covering himself. "Think you can get the bandages from the bathroom for me?" He started to unwrap the soaked dressings on his stump.

I got up and retrieved what he asked for before going and cleaning myself up. After a quick shower and refreshing my mouth, I came back into the room. Mikhail was in shorts, but no shirt and his stump was freshly covered. The bed had also been stripped clean and the washing machine rumbled from the other room.

A set of loose shorts and a T-shirt had been left on the chair, and he pointed. His jaw tightened and he glanced at me. "I'm sorry for..."

I cocked my head and he stopped talking. I didn't need to repeat his words back at him, and I slipped on the offered clothing. "I was the one who screwed up."

"Yeah, but that was uncalled for." He nodded toward the bathroom as he balanced on the crutches.

"You regret it?"

He stared at the floor and then glanced at me as he chewed on his lower lip. "That wasn't... I've never acted like that before."

"You've never had angry sex?" My eyebrows rose.

He shook his head. "No. And that wasn't right, Holly." He met my gaze. "That was me trying to wipe out the memory..." He closed his eyes and growled. "Damn it. I was trying to..." Frustration filled his face.

"You were trying to get back at me the only way you knew how. To make me regret my choices even more than I already do." I knew exactly what he was doing. It had occurred to me a time or two when men had pulled the same shit on me.

His eyes opened and darted to me. "Yes, and it backfired. That was meant to be it, the end of our story. That was meant to be all you ever got from me. And then you came in here..." He raked his hand through his hair and turned his back on me. "I just wanted the lewd images my imagination kept drawing of you and that asshole to stop." He shook his head and let out a low laugh. "Well, it didn't totally backfire. It completely eradicated any images of *those* scenes from my mind, but now I'm more fucked than I was before."

He crutched out of the room, leaving his exasperation trailing behind him.

I followed, digesting his words. He stood at the window where I had been last night. I had no idea whether his little declaration meant we were over.

"Are..." I paused as he turned. I cleared my throat and continued, "I'm not sure I understand what you are saying."

He turned away but I could see his reflection as he stared at the streets below us. "I'm saying I cannot have this shit hanging over us and concentrate on wiping those bastards out." He pointed at the street. "Building bombs is not an activity where one's mind cannot be any less than one hundred percent focused on what is in front of him. That's a prime way to ensure our death."

"So, everything is on hold." *Again.*

He laughed and wiped his face and just shook his head. He turned and crutched toward the door without acknowledging me.

"Where are you going?"

"To my gym. I can't very well do what is needed unless I figure out how to land and take off on one leg." Bitterness laced his voice. "And I can't move without making noise, so until I can figure out how to make these damn things silent, we can't go out to retrieve the rest of the bleach."

I followed him. "You think we'll need it?" I didn't really want to go out on the streets either. Not when I wasn't at my best. It was a fluke that I had killed five men. I had the benefit of surprise on my side.

He glanced over his shoulder at the next landing and nodded. "Why are you following me?"

"You said you had a gym. I am in shit shape, too."

"Maybe we can spar together," he said softly. "I should know how to fight on one leg as well."

"Couldn't you make a prosthetic or something?"

"If we had months, probably, but we don't have that kind of time. So I have to train in between trying to figure out the right materials for the bomb and how we're going to deliver them now that I'm fucking crippled."

"Them?"

He nodded. "It's impossible to get the leviathans into a space big enough for all of them, and deliver a bomb that will cover that massive ground. Well, it is possible, but I would be in range of the blast."

I jolted and he glanced at me.

"So, that leaves us with the option of multiple devices stretched out for blocks down Broadway, and the granddaddy of bombs in Time's Square." He stopped on the eighteenth floor and punched in a code that didn't follow any of the others.

"You have different access codes for different floors?"

"Just my personal spaces. You have all the rest of the codes."

"And what else are your personal spaces?"

"Floor twenty-six and up." He crutched into the room and waited until the door to the hallway closed before he flipped the light on.

"What's on the other floors?" I asked slowly as my gaze traveled from one side of the floor to the other. Mikhail St. Clare had a state-of-the-art gym that included strength training weights, cardio machines of every conceivable type, a boxing ring, and an array of bags, from the small speed bags to the heavy punching bags. The walls were painted with every imaginable martial art form progression, from the lowest level to the highest level.

I was more impressed by this space than I had been with his apartment when I had first seen it.

Mikhail crutched forward and his voice droned for a moment.

"What?" I had been so enamored with this room that I didn't hear what he had said.

"You weren't listening, were you?"

I shook my head and looked around the room. "No. I was in the grips of awe." When I looked back, I caught a genuine smile before he suppressed it.

"The upper floors are where I store my food."

"And twenty-nine?"

"My treasures," he said. "That's off-limits to you."

"Why?" He had my full attention now.

"I am not willing to share *with you*."

His statement was delivered with a finality that stung the awe right out of my bones. He crutched away from me toward the ring leaving me looking after him with a slack jaw.

He glanced over his shoulder.

"Are you coming?" He climbed into the ring and set one crutch in the corner, using the other for balance. "This may very well be the *only* time you'll ever be able to kick my ass."

I bit my lip. He was still technically injured. "Are you sure you are in fighting condition?" I asked. "What if something tears or your back..." I couldn't finish, but I found my feet were already moving toward the ring regardless of my reservations.

"My back is fine now. As for the rest, if something tears, you'll stitch it up. That's if you can even land a hit."

"And if you break my arm or leg while you're at it?" I climbed in the ring opposite him.

His eyes narrowed. "That will be an added bonus, and maybe I won't be so pissed at you."

Steam rose inside me, and my worry turned into a feral need to beat the crap out of him just to prove I wasn't some useless human.

He grinned, but there was no humor in it. As a matter of fact, his eyes held that same dangerous quality they had when I first squared up against him in his apartment. I had grazed his chin then, but he knew me better now, so I didn't think my ambidextrous fists would matter.

He threw a pair of boxing gloves at me. I caught them on my chest and stared at the soft bags on the end and then looked up at him.

"There's also a head protector hanging from the corner." He nodded toward the corner and pulled on his own gloves.

I had seen what a punch from Mikhail could do, and I started to second-guess my getting into the ring with him, even in his condition. Cold fear tightened every muscle.

He must have seen it because he dropped his hands to his side. "I'm not here to kill you. Beat your ass..." He gave me an emphatic nod mixed with a shrug. "Maybe, but mortally harm you..." He shook his head. "No matter how mad I am at you, I still could not truly harm you."

"Oh, but you can rip my heart out and stomp all over it?" I pulled on one glove and then the other, hitting them against each other.

"All's fair in love and war." He tossed his remaining crutch into the corner. He shifted from his toes to his heel, testing out his balance and maneuvering enough to stand with his injured stump protected. He put his hands up and stared at me expectantly.

All I really needed to do was sweep that leg from underneath him and he'd go down. *But could I?*

His gaze narrowed. "Are you chickening out on me?"

"Fuck, no." I stepped in and instead of circling, I threw the first punch.

He parried, knocking it to the side, and delivered a punch to my stomach, which did nothing but send me back a step with a sting and a bruised ego. Until I shuffled away and spun low enough to sweep his ankle.

He jumped and my sweep missed him, but he didn't come down straight and pinwheeled right onto his side, wincing as he hit the mat hard on his shoulder. Mikhail rolled onto his back and stared at the ceiling as if he had never seen this view before.

He glanced at me. "That was pretty low."

I shrugged and threw his words right back at him. "All's fair in love and war."

My back hit the mat, and I yelped. I hadn't even seen his sweep. I looked over at him while I tried to get the breath he just knocked from my chest back. Once I drew in air deep enough for my back not to hurt, I said, "I guess that's better than being thrown into the back of the couch."

He looked at me in confusion and then his forehead smoothed out as the laugh started. "Well, if I chained you to the bed again, you can be guaranteed that I wouldn't just ignore you and go to sleep this time."

I stared at his profile as he studied the ceiling. The laugh lines faded, and he turned to look at me. "We have a plan for the leviathans, but we need to talk about the serpent king."

His change in gears made me blink at him. "How the hell did you get to the serpent king from binding me to the bed?"

He glanced at me and continued, ignoring my question. "There is a single serpent king that the many are derived from, and if we kill the primary, the rest will fall. I think the one here is the primary. But if he isn't, we are screwed."

I digested his words as he stared at the ceiling.

"But I don't know how to kill him."

His quiet admission chilled me. "But if his army is destroyed..."

"He can multiply at will. At least, that's the rumor." He lifted into a sitting position and attempted to get up with one leg, but fell back on his ass. "Think you could lend me a hand?"

I thought about being sassy and clapping my hands together to lighten up the mood, but that kind of humor would be lost on Mikhail at the moment. His brow was deeply furrowed, like his thoughts were taking as much of a toll on him as his new physical limitations.

I peeled off the boxing glove and stood, offering him my hand. He took it and used me to keep his balance while he lifted himself onto one leg.

"I'm worried about trying to get the bleach," he said, busying himself with removing his gloves.

"I can make the trek alone."

My offer was met with a glare and a shake of his head.

"Why not?" I asked before he could launch into a tirade. "All I need are night goggles, a spray bottle of bleach, and an empty backpack."

His jaw tightened. "And what if you find yourself surrounded?"

My mind went back to the soldier who had fell behind our merry band when we came to this building. He had a super soaker, but he didn't have any firepower to follow through once he had compromised the leviathan's skin.

"Then I guess it's my time." I met his gaze.

His lips pressed together. "No."

"Yes. If we go together, you are more of a liability than I am right now. At least I can run and find a suitable hiding place."

"They know who you are, Holly. They know that if they parade you out there for all to see before they kill you, it *will* draw me out."

"Then you stay the fuck inside no matter what." I pointed at him. "Even if I'm begging for you. You stay safe and follow through on this. I will never give up this place. Ever."

"And what if it's humans who grab you instead? Humans haven't exactly instilled any level of trust in me lately. They seem all too willing to turn on their own."

I did not have a snappy comeback this time. They hadn't instilled confidence in me lately either, but those who were left were untrained and scared. And scared people do an awful lot of stupid things. So that was another wild card I'd have to deal with, but if it played out, Mikhail could not stop. "You still follow through on your plan," I finally said, because without that plan, the world was doomed.

He hopped to the corner and grabbed his crutches. "Come on, Miss 'I've got an answer for everything.' It's time to figure out exactly what we're up against."

"And how do you suggest we do that?"

"First, we look through the archives I have upstairs in case I've got something I overlooked, then we search on the archives I downloaded before everything went to shit. Then, if that is a miss, we'll have to try to get to the New York Library up by City Hall, which is just as dangerous as trying to get the bleach." He wiped his face. "I need to do some research on bomb making, too."

"Don't you wish we still had access to the internet and all that information just at the touch of your fingers?"

He sighed and nodded. "That would be convenient right about now."

"Are you sure those resources are gone?"

"We took out your communications and satellites." He paused and looked out the window before continuing. "There's no way to access whatever databases still hold information. Without power, they are very large, very dead paperweights.”

“So, books it is.” I climbed out of the ring with Mikhail.

“After strength training.” Mikhail pointed me toward the upper body section while he went straight to the leg press.

I sat down at the universal weights and reached for the bar above my head, wondering why the hell I was building muscle for it to be torn from my bones by the beasts in the streets.

Dragon Dawn
Chapter 4

INSTEAD OF TAKING ME to his study, Mikhail first went down to the tenth floor and pressed a panel on the wall by the door. It opened and he typed in the familiar code that opened the front door and the fifteenth floor where the soldiers had stayed before I decimated them.

This floor made me gasp. It was a full-fledged lab, with some areas out in the open and others behind glass partitions that were branded with a hazardous sign.

"This is where we'll be making the bombs, and on the floor above is where we can test in the steel rooms." He crutched into the center of the room and glanced around before looking at me. "There can be no mistakes in here. No sidetracking me, either. In here, it's all business because if I fuck up here..." He closed his eyes for a moment. "I'll be handling highly unstable chemicals, so if I fuck up, we die." His gaze landed on me. "Can you follow directions without question?"

I glanced around at my surroundings. In this venue, yes. I could follow directions without arguments here. I nodded and met his gaze. "Here, yes."

His lips twitched. "From that answer, I gather total cooperation is reserved for this room only."

"You read that right." Although I would do almost anything to try to make up for my past mistakes, I wasn't about to let him boss me around outside of the lab.

"So much for my little 'I am the only say' rant." He turned away from me and sighed. Then he nodded and headed toward the door. "Time to hit the books. With two of us, hopefully we can find something in the archives here, today."

"I might need some caffeine."

"Well, grab the coffee and the coffee machine from fifteen on our way up." He stepped out onto the stairs and started the slow ascent back to the penthouse on the thirtieth floor.

At fifteen, he kept going, and I opened the door, stepping inside. My heart clanged as I reached for the light switch, half expecting a hand to grab my wrist. When the lights turned on, only the bright and clean floor shined back at me. None of the gore from yesterday was present. The only indication of anything being off was the thin hole in the cabinet near the cots.

Mikhail had even stripped the cots and thrown the linens in the washing machines. I crossed and moved the bundles to the dryer because if they remained in the machines, they would get moldy and ruin the washers. With the dryer running, I turned my attention to the coffeemaker on the table near the cafeteria. It was one of those that used a coffee pod instead of a filter and the metal tree next to it was nearly full, except for a handful of missing pods. I unplugged the coffee maker, grabbed the pod tree, and headed toward the door.

I didn't look back as I exited and swiped the lights. I moved up the stairs quickly and caught up with Mikhail on the twenty-eighth floor.

"What took you so long?" he asked.

"I moved the sheets from the washer to the dryer before grabbing these." My breath labored from the sprint up the stairs, but I was glad not to have to juggle the machine and pod tree while trying to plug in the code for the penthouse.

Mikhail opened the door and leaned on it, allowing me to enter before he maneuvered inside. "I'll meet you in the study."

I headed for the kitchen and set up the coffee machine in the corner by the sink, far enough out of the way of the cooking area not to be a hinderance. I found a cup that would do and made myself a fresh brewed coffee that smelled as heavenly as it tasted.

With the warm cup of java in my hand, I crossed into the study. Mikhail had already pulled books from the lower shelves. A half a dozen books on the upper shelves had been pulled over, too. And as Mikhail read more titles, he lifted his crutch and pulled a couple more over.

He glanced at me and nodded toward the bookshelves. "Do you mind grabbing the ones I've pulled out?"

I climbed up the shelves and grabbed the books he had tilted, tossing them onto the growing pile of books. The last one I pulled, I actually could read the spine. "Myths and legends?" I asked, waving it at Mikhail.

"There isn't going to be a how to kill a serpent king manual, especially since man didn't believe in him until he came crawling out of the sea with all his fucking demands."

"And don't forget his army of thugs. You included."

"Gee. Thanks." He didn't smile or roll his eyes at my dig. Instead, he sat down next to the massive pile and took the first book.

I climbed down from the shelves and settled in on the other side of the massive stack of at least twenty books of various sizes and bindings. Some were soft cover, some hard, some worn, and some like the one in my hand seemed ancient. It was leather bound, and I opened to the first page. Even the font was of ancient times and the paper was whisper thin. It kind of reminded me of the old King James Bible I used to have as a little girl.

"What am I looking for?"

"Anything to do with Hydra."

My gaze jumped to him, and my mouth dropped open. He was too busy sweeping through the pages of his book to notice my shock. "Like in if you cut off its head, two will grow back?"

Mikhail nodded. "If it isn't the primary, yes. But we need to know what will kill it."

"Hercules killed the Hydra with a golden sword that was given to him by Athena."

"Gold doesn't do anything. One of my dragon kin had a golden dagger and tried to use it. It didn't even pierce his slimy skin." He glanced at me. "It had been a theory, but it was disproved that day."

"If memory serves me, the Hydra spits acid."

"Yup." He flipped a page.

"The serpent king does the same?"

He glanced at me with lips pressed together. "How the hell do you think they got me out of the sky? Do you think I just landed in the midst of them and let them all take a swing at me?"

"I don't know. I've never seen the serpent spit." I had never seen the serpent king attack on his own. He always sent the leviathans into the fray.

He blinked at me and took a deep breath as if he just realized I was missing the info he had in his head. "Yes. The serpent king spits acid, just like the fabled Hydra in Greek mythology." He wiped his face. "I don't know that these texts here will help." He waved at the books.

"What were swords made of in ancient Greece?" I asked, because gold was soft and wouldn't do well in battle at all.

"Iron. But they didn't gleam like gold or like..." His head snapped up, and he glanced at me before he looked up at the top of the bookshelves.

I followed his gaze and shivered.

"It's ancient and made with iron and steel. The fabled golden sword could very well have been a katana." His eyebrows rose.

"You're reaching." I went back to my book.

He sighed, with his gaze still locked on the sword. "Maybe, but if all else fails, we will have to rely on that and your mad skills." He looked at me and a dimple appeared. It was the first real point of levity he showed since before I nearly poisoned him to death.

I truly missed that dimple, along with the impish quality dancing in his eyes when they reflected humor. I knew I shouldn't ruin the moment, but I needed to ask. "Are *we* over?"

He looked down at his book and let out a long sigh. "Were we ever...*we*?" He glanced at me with that quizzical crease between his eyes.

I didn't know how to answer his question.

"Or was it just a mutual attraction that turned into something unhealthy and possessive over the time I nursed you back to health and vice versa?" He closed the book in his lap. "There is a lack of trust between us outside the battlefield. We are both guilty of that. So, I ask again, was there ever truly a *we*?"

I glanced at the floor with my throat tight and then shook my head. In the sense of a couple, we had never been, even with his first growling kiss here before I stabbed him in the back.

"The question you *should* ask is if there is a possibility of a 'we.'"

That pulled my gaze back to him. He still stared at his book and his lower lip disappeared through his teeth for a moment. Then his sharp eyes glanced my way.

"I need to be able to forgive you in order to get to the point I can answer that question."

I swallowed hard and nodded. "So, telling me you loved me was just your libido talking?"

He chewed on his lower lip, as if he were inspecting his feelings. The longer he didn't acknowledge the question, the more it burned. He slid his eyes to me again and shook his head. "No. That was my heart talking before I was reminded of how monstrous humans can be."

"And now?"

"My feelings for you..." He cracked open the book in his lap and his jaw tightened as he stared at the pages. "They are all over the fucking map. One moment I'm angry as hell and I don't even want you in the building with me, and the next I want to take you in my arms and forget the rest of the world exists." He closed his eyes, leaned his head back against the couch, and wiped his face. "Basically, I'm in love with you and I hate you at the same time. It's fucked up."

He put the book aside, got up on his crutches, and crossed to the window. "This just adds to all the turmoil building inside, too." He waved to his bandaged leg. "I can't have all this shit in my head, tearing through my thoughts like a child in an all-you-can-eat candy store."

The imagery made me smile, and I put aside my feelings for the moment because mine were just as complex as his, except my crutch was guilt, not anger. I needed to be patient.

"What do you need from me?" I asked softly.

He turned with his eyebrows raised, as if my question surprised him. "Time." He let out a laugh laced in sarcasm. "Something we don't have."

I wanted to go to him, to wrap my arms around him and apologize, but I stayed put and focused on the myths and legends book in my lap, giving him the time he needed.

Dragon Dawn
Chapter 5

NOT ONE OF THE books at Mikhail's disposal had any more information on Hydras. They did have some interesting information on dragons, though. According to the lore, dragons were mentioned in almost all civilizations. But they varied between Western and Eastern depictions.

"Are the dragons in the Far East wingless?" I asked as I read the text.

"No. We all have wings, but some of the ones in the Far East don't have the wingspan we do in the West. And some can't fly at all, so they slither with their wings folded like a giant serpent. Consider the differences between humans of European descent and those of Asian descent, or African descent for that matter. It's all in the genes. Same principle with dragons. Some of us have shiny scales, others are as black as the night sky, and still others had all the colors of the rainbow represented throughout their scales." He sighed and sat down at the computer.

"But only one can shift." I stated the obvious.

He nodded. "As far as I know, I'm the only hybrid out there." His voice carried the weight of his uniqueness. He booted up the computer and moved the chair over so I could squeeze in next to him to see what he pulled up.

"You have archives of St. Catherine's Monastery?"

He smiled and glanced sideways at me. "I figured the oldest library in the world was worthy of pulling archives for. I made sure it wasn't targeted and it's far enough away from civilization to potentially still be standing. So yes, I copied their archives into my network here in the event it was inadvertently destroyed."

"Did you do that with the Vatican, too?"

"No. There was no way to do that. Especially in the time I had to get this all together before the internet was taken out."

I stared at him, and a disturbing thought surfaced. "How much warning time did you have before they came?"

"I had an inkling when lockdowns went into effect and people stopped going out and started dying. The extended silence was enough to interrupt their sleep. And God help me, I felt it when they woke. It was as if an urgent SOS went out to all the creatures in their path." He glanced at me. "Do you remember the reports of an anomaly in the deepest part of the ocean?"

I vaguely remembered and gave him a half nod mixed with a shrug.

"Well, that took the news headlines for a few days before it fell back on the pandemic. I didn't know how long I had, but that is when I started preparing for the worst." He waved at the room surrounding us. "I made this building self-sufficient and set up the façade to mirror the buildings around both day and night. The night being much more critical. And then I downloaded everything I could onto my closed-circuit servers before the serpent king crawled out of the ocean with the leviathans." He took a deep breath. "I was met with the same ultimatum as you were: serve or be annihilated."

"They knew you were here?"

He let out a laugh. "Yes. They knew I still walked the earth. They knew where my home was, but they did not know about this place." He opened the list of documents and books for the library that he downloaded. "They had my family." He stared at the computer and let out a heavy sigh. "If my family had been here, they would still be alive and I would have never been forced to call my brethren, either." His fingers banged on the keyboard harder than necessary.

I kept my mouth shut as I watched document after document be pushed into a waiting folder:

myths, fables, old parchments, anything that had reference of Hydra or fabled serpent in it.

He paused and looked out the window and then over at me before his eyes fell back on the keyboard.

"You can't live by what-if's." I touched his arm.

"That's easy for you to say. You didn't participate in the quest to wipe humanity off the earth." He met my gaze. "Or witness the annihilation of your species." He wiped his face. "I could do nothing." His eyes blazed. "I'll be damned if I do nothing this time."

I squeezed his arm in support and then we pored over the text on his computer until the darkness wrapped around the apartment.

My stomach rumbled and Mikhail glanced at me and then the clock on the desk. "You need to eat." He leaned back in the chair, rubbing his eyes.

"So do you." I stood and stretched my stiff body. "What can I cook for you?"

"There should be some hamburger patties in the freezer," he said as he went back to scrolling. "I don't know what else I have up here that would still be good." He sat forward, studying the screen without looking up at me.

I took that as a sign and left him to continue researching. I headed into the living area and blinked my eyes to clear the afterglow of the computer from burning into my irises. I swung open the refrigerator. He had been right: there wasn't much else that could be easily cooked up in a flash. Although he did have a package of bacon, along with a tomato that had seen better days. The tomato went into the garbage.

Then I was grilling up the bacon in one skillet and three burgers in the other. After a few minutes, the thump-shuffle of Mikhail's crutches broached the living room. I flipped the burgers, turned the bacon, and set plates out, along with large glasses of water. Neither of us had anything most of the day and I knew just how famished I was; I couldn't imagine how hungry he must be.

"Do you want eggs, too?" I asked as I moved the bacon around in the pan so it wouldn't burn.

He took a seat at the counter. "What you have is fine," he said without an ounce of enthusiasm.

I glanced up from cooking to find his tired gaze following my every move, but there was an underlying despair reflected in his eyes. "Why such the long look?"

He met my gaze. "We have to go to the library."

Who would have thought going to a library would strike terror inside anyone? But I gulped. New York's biggest library was near City Hall. That was far enough away from Mikhail's to dry out my mouth and cause my stomach to clench.

His lips twisted into a smile that agreed with whatever my face had given away. "I'm not thrilled with it either, but there wasn't anything beyond what we already knew in those archives." He hooked his thumb toward the study. "So, we need to figure out how I can move silently. Through the tunnels not the streets."

I focused back on our food as my mind went into a flurry. I focused on how to get Mikhail to move silently. The crutches had a distinct noise and that would call the leviathans from miles away. Even if we padded the bottoms with something that had less of a grip, the damn things creaked with his weight.

Although I was confident in getting the bleach myself, I was not confident that I could get to the library and back without any sort of confrontation.

"Can you fly?" I asked as I plated our meals and pushed the plates to the other side of the counter. With the stove burners turned off, I grabbed the condiments from the refrigerator and walked around to take a seat next to Mikhail.

He ate slowly. Almost as if it were his last meal. "I don't know."

"Not even in miniature form?"

He glanced at me. "I. Don't. Know," he said with more force. His lips turned down into a scowl.

"If you can fly at that size, they will never know it's you. You'd blend with the other night birds."

"And what about you? I cannot carry you while I'm that size."

I glanced down at my plate and picked at the food just as much as he was at this point. "You can also see in the dark. I can't. You could find what we need and bring the book back. And I can make at least one or two bleach runs. Divide and conquer."

He focused on his food, pushing pieces around with the fork I had given him, but he didn't eat any more. He finally pushed the plate away and covered his face with his hands, drawing them down slowly.

"If I go alone..." His voice was barely a whisper, and he looked down at his leg. He shook his head slowly. "I'd still be hopping around the library, making a fucking racket."

"Not if you take a crutch."

He bit his lower lip, debating. "It's not a bad idea," he said after some time and started eating again. "But you going after the bleach alone is." His gaze slid to mine. "If something were to go wrong..."

"You can't take that trek with me, Mik. I need both hands and an empty backpack to get to that hole and climb down. Coming up will be worse with a full pack. I'd go with a super soaker and that katana on my back."

His fork dropped on his plate, and he raised an eyebrow at me.

"It's quiet, whereas a gunshot would bring the entire pack." I went back to my food, eating instead of picking this time.

"You would have to get within striking distance." He shook his head. "That's suicide."

"Then what the hell is your grand plan to get this shit done?" I slammed my silverware down on the counter and turned toward him. "Huh? Mr. Smarty Pants?"

He recoiled and now both eyebrows were raised. He blinked a couple of times and then snorted a laugh. "What the fuck did you just say?" he mumbled through the laughter now echoing off the kitchen appliances. "Mr. Smarty Pants?" Another snort came out, and this one had some smoke with it, as if Mikhail were losing complete composure.

"It wasn't that funny." I pouted, refusing to let the laughter winding up inside me to surface. It was truly as if we had come full circle—well, at least on the language part. I was usually the one dropping f-bombs like a drunken sailor.

He wiped at his eyes and leaned back on the chair, trying to stop his guffaws. "Yes, it was," he said as he wound down. "But you're still not going out there without me in some capacity." He leaned over on the counter. "Oh, man. I don't remember the last time I laughed like that."

"When you heard my first name," I said. He had laughed almost as emphatically, but his eyes didn't shine the way they were now.

He glanced over at me and shook his head. "Not even close." His dimples showed and his eyes sparkled with humor.

Instead of arguing with him, I just took him in, allowing a smile of my own to surface. Just for this brief moment, joy reflected in him, and I wanted to savor it, because God only knew how long it would be until I saw it in his eyes again.

He finally sobered enough to eat his meal. By the time he finished, that smile and glint in his eyes had passed.

"Your idea of me flying in miniature form to reach the library is actually pretty good. But that also means I need to take off from the roof, not street level." His mind was at work again and he glanced at me. "And if you wait for me to get back, at least I can give you air support if you get in trouble. But if that happens, we have to find a place to hunker down until the threat passes.”

“Because you can’t compromise this building,” I added.

“Right. But I also don’t want you defenseless on the ground.”

“Do you have a crossbow?” I figured the question was warranted.

“No. But I might have a regular bow with some arrows tucked away somewhere.”

“Well, find it, because that would work. They offer quiet deaths, especially when the arrows are dipped in bleach. All it takes is a clean headshot.”

“You sure you weren’t trained in the military?” He narrowed his eyes at me.

Heat crept into my cheeks, and I grabbed his empty plate. “Go find me a weapon, and I’ll do the dishes.”

“Yes, ma’am.” He climbed to his feet, adjusting the crutches under his armpits before he headed to the door and disappeared.

I wondered whether the bow might be stashed in the floor that was off limits. But before I could start obsessing about what was in that floor, I dug into cleaning the mess I made in the kitchen, ignoring that itch that crawled right between my shoulder blades.

Dragon Dawn
Chapter 6

I STRETCHED OUT ON the couch waiting for Mikhail to come back from his weapon finding adventure in the building. My eyes were too heavy to stay open, especially after the sleepless night last night.

My eyes adjusted to the dark and a shadow rose, blocking the moonlight. I slowly turned, facing the beast that snuck up on me. The flaming sword in my hand made me pause but the growing height of the monster made me turn the rest of the way.

The serpent king stood over me and something fell from between his razor-filled maw. I stepped back and Mikhail's body landed before me. Twisted and maimed, with half his face eaten by the serpent's acidic saliva.

I couldn't tear my gaze away from him.

A hiss finally ripped my eyes from Mikhail in time to see the serpent king's dripping mouth coming at me fast. I swung the burning blade and stumbled as my cut missed.

Death approached like a rocket.

"Holly."

Mikhail's voice knocked me out of the dream.

My eyes flew open to Mikhail standing by the couch on crutches, with a bow in one hand and a quiver over his shoulder. He stared down at me in the low light still emanating from the kitchen.

"I hate nightmares," I mumbled and rubbed my face, even as the horror receded back into my subconscious.

"Well, I think this will cheer you up." He shifted a crutch and handed me the bow. Next came a quiver of at least fifty arrows. And then came a bag that I hadn't noticed in the dark. He set that on the table and then crutched over to the chair with the ottoman and collapsed into it.

"What's in the bag?"

"Arrows with foam tips and a practice bull's-eye."

My head spun to look at him as my eyebrows rose in surprise. "Excuse me?"

He smiled. "My son went through a Robin Hood stage."

"Seriously?" I unzipped the bag and stared at the contents. I picked up an arrow and inspected the nock and then the foam. Each end had a patch of Velcro on it. Some of them were a little more worn than others, but the weight of them felt comparable to a real arrow, so the practice wasn't in vain. "This is awesome."

"You can hang the target on any of the doors you'd like. They're more sturdy than the walls and I'd rather not have to patch up drywall again."

"I wouldn't miss the target," I said offhandedly, still studying my newest gift from Mikhail. "But I'll put it on the laundry room door since that door gives me the longest line of sight throughout the apartment."

"So, what was your nightmare about?"

I glanced at him and then out the window. "Both of us being killed by the serpent king." I brought my gaze back to him. I shrugged.

He just nodded. "It is a possibility." His sigh followed his words. "Assuming we don't kill ourselves creating the bleach bombs." He offered me a weird smile-shrug combination. "Or get killed while trying to get more information on him or retrieving the bleach, or just falling down the damn stairs," he added. "It's all a crap shoot at this point."

"That was quite the pep talk."

"I'm sorry. I'm just as tired as you are, and my mind won't stop like I need it to." He leaned his head on the back of the chair and closed his eyes.

My mind drifted to a certain activity that guaranteed us sleep afterward. I opened my mouth.

He pointed at me. "Don't say you know a way to tire me out even more."

How he knew that's where my mind went, I'll never know, but his lips twitched as if he tried to suppress a smile.

"Then I'm out of suggestions." I grabbed the bull's-eye target and turned it to see what type of fastener it had. All I would need was one sturdy nail to catch in the eyelet opening.

"Do you have a hammer and nail?"

He pointed toward the bedroom. "Bottom drawer of my nightstand. If it's not in there, it might be in a small hardware bag in the bottom of the closet."

I retrieved the items and pounded a nail into the center of the door at close to seven feet high. Although that was lower than a kill shot for a leviathan, at least it made it so I had to raise the bow higher than just straight out. With the target set, I grabbed the bow and the bag of practice arrows and went to the farthest corner of the apartment.

From this angle, I'd have to shoot directly over where Mikhail lounged. His eyes were no longer closed, either; they were intently watching me.

I nocked the arrow and pulled back. The muscles between my shoulder blades cried out at the motion. I ignored it and focused on the target. Blowing a slow stream of air, I released the bowstring. The arrow flew true and hit the target with a soft bang.

Mikhail looked over his head at my dead-center bull's-eye and then back at me, nodding in appreciation.

I rolled my shoulders. "I need to get in shape," I muttered. My back was still fragile from the burns and the lack of endurance I had was laughable. I pulled another arrow from the bag and repeated the motions, although this time, the protest in my back was more pronounced and that pulled my aim off. The arrow hit the corner of the door and bounced off onto the floor.

I lay the bow down next to the bag and crossed to the fallen arrow, picked it up, and dumped it onto the coffee table before I sat down. "I need some serious work on my arm and back muscles."

"The first shot was dead on." He sat up. "I need sleep. And you do as well. Tomorrow we can do some more in the gym and while you're bulking up your arms and back, I'll attempt to shift and fly." He got to his feet and started toward the bedroom.

My heart jumped in my chest. *Hadn't he said he'd have to take off from the roof earlier?* "You're going on the roof?"

He turned toward me with an amused grin. "Not quite yet. We have to find out if I can still fly before I decide to jump off a thirty-story roof. Don't you think?"

I chuckled. "Yeah. I'd hate to see you as a road pancake." I stretched out on the couch again.

He stopped at the bedroom door and, without looking at me, he said, "You don't have to sleep on the couch. The bed's big enough for both of us."

Although the couch was comfortable, his bed was like sleeping on clouds. I did not need to be told twice.

Dragon Dawn
Chapter 7

I WOKE WITH A start as the sun filtered into the bedroom. But I couldn't move, because at some point during the night, Mikhail pulled me into his arms and had them wrapped around me in a tight grip. I wasn't sure whether he was trying to protect me or suffocate me. I tried to wriggle free, but his grip tightened to the point of pain.

"Mikhail," I hissed and jabbed my elbow into his chest.

His head popped up and his gaze darted around the room, then he looked down at me.

"You're crushing me."

"Oh, sorry." He released me, rolled onto his back and ran his hands through his hair, tucking them behind his head as a loud yawn ripped through the morning. "I haven't slept that soundly since before the pandemic." He rubbed his face and looked at the clock. "Shit. It's almost noon."

"What?" I spun to look at the clock and my heart clattered in my chest. Indeed, it was a few minutes before midday. With the exception of when I was healing, I had not slept the morning away since high school. I was up and out of bed as if the room were on fire.

"What is your rush?" Mikhail stretched languidly, as if we had all the time in the world.

"We have things to do."

"People to see. Places to go?" he teased from the bed.

"Get up," I huffed and headed toward the bathroom with an eyeroll in progress.

His sigh followed me and then a shuffle of crutch-step, crutch-step moved away from the bathroom.

I brushed my teeth and then tied my hair in a ponytail before I splashed cold water on my face. I needed to work on my arm and back muscles today. I needed to get to the point two tries on a bow didn't exhaust me. And Mikhail needed to attempt flying in miniature form.

Mikhail was already in the kitchen, cooking us up some eggs. His bare chest greeted me as I stepped out in clothes more tailored for a workout than lounging. I climbed up onto the chair and my gaze couldn't help but wander down behind the counter. His sweats hung on his hips.

He caught my curious inquiry and his face morphed from concentration to amusement. "Were you hoping I wasn't wearing anything?"

"Aren't you chipper this morning."

He turned, grabbed a cup that was under the single-brew coffeemaker, and slid it across the counter.

I stared down at the dark coffee and let the scent waft into my nose. I closed my eyes, inhaling. I felt more alert already. "Thank you."

"I wouldn't thank me quite yet," he said. "Today, I'm going to kick your ass in the ring."

"Oh, you think so?" I sipped the coffee as his eyes rose to meet mine.

"Yes. I had a decent night's sleep. I should be able to conquer the world today."

"But can you fly over it?" I said, goading him as much as he was trying to get under my skin.

He shrugged and poured scrambled eggs on the two waiting plates, pushing one to me and the other he moved to the side of where he stood. After handing me a fork, he dug into his as if he hadn't eaten in much longer than it'd really been.

"Eat up. You're going to need all that fuel." His eyes twinkled with mischief at a level I'd never seen.

This playful side of him was...refreshing and it took me by surprise. My insides swirled with a combination of emotions, all of which would land me on my back in a sheen of sweat. For all

I knew, that could be his goal. My heart rate picked up. But with my luck, it wouldn't be in any sexual context. More like a dose of pain and a whole lot of sore muscles.

After breakfast, he cleaned up the kitchen and then wiped his hands on a dish towel. He flashed that brilliant smile in my direction as he steadied himself on his crutches. "Ready?"

I downed the rest of the coffee and set my cup near the sink. "Ready as I'll ever be." Although I had doubts about what kind of beating I was in for today.

We made our way down to the gym and as soon as we were inside, he headed toward the ring. This time, he leaned a single crutch on the side and came to the center with one for balance.

I raised an eyebrow as he pulled on his gloves. "Just as long as you don't use that as a weapon." I pointed at the crutch.

"I didn't do so well without a way to stabilize myself yesterday, so..." He waved at the crutch. "It also means I only have one arm to block or throw punches, but I'm not limited to just my fists."

Oh, great. He literally meant he was planning on kicking my ass. Well, we'd just have to see about that. I had two feet and two hands and a frighteningly accurate aim. When he waved me in, I didn't hesitate; I stepped in and went to throw a punch when he started a crutch-enabled roundhouse.

I ducked and swept the crutch out from under him. He hit the mat with an "oof" and glared up at me. I was not above taking advantage of his disadvantages.

"That was pretty low," he muttered and rolled onto his hands and knees, using the crutch to get himself back up.

"You opened yourself up to that."

He pressed his lips together and waved me in again. I launched at him and this time he dropped the crutch and parried enough for my swing to only graze his shoulder. Then he grabbed both my arms and fell backward, pulling me down on top of him before he rolled and pinned me to the floor.

I looked up at him, blinking as he held my wrists hostage in his grip. He huffed and then crushed his lips to mine in a rough kiss. I balked and tried to roll us, but he held fast, even with my legs pressing the floor to gain leverage.

When he broke the kiss, he chuckled, and his eyes sparkled with tiny flames that changed from yellow to blue and back.

"You are not going to get anywhere trying that on the leviathan."

He tossed his head back in a full laugh. "True, but I'm not sparring with a monster. I'm sparring with you."

"What happened to the love me, hate me thing?" I cocked my head. "Not that I'm complaining, but you're doing the mixed signals again."

His smile faded, as did the dancing flames in his eyes. "You are just going to have to live with the mixed signals for a while." He rolled off me and retrieved his crutch, getting up to his feet again. "In the meantime, get used to that view from the mat."

"Those are fighting words." I climbed to my feet and squared myself. This time when he nodded, I waited, measuring the distance and the tightness of his muscles. I faked left and jumped to my right, swinging for his jaw. He didn't parry, but his hand came up and he grabbed my fist, yanking me against his chest before he lifted me and rolled me over his back.

I landed on my butt on the floor. He spun with the crutch and faced me with a cocky grin.

From my position on the ground, I swept my leg, trying to topple him like I had before, but he easily jumped it with the help of the crutch. I hopped to my feet and went at him with slashing punches from both hands, and ended up slamming his shoulder and knocking him off-balance.

He fell on his ass this time with his mouth open in an O of surprise. He glanced up at me and reached for his crutch, sweeping it toward my legs. I jumped like he had, even when he tried to reverse course.

When I stepped out of his reach, he laid down on his back, huffing.

"You weren't supposed to use that thing as a weapon."

He grinned and glanced at me with a shrug. "It seemed like a proper response."

"Proper, my ass. If you hit me with that, it would have broken my leg."

His grin disappeared as he glanced at the crutch and then me.

"Unless that's your plan." I slammed my fists into my hips and narrowed my eyes. "Is that what you're trying to do? Make me an invalid so I can't go collect the rest of the bleach?"

He sat up and met my gaze. "That would be like signing both our death warrants." He glanced down at his hands and then the crutch again. He met my gaze and sighed. "I keep forgetting how fragile you truly are."

"Don't bullshit me, Mik."

"I'm not. It didn't occur to me that I could break one of your legs."

He started to pull off his gloves, and I stepped closer, half expecting him to sweep my legs. When I stood over him, I offered my hand to help him get up. He smiled up at me and took it, but instead of using it as leverage to stand, he pulled me off-balance and then swept the foot my weight was on. I fell headfirst into his lap, pulling a hissing groan from his lips.

With my arms all akimbo, I yanked my hand from his and situated myself into a sitting position that had both his thighs pinned underneath me. I closed my knees, pressing his thighs together, but he was still red-faced from my cannon into his nuts. I rolled my neck, getting the kinks out, reaching up to massage the sore muscles.

"You broke my balls," he muttered.

"That's what happens when you pull and sweep out someone's leg at the same time. You are bound to knock heads."

He snorted a laugh and met my gaze. "You knocked my head into tomorrow."

"Aw. Do you need me to kiss it and make it better?" I pouted and widened my eyes, feigning innocence.

He blinked rapidly and opened his mouth, but closed it and just raised an eyebrow.

"No comeback?"

"No. I'm waiting for you to follow through." He dropped back on his elbow with a half grin on his lips.

I leaned over, kissed the crotch of his shorts, and then sat back up. "Better?"

"Eh." He waffled his hand back and forth.

I sighed. If I started this, I wasn't going to end it until I was riding him into oblivion. And I knew how he felt about any possibility of me getting pregnant. That was as deadly an endeavor as anything we'd planned to date.

"Mikhail, I don't want to start something you are unwilling to finish."

"Have you not heard of the rhythm method?"

"Yes." I drew the word out hesitantly. Because, honestly, if I was driving, I'd get lost in the feel of him and open myself up to disaster.

He searched my eyes. "Are you capable of stopping when I tell you to?"

I laughed, because for me, that was as sure as stopping a hurricane. Especially considering talking about having sex had already made my itch kick up. "I honestly don't know," I said through the chuckle.

His gaze grew stormy, and he tried to scoot out from between my legs.

I tightened my knees, halting his attempt to get away. I didn't want to dismiss the opportunity. Instead, I pushed him down the rest of the way to the mat and pressed my lips to his. I inched my knees up high enough for our hip bones to be flush and to feel his hardness beneath me.

"Holly," he said against my lips and grabbed my arms, pushing me away.

I circled my hips, grinding against him.

"Bloody fucking hell," he muttered and flipped me over, covering me with his body. He shredded my shirt and devoured my mouth, and then my breasts. When he moved lower, I moaned his name. He stripped my shorts as easily as he dispatched my shirt, and then my dream flashed through my head as he attacked my core with his tongue, his lips, and his fingers.

Every sensation drew gasps from me. I threaded my hands in his thick hair as he toyed with me, bringing me from plateau to plateau until I was drenched and screaming his name. My body trembled with aftershocks of pleasure. He crawled up my form, licking, kissing, sucking until he claimed my mouth the moment he entered me.

I arched into him, meeting his thrusts with heated passion. And then Mikhail pulled out and rolled onto his back, his breath ragged as his gaze locked on the ceiling.

Instead of letting him remain frustrated and unsatiated, I sat up and leaned over, taking his hard, throbbing member between my lips. He groaned and grabbed a handful of my hair, guiding me up and down his shaft until his entire body clenched and he flooded my mouth.

Out of breath and sweaty, I shifted, laying the back of my head on his stomach, and turned to meet his gaze.
He still stared above him, and his heart hammered in his chest, just like mine. He looked at me and smiled, running his fingers gently through my hair. "You certainly will be the death of me."

Dragon Dawn
Chapter 8

WORKING OUT WITH MUSCLES that felt like gelatin was nearly impossible, especially considering my shirt was more like an airy shredded mess. At least Mikhail hadn't torn my shorts to pieces. He gave me the option of getting a change of clothing, but I knew if I went upstairs, the bed would look way too comfortable to pass up. I needed to strength train if I had a prayer of shooting more than one arrow a day. And it was the only way Mikhail would let me make the bleach run.

Mikhail's idea of coaching me on the weights reminded me of my first drill sergeant. He pushed me to do almost double the reps I would have on the machines. I concentrated on the seated arm press, seated arm rows, and the seated lat pull, all conditioning my chest, arms, and back. I only started whining on my last machine because by that point, I thought I'd just fall on the floor in a quivering mass.

But then it was my turn to take the reins. That perked me up, and I returned the favor, pushing Mikhail past the point of complaint. And I made him do the entire weight circuit: arms, legs, and abs. And boy did he start cussing me out on the leg press.

"Look, you need to be in better shape than you've ever been in," I growled at him. "You have to land on a single leg." I moved the pin from the four-hundred-pound mark to five hundred pounds. "Five more."

"This is one of those times that I intensely dislike you," he muttered with a glare. But he did the full reps, with his leg shaking through each one. "What next?"

I smiled. "Attempting to fly."

He blinked at me as though I had lost my mind.

"Come on. You have to try some time," I said.

"Preferably when I'm not ready to pass out from exhaustion," he balked.

"Why?"

"I don't feel like landing on my face," he said. "And worst case, I break the only leg I have." He curled himself out of the leg press and swung his foot onto the ground. "Hell, I don't even know if I can navigate the stairwell right now." He wiped the sweat from his forehead and flicked his wrist, sending droplets across the room. "Where the hell did you find energy, anyway?"

"I blazed through the endorphin mark." I grinned. "And then you gave me the opportunity to drill you just as hard as you drilled me."

"Evil woman." He reached for the crutch, but I grabbed it, moving it out of reach.

"How high do you need to be to attempt to fly?"

He sighed and scanned the room. "It depends on how small I force myself to get. But I think if I make myself a little smaller than I did before, I could get away with trying to launch from up there." He pointed toward the rafters that held some of the punching bag chains.

I followed his finger and sighed. "And how exactly do we get you up there?"

He huffed a laugh and pointed toward the far wall, where a metal rung ladder traveled up to the ceiling. "And then I have to shift without falling off the girder."

I glanced at him. His gaze was still locked on the spot where the ladder met the joist and his brow furrowed with worry. When he looked at me, that worry still hadn't abated.

"I can hardly stand right now, so climbing that isn't on the to-do list today." He mopped his face. "I need a shower and a nap before I attempt to fly."

I glanced at the ladder. Twelve rungs. I wasn't so far gone not to be able to manage that. Especially after some of the herculean efforts I was put through the last month. "And if I carry you up?"

He met my gaze and looked between the ladder and me. "Seriously?"

"Yes. You need to try. I can catch you if something goes wrong."

That prompted a snort of laughter. "You overestimate your talents."

"Fuck you. Now shift into that little, endearing creature I carried for blocks." I waved at him.

He crossed his arms and lowered his eyebrows at me. Mikhail looked like a sulking child, so I matched his pose, but did one better: I put my foot forward, tapping it with impatience.

"Holly. I. Am. Tired."

"So. Am. I." I stomped my foot just to make my point.

He deflated and stared at me. "We aren't leaving until I try, are we?"

"Considering I'm the one holding your crutches, nope."

"Bitch," he whispered and closed his eyes.

His shift was instantaneous, which meant his injuries were all but healed. Now it was all a mental game to get over the leg loss, and I hoped this little exercise would give him a little more confidence in his skills. He shrunk down to a hair smaller than what he had been before we left that stairwell.

I leaned the crutches on the nearest machine and scooped him up under my left arm. When I reached for the first ladder rung, Mikhail bit down on a trail of shirt ribbons.

"Just in case," he said through his teeth.

I rolled my eyes. "If I drop you, what's left of this shirt is going too."

"Still." He kept the torn fabric tightly between his teeth.

I hoisted us up, stepping cautiously and centering my weight before I reached for the next rung. It took a good ten minutes to climb to the top. I hoisted Mikhail up onto the joist and his dragon foot clasped onto the metal as if his very life depended on him not letting go.

I made my way down and stood under the girder. He moved slowly, using his wings for balance until he was far enough from the wall not to knock his wings when extended.

Mikhail glanced down at me and even from here, I saw the worry.

"Just glide to the ground," I said, not knowing whether that was even possible.

He launched off the rafter, extending his wings at their full length. He gently drifted across the expanse, dropping closer to the ground as he went. Then he flapped his wings, gaining altitude until he circled back around and above the joist. He went around the room again, and his dragon grin met my gaze as he flew by.

He was grace incarnate as he banked and used the space to fly as if it were an open area. However, after a few minutes, his wings slowed, and he aimed for the ring with the rope barriers.

He did not stick the landing. Instead, he hit the padded floor and tumbled head over ass into the ropes.

So much for grace.

I crossed over to him. "Are you okay?" I asked as I untangled him from the rope and set him on his foot outside the ring.

"Yeah. I just came in too fast." He shifted into human form and held the rope for balance. "I used to be able to stop within a few strides, but since I only have one leg, rolling is my only option now."

"Before you go to the library, you have to stick that landing." I could envision a swarm of leviathan in seconds if he tumbled down the street or worse, smashed the glass at the entry of the library. Just the thought of him being at risk set my skin cold.

"Get my crutches, please," he said. "You've got some target practice to do while I clean up and make us something for lunch."

"I'm calling the shower first considering what you did to my clothes." I crossed, retrieved the crutches, handed them to him, and then headed toward the door.

He followed, thumping the crutches into the ground as he tried to catch up with me. "Maybe I like the view," he said as he settled in alongside me.

"You can be so obnoxious sometimes." I held the door open for him and swept off the lights before I closed it behind us.

Going up the stairs was slower today because both of us were feeling the workout. By the time we got to the penthouse, my lungs felt as if someone had wrapped them in rope and squeezed. Mikhail didn't seem all that much better.

He collapsed onto the couch as I headed into the bedroom to clean the sweat from my body and get clothing that was not in shreds. When I went back out into the living room, Mikhail was hunched over the counter, with papers strewn across the space.

I crossed and looked over his shoulder at what he was doing. Several mathematical formulas were written and crossed out, along with drawings. I picked one up and studied the hand-drawn sphere.

"That one won't work." He glanced up at me and went back to the paper in front of him.

"Why not?"

"The blast will vaporize the bleach." He put the pencil down and pressed the heels of his palms to his eyes. "I need a shower."

With that, he grabbed his crutches and left me to stare at the partly finished picture of our bomb. The section he drew kept my focus. He had the explosives in the innermost cavern, followed by a layer of debris. Mostly nails but also some glass slivers and anything sharp that would fit in the compact area. And then he had a section of bleach wrapped in thin plastic or rubber, almost like balloon material. Something that would easily shred and break away, allowing the bleach to be dispersed in the blast radius.

It was sophisticated enough for me to blow an impressed stream of air from my lips. My gaze went to the ingredient list, and I wondered whether we would have to make a shopping run.

Making a run for the bleach and for information was enough of a deterrent. But finding some of the things I didn't even know how to pronounce, let alone know what they were, was going to be a huge problem. I stepped away and made my way into the kitchen to see what was available for food.

I really wanted my cereal that was stuck at the bottom of the stairwell with the rest of the bleach. The debris on top probably had shifted at least a few more times since we all navigated out of that hole after it collapsed on Mikhail. I'd have to try to make my way back down in the dark, too.

It was not something I was looking forward to at all.

Dragon Dawn
Chapter 9

AFTER WE ATE, MIKHAIL grabbed his drawings and took me down to the eleventh floor. As we walked in and he turned on the lights, my gaze moved beyond the lab stations, falling on the bank of metal doors. One of which stood open, and the inside walls were charred black.

I shivered. "That's where you burned me. Isn't it?" I pointed.

"Yes." He headed toward the right side of the lab. To the wall of cabinets. Before he opened them, he handed me an empty waste basket. And then he glanced at his drawings and started opening doors and putting things into the basket I held.

The garbage pail nearly overflowed by the time he got to the last cabinet. After balancing a couple more items on the pile, he closed the closet and headed to a wide and neat station in the middle of the floor. The only item that told me this might have been his workstation was a small photograph of his family taped to the edge of the computer terminal.

I put the pail where he pointed and then he started taking things out and putting them in piles. I didn't question him, not even when he handed me the empty pail. I placed it on the ground and turned back as he pulled the drawings out of his back pocket and spread them out on the clear area of the desk.

He took a deep breath and glanced at me. "I have to take a look at my stash to see just how much explosive materials I have, which will tell me how many trials we can run."

"Okay, we—"

"No. Not we. Just me. You stay put."

I narrowed my eyes at him.

"I'm still not ready to share my treasure troves with you."

"When you said treasures, I thought it was things like gold and jewels."

His lips tilted into a half grin. "You've been reading too much Tolkien."

How he knew I liked J.R.R. Tolkien, I'll never know, but the smile and mischievousness playing in his eyes made me feel lighter, despite the rebuff. He crutched away, leaving me in the lab alone.

I glanced around and wandered from workstation to workstation to see what kind of people he had been associated with before the world went to shit. If the paraphernalia left on the desks told me anything, it was these people were family friendly. Pictures of children and pets were prominent on almost every station. But the one that caught my eye had a couple of pictures of Mikhail taped to the computer monitor.

I stopped and stared at his likeness in a colorful bathing suit on some tropical beach, with a grin and holding an obscenely large margarita. He nearly glistened in the sunshine, with his hair windswept and his eyes sparkling more than the sea behind him. I had never seen such a carefree expression on the man, and he wore it well. I could see why his wife fell madly in love with him. His charisma came through in the photo, along with a playful nature that I prayed I would see at least once before we died.

The other photo was of him in a tuxedo, leaning on the railing of a ship as if it was the most normal thing in the world. His expression more thoughtful as he looked out at the water. That was an expression I had seen before and while it suited him just as much as the other photo, my gaze kept going back to the man on the beach.

I scanned the desk and my gaze fell on a wedding photo. I sighed at the couple pictured there. Their happiness shined through the photo like a beacon, and my heart twisted. The way he looked at her was so full of love that my throat tightened.

He had never looked at me like that.

I turned away from his late wife's workstation and looked right into Mikhail's gaze. I hadn't heard him come in.

I forced a smile and pointed to the photo of him on the beach. "That's quite the drink."

His gaze dropped to the desk and then came back to mine, but that mischievous glow was missing. It was almost as if I had violated some sacred space by standing where I was. He smiled, but it was as forced as mine. Although, it did relax a little when I stepped away from her desk.

"I don't even remember her taking that picture. I think I was on my fifth or sixth drink." His lips curved into a smile of reminiscence and his eyes took on a faraway look. "That was one wild vacation." He glanced down at the bag in his hand and his smile faded. "But enough of the past. We don't have a lot of explosives to spare, so we are only going to get a couple trial runs."

I wondered if we won this war, would he ever be able to smile and look like he had no worries in the world again, or whether his eyes would always carry that haunted quality in the background.

"What do you need me to do?" I stepped closer.

He turned toward his workstation and I followed. "Right now, just hand me things when I ask for them." He pointed at the array of items and stepped to the clear part of the workstation counter, carefully unloading the single piece of C-4 that he had in the bag. "And try not to distract me, please, for both our sakes. Working with explosives is not normally what I do, so I'd rather not be blown to bits because I was distracted." He met my gaze.

I gave him a nod. I wouldn't distract him in any way. Not when both our lives were in jeopardy.

"You can ask questions after, okay?"

"Yes. I'll let you do what you need to and hand you whatever you need. Other than that, I'll keep my mouth shut." I could follow orders just as efficiently as the next soldier, especially considering I knew this would bring us a step closer to taking down the monsters.

"The goal is to replicate the picture in miniature form." He stared at the drawing and then looked up at me. "In doing this, I can get a feel for the impact and adjust accordingly."

"Is one large bomb in Times Square going to be enough?"

His lips pressed together, and he shrugged. "We'll see." He focused on the clay-like substance before him and took enough to roll it into a ball that was an inch in diameter. He repeated the exercise until the piece of C-4 was gone. "This is a fraction of the size we will need in the real bombs, but we need to be able to test what kind of buffer we will need between this and the bleach."

"What material were you thinking?" I looked at the array of items on the desk. It ranged from metal to rubber, and I didn't know which would be best.

"Metal around the C-4, but I'm not sure how thick we need to make it so that the explosion doesn't render the bleach into an aerosol while still being able to spread the bleach and debris to the most optimal range." He pointed to two half-sphere iron molds. "Hand me those, please."

I did as he asked and when he pulled a silver necklace out of the bag he had retrieved, I gave him a sideways look.

Mikhail stopped and glanced at me. "Okay. So, I do sometimes collect shiny things," he said. "Just stop staring at me like that."

I couldn't suppress my smirk fast enough.

He rolled his eyes and refocused on the half-orb molds. He ripped the chain in two and dropped the pieces into each of the iron molds. He picked one up by the rubber handle and placed his hand underneath the sphere. Blue flame danced on his fingers, and soon the chain was melted in the half-sphere. He rolled the liquid around, coating the sides.

"Keep doing that until it cools." He handed me the first sphere.

I took it and slowly rotated it like he had, coating and recoating the sides while he melted the other half. Once we finished, he brought me over to a sink and filled a metal container with cold water. Then we doused our molds with the water. It sizzled and a weird ozone smell emitted from the can.

Mikhail led me back to his workstation and slid a small vial with a cord on the end into the clay sphere before he knocked the two silver halves out of the molds. Carefully, he fit the sphere into one of the halves and pressed the other half on the top, and then soldered the silver together with his finger.

I was impressed.

He took a seat and stared at the small bomb, keeping the two wires that were sticking out to one side. "Now comes the hard part: figuring out how to do a subsequent layer that we can fill with debris and bleach. The wires will have to be hooked to a battery and to something that will receive the detonation signal."

"It won't all be enclosed in the bleach sphere?" My translation of his drawing had the explosive inside the bomb completely so it would explode in all directions.

Mikhail shook his head. "We don't want bleach to get into the inner sphere. Plus, with this design, the explosion is expected to be outward, away from the detonation. So, instead of a full three-hundred-sixty degrees of destruction, we are only looking at two hundred and seventy at the maximum. That way, if we plant it on the ground, the destruction of the building it is against is minimized. If it is hanging in the air, there should be minimal upward blowback." He glanced at me. "If I have to fly to deliver the bomb, I would rather not get blasted with what we are putting inside the real deal."

"I would prefer you not to be in the blast radius either."

He smiled at me and then glanced at his array of items. He sucked his lower lip between his teeth. "You mind grabbing me one of the containers of bleach while I attempt to put together the bleach portion?" he asked after a few minutes of surveying the items.

"Sure. Don't blow yourself up while I'm gone," I said, but he just gave me a half nod, as if he no longer listened. I glanced over my shoulder as I opened the door.

Mikhail's concentration was total as his hands moved over the items, crafting what we needed. I sent a prayer to watch over him while I was gone because it would be just like him to send me away, out of harm's way.

Dragon Dawn
Chapter 10

THE FIFTEENTH FLOOR STILL gave me the chills when I walked in. After all, I killed four men in this room. I flipped on all the lights, making it bright as I crossed to the lockers where we stored all the bleach bottles we had. Although we had thirty bottles here, the stairwell held at least double that. We had close to one hundred bottles from the warehouse in Penn Station.

I grabbed a bottle and closed the locker door. I turned and my gaze landed on the pile of chains in the corner. I shivered at the sight of them. Those were meant to keep me hanging from the ceiling in whatever position those men dreamed up.

I shook the morbid thoughts from my head and headed back down to the lab. Halfway down the stairs, the building shook. I flew the remainder of the way and punched in the entry code. I threw the door open.

Mikhail was on his back, in the middle of the floor. The door to the room that he had burned me in hung on a single twisted hinge. The rest of the door was bent as though Superman had punched the center of the door. The desks closest to the room were blown over and charred.

His station was untouched, and in the center of the desk sat a bottle of bleach.

He had done exactly what I had been afraid of. "What the fuck?"

Mikhail glanced back at me. "I wasn't sure if silver would be enough of a buffer," he said over the noise of the fans sucking whatever toxic air the aerosol bleach created right out of the room like a giant vacuum.

"You could have been killed!" I pitched the bottle of bleach at him.

He caught it and sat up, grabbing his crutch to help him climb to his feet. "I don't want you in here when I do the actual experiments."

"Bullshit!" I marched over to him and swung my fist.

He blocked my punch and grabbed my arm. "You would have been injured in the blast." He pulled me close. "I heal quickly. You do not."

Although he had a point, it still did not settle well. "You could get mortally wounded," I said through clenched teeth.

"No. Just thrown across the room. I can deal with a few bruises."

"You've got stitches and cuts you're still healing from," I argued.

He closed his eyes and took a deep breath. "I still have dragon blood at my disposal. You cannot be in this lab when I do a test. Understand?"

"No. I do not understand." I stepped into his personal space and glared up at him. "We are partners in this insane idea." I poked his chest. "Where you go, I go."

He pursed his lips. "Like getting the rest of the bleach?"

I blinked at him. "No. That's my task. Besides, we already discussed that."

"Yes. It is just like that. I can't go with you because it is dangerous for me to go in human form. You can't go with me to the library because of the distance. This is the same thing. You can't be in here because your fragile body cannot absorb a blast. Mine can."

"But you said you didn't want to be in the debris zone," I said.

"Exactly. I'm not putting debris in the test bombs. Just bleach to make sure it doesn't get blown into an aerosol. Once I get that right, we can work on scale and figuring out the detonation method, especially since we need multiple bombs to serve our purpose. But until I get the explosion right, we aren't going to be able to do any damage to the leviathans." His face was an inch away from mine and his eyes flamed with irritation.

I hated it when he was right. And I hated the fact he could get hurt beyond my ability to repair. Just like I hated the idea of him flying to the library to get research on the serpent king. Even so, I didn't back down from my stance. I remained staring at him with as much frustration etched into my features as I could muster.

He closed the distance and crushed my lips beneath his, hard enough to almost topple us both over. His hands threaded through my hair and his crutch fell to the ground. I stepped away and he teetered, off-balance until I reached out to steady him.

"Kissing me won't get me to agree."

His jaw muscle jumped, and he hopped closer. "Maybe I just want to have angry sex with you."

"You don't fuck in anger," I replied, jutting my chin out in defiance.

"Since I met you, I seem to have failed on keeping that personal ideology." He pulled me against him and stared down at me with a combination of hunger and fury, all wrapped up in the tightness of his muscles.

"No. We have work to do." I stared up at him, refusing to give in to him even though he now had my motor running. It would be so easy to drop to the floor and get busy, but time was not our friend.

His low growl of frustration filled the space between us. "Fine." He reached down and grabbed the crutch without wobbling. His balance on one leg was better than mine on two. He crossed to the door and ripped it the rest of the way off the hinge. The steel door had to weigh a ton, but he dragged it across the room as if it were made of paper.

"What are you doing?"

"I need steel." He dropped the door at the side of his cubicle and then grabbed his chair, lowering it as low as it would go. He rubbed his fingers together before he fired them up, cutting a chunk out of the bottom corner of the mangled mass.

I stood to the side, feeling like an outsider. But I didn't dare speak as he crafted the same outer shell with steel that he had made with silver. When he handed me one of the molds, I mimicked what I had done before until after he sealed the ball around the C-4.

He gave me a sideways glare as he made a plastic ball with a hole in it wide enough for the explosive to fit snugly in. He poured in bleach and then plugged the hole with the bomb, sealing it with crazy glue. He waited a moment and then picked up the entire thing, turning it so the wires were on the bottom. He pulled out a walkie-talkie and wired it to the bomb.

"Go." He pointed at the door as he headed toward the second steel door.

He disappeared into the room and then came out again, closing and locking it before he turned to me and leaned his back against the steel door. "Seriously, go." He waved me away.

"If I felt the building sway, don't you think an explosion will bring the leviathans?"

He blinked at me and bit his lower lip. "If we don't get this right, it won't matter. Just go up a couple floors like before."

"Mikhail—"

"I can't have anything happen to you because I gave in to your stubborn resolve. I will survive being thrown by a steel door—you won't." Desperation reflected in his fiery irises.

"What does success look like?" I asked as I slowly backed my way to the door.

"The walls and ceiling dripping with bleach despite the blast."

I gave him a nod and turned toward the door.

"Holly?"

I glanced over my shoulder. "Don't blow yourself up." I repeated the same directive I gave him before and slipped out the door with a heart full of reservations.

Dragon Dawn
Chapter 11

I SAT ON THE landing of the twelfth floor, only going up one flight instead of more like he wanted me to. My heart pounded, and I took long slow breaths to try to calm the mounting panic. Trusting Mikhail not to harm himself was like giving a baby a blowtorch. It was not a smart move, but the shit thing was I had to. He was right: I would be killed if that door flew into me.

He was a dragon, after all.

I jumped at the muffled boom, but I didn't feel the building list like before. Perhaps it was because I was sitting down. I rushed below and punched in the code, swinging the door open to another war-like zone.

The desks near the room were on fire. Mikhail aimed a fire extinguisher at them, dousing the flames. He glanced at me with a grin that did not belong with the smoke and the scent of bleach in the air.

The door that had been hinged on the steel fire room he put the latest charge in was embedded in the wall to the right of the door. I'm surprised it didn't barrel through the wall into the stairwell.

"I triggered the blast from the third room." He nodded to the only room left with a steel door.

Inside the blast zone, the metal still glowed red, but the walls seemed slick on initial inspection. I stepped closer to get a better look.

"Don't. It's too hot, but most of the bleach remained liquid."

That explained his maniacal smile.

Thankfully, his desk was outside the blast zone and all the items remained undisturbed. "Do you have enough materials to make what we need?"

"That's what I need to figure out. I've got enough steel here." He nodded toward the rooms as the last of the flames went out. Just for good measure, he covered the area in the thick foam from the extinguisher. "But the plastic is a different issue."

"So, plastic and delivery are our only things to work out?" I asked as I stared at the room. A drop fell from the ceiling, sizzling on the floor, and my nose itched from the bleach scent wafting all around me. It was worse than when I sprayed myself down to cross the city.

He picked up his drawings and headed toward the door. "I need some computing power to figure out what the range of destruction will be and how many of those we will need to do the kind of damage we have to do to get this right."

"Are you sure the fire's out?" I scanned the thinning smoke and the foam covering half the floor. I did not want to end up in a building fully engulfed in fire with no real way out that wouldn't put us right in the direct path of the leviathans.

"Yes." He still surveyed the room to be sure and before we left, he flicked a button that turned on the fire prevention system on the floor just in case. "Now, even if it smoldered, the system will stop it."

I followed him up the stairs. The progression was slow with his crutch, but I matched his crawling pace. The creases in his forehead announced his deep in thought mode, and with each step, they seemed to only increase. I remained quiet, letting him mull over the results of his last successful test.

When we entered his apartment, he went directly to the kitchen and grabbed a cold beer out of the refrigerator.

"Would you like one?" He nodded toward the beer in his hand.

I debated and opted against it. "I'm good for the time being." I needed to be sharp as well in order to plan out my trip to the hole in the ground that housed the bleach, along with some of the food we pillaged from the superstore warehouse in Penn Station. The thought of the sweet cereal boxes stuffed in the corner had my mouth watering.

"I think I'll make myself a sandwich while you go crunch numbers." I sidestepped him into the kitchen. "Did you want something, too?"

"I'm not hungry yet." He crutched away, staring at the drawing in his free hand.

I busied myself with making a grilled cheese sandwich and then I went into the study, grabbing a pad from Mikhail's desk and a pen from a cup holding at least a dozen writing utensils on the corner of his desk, and parked myself on the sofa behind him.

The clicking of the keyboard got lost in the swish of my pen across the paper in my lap. I nibbled on my sandwich as I started to outline my plan for retrieving the bleach. There was more than three times the amount of bleach we had downstairs still sitting in that stairwell. I figured I would be able to haul two backpacks or close to ten jugs each trip.

At least, I thought I'd be able to haul one hundred pounds on my back, but the climb up the debris might be iffy. I hauled fifty pounds and carried Mikhail last time, and I struggled to gain the right footing at times.

I stared at my calculations and exhaled, unsure of how many were still down there. For a moment, I wished Mikhail was whole and could carry a cart back with zero effort. It would take me at least five trips if I hauled ten of them back each time. Making one trip was daunting enough, but multiples made my blood run cold and my hands shake.

I put the pad aside and finished my sandwich. Mikhail still pounded away at his computer, grumbling under his breath. When he ran his hands through his hair and leaned back in the chair, I could relate. That was exactly my inner reaction to the number of trips I'd have to take to the pit.

He twisted the chair toward me and met my gaze. "As much as I want to do this with one bomb, I really can't. It would level most of midtown and probably us in the process."

"You mentioned that before."

"I know. I just wanted to make sure it couldn't be done." His gaze flicked to me then back to the computer screen.

"What about Central Park?"

"It provides too much cover for them, and we run the risk of missing some. Besides, Times Square is the place the serpent king likes to gather for his ultimatums. So, getting him there won't be as much of a hurdle."

I slowly nodded, soaking in his words. The serpent king did seem to use Times Square as his own bully pulpit. "So, how many blocks down Broadway were you thinking of lining bombs?"

"At least six blocks. Realistically, we should have them set up over a ten-block radius to make sure we don't miss any."

"So, ten bombs?"

He shook his head. "Twenty small bombs. I want both sides of the street armed, so there is zero chance of a misfire. And then one larger bomb to cover the radius of Times Square. That's where most of them will be concentrated, so while I don't really want to do a lot of damage to the buildings, it's unavoidable with the size that is needed to douse every last one of those bastards."

Now my trip to the stairwell to retrieve the bleach seemed much less of a problem than delivering twenty-one bombs without being caught.

"And how much of the bleach in the stairwell do we need?"

His gaze locked on mine. "All of it." He rubbed his face. "And we still have to figure out how to get them there and trigger all the bombs once they've arrived."

Well, shit.

Dragon Dawn
Chapter 12

I STARED OUT THE window at the street below as the sun dipped under the horizon. The colors of the sunset were stunning to say the least, but a bitterness swept through me at the change of the guard. We had started marking down the times they switched up sentries. As well as the patterns of the perimeter marches. Every evening, they replaced the day shift with the night shift and replaced it yet again when the sun started lighting up the night sky.

Twilight.

That was our target for the first bleach run. Although I wanted to do it all in one night, Mikhail cautioned against it because he felt there was too much risk. However, with the amount we needed to retrieve, he conceded that two runs would be within reason, but any more than that would be akin to suicide. Even so, that would take me the better part of a week to retrieve the bleach. And he still had to make that library run to see what he could find out on how to take down the damn serpent king.

Mikhail stepped beside me and handed me a cold brew. This time, I took it and we silently watched the leviathans climb out of the river and head uptown and then, after a few minutes, the line of those exiting back to whatever muddy depths they hid their numbers in.

"What if we use blood to attract them?" I asked as the beasts disappeared into the Hudson one by one.

"That will only attract those nearest to Times Square." His gaze never left the street.

"Not if it's dragon blood. You said they could smell that for miles."

Mikhail looked at me with a cocked eyebrow. "Haven't I already bled enough for the cause?"

I rolled my eyes at him. "Don't you have a couple more jars tucked away?" I thought I remembered at least one more tucked in the back of the cabinets on floor fifteen.

He bit his lower lip. "Those are my insurance policies."

"If we beat the serpent king, you won't need them."

He let out a laugh and turned away, heading toward the couch, where he flopped down. "You expect me to believe I won't be hunted like a rabid dog once the immediate threat has been taken out? After all, I am a dragon." He sent a glare at me, using my own words against me.

"We don't need it all. Just enough to bring the beasts running." His crutch leaned on the coffee table, blocking me from getting any closer, so I took a seat in the chair he usually occupied and stretched my legs out onto the ottoman.

He glanced back at me. "I still would prefer not to use that."

"But it would bring them all running, right?"

He crossed his arms over his chest. "Yes. But—"

"No buts. There is no other way to bring them all running."

"A scream would do just as well."

"I'm not setting someone up to be killed by a rabid pack of leviathans."

"I can tape you screaming."

"Smart ass." But his comment started the gears turning in my head.

He smiled at me and raised his beer in my direction.

"Why not use the combination of a scream and dragon blood?"

"I told you why. I'm not parting with the only thing that may mean my living or dying." He glanced at me. "Not with how fucking fickle the human race is."

"I'm part of that race, if you haven't forgotten," I replied. Heat raked over my skin with the burn of irritation.

"I have not forgotten."

The warning in his voice told me he was in that volatile space between loving me and hating me for my shitty choices. I guess I couldn't blame him for his lack of being a willing sacrifice to save the world. Especially with the encounters he'd had with humans since I crossed his path. But unlike Mikhail, I would give my life if that meant the human race survived.

Instead of hammering him with a plan for the bomb, I needed to refocus our energies into something productive. Arguing with Mikhail over anything was unproductive. We both dug our feet in and neither of us would back down, not in the heat of it. But given a little time and reflection, we might be able to meet in the middle. Of course, if the middle did not include dragon blood, I was going to be pissed.

"When were you planning on taking that trip to the library?"

"As soon as I stick the landing consistently. I can't misstep, and I have to be quick. Quicker than I currently am with this thing." He waved at the crutch. "And as soon as I catch a quick nap, I'm going downstairs to practice landing."

"When can we start doing the bleach runs?" I changed the subject again.

He glanced over at me. "When I can stick the landing."

"I can do this without you." I crossed my arms.

"We've had this conversation. I do not want you risking it alone. And I have to be able to land somewhere high enough to be inconspicuous. And that does not include a crash landing." He chewed on his lip. "Plus, I think I need to do the library run first because, if for some reason the shit hits the fan on the bleach runs, they will figure out that I'm in miniature form and that will screw with my chances to get across town to the library without some altercation."

I raised a challenging eyebrow.

"If the serpent king figures it out before we set our trap, I am a dead dragon. You think what they did before was bad? It is nothing compared to being torn to bits, and I promise you, it will not be quick. He's a spiteful bastard, and I will suffer greatly if he catches me."

Any argument I had lined up failed at the thought of him being harmed in that manner. If the leviathans or the serpent king figured out Mikhail wasn't a bird, we were fucked.

"Get some rest. I'm going to go work off some of this excess energy." I headed for the door.

"I'll be down in a while," Mikhail said as I opened the door. "So don't get yourself so exhausted that you can't help me up to the rafters."

"I'll try not to. Sweet dreams." I closed the door on his sleepy smile and headed downstairs to get my adrenaline pumping.

Dragon Dawn
Chapter 13

THE FIRST THING I did when I entered the gym was head to the punching bags, where I pounded the living shit out of them, releasing every ounce of pent-up frustration that I kept inside since that first test bomb went off.

"I'm not a weak human," I muttered under my breath with each punch. But compared to Mikhail, I would always be the weaker one. Even with his new disability. I might have the advantage of two legs, but he had the strength and the ability to withstand being tossed across a room by an explosion and not be the worse for wear.

I paused mid-punch. Even though he had been healing nicely, maybe I should have taken a look at his leg to be sure the explosions hadn't ripped anything open. I debated on running back up to check on him but refrained. He hadn't been pale at all. He just looked tired, which wasn't a far stretch considering he used a lot of brain power along with brute strength to figure out our bomb ratios and what we would need to wipe out the entire leviathan army here in New York City.

I peeled off the gloves and crossed to the treadmill. Running would take my mind off Mikhail and ailments that were probably just a figment of my active paranoia. I focused on making my steps as light as I could possibly make them while still keeping up a good pace. Unfortunately, they still were not silent. If I ran like this across the pavement, my steps would echo in the empty streets and bring on the death machines.

Moving fast was not an option when being quiet was of the utmost importance. I turned up the speed on the treadmill to a fast run, resigned to never being as stealthy as Mikhail. My endurance needed work, and I sprinted until I thought I'd either pass out or throw up, making me regret having my sandwich earlier.

I dialed down the pace, cooling off. Sweat rolled off me and my hair lay in tacky strands on my cheek and neck, saturated. While we had run in the tunnels, it had been cool enough to keep me from sweating profusely like I was now.

It was almost embarrassing. I swiped at the wetness on my forehead, and kept walking, forcing my breathing to slow enough so I wasn't wheezing.

The door clicked open, and I glanced over my shoulder.

Mikhail crutched into the room and gave me a nod.

"You look a little pale," he said as he got closer to me. "Are you okay?" Concern flushed his face.

"I overdid it." I forced out the words. "Trying to cool down and not throw up." My breathlessness overtook my speech, and I flipped the treadmill off. I stepped onto the floor with legs that felt like those wavy balloon people I used to see at gas stations during the holidays. I walked around the perimeter of the room, still struggling with that sandwich.

"Did you have any water?" he asked, trying to keep pace with me.

"No."

He pointed at the water cooler by the door. "Drink."

I let out a high-pitched laugh. Anything that went down would come up just as fast. I needed to win the mental game before I could deal with the physical effects, and he was not helping me right now.

"Go work out." I concentrated on my footsteps and breathing long, slow, deep breaths until my chest eased up. My stomach would follow, but not if he was hammering me like a fucking mother hen.

He stopped following me. "A little water—"

"Zzzt." I hissed at him and snapped my index finger and thumb together in the universal "zip it" signal. I would grab water when I was good and ready. But right now, I just needed to keep up this slow pace and concentrate on breathing.

He left me to deal with my situation and started his exercise routine with the leg press.

It took me a good ten minutes of walking to cool down enough that I thought I could stomach some water. Mikhail had those water dispensers with the upside-down five-gallon tanks on top and the little cone-shaped cups on the side. I pulled one out and filled it with cool water.

The first sip hit like a bomb, and I closed my eyes, willing the churning to settle. I took another sip, hoping it would soothe the raging seas of my stomach. It took nearly a half hour to finish that cup and thankfully I was able to keep it all down. But now all I wanted to do was drop to my knees and put my mouth under the spigot and let the water flow down my gullet until this crazy thirst evaporated.

Instead, I took another full cup and chugged it.

Mikhail started to chuckle as I reached for the third cup. "You've entered the thirst zone, I see."

I sent a nod his way while I took the third cup in nearly one long gulp.

"Just go easy. That sour stomach can backlash if you have too much." He did another rep on the leg press.

I crossed to him with the fourth cup, but I heeded his advice. I sipped this one as my body rewarded me with a small stomach roll before it settled into grateful quiet.

Mikhail slowly released the press, curling up again as he blew out another breath. He turned to me with a sweaty brow. "You about ready to help me up to the rafters?"

I glanced at the ladder and then at him. "Did you want to try to fly up there and try to grip the girder?"

"Not particularly."

"Well, what if you have to launch from the ground outside the library?" I wasn't convinced he would be able to get to the roof.

He crossed his arms and challenged me with a sour look.

"Just humor me so I have a little peace of mind that if you had to, you would be able to." I reached out the water as a possible bribe to get him to try for me.

He reacted like I would have: a single eyebrow slant that basically screamed, *What the hell are you babbling on about?* But after a moment, he swung his leg out and hopped off the machine.

"Finish that up so you can catch me if I miss the rafter." Without waiting for an answer, he shifted into the miniature dragon and waved me back. Spreading his wings, he bent his standing leg and then launched himself into the air. Although he started at a few inches from the ground, the pounding of his wings quickly gave him the height. Soon he was skimming the ceiling and weaving in and out of the rafters.

I positioned myself a few paces back from the center of the rafter as he made another pass around the room. When he approached the rafter, he stuck his talon-like foot forward. As he reached it, his foot grabbed onto the metal. But just like before when he tried to land, he tumbled forward and landed on my chest, knocking me onto my back.

Dazed, I looked at him with his wings all spread out over me and his face between my breasts. He picked up his head and met my gaze, but there was not an ounce of apology in his eyes. In fact, I would say his dragon form was holding in a laugh.

"Get off me." I threw him to the side, and he transitioned, pulling me on top of him with a grin I wanted to wipe off his face.

"Did I prove I can take off from a standstill?" he asked, still gripping me tight against his chest.

"You just proved how much of an asshole you are," I shot back and tried to wiggle out from his arms.

He just clamped down tighter. "I think I proved that part just fine. And I proved I can land wherever I want. It just isn't as pretty or graceful as I'd like." His dimples appeared. "I quite like soft landings." He glanced down at my breasts that were crushed between us.

I let out a scream of frustration and tried to push myself up, but I was too tired to fight his hold. So, I collapsed on top of him instead. Letting every muscle go into relaxation mode and becoming a virtual rag doll.

He let out a soft chuckle and moved my hair out of my face. "Giving up so easily?"

I looked up at him with my best cross expression. I was not pleased to have a dragon at any size plow into my breasts. "I take issue with using my girls as a landing strip."

Mikhail threw his head back and let out a guffaw that echoed on the rafters. "Duly noted." His hands moved to cup the sides of said body part. "Do I need to kiss them and make them better?" He batted his fucking eyelashes at me.

"Fuck you, Mikhail!" I took the opportunity and pushed myself to my feet before he could ensnare me again.

He still smiled from his position on the floor. "That can be arranged, too."

"Oh my God!" I threw my hands up in the air and headed for the door. I needed a shower and a drink before I started practicing with my bow. Maybe I'd paste a bull's-eye on his ass and use that for my target.

Dragon Dawn
Chapter 14

MIKHAIL STEPPED INTO THE bathroom after I had been there long enough to create a thick, hot steam.

"Are you really angry with me?" he asked as he popped his head inside the shower entrance.

I opened my eyes, taking in the sincere worry etched into his face, making his lips almost pouty.

I tried to suppress my smile, but I didn't do a very good job of it. "No, Mik. I'm not angry. But I was serious. Using these as a landing strip does not get you any sort of warm and fuzzy reaction." I held my breasts in my palms to make my point.

"But they provide such a soft landing." He crutched the rest of the way into the shower. "And I needed some sort of a release." He came close enough to crowd me.

Mikhail reached over my head and pressed a button on the back wall. The stream of water switched from the showerhead to rain down on us from the ceiling.

This was new. *Why hadn't he shown me this bliss before?* I glanced at Mikhail.

He grabbed my face and planted a kiss that was as hot as the steam filling the bathroom. Then he picked me up and pressed me against the back wall. His entire form leaned into me, and I wrapped my legs around his waist.

There was no foreplay this time. Just the sudden thrust of his hips once we lined up perfectly. I gasped under his lips and he smiled, but didn't stop the soul-searing kiss.

And I did not want him to stop. Not the kiss, not the fucking, not the teasing. If he had continued with the overbearing protector routine, we would not be having hot shower sex like this.

Mikhail pulled away from my lips and stared into my eyes. Water drizzled down onto him, sliding over his skin as his eyes flashed blue for a moment before sliding back into the citrine. One hand braced the wall and the other held my ass as he pumped hard and fast. His lips remained parted, as if he wasn't sure whether he was going to kiss me again or not.

Either way, a dragon captured by passion was the most beautiful thing on this earth. I could get so damn used to this view.

I thrust with him, holding onto his shoulders as I arched into him. I crossed my ankles behind him, riding him as hard as he was riding me.

"Holly, I've got to..." He grabbed my hips, trying to stop, but my grip around his waist was solid, and I was almost there. Almost to the plateau I craved. "Fuck, Holly," he said with a growl.

I tilted my head back and pushed into him with all I had as my orgasm ripped a groan from my lips. He pumped through it and then when I relaxed, he pulled out, shooting semen all over my legs with that growling groan of his that made my day.

He leaned his forehead against mine as his hands planted on the wall behind me, and he shifted his leg a little to get more centered. "That was too close," he whispered and pulled away. "You cannot do that to me."

I looked up at him with a satiated grin. "Apparently, I can." I bopped his nose and reached down to grab the crutch that had fallen on the floor, handing it to him as I stepped out from under the tent of his arms.

I ran the soap over myself once more under the rainwater and then rinsed before I stepped out, leaving Mikhail to clean himself up. He proved he was more than capable of taking care of himself today. He didn't need me doting on him either.

I dried, dressed, and twirled my hair into a bun before I headed into the living room to start my evening practice. The after-sex euphoria faded. The more I thought about how close he came to coming inside me, the more I realized I truly must have a death wish. I was not as scared of that happening as I should be.

With my luck, I'd get pregnant the first time that mistake happened. I held the bow and arrow in my hand as I stared at the ground, berating myself for my stupidity. I was so concerned about my climax that I didn't even consider how close he already was to his.

"Why such the somber look?" Mikhail asked when he stepped in the room.

"I'm sorry about that." I nodded toward the bedroom. "You just totally swept me away."

Dimples appeared and he nodded. "I was nearly in the same boat." He cleared his throat and made his way into the kitchen. "We really, really need to be more careful."

"You mean me."

"No. I mean both of us. It is so easy to get lost in each other." He closed his eyes. "It's so damn easy to get lost in the feeling of you that I have to be much more aware of my...reactions."

"What if I did get pregnant? You have the facilities downstairs to do a C-section earlier than the normal gestation."

He pressed his lips together, but the way his gaze met the floor and studied it meant he had never thought of that as a solution. But then his head started a slow shake back and forth. "I have the facilities, but I do not have the skills." His eyes narrowed at me. "It's not a feasible solution, Holly. There are too many risks. Besides, I don't have neonatal facilities here."

I stared at him and cocked my head. "That could be remedied." I gave him a shrug.

"Where is this coming from?"

"It just occurred to me that before everything went to shit, women scheduled cesareans when needed." I met his gaze. "If we stop all this, it's something to consider."

"No. It's not. It will be years before we can rebuild the hospitals, and that's assuming there are medical professionals still alive." He grabbed the fry pan and slammed it on the stove before taking a deep breath. "It's too great a risk," he said softly.

I wasn't so sure about the risk. Especially when it meant the dragon bloodline would not end with him. But I let it go and concentrated on the bull's-eye across the room, raising the Nerf arrow and letting it fly.

I ignored the clanging in the kitchen and continued shooting arrows. Today I was able to get fifteen shots without my arms turning to jelly. And they all were clustered in the center of the bull's-eye.

"You are pretty good with that." He pushed two plates of burgers and salad across the counter.

I dropped the bow on the coffee table and approached the counter as Mikhail crutched around to join me.

"I think in another day or two, I'll be ready to make that library run." He picked up his burger and nearly devoured it in one bite.

My stomach clenched at his words. Him crossing the city scared me more than getting pregnant with a dragon's child. I stared at the food as that fear bloomed in my blood. I swallowed it and tried to smile as I reached for the meal he had cooked me.

"The thought of you going out there, unprotected, scares the hunger right out of me." I nibbled on the patty and that seemed to kickstart my stomach. I took a bigger bite, resigned to being a basket case until he arrived back home. "What happens if..." I could not finish the sentence.

He finished his last bite and turned toward me. "I can't fail. If I do, it means you need to figure out a way to use the diagrams to at least take out as many of those fuckers as you can. And if they try to flush you out by using my broken and beaten body as bait, you ignore it. I'm dead anyway. That is a foregone conclusion, so you just lay low until you can destroy them. You understand?" His eyes blazed as he spoke. "Before I go, I'll give you the access codes to every floor in this building, so you have exactly what you need to build the bombs I designed."

"I won't have your fire to manipulate metal."

He closed his eyes and pressed his lips together. "Then you find a soldering kit out there." He pointed at the windows. "You have the skill and the mind to do this, just as I do." He glanced at the arrows still stuck to the bull's-eye. "You don't need my fire to decimate their army."

"There are only so many bullets and arrows left." I took a deep breath. "If you die, we will all die."

"Then go out with a fucking bang." He grabbed his crutch and his plate, and moved around to do the dishes, as if just sitting there doing nothing was contributing to humans' extinction.

With all the bleach and C-4 at my disposal, I could go out with a hell of a bang.

Dragon Dawn
Chapter 15

THE FOLLOWING DAY AND a half were strained between us as my anxiety peaked. Mikhail launched from the floor easily and was now sticking the landings every time, whether it was on the rafter, the floor, or the boxing ring. Each time he landed perfectly, it felt like a knife was shoved into my abdomen.

My endurance seemed to be growing at a snail's pace in comparison to his, and I was still stuck at fifteen arrows before fatigue hit and my muscles protested.

"Fifteen accurate shots is nothing to scoff at." Mikhail handed me a plate of eggs over easy, bacon, and toast.

"You took, what, three days to get enough strength in your leg to be able to land almost anywhere without it being a crash landing?" I picked up the bacon and took a bite, savoring the flavor.

"I'm a dragon. It's not a fair comparison. Besides, we have not attempted the same landings with a crutch strapped to my back. We need to do that for both the launch and the landing to make sure I don't have any issues with the weight of it and my small frame."

"That won't slow you down at all," I said. As much as it stressed me, we needed something to help us figure out how to kill the serpent king. And the New York Library had enough mythology books to warrant an entire section and some, if I recalled correctly, were quite old. "The bag we tie to it might give you some drag, though."

He nodded. "We'll have to get creative with how we tie that to the crutch, because a bag billowing behind me would be noisy enough to warrant exploration."

"Won't carrying it back be the same?"

"Maybe not. It's cloth, and I'll have it around my neck, so it could look like something in the bird's mouth. Besides, I'm only traveling at night and I'm not bringing the crutch back. I don't necessarily need to stick the landing on the roof here, either."

"How long do you think it will take?"

"Well, it took us the better part of the day to go through what I had online and that wasn't a huge array of things to dig through."

"Basically, when should I start freaking out?" I needed to know when I should take action. Just slumming in the building was not going to keep my mind off him and his situation until he was back in the building safely.

He sighed. "You shouldn't unless they drag me through the streets. It could take me a few days, maybe even upward of a week to find the right information and then, depending on the number of books I need to transport back, it might mean making my form bigger, which would mean making sure there is no chance of being seen."

"So, I just wait." I finished my meal, but it did not quell the uneasiness filling me.

"Yes. And you promise me not to do anything stupid, like venture out to get the bleach, or if more time than you think is reasonable has passed, coming to try to find me." He pointed at me and cocked his head. His eyebrows rose, waiting for me to respond.

I just stared at him, unwilling to agree to those terms.

"Promise me, Holly." His gaze turned to a glare the longer I took to concede.

"Fine. I promise!" I threw my hands up in the air and stood. It was my turn to clean up the kitchen and bang pots around to release this frustration building inside me. But by the time I had the pans scrubbed and the plates rinsed and put in the dishwasher, my insides felt as if someone had scrambled them.

Mikhail sat still in the chair, watching me as he chewed on his bottom lip. "You're not going to break my trust again, are you?"

I halted and slowly turned toward him. I thought we had moved past my deception, but the hesitation in his eyes told me otherwise. It burned deep down but I understood his doubt. I crossed back to my seat and took his hands, swiveling the chair so he fully faced me. Against every fiber of my being, I met his gaze and said, "I promise I will not leave this building until you come back."

Relief swept through the tense muscles in his face, but his eyes still had doubt clouding them. He pulled me in for a soft kiss, and then sighed and kissed my forehead before he released me. "Thank you for that," he whispered. "If you get bored, you can always check out my stash."

The forbidden dragon stash. The appeal of sneaking through Mikhail's trophies and whatever his dragon heart collected gave me a warm feeling all over. "I thought you weren't ready to have me milling about in your private things?"

"I'm not." He gave me a halfhearted shrug. "But you deserve to know what's in this building and not just those areas that I'm comfortable with you exploring. I need to let you see everything, including the areas no one but me has ever stepped into."

"Not even your wife?"

He shook his head. "Not even my wife."

I leaned back in the seat as my nerve endings buzzed with the ramifications. I licked my lips. "Why not?"

That sardonic smile of his appeared briefly and then he glanced toward the windows, avoiding eye contact. "Let's just say she might have taken issue with some of the things I collect."

"Mikhail, what do you collect?" Cold pressed down on my shoulders.

He raised an eyebrow. "If I told you, where would the fun be in that?"

"What floor is it on?" I pushed for more information. Otherwise, I would go batty until he gave me all the access codes to every nook and cranny of this damn building.

"I need to go try to fly and land with this on my back." He held the crutch up so I could see it.

"Damn it, Mikhail." I stomped my foot on the ground, trying to make my point all the more serious, but all it ended up doing was getting a chuckle from Mikhail before he left me stewing in the apartment.

Dragon Dawn
Chapter 16

I WAS RIGHT. MIKHAIL had no issue with taking off and landing with the crutch strapped to his back. Or in accessing the crutch once he shifted into human form. And he conveniently had foldable crutches in the storage space on the medical floor.

Which meant it was time for him to take this adventure on, whether I was ready for him to or not.

"What if the library is locked?" I asked as we climbed the stairs. "We should wait one more day," I added and put my hand on his arm as he pressed the code to unlock the door to the roof.

He stopped and took a heavy breath before he turned his annoyed citrine eyes my way. "One more day is not going to change things. This is still dangerous, and we both have to deal with it." He peeled my hand off his arm and turned off the lights in the stairwell before he opened the door on the breezy night.

I stepped out on the gravel with him and glanced around at the barren section of roof. The back half seemed to rise up another floor, but it was all reflective glass, like the rest of the building. My apprehension took a back seat to my curiosity.

His gaze followed mine. "Greenhouse," he whispered and adjusted the strap that held the foldable crutch with the tote tied securely between the two halves. "Both the greenhouse and the stairwell take the code to my apartment." He offered me a smile and stepped close, leaning down to give me a soft kiss. "Remember your promise." He handed me the crutch he used to get up the stairwell and then shifted.

I bit my lip as he launched into the air, and at the edge of the building, he disappeared into the night. I stared in the direction of the library as my eyes adjusted to the moonlight. I thought I caught view of him gliding over the buildings, but I couldn't be sure. He looked more like an eagle than a dragon, and my heart squeezed.

I hoped if the monsters below caught sight of him, they'd think he was one of the predator birds and not Mikhail. I retreated into the stairwell and made sure the door was closed tightly before I flipped the lights on and descended to the apartment.

On the coffee table were a couple of printed papers that had the entry codes for every floor and every locked cabinet and door on it, along with a short description of what they contained. My gaze went to the twenty-ninth floor and to the words next to it: My private stash.

I took a breath and sighed. If I hit that first, that would only entertain me for a few hours, depending upon what was so bad he couldn't show his wife. Nerves ate at my stomach, and I made a decision to bide my time while I waited for Mikhail. So, instead of going from the top down, and learning a secret about him that might change the way I viewed him, I chose to explore the building from the ground up.

I stared at the paper, plotting my plan to draw this out as much as I could. Thirty floors to explore and who knows how many days to do it in. I glanced at the living room. I knew where most of the things were, but tonight, until I finally fell into a knotted slumber, I was going to shuffle through his apartment first. And maybe rearrange things a little to be more to my liking.

It was also time to claim space as my own. Which I was sure would piss off Mikhail, but I needed to do something to erase this anxiety making my body perpetually have to move, to satiate it to a manageable level.

I started with his side of the closet, rearranging clothing according to type, formal to casual, and then within those categories by color. When I had successfully color-coded by fashion everything hanging on his side, I pulled down the boxes at the top of the closet and the footwear at the bottom. The footwear was easy. Mikhail had dress boots, regular boots, and work boots. He had a few pairs of loafers to go with the suits but for the most part, he was a boot man.

That gave me a new appreciation for his style.

The boxes were labeled summer and I opened the tops. A smile spread on my lips at the array of swimwear and tank tops shoved inside, reminding me of that picture on his wife's desk in the lab. I returned the box with his stuff back to the upper shelf and then closed his side of the closet. I went back to the other box and started pulling out bikinis and one-pieces that were not my style. Anything with a thong did not belong on me. But there were a few non-thong items that I tried on in the bathroom, moving this way and that as I criticized my reflection.

I kept everything I tried on and piled everything else in the to-go pile. One suit caught my eye: black with cut-outs on the sides. Even though it had more of a thong on the backside, I still tried it on, just because, and I wasn't disappointed. Plus, it was not as uncomfortable as I thought.

That gem landed in my keeper pile.

Next was her side of the closet. I stared at it for a while, debating. Mikhail had given me free rein to what clothes were here, so it was time to thin the hoard with those things that I would wear. However, I couldn't just discern by looking at something. I had to try on every last item to see if it jived with my complexion and whether it was comfortable or not.

Anything that scratched, itched, or was just plain not my thing went into the garbage stack. I kept quite a few of the dresses, despite my initial chuck-them-all reaction. The ones that felt like silk on my skin stayed. And the ones that I knew I could make Mikhail salivate by wearing stayed as well. Every pair of pants and jeans fit like they were meant for me, and now that my burns had healed, I could pull them on without issue.

Near the farthest wall from the opening, I found an array of velvet dresses, some long like the one he had given me to wear on our trek across the city and some knee-length and some short, but they all felt like a cloud. Those were keepers, too.

The pile of to-go items mostly gleamed with sequins and beads, which were totally not my style, even though some of them did look decent on me. The chiffon, silk, and velvet stayed, as did all the jeans and any T-shirt the woman had.

Her sweaters were hit or miss as well. Some were my style, but some I'd categorize in the ugly sweater group and those went into the crap pile as well.

The amount of clothing that was here was incredible considering this was not their full-time home. I couldn't fathom trying to clean those closets out if his home still existed.

The shoeboxes were next, and most of the high heels went in the throw-out stack. I found a pair of comfortable flats near the back and at least three pairs of high-heeled boots that fit, along with a pair with fur lining like the ones I left at my apartment. If we won this war, I'd have to have Mikhail take me to my place to get whatever hadn't been picked over so I'd have my comfortable underwear and leggings and all that I kept there.

I pulled down the last box, the one with all the fine lingerie inside. Sifting through this box felt like I was violating someone's privacy and after a moment, I replaced the top and put it back. Maybe at some point, I'd feel comfortable enough to trash the items that I would never be caught dead in, but right now, I figured I'd probably done enough to send Mikhail into a tirade.

I closed the closet and glanced out at the dark night, wondering whether Mikhail had gotten into the library without incident. My nerves lit again, creating a hot fire just under the surface, and I shifted. My gaze went to the bureau, and I bit my lip.

"Fuck it," I muttered to myself and started the process of cleaning out that piece of furniture in the same manner I had with the closet. This was where Mikhail kept his undergarments and his old T-shirts. Basically, drawers full of things that I would rather bum around in on a day-to-day basis. And it was neat, like clothing store bin before the doors open to the public neat.

The way things lined up in pristinely uniform piles made me have to squash the urge to mess up the drawers just to fuck with him. *I mean, who stacks underwear and socks that way?*

The thinner top drawers weren't as organized. The left drawer had jewelry and wristwatches.

The middle drawer was filled with loose change, which made me laugh. I had a change drawer at home, too, but it would probably be years before this type of currency was used again. The last drawer held a few belts.

Everything was so ordinary. So domesticated. And it reminded me of the past when everyone was just going through the daily motions, thinking they were truly living.

The nightstands were more of a hodgepodge of things, from batteries to candles to notepads and pens.

I yawned and glanced at my garbage pile, wondering whether Mikhail would even notice if I took it down to the incinerator. I guess we'd find out when he arrived back from his library adventure.

Dragon Dawn
Chapter 17

SLEEP HAD BEEN FILLED with too many nightmares, but thankfully I was able to get a few hours of solid rest after I finally removed the pile of to-go items in the bedroom. Once I dropped them into the incinerator, the anxiety of having that messing up the bedroom floor lifted, and sleep actually took hold.

Breakfast was a simple pair of eggs over easy with toast. Then I was ready to tackle the building. As I descended the stairs, the twenty-ninth floor called to me, but I resisted. I didn't want to encounter something that would alter my view of Mikhail. I stood before the door with the passcodes in my hand.

Biting my lip, I stared at the door, debating on screwing up the plan I had to start at the bottom and move upward. Instead of entering, I continued down to the first floor and the door to the right of the stairs in the lobby.

His list stated this was where office supplies used to be delivered. It also had a note not to turn on the lights. There was enough natural light filtering in during the day. That was the only area of the building that didn't have light filters on the interior windows.

I carried a small flashlight just in case it was dark, but I would shade it if I had to use it. The moment I opened the door, I realized carrying the flashlight was not necessary.

Metal shelving filled the room and boxes of reams of paper for printers covered many of the shelves toward the back. The closest two shelving units had all sorts of supplies, from staplers, to pens, to pads, to staples and staple removers. It looked like a mini office-supply store.

I closed the door and headed to the second floor, tagged on the list as office space. He had codes for the ten doors on this floor. Five on each side of the hallway. I inspected them all and found nothing out of the ordinary.

Floors three through seven were marked as apartments. The apartments on the third floor were marginally bigger than mine had been, but they were better equipped, with granite counters and stainless-steel appliances. Much like the countertops and appliances in Mikhail's penthouse. At least he was consistent in his choices of décor throughout the building.

It made me smile.

The fourth floor had a mix of one- and two-bedroom apartments that were marginally bigger than the third floor. As I went up, the apartments got bigger, transitioning the one-bedroom apartments to two- and even three-bedroom apartments. The seventh floor had the nicest layouts, but they were still smaller than the total space of the penthouse.

Floor eight through fourteen were labs, but eleven was the only floor with the steel rooms. Rooms Mikhail had said were built so his children could let out their pent-up frustrations.

Which meant whatever work his laboratories had been used for, the lack of any testing facilities beyond the steel rooms told me that they were not in the business of testing explosives.

I leafed through a few sets of papers on desks as I passed through each room. Most of them read like a Russian textbook to an American with zero language skills. I couldn't decipher what I was reading. It was either too scientific, or the math on the paper was far too sophisticated.

After wandering uselessly around the labs, I escaped into the fifteenth floor. Memories of death accosted me, and I turned on every last light in the place. Even with the overhead light shining away every possible shadow, this floor still haunted me. Thankfully, Mikhail had taken the chains down and piled them in the corner the night we scrubbed this place down. Otherwise, I wouldn't be able to set foot on this floor.

Even now, my feet did not want to move from in front of the door. I had been through all the cabinets before as we had emptied the backpacks and found where Troy had stowed the last few vials of antibiotics, returning all the medical items he had lifted.

I let out a strangled laugh. "This is ridiculous!" I shook my hands and my head, ridding myself of this anxiety, and headed to the entry to the kitchen area. I still hadn't explored that area, even with Mikhail with me. Besides, I had already searched through half the building and my stomach was making ungodly noises.

The kitchen was like a fully equipped gourmet restaurant, with different prep and cooking stations. Three large metal doors graced the back wall. I started with the far one. Dry goods and jarred goods covered the shelves. Varieties of pasta, rice, and various jarred sauces covered most of the shelving, along with what looked like unopened jams and peanut butters. I picked up a jar and looked at the expiration date. A sigh followed and I replaced the jar. It was over two years past the date printed on the canister.

The next was a refrigerator unit. Inside was barren. Nothing graced the shelves but there was a lingering sour milk smell that had me exiting just as quickly as I entered. Although the refrigerated unit was empty, the last door revealed a packed freezer. As I scanned the shelves, my eyes landed on a section of shrink-wrapped packages of unopened peppermint stick ice cream. I should have had something more reasonable, like one of the burger patties or hot dogs from one of the tightly sealed packages that did not look like freezer burn had eaten it, but I reached for that sweet, creamy option instead.

I closed the freezer, found a sharp knife in a drawer, and cut open the wrapper, peeled the top off and undid the vacuum-packed top. It took me a few moments to find a spoon but when I did, I sat on the floor and took my first spoonful.

Creamy peppermint burst in my mouth, and I moaned at the exquisite taste as the coolness coated my tongue. The fact it still held its creamy consistency amazed me. I glanced at the sell-by date and shrugged at the long-passed date. This baby had not lost an ounce of its original consistency.

I enjoyed the entire tub of ice cream in silence, savoring every single bite. It was as good as anything I had eaten while in this building. Truthfully, I nearly hit nirvana. When I finished, I cleaned the spoon, and dropped the container and the wrapper down the incinerator shaft.

With a massive dose of sugar infused in my body, I was more than ready to check out the other floors of the building. In my mind, I'd quit at the surgical floor and head back upstairs for some target practice and then sleep before I checked out the other floors.

Floor sixteen started out interesting. The entry was similar to the surgical unit, but there were hazmat suits hanging on hooks and the doors would not open without putting on a full suit. Once I did that, the scanner allowed me inside. Another lab sat before me, but this one had a wall of vials with different colored liquids. And each cabinet had its own keypad.

Mikhail's warning of not touching anything in the labs when we arrived echoed in my head. I turned and left without any more inspection. Chemicals scared me enough not to mess with them, and having to put on a hazmat suit did not instill calmness. Once back inside the air lock, I stripped and hung the suit back up next to the others. I made a mental note to ask Mikhail what exactly that lab had been doing before the world went to shit.

With unease crawling on my skin like an army of biting red ants, I headed to the seventeenth floor. I didn't even look at the tag next to the floor number. I just punched in the code, stepped inside, and flipped on the light, thinking this might be another unpleasant surprise.

A surprise, yes, but not unpleasant. Four comfortable, low-backed chairs sat in what looked like a mini-lobby. A reception desk sat a few feet away, with the word *spa* scrawled in script on the wall. Hallways led away from the lobby on both sides of the desk. Soothing paintings hung on the wall of calm ocean sunsets and beautiful waterfalls with lovely fall colors.

This was certainly unexpected, and I made my way down the hall, engaging every light switch I came upon. Mikhail had a dry sauna, a few private whirlpool tubs with jets, and several massage stations. There was even a pedicure chair. The back wall had an array of oils, diffusers, candles, scented soaps, and a few nail polish colors on a small shelving unit.

I crossed to the oil blends and took a sniff of a few of them, finding one that was soothing, with tones of citrus. I pocketed one of those and then made my way back out. Glancing at the list, I was through for the day. The floor above this was the gym and if I really got curious as to what was included in the medical supply floor, I'd check it out in the morning, and I already was more than familiar with the surgical floor. That was the one I wished like hell I hadn't been introduced to, but I had no choice in the matter.

I saved the floors tagged as entertainment and food for tomorrow. Along with his private stash. As I climbed the stairs to the penthouse, I glanced at the twenty-ninth floor, slowing as I stared at the numbers. My sugar rush was fizzling out, and I needed a little bit of shut-eye before I discovered Mikhail's deep and dark-enough-not-to-tell-his-wife secret.

Dragon Dawn
Chapter 18

WHEN I OPENED THE penthouse door, it was dark. I hadn't turned on any lights when I left earlier, and the night sky greeted me. I turned out the stairwell lights and crossed into the den to the window that faced the heart of the city. I scanned the sky, looking for any sign of Mikhail. Nothing but stars and moonlight graced the night.

I glanced up at the ceiling, wondering whether he had landed and had an issue getting down here. My heart fluttered, and I started for the door, stopping to lean on it as Mikhail's assurances echoed in my mind. He promised he could get to the penthouse without an issue. It was only one flight; if need be, he'd go down the stairs on his butt.

My hands shook with the sugar crash bleeding me of strength. I needed to take advantage of the sudden wave of exhaustion. If I waited too long, I'd be staring at the ceiling all night.

I grabbed a water on the way to the bedroom and then brushed my teeth. With a great yawn, I stripped out of my clothes and climbed under the silky sheets. Sleep came with a vengeance.

LIGHT BLINDED ME, AND I rolled away from it, covering my head with the blanket. Awareness filtered in and I sat up, throwing the blankets away, thinking maybe Mikhail was back. Disappointment raked through me as I squinted at the sun blazing through the window. I glanced at the side of the bed just in case, but it was still as empty as it had been when I fell asleep.

I took a deep breath. It was now more than twenty-four hours since he flew off the roof in search of information. I bit my lip and threw myself back on the pillow. Worry wormed its way into my head despite knowing there wasn't a thing I could do until he either came back or they dragged his broken body through the streets.

With a deep breath, I forced myself out of the bed and straightened it neatly, so it looked like no one had slept there. Something about making the bed in the morning satisfied me. It made me feel like if I accomplished nothing else, at least I had straightened up my bedroom.

With a nod, I headed to the bathroom to clean off the cobwebs still lingering in my mind and hopefully keep the worry at bay. Unfortunately, it only proved to allow my mind to wander to worst-case scenarios, leaving me feeling clean but hollow without Mikhail here.

I stood at the mirror, running a brush through my hair. *Maybe if I made an effort to look good, Mikhail would end up coming back today.* My eyebrow rose at my reflection, and I opened the cabinet under the sink. Sitting in a bin toward the back was a blow-dryer, and I pulled it out. For the first time in years, I styled my hair. The process felt both awkward and soothing as the heat stripped my locks of dampness and tamed it into a smooth crown of hair.

I chuckled as I put the dryer back where I found it and then hand-combed the stray hairs back in place. I had forgotten how much I liked the soft waves of my hair when I dried it that way. With a sigh, I went to the closet and opted for jeans and a nice aqua-colored T-shirt. I pulled on a pair of Mikhail's socks, which were about three sizes too big, and then put the worn pair of his wife's flat boots on.

Do I eat or do I do some target practice since I bailed on that last night?

My stomach made the choice for me, and I sauntered out of the bedroom and into the kitchen to make me some eggs to start my day.

Although my mind jumped to the shelves on fifteen with the ice cream.

"Later," I said softly as I put two pieces of bread in the toaster. "You can reward yourself after we go through the rest of the floors." I flipped the eggs in the pan and chuckled to myself when I realized I had been speaking out loud.

"Oh, Mikhail, if something happens to you, I'll become batshit crazy in no time."

The eggs slid onto the plate and the toaster popped up at the same moment. I smiled at my timing. I hated waiting for one or the other, so having them both come out in unison pleased the hell out of me.

I came around to the counter and climbed up on the chair, pulling both the plate in front of me as well as the paper with the codes. Entertainment, food, and his stash. My foot tapped on the chair rail as I debated how to tackle the rest.

I took out a pen and scribbled the only question from yesterday that still bothered me. *What sort of things were you experimenting with to have a secure lab like that?*

I put the pen down and finished my breakfast. I had the rest of the day to kill because Mikhail wouldn't make the trip back during daylight hours. That much we had agreed upon.

I cleaned up the kitchen with my mind still swarming on what to tackle first. It continued to oscillate while I did target practice. Today, I successfully hit thirty bull's-eyes before my arms felt like jelly.

Satisfied, I collected my Nerf arrows and put them away, along with the bow, leaving the place just as neat as it had been when I awoke. I picked up the list and headed out.

"Food first, entertainment next, and then maybe I'll get the nerve to wander through Mikhail's stash," I said as I passed the twenty-ninth floor. The numbers mocked me in a way that almost had me diverting my plans of working my way down and leaving that for last.

I stopped at the twenty-eighth floor, punched in the code, and stepped inside. There was a tiny lobby area probably as big as the entry in the surgical floor or the lab, and before me stood a wide metal door that reminded me of a freezer door. I unlatched it and pulled it open wide.

Frigid air rolled over me. I shivered, waving away the white mist that flowed out into the entranceway. I set the stop on the door because I could see it closing on me, and me freezing to death inside before Mikhail found me.

Inside hung at least a thousand cleaned and shrink-wrapped carcasses. From cattle, to deer, to pigs, and lambs. Near the back sat a gleaming stainless-steel counter and all manner of cutlery used to pare down the meat to serving portions. I inspected some of the hanging meat and nothing looked like it had any freezer burn. Impressed was an understatement.

I made sure the doorstop was folded back up and the door latched tight before I left the twenty-eighth floor. The twenty-seventh floor amused me from the moment I stepped inside. Beyond the small, gated entrance surrounding the door was a field of what looked like wild grass, and more unbelievably, live chickens milled about. The edges of the walls held henhouses and every so often, sifters from the ceiling opened to scatter seed in different parts of the floor.

I nearly laughed at the thought of what it took to grow grass inside a building. The sheer amount of soil and sod that would have been needed to cultivate this. Just as I wondered how it could continue growing without sunlight, overhead sunlamps switched on, giving the grass what it needed to grow. Mikhail had enough chickens and eggs to never need anything else. Instead of stepping inside the fence, I headed out, laughing under my breath.

The twenty-sixth floor was another freezer floor, but this time, this seemed to be more freeze-dried items, like milk and those old rolls of frozen juices, with everything shrink-wrapped for longer shelf times. Milk, juices, single-serving meals of lasagna, beef stroganoff, and things of that sort that normally would have gone bad if they had been refrigerated. There were also freeze-dried fruits like strawberries and blueberries, and my mouth watered at the sight.

The last food storage was filled with dry goods and MREs. Pasta, dried potato mixes, noodle mixes, some canned goods, but not many graced these shelves. I suspected, based on what I saw, that we could last indefinitely in this building if we had to, and I glanced at the ceiling, wondering what he had in that greenhouse on the roof. Eventually, I'd check that out, too.

I decided to do the rest of the floors from the lowest to highest and headed to the twenty-first floor. Imagine my surprise when I opened the door on a bowling alley, of all things. There were five lanes, seating and scoring pads for each, and a wall full of shoes and balls. A soda machine that had long since been emptied sat against the wall to my right, and restrooms for men and women lined the wall behind the soda machines. Beyond the restrooms sat at least a dozen old-school pinball machines.

The outside windows were blocked with different art pieces and very little natural light bled into this floor. On the wall behind where the door opened were the controls. I was tempted to turn a lane on and try my hand. I had never bowled in my life. But before I could, an old circular iron stairwell in the corner caught my eye.

I crossed and climbed up it, engaging the light switches on the wall at the top of the stairs. This time I did laugh out loud. At least a dozen pool tables littered the floor, and on the outer edges of the room sat a couple of poker tables with chips and packaged card decks sitting on the leather fabric. On a few of the walls were dartboards and finely polished cabinets holding the darts and cues.

Damn. I glanced around, blinking as a memory surfaced. In the days of television news, I recalled a story on one of the perks of working for the St. Clare foundation. In most of their buildings, there often were game rooms, billiards, theaters, and other places where the employees could let off steam, and the employees even had competitive leagues after work hours. I laughed out loud. Had I been old enough at the time, I would have marched down to the nearest office and applied for a job.

I still had two more floors before I got to his private stash, and I scurried out the door, turning the lights off as I went. When I walked into the dark seating area on the twenty-third floor, I had an inkling of what this actually was based on the memory. And I was not disappointed when I turned on the lights to a mahogany-walled theater with a screen that must have been nearly two stories high and nearly the length of the building. Speakers lined the walls and three tiered rows of the most comfortable lounge chairs faced the screen.

I took a seat and pushed back, feeling the wide leather seat hug my backside. I sighed and closed my eyes, trying to recall the last movie I actually watched in a theater. I had to have been about sixteen, and I believe it was one of those Marvel adventure movies that I loved.

I stood and looked at the back wall. One of those old-fashioned popcorn machines sat in the corner under an overhang, empty and shining as if it had been new. A counter stocked with candy sat open to the floor as well, and I crossed, picking up a package of Twizzlers. They were as hard as a rock, and I dropped them back into place as I gave the theater another glance.

I glanced up at the lower ceiling in this section of the theater. I bet the control rooms were upstairs. There wasn't a clear way to get up there from where I stood, so I exited the theater, turning off the lights before heading upstairs.

The twenty-fourth floor consisted of a small landing, a projector room that was lined with

DVDs and Blu-rays and a large multi-disk player that could run either format. I flipped on the power and the screen came to life with a movie that had already been in the player. I stared at the screen for a few minutes as credits rolled, before I shut it off.

A door sat in the corner, and I opened it to a darkened stairwell that led down. I flipped on the light and descended to the landing and then down another short set of stairs. The door opened to the theater right behind the third row of seats. I looked at the outer part of the door and caught an indented latch that I hadn't seen when I was in the theater. Basically, the door was hidden unless you knew where it was.

Genius.

I headed back up, shutting off lights as I went. I'd have to come back and watch something if Mikhail wasn't back tonight. Between the gym and the entertainment rooms, I'd actually have something to keep me busy without just pacing the penthouse, waiting to see whether he survived his dangerous endeavor.

I climbed past the food storage floors and stood in front of the last door. The one that held Mikhail's secrets. Biting my lower lip, I glanced at the code again. This one did have a different entry key from the majority of the rest of the floors. I touched the door as if a fire burned on the other side, but only cool metal stroked my palm.

I snarled at my own hesitation, hating this world of doubt swirling in my blood that made my heart beat faster and my palms sweat. I shook my hand and then punched in the code before I chickened out.

Without pausing, I threw the door open and reached for the bank of light switches. I stepped inside, closing the door behind me as the banks lit up row after row of stuff. Smaug had nothing on Mikhail, except it wasn't just jewelry. Mikhail had the walls covered in art. I ignored the piles of stuff throughout the room and just walked the perimeter, staring at the paintings. Picasso, Monet, Dali, Munch, Pollock, Matisse, Michelangelo, da Vinci, Van Gogh, Warhol, and so many others. The little tags on each had the year and artist next to it. Some even had handwritten notes to Mikhail alongside the paintings, framed in glass to preserve them. He had a few silk murals encased in glass, and I stared at the date next to the small oriental and blinked. This one was painted before Christ.

My stomach tightened at the reality of how old Mikhail really was. This art should be in a museum. They were lost pieces that no one had ever been privy to. I was sure I was looking at what amounted to billions of dollars' worth of fine art.

I wondered whether this was what he kept from his wife. She was notoriously outspoken about those that hid things that should be shared with the world. This certainly would qualify. I didn't have the same hang-up. I believed in preserving history as best we could, even if that meant private collections. Especially with how greedy people had turned out.

I turned my focus to the various piles stationed around the room. Silver, gold, and gemstones made the outer perimeter of piles. Paths through them seemed more mazelike than organized, but the minute I got to the inside, my eyes widened. Mikhail had a large collection of swords. Racks of them, from ancient iron, to katanas, to those of the Middle Ages, to modern-day military swords. It was an impressive collection, but none of them were as balanced or efficient as the one he kept in his study. I tried them all and by the last one, my arm ached from the weight.

Inside the racks of swords was a metal room like the ones down in the lab, but this one wasn't quite as big as it did not go floor to ceiling. I looked at my sheet of paper. There was a second code written next to the word *safe*. I looked at this again as I walked around it, ascertaining this was the safe. I punched in the number; the door unclicked and slowly moved outward. It was at least two feet thick and inside, a light shined down on top-to-bottom shelves of explosives. C-4, TNT, grenades, land mines. I took a breath and smiled. This might be what he didn't want his wife to find, but even this did not sway the way I felt about the man. If anything, it increased it just a hair.

I closed the vault, without taking a closer look at the contents. I'd rather not inadvertently set something off and end up leveling what was left of downtown Manhattan.

I wandered around looking at the piles of jewels and precious metals before I left the floor of his stash. I made my way upstairs as his words echoed in my head. I chewed on my lip. In the penthouse, I picked up my bow to continue target practice, but I stalled.

"Oh. He's good," I said, realizing Mikhail had baited me with that little tidbit of his wife not allowed into his private stash because it would have upset her. That bastard knew exactly how to keep me from focusing on my worry for his well-being by dangling that imaginary carrot in front of me.

I shot my arrows with vengeance brewing in my blood. This time I hit the bull's-eye fifty times, fueled by my irritation of how accurate his ruse was in sidetracking me.

Dragon Dawn
Chapter 19

WITH NOTHING ELSE TO do but worry, I moved my attention to his study—the only room I hadn't really touched in my cleaning frenzy after Mikhail had left. I dusted and then rearranged the books in order of genre, author, and alphabetical. Reference books went on the bottom shelves.

Next, I went through the desk drawers, organizing. I didn't dare get rid of any of the knickknacks stowed in the drawers because I wasn't sure whether they had been gifts from his children. Although I was quick to dispose of his wife's clothing, this was a bit more personal.

Nightfall came as I finished the last drawer and with it came that gnawing sensation in my belly. I fixed a burger to quell the hunger pangs and then went back to the study to see whether there was a book that would captivate me and keep the worry at bay.

This was the third night. Close to thirty-six hours. That thought dragged the bite back to the surface, and I turned away from the bookshelf, knowing my concentration was shit right now. Instead, I took to pacing the length of the apartment instead.

Sleep wasn't going to come. Not with this nervous energy blooming in my belly despite my weary muscles. I had a plethora of entertainment options at my fingertips. I headed down to the entertainment floors and stepped inside the bowling alley. Throwing a ball at pins might prove to be fun, except both my arms were already sore from practicing with my bow and arrows, and I didn't want to aggravate them further.

I sucked at pool and that would only serve to frustrate me. Darts, although in my wheelhouse of fun things, didn't seem to entice me even as I walked through the space and inspected the fine tools he had in each cabinet. Mikhail spared no expense for his employees, and it was evident in the craftsmanship of the darts, the pool cues, and even the pool tables themselves.

I found myself in the projection room, staring at the array of movies lining the wall. I wasn't sure anything here could keep the tightness in my muscles from becoming painful, or the worry clouding my thoughts from festering any further, but I had to try.

I chose two movies and slid them into the slots, pressed continuous play when the system asked, and then paused. If I was going to watch movies, I needed a movie-worthy snack. My mind drifted down to the freezer on the fifteenth floor.

I smiled and exited the theater, taking the stairs two at a time down. On fifteen, I ran into the kitchen and grabbed another tub of ice cream. After unwrapping the quart, I grabbed a spoon and jogged back up to the projection room.

The machine blinked for me to press the start button, and I punched it with my index finger and headed down to the comfy leather seats with my ice cream.

The screen filled with the first movie. A comedy about a boss who propositioned her assistant so she wouldn't be deported. The second one I hadn't seen before but it was in the comedy section along with the first one I chose. I had heard the title, but had no idea what it was about beyond having a couple and a golden retriever on the cover. I hoped the second one was as good as the quotes on the cover, because I needed to be fully involved in the movie to kill time.

It was funny how a romantic comedy could lighten my heart. It had been so long since any form of visual entertainment existed, and society really needed it. At least, *I* really needed this type of immersive entertainment. I wondered whether any of the actors in the movie had survived the monsters.

I blinked and shook my head, refocusing on the movie. Anything outside of this was unwelcomed. I needed the suspension of reality. I took another spoonful of ice cream and closed down the whispers of worry trying to grab my attention.

With the ice cream carton long empty and my stomach hurting from laughter, the first movie transitioned to the next one.

Marley & Me flashed onto the screen, along with the actors' names before the opening credits transitioned into the movie itself. I never laughed so hard as I did for the first half of the movie. But then it turned serious and heavy, and near the end, the tears just wouldn't stop.

Hands descended on my shoulder, and I let out a yelp, swiveling in my seat. Mikhail smiled down at my tear-stained face, as if I were the most beautiful thing this world had to offer.

I turned back to the screen, sniffling and wiping my tears away. "They should have a warning on the movie case." I waved at the screen and then looked back at him.

He didn't speak, and his gaze was on the screen as well. His eyes teared up too as the final scene played out.

When the credits started, I stood, and picked up the empty ice cream carton that I put on the floor. "Did you find what we need?"

"I think so." Mikhail cocked an eyebrow at the ice cream container.

"Don't give me that look. I haven't had ice cream in years, and this happens to be one of my favorites."

He grinned. "Something else to argue over," he said. "It's my favorite, too. Thus, the collection of containers in the freezer."

"Why on fifteen and not in the upper-level food storage?"

His cheeks turned rosy. "I was hiding them from my wife."

I burst out laughing as the screen went white. I held the door for Mikhail, and he pushed a button on the control panel next to the door. The room went dark again.

In the light of the hallway, I got a better look at Mikhail. Dark circles encased his eyes, and he moved slower than usual, as if his entire body was operating on empty.

"Have you eaten?" I asked when we neared the penthouse.

He nodded. "That was the first thing I did before I went in search of you."

"How long have you been back?"

He looked at his watch. "Not quite an hour." He glanced at me. "I did have a moment, though." He opened the door to the penthouse. "But then I saw the full quiver of arrows still sitting here. You wouldn't have tried for the bleach without them." He nodded to the corner where my bow and the real arrows sat.

"I promised I wouldn't leave the building." I closed the door as all the sentimentality of the movie vanished, replaced by hot irritation.

He shrugged. "I'm still hesitant to trust you fully."

"Yet you gave me the code to your stash." I leveled a glare. "And baited me so I'd worry more about what was behind that door than you being gone." I crossed my arms.

A smirk appeared on his lips. "Did it work?"

I rolled my eyes in response and headed toward the bedroom, ignoring the bag of books on the coffee table. "I'm tired. We can look at the books you brought back in the morning."

He followed, turning out the lights in the heart of the apartment as he stepped into the bedroom. "I need to clean up. Then I'm sleeping for the next twenty-four hours." He headed to the bathroom and closed the door, leaving me to crawl into the bed.

With all the sources of my stress relieved, I didn't even hear the shower shut off or feel Mikhail crawl under the covers next to me.

Dragon Dawn
Chapter 20

I STRETCHED AS THE sun bathed the room in light. Mikhail snored softly next to me, and I smiled as I watched him sleep. Without the stress tightening the skin around his mouth and eyes, he was a stunningly handsome man. I sighed and slipped from bed, pulled on a bathrobe, and headed into the living room.

I pulled out the thick and very old book from the top of the pile in the bag, laying it on the table, and then did the same with the rest. Mikhail must have found sticky tabs at the librarian's desk because he had several passages in the four books he came back with marked.

I thought about grabbing coffee, but I did not want Mikhail to wake with the scent. He needed sleep. So, I settled into the corner of the couch with the oldest tome in my lap and opened it to the first tab. According to this particular book, the only way to kill a Hydra was to behead it with old-world steel. But the trick was to behead the primary beast; otherwise, it would just keep multiplying.

I shivered. The thought of us getting close enough to actually slice that thing's head off just gave me the willies.

I moved onto the next section he had marked. I read and re-read the description of a dragon. It was true to a fault; it even mentioned that when they eat certain beans, their fire becomes unstoppable. However, there was only one species that was impervious to the flame due to their granite-like skin. The book went on to describe the lizard-like beings with teeth like sharks and scales made of iron.

I turned to the last tab. Another myth of the sea serpent, which paralleled that of the Hydra.

The other books reiterated a lot of what was in the oldest book, except one went on to describe the steel needed to penetrate the Hydra's neck. When I was done reading, I sighed. That collection of weapons Mikhail had stashed away would likely provide us with our blade. But the more pressing part was the creature's acidic spit, especially considering some of the books said the sea creature's saliva burned through anything it touched. Unease filled my stomach, along with hunger pangs.

I climbed off the couch, glancing at the clock in the kitchen. It registered a little after one in the afternoon. No wonder I was hungry. I whipped up a heaping plate of scrambled eggs and buttered four pieces of toast. With the plate and a couple of forks, and a large glass of orange juice, I headed into the bedroom and sat on my side of the bed with the plate in my lap.

Mikhail's eyes slowly blinked open, then landed on the plate. A slow grin formed as his gaze moved to mine. "Breakfast in bed?"

"Actually, it's lunch in bed, but whatever." I held out a fork for him and waited until he got situated with his back to the headboard before I offered him the plate.

"You better hold the plate, otherwise you might not get a bite." He took a piece of toast and stabbed a forkful of eggs, making his point as he nearly inhaled both.

He went for another bite, and I let him, taking a forkful myself. I did not need as much as he did. Although I held the plate, I still only got three bites before he inhaled the rest. I took a sip of juice and then handed him the rest as I nibbled on the last piece of toast.

He drained the glass, and then took both the plate and fork from my hand and set the dishes on his side table. Without another word, he turned and cupped my face, pulling me into a good-morning kiss.

"Thank you," he whispered. "For breakfast. For keeping your word. For everything." Each phrase was accompanied by another kiss.

I pulled away and smiled at him. "Now it's my turn to go on an adventure."

His playful grin faded away and his hands fell from my cheeks. "Not until we come up with a viable plan."

"I have a viable plan. A quiver full of bleach-dipped arrows, a super soaker and two empty backpacks, and be as quiet as humanly possible."

"We need to discuss what the plan is for taking out the serpent king," he said as he scrunched back down under the sheets.

"I read the passages in the books marked with sticky notes. The only thing I'm unsure of is what sword needs to be used and how do we get close enough to chop off its head." I hunkered down next to him and rolled on my side so I faced him.

He stared at the ceiling and sighed. "The katana you used is the only sword I have that is made of the pure metals listed in the reference materials I found. I couldn't bring those books with me—they were too big—but that's the only weapon I have that is deadly enough to do what they say is needed." He turned his head and met my gaze. "You need to be the one to wield it while on my back."

I blinked. "I get to ride you?" Oh, the thought of flying through the air with my legs around his neck and the wind whipping through my hair brought forth a childish glee.

His lips twitched into a smirk, and he cocked an eyebrow.

I swatted his arm as my fantasies morphed from dragon riding in the skies to riding Mikhail in this bed. Both of them heated me, but in very different ways.

With another breath, that mischievous light fled from his eyes. "I think I might have something that will protect you in one of my stashes." He sized me up with his gaze.

"Like Kevlar?"

His gaze jumped to mine. "No. Something even better."

"Why do I need protection if I'm on your back?"

"You're human. And the heat could be as damaging as the serpent king. Plus, what I've got in mind will even protect you from any rogue bomb missiles." He shrugged. "Besides, I have to make a suitable saddle for you to sit on, so you don't just go flying into the wind. And it needs to be something that won't just melt right off me in high heat."

"So steel," I said but he shook his head.

"No. Whatever I have to attach you to me with needs to be more like cast iron."

"That's going to be heavy as hell."

He nodded as he chewed on his lower lip. "I might be able to thin it out enough so it does the job without weighing me down."

"Do we have time for you to do that?"

He looked down at his hands and then over at me. "It depends on how long it takes you to get the bleach and for me to figure out a viable trigger method. And we do not have unlimited time. Sooner or later, they will find all the humans in the city and stamp them out. People can't hide forever like we can here. They need to eat and have drinkable water." He closed his eyes. "And when they venture out..." He didn't finish. Instead, he shook his head slowly. "Unfortunately, I have to put you in a position of vulnerability. But it is the only hope we have of ending this war."

"I want to start getting the bleach tonight."

He tensed beside me, and instead of commenting, he climbed out of bed, grabbed his crutch and a pair of sweatpants, and headed into the bathroom. The sink turned on and I crossed, opening the door.

"By the way, why do you have a high security bio-lab?"

Mikhail spit out the toothpaste in his mouth and rinsed his toothbrush, sliding it back into the slot next to mine. He wiped his lips with the hand towel and then adjusted the crutch under his arm so he could face me. "What do you know about St. Clare Industries?"

I shrugged. "Technology. I know more about the St. Clare Institute than your other companies."

"St. Clare Industries was into all forms of technology." He waved at the building around us. "Sustainable energy was just one facet. We also worked with biotechnology. Before the monsters surfaced, we were trying to find a cure for the virus. Thus, the higher protocols put in place for entering and leaving that lab."

"Did you?"

He shook his head. "No. Even after martial law was declared here, people still found a way to come to the office. Until the monsters came. And by that time, anyone who lived in the building had gone off to other parts of the state and even some to other parts of the country that were less populated.”

I remembered the exodus from the city. So many people sold their homes and moved to the country, hoping for a reprieve from death. I often wondered whether they found their sanctuary or whether they died trying to get to paradise.

“Then the monsters rose up and you know the rest.” He crutched out to his office and opened the drawer to the desk. He glanced around the room more closely and then turned to me. “You cleaned?”

I smiled. “I kept myself busy.” I neglected to tell him just how thoroughly I cleaned the apartment. Especially the closets.

“Huh.” He reached in and grabbed the top notebook and a pen, and took a seat in his swivel chair. He pointed for me to sit on the couch. When my butt rested on the leather, he handed me the paper and pen.

“Draw the path you’re going to take.”

I stared at the paper and then drew a grid of the streets and avenues in the area. And then I marked an X where this building was and traced the route from here into the alley we had come out of. I didn’t know how far the switchbacks went, but I did know we traveled back and forth a few times. I thought it was the equivalent of a couple blocks, and then I marked another X where I thought we had come out of the tunnels.

Tentatively, I handed it back to Mikhail. “I was carrying you, and I was behind Troy, so I am not sure how many switchbacks were blocking that alley.”

He studied the picture and nodded. "Your marker is about where I thought the exit of that subway was. I need to rummage through one of the storage rooms on the twenty-ninth floor to see if I have night vision goggles."

"Wait. Storage rooms?"

"Yes. Don't tell me you didn't find them." He smirked. "The oldest paintings are on the doors." His smirk morphed into a grin.

"So that's where you hid stuff from your wife?" I crossed my arms.

A dimple appeared. "What do you think?"

"I think the paintings themselves would have upset your wife."

He raised his eyebrows and pursed his lips. Finally, he nodded slowly. "She probably would have been upset with me for keeping them from the world."

"But that's really not what would get her panties in a wad, is it?" I narrowed my eyes at him, studying his reaction.

"No." He climbed to his feet. "Come on." He headed toward the door. "While we are in there, remind me to look for the night vision goggles for you."

I scrambled after him.

Dragon Dawn
Chapter 21

MIKHAIL OPENED THE DOOR to the twenty-ninth floor and flipped on the lights. He turned to the right and crutched halfway down the wall to where one of Picasso's pictures hung. Just like the door in the theater, there was a small tab below the picture, and he pulled it open.

Inside the room, lights automatically went on overhead, and I gawked at the display. Guns of every make and model ever made hung on the walls.

"You said you didn't have any guns!" I smacked his arm as he headed to the tables and cabinets in the middle of the room.

"Yes. I have guns, and while I could make ammunition, I do not have the proper materials to make smokeless gunpowder. So they are pretty much useless hunks of metal. The swords and explosives would have sent my wife into a tizzy, but these would have had her hiring a lawyer and filing for divorce. She hated guns. She thought they were the very embodiment of evil, no matter how many times I tried to tell her that it was the person holding the gun who was evil, and not the weapon itself." He opened drawers in the cabinet, rifling through all the stuff inside. He pulled out a pair of night vision goggles and handed them to me. "Those should help you see at night."

Although I was curious as to what else he had stored in this room, it was evident it was military in theme, so I would come back and make my way through it and probably neaten his piles up into some semblance of order. "Why do you collect all this shit?" I waved at the room we were in and then the outer room. "I mean, I get the paintings and some of these antiques, but..."

He shrugged. "It's a dragon thing."

The lore I read bubbled up in my mind. Dragons collected whatever tickled their fancy. Usually gold, silver, and gemstones, but anything that shined was up for grabs. "Is this the only thing you have hidden?" I asked. Because, at this point as I glanced around his private stash, I thought he was a goddamn gift from heaven. Even without the ammunition.

He looked down at the floor and shook his head, but made no indication that he was going to move.

"No secrets between us, right?"

He met my gaze and nodded.

"Lead the way." I waved, forcing him to come clean with whatever was behind the other doors.

He swallowed hard before doubling back toward the door and following the other wall to the space directly across from the guns. He hesitated at this door and bit his lower lip, as if what was behind it would change my viewpoint of him.

"It's okay. We all have skeletons in our closets." I reached out and put my hand on his arm. His muscles twitched under my fingers.

He started to laugh and opened the door. "I bet you don't have a closet like this one." He glanced sideways at me.

My gaze moved from his face into the low-lit room. I gasped and my hand flew over my mouth. But that didn't stop me from stepping inside. Skulls lined the walls. There must have been at least a hundred human skulls mixed in with what looked like a handful of dragon skulls.

"What is this?" I asked when my mind finished stalling like an old car.

He cleared his throat and if he could have shuffled his feet, I bet he would have. "Skulls of my enemies," he muttered under his breath.

I glanced back at the array. "For someone who has lived for thousands of years, this seems...light." I glanced back at him. A part of me was totally weirded out by it, but most of me was fascinated.

Mikhail chuckled. "I try very hard not to amass enemies." Then he nodded to one of the skulls. "I hope you aren't freaked out by this, but Troy's head is in here, too."

I turned to stare at him and then glanced around again. His head would not have been decomposed by now, which meant Mikhail fried the flesh and brain matter out of the skull before hanging it on the wall. My throat tightened, and I stepped outside the room, taking deep breaths to quell the sudden twist in my gut. "I thought he went into the incinerator," I finally squeaked out of my tight throat.

"His body went down the incinerator." Mikhail stepped out and closed the door behind him, shutting off the view of the remains of his enemies. "Are you okay?" His hand landed on my shoulder with a gentle squeeze.

I wasn't sure how to answer him. "What else?" I glanced back at him.

His gaze went to the back wall; he closed his eyes and his chin dropped to his chest.

My heart jumped in my chest. There was something else, and from the look on Mikhail's face, this one must be tons worse than the skulls of his enemies. I didn't know if I could see what he had in this last room, and I almost stopped him when he crutched past me.

"While my wife would have divorced me for either of those rooms, this is the one she would have actually shot me for." He stopped at the last door and without pausing, he swung the door open. Trepidation etched in the lines around his lips as he looked at me.

I blinked. I didn't understand what I was looking at. It looked like a greenhouse, with sun lamps and plants that had grown out of control. I turned to him and waved inside as my brow crinkled in confusion.

"Coffee trees." He licked his lips. "You know what caffeine does to me. But you don't know that I had a serious addiction to it once upon a time."

"Coffee trees?" My brain couldn't wrap around this either. *We had an unlimited supply of coffee?*

He nodded and his cheeks flushed a hot red, as if he were embarrassed.

It took a moment for everything he said to sink in. "Addiction?" I finally said after my brain homed in on that word. *A dragon with a caffeine addiction. Holy shit.* "When were you addicted?"

"The early years. I took out quite a few civilizations before I got a handle on it, but as you can see, I still have somewhat of a problem. And having to fuel up to take out the military installations across the world didn't help."

My shoulders slumped. "And you need to be caffeinated up to destroy the leviathans."

He stared at the coffee plants and nodded. Longing shaded his eyes, and he closed the door on the plants. "When we are done, you may need to burn these to the ground for me."

"Do I have to?" I stared at the door. The idea of having my own home-grown coffee beans was just too appealing.

He let out a laugh. "Caffeine isn't good for either of us."

"I beg to differ. It wakes my ass up." I planted my hands on my hips and gave him a look that conveyed my train of thought: *Do not try to take my coffee away from me.*

He grinned at me. "So, this all doesn't have you running for the hills?" His eyes moved across the room and then back to me.

"The skulls of your enemies kind of freaked me out at some level, but it also intrigued the hell out of me. I would have thought that room would be overflowing with skulls." I lifted a shoulder. "The rest does not bother me at all. Especially having our own coffee trees. While I know it's a problem for you, that actually thrills the shit out of me."

I glanced around the room. "While we are baring our souls, I kind of cleaned out the closets upstairs."

"I noticed."

I nodded. "The things I didn't want went down the incinerator." I met his gaze.

His lips tightened and then he licked them. "Like what?"

"Like the sequin dresses that are just not me, and some of those spiky high-heel shoes." I cringed away from him as if he were going to explode.

He inhaled and then smiled. "Okay." He started crutching toward the door with his shoulders tense.

"You're not mad?" I followed him.

He stopped, and I pulled up before I walked into him. His gaze moved around the room and then back at me. "I wish you had waited for me to be here."

"So, you're angry."

He took a moment and looked down at the floor as if inspecting exactly what he felt inside. Then he slowly shook his head. "No. You kept the things that are more you, and I have to respect that. While you may be the same size as my wife was, you are definitely nothing like her."

I wasn't sure how to take that comment, and I opened my mouth on some snide remark.

"Which is a good thing," he added before I could level any sarcasm in his direction.

"It is?" I had not expected that from Mikhail.

Mikhail smiled as we headed out the door to the stairwell and started our climb to the penthouse. "I don't have to pretend at all with you."

"You pretended with your wife?"

He chuckled. "I didn't realize it until I met you, but yes. I pretended to be civilized. I hid my dragon side." He sent a wicked grin my way. "Truth is, I'm not at all the pretentious billionaire I used to project."

I noodled on his words, mulling them over, but my mind kept going to the room full of skulls instead. "So, are you going to add the serpent king's head to the collection?"

"You seem a little preoccupied with that room. Are you sure you are okay with everything?"

"Yes. I just want to know if the serpent king's head will end up stored away in the building we are living in." The thought did not settle well. It was enough to have Troy's remains still here, but having the serpent king's remains in the same space our home occupied—I wasn't sure I could deal with that.

His smile faded into his expression of serious thought. "If we succeed, I'm not sure there will be anything left but dust."

Thankfully, my brain let go of the thought and glanced down at the goggles in my hand. I paused as Mikhail reached for the keypad. "Hold up. I want to try these out." I slipped them on my head but didn't pull them over my eyes in the bright stairwell. I met Mikhail's gaze. "Turn out the lights, please."

A moment later, we were drenched in blackness. I could only see Mikhail's citrine eyes glowing in the darkness. When I slipped on the night vision goggles, his magnificent male form stood before me, with his bemused grin on his face.

"Those are possibly the least sexy thing you've ever put on," he said.

I snorted a laugh and peeled them off my head. They would do just fine out on the streets once darkness fell. "I need to get my head in the right space for tonight."

"What do you need?" he asked softly.

I glanced at his citrine eyes and the sincerity displayed in those soulful wells. What did I need to try to go through the maze that led to the bleach and back? I needed my muscles to be stretched out enough for them not to cramp up in the cold. I needed my mind clear, with only the goal of getting the left-behind liquid gold that would fuel our attack on the leviathans.

"A massage." The words slipped out before my brain finished categorizing what I needed. His eyebrows rose. "I thought you'd say sex," he said. "But I happen to have a full-service spa downstairs. Unfortunately, you will just have to settle for these hands." He wiggled his fingers at me and held the apartment door open for me. "But I need to get dressed before we head down to the spa."

Dragon Dawn
Chapter 22

OH, MAN. MIKHAIL KNEW exactly how to knead the knots out of my back. He sold himself short. He was about the best masseuse I have ever had. With the light citrus blend oil that he chose, I was drifting into nirvana by the time he moved from my back to my legs.

I purred my approval as he continued to wipe out all the stress of the last few weeks from every muscle in my body. He even used the sheet like they did at a real spa. Moving it aside to only concentrate on one appendage at a time.

When he got to my feet, he wrapped the one he wasn't working on in a warming towel, and it was as if my relaxation took flight into the stratosphere. Truthfully, I may have drifted off, because I never felt him wrap my foot when he was done with the other one.

The sheet that he had draped over my lower body fell across my shoulders. "You may roll over whenever you are ready."

I blinked my eyes open to the floor below me in a fog. I scooched down on the table and rolled onto my back, fitting the sheet across my chest like I had at the spa I once frequented before the world went to shit. When my gaze landed on Mikhail leaning on his crutch, I offered him a smile before I closed my eyes again.

He situated the sheet under my right leg and then he started at my ankle and worked his way to my hip. He had magic in those hands of his, I was sure of it, as I drifted to that plane between awake and asleep.

He repeated his manipulation of my muscles on my left leg and then covered my lower body under the sheet before he started with my right hand, tenderly working out the knots in my forearm and upper arm. He even stretched my shoulder, too. Rinse and repeat with my left arm.

Then he went behind me and rubbed my shoulders, neck, and scalp with tiny rotations of his fingers that nearly had me dropping into sleep.

"Relaxed?" he whispered in my ear as his hands trailed from my shoulders over the upper part of my chest and out to my shoulders.

"M-hm." My body was so loose that I did not want to move from the table, and I did not want Mikhail to stop.

He slowly slid his hands back to my neck and then slid his fingers behind my ears, almost tickling me. And then his warmth left me. My eyes blinked open, and I stared up into his hooded eyes. Mikhail's irises burned bright, and he gave me a strained smile.

"Are you okay?" I asked, and darn if my voice wasn't as groggy as I felt.

He nodded. "Just aroused as hell and trying my best not to ruin your state of relaxation."

I blinked at him and slowly smiled. My body felt fluid and languid, and even though I was relaxed into a puddle of flesh, my core tightened at his admission, sparking my own need. "There are some areas that you missed," I said with a husky voice and batted my eyes at him.

His grin became more natural. "I'm sorry I missed a few areas, ma'am. Care to show me where?"

His tone was like honey, and the role play did more to heat me up than the warming towel he had wrapped my feet in. I moved the sheet down, uncovering my chest. "I think you missed here and here." I touched my breasts.

He closed his eyes and his hands returned to my shoulders. He gently stroked my skin, moving his hands like an expert, until he had my breasts cupped in his palms. He rubbed his thumbs gently over my nipples. Then he diverted from any spa behavior. He leaned over and took one of my nipples in his mouth. He shifted to my side, continuing to work knots out of my sides with his hands as he toyed with my breasts using his mouth and tongue.

He turned his heated gaze in my direction. "Where else?"

"Lower," I whispered.

His hands trailed to my hip bones, to one of the erogenous zones, and he used it to his advantage as he ran his hands from my sides to the front of my body, heightening my arousal as he loosened my muscles.

When his fingers brushed my pussy, I let out a soft moan, letting him know he had found the right spot. The sheet went flying behind him as he bent down to taste me and he kneaded the tightening muscles in my thighs.

His finger entered my wet path. "Fuck," he whispered in that husky, drawn-out way that lit my libido on fire.

"Yes." I swung my leg around him so I could sit up on the edge of the table.

Mikhail stood up, and I'm not sure how he did it, but his pants were down around his ankle and his hard cock inside me before I could blink. The crutch still supported him, but his hands gripped my ass as we moved together.

My body responded immediately, and I threw my head back with the force of my release. His lips skimmed along the line of my throat as he let out a possessive growl and arched into me, capturing my mouth with his in a kiss that left me sizzling.

And as soon as it started, his pressure moved out of me, and he groaned my name as his hot seed covered my belly. He trembled as he held me to him. "Damn, I missed you," he finally said as he pulled away and laid me back down on the massage table.

He cleaned my stomach with the warm towel and then pulled up his pants.

"I hope that didn't fuck up your nirvana." His tilted smile appeared.

I shook my head. If anything, it only increased my state of pampering. "I really don't know if I can walk. You've made me a total puddle of flesh here."

He grabbed the sheet off the floor and draped it over me again. "Good." He caught a quick kiss and then sat in the chair in the corner, looking even more wiped out than he had when he found me in the theater last night.

His expression turned serious as he studied me. "I wish I could go with you."

I wished he could, too, but crutches made noise on the pavement. He would put us in more danger by being with me, and navigating down the debris would be hazardous enough with two legs. I couldn't imagine him being able to make it down that with one leg.

"I know." I wasn't going to promise him I would be all right, either. I didn't know whether or not I would get into trouble.

He took a deep breath and got to his feet. "Take your time. I'll wait in the lobby for you."

He left me to stare at the ceiling as every muscle tingled back awake. After what seemed like forever, I got to my feet, dressed, and then headed out to find him sitting in one of the chairs, just staring at the floor. When his gaze lifted, I could see the desperate plea locked inside.

"What will you do while I'm gone?"

He laughed. "I'll be pacing the lobby."

I challenged him with a raised eyebrow. "You can't make noise in the lobby." I pointed at his crutch.

"Well then, I will sit by the door, waiting for you." He huffed and stood.

"Why don't you start making the bombs with what we already have here?"

"Because I'll be too nervous to handle that shit while you're gone."

Well, at least he was honest. "Okay, then how about trying to figure out how we are going to set those mothers off?"

"I'll bring a pad and pen down with me." He opened the door to the stairwell and waved me through.

As I climbed the stairs back to the penthouse, the tension he had released over the last couple of hours returned with a vengeance.

Dragon Dawn
Chapter 23

DARKNESS SURROUNDED US IN the lobby. Mikhail put the pad and pen he had carried onto the floor and then wrapped his arms around me in a hug. He kissed the top of my head and then pulled away.

"Godspeed," he whispered.

I adjusted the strap holding the quiver on my back and nocked an arrow into the bow. The scent of bleach drifted off me in a cloud of toxicity that we hoped would keep any beasts from being too curious. I gave him one last look, flipped down the night vision goggles, and headed out the door. I had ten minutes to clear this area before the leviathan patrolling returned.

With my heart pounding in my ears and sneakers on my feet that were light enough not to squeak or trail sound, I navigated up the road. With the goggles, it was a whole new experience than the near-blind trudge we had made before. I was able to find the narrow entry we had come out of and slid inside as the ground started the familiar tremor of a sentry. I moved farther into the alley, hugging the wall with a small overhang. I raised the bow, aiming the arrow skyward where I thought the leviathan would appear.

If that thing so much as looked in my direction, I would let the arrow fly. With the tip doused in bleach, it would pierce through the beast's skin. But I would have to make sure it was a kill shot. Otherwise, I'd just piss him off and he could easily flatten me with one stomp of his foot. And God help me if he called for backup.

My arm ached as I held the bow at the ready. The shaking in the ground grew near and then the profile of the leviathan came into view. He didn't even swing his nose in my direction. But he did crinkle his nose, as if my path had left residual bleach fumes.

As he left my view, I released tension on my arms, lowering the bow. I took a few deep breaths and glanced at the clear sky above. This was different than the cloudy night when we arrived here. The darkness surrounding us made the galaxy above seem so vast, and I had a moment to wonder whether we would go back to all that light and noise pollution once this war was over.

The sky calmed my shaky nerves, and I started down deeper in the alley, coming to the first switchback. Seeing it was interesting, considering Troy had been using his hands to navigate instead of any semblance of vision. What we thought was a switchback was actually a gaping hole, as though one of the baby leviathans had run right through the fence.

I slid through the space and from memory turned to my left, following the length of the barrier to another switchback, which was actually another narrow alley that led to a bigger opening. I continued retracing my steps until I came to the mouth of the alley and the rubble of a building on the right.

Instead of rushing out of my hiding spot, I waited. If I was caught climbing down into the stairwell, I would have no true recourse, so I waited for the patrol to go by. Usually, they were on a ten-minute grid, but I wasn't sure about this side of the street. I needed the maximum amount of time possible to make it into the stairwell without falling and breaking something.

The ground shook under my feet, and I attempted to blend into the shadows with my arrow at the ready. My chest constricted at being in a more open alley than the one by the apartment building, but with the bleach scent still wrapped around me, and my goggles giving me a wider view of the city streets, I was in a better position to fight if I had to.

Two leviathans walking side by side crossed into view, and I held my breath. Killing one would be easy, but killing two without a warning shout from the monsters was nearly impossible. They slowed; one lowered their snout to the hole and promptly sneezed.

"It still reeks," the nosy leviathan said as they passed the hole.

"Why do you keep doing that?" the other asked.

"Because I really want a snack. We haven't seen a human in days and I'm getting hungry."

Shit. Just what I needed. Hangry leviathans.

I waited until they were out of view and slowly crept forth, picking my steps carefully. Any shift in the debris would bring those monsters running. But I could not go as slowly as I wanted, either. I only had minutes before I would be in their line of sight. Assuming they could see me at all in the darkness.

I made it onto the metal door on the top landing and picked my way through more debris as I descended the stairs. When the pieces of brick and other rubble started to dance on the ground, I moved faster, skirting around the edge of the opening onto a lower stairwell. Moving inch by inch and stair by stair, I descended into the darkness, barely pulling in more than a shallow breath. By the time I reached the lowest platform where the bleach had been stashed, I was bathed in sweat and the tremors above had subsided.

I stepped behind the blanket that had been draped to muffle noise and human scent from drifting upward. The carts were still piled on top of each other in the corner and the original contents of backpacks were neatly lined up on the floor. None of it had been disturbed.

My gaze landed on my cereal box.

Even though my stomach was in knots, I scurried over to my pile, stripped the backpacks from my shoulders, and took a seat on the ground, indulging in the remaining cereal. That first bite locked up my jaw, and I inhaled through my nose, sucking enough oxygen in to loosen the sudden clamping of my teeth. The second handful was gloriously sweet. I closed my eyes and let the sugar rush commence. When I finished the rest of the box, I climbed back to my feet and focused on the bleach.

I could easily fit five bottles in each bag. The hard part was stacking them on my back and then getting the quiver in place. I moved it in front so I would at least have access to the arrows.

I stood up and nearly tilted backward and was thankful I moved my quiver because otherwise they would have spilled out all over the floor at my angle. As it was, it would be almost impossible to shoot if I had to. I'd just have to figure that out if I got into that situation.

I slowly climbed the stairs with my bow in one hand and using the other to guide myself along. When I got to the upper-most landing, I waited around the corner, leaning my back against the wall for support. I didn't have to wait long before the debris started to dance at my feet.

The telltale sniff came, but it was not followed by a sneeze. Another sniff followed and then a grumble.

"Does this smell different to you?"

I reached for the small bottle of bleach I had attached to my belt and let off a quick spray around the corner and replaced it just before the beast above sniffed. The air in the stairwell seemed to be sucked out with that breath, including the bleach mist I just sprayed. The sneeze that followed nearly tumbled me down the stairs. Thankfully, I had regripped the handrail in the event they decided to reach inside or something equally as stupid. Like send a sneeze down an already compromised pile leading out.

"Asshole," the leviathan cursed.

"It smelled different to me," the other one said.

"Smelling that stuff has done something to your sense of smell, because that is all I could make out."

A rumble echoed as more debris moved, and then the ground tremors started again as the beasts' arguing voices got farther away.

I didn't wait until the tremors subsided altogether. I picked my way up the rubble, testing each step to make sure it was secure. I almost got to the top when the familiar vibrations started again.

I would never make it into the alley.

My gaze darted around and landed on a piece of wall leaning in a way I probably could slide behind. I took my spray bottle and doused myself and the path behind me, and then moved as though the ground beneath me was actually solid.

It shifted as I moved, stopping my heart in my chest. I jumped, landing on the tar, but I teetered with the weight on my back. If I went over backward, I'd be just as screwed as a turtle on their shell. I threw my weight forward and crashed down onto my hands and knees. I winced at the impact but crawled forward into the space between what was left of the building and the fallen part of the wall. I prayed I hadn't made too much noise. I maneuvered so I faced the entry and sat on my heels, waiting. Thankfully, my bow was still clasped in my hand, but the arrow I had nocked had fallen. I grabbed another arrow and held my breath.

"I can smell that toxic shit from here." The leviathan came into view, but they both stayed on the other side of the street, as far away from the hole as possible. "It's just as strong as the first night that it caved in. Your damn sneeze set it off again," the closer leviathan said.

"Just keep moving," the other one said as he passed the first one.

This time I waited until the vibrations in the ground faded and then I crawled out of the space and picked my way to the alley. Navigating back to the apartment, although slow with the backpacks, was faster than climbing up the rubble.

I stopped in the alley across from Mikhail's building, winded from both the weight and my pounding heart. I put my hands on my knees to catch my breath and waited for the downtown sentry to pass. I forced shallow breaths, opting for silence as air rushed in and out of my mouth.

That familiar vibration started, and I closed my mouth, breathing through my nose as silently as I could. When the ground felt like an earthquake was upon us, I held my breath, with my gaze locked on the opening. The beast stepped into view and seemed to pause.

I turned my head as far as I could without losing balance. The beast was sniffing the air.

Fuck.

Without taking it off my belt, I slowly depressed on the bleach trigger. Bleach stung my palm, and I closed it. My eyes widened with realization. I didn't dare open it. The bleach did the job, because its nose crinkled and then it started to move again.

With my fist clenched tight, I waited until the earthquake-like movement subsided and poked my head out of the alley. I glanced both ways and then put on the speed despite the bleach containers sloshing on my back. I rounded the corner and the door opened halfway down the building.

Mikhail's eyes glowed and the expression on his face matched mine. Panic. Pure and absolute. If he had that door open, then he knew. He could either hear or smell me. *And if he could...*

The ground started to shake when I was a few steps away from the door and he reached for me, yanking me inside and shutting the door. He hauled me across the floor and into the stairwell as the entire building shook with the number of beasts converging.

"M—"

His hand clamped down over my mouth as he pulled me into a sitting position on the stairs. He lowered his crutch and silently set it on the ground.

I peeled the night vision goggles off and held them out in the absolute darkness. They disappeared from my hand. The rumbling on the street moved on, and Mikhail let out a long, drawn-out sigh.

"What happened?" he whispered as he unclasped the backpacks.

The light went on and I blinked, squinting up at him before I looked down at my closed fist. A drop of blood dripped from between my fingers and landed on my jeans. I slowly opened my hand to a nasty gash that crossed my hand.

"I must have cut my palm when I was climbing out of a hiding place."

Mikhail took both backpacks and slung them over his shoulder as if they weighed nothing. He grabbed his crutch and started up the stairs. "Let's get you patched up and out of those jeans." He pointed at my knees.

I glanced down and surprise raked sharp nails across my back at the maroon splotch marring my right knee. "I'm not sure if resting with my hands on my knees to catch my breath or spraying the bleach saved my ass."

"I would say it was a combination of both," Mikhail said. "The fresh bleach overpowered the smell of your blood for just long enough to give you a shot at making the building before they got you in the street." He wiped his face with a hand that shook.

"I'll be more careful next time."

His gaze shot to mine. "There will not be a next time. Whatever you collected in these bags will be enough."

I stopped and he continued up the stairs. He didn't slow; he just kept climbing with that stubbornly tense set of his shoulders.

"This isn't a dictatorship."

That stalled his step, and he slowly turned. "Yes, Holly, in this case, it is a goddamned dictatorship. You are not going out there again." He stabbed his finger toward the outside world. "And this is the end of this conversation." He turned his back to me and marched up the stairs as he muttered colorful curses under his breath.

Dragon Dawn
Chapter 24

I STEPPED INTO THE medical room. Mikhail had already ditched the backpacks in the outer room and was inside, slamming things on the table, still muttering like a damn lunatic. He didn't even look up when I entered. He just pointed at the table.

"Up," he commanded.

"I can wash and dress my own wounds."

His gaze finally snapped to mine and under the aggravation pulling his lips into a frown, his eyes still held that frantic panic I had seen when I was running toward the door.

My stomach tightened. He was masking his panic into this crazed monarch shit. "Stop, Mikhail," I said softly as I approached.

He stilled and stared at me. The carefully crafted anger fractured, and underneath desperation screamed. His lower lip trembled, and he pressed his lips tightly together. He blinked his eyes and looked away.

"What if..." His voice cracked. He shook his head and turned away.

"What if they had caught me? I still had a quiver of arrows. I would have taken down as many as I had arrows for." My words were not helping. "We knew the risks. We need the bleach, Mikhail."

"If I lost you—"

"You would have carried on and done what was necessary to save us." I wasn't going to let him wallow in this perpetual fear.

He shook his head. "I would bomb the shit out of the leviathans, but I'd probably take out a good part of the city, trying to wipe them out. And as far as the serpent king, he's already grounded me twice. In a fight to the death, I don't know that I can beat him."

"But your fire?"

He laughed in that tight way that he always did when he was on edge. "My fire does shit to him. Even the caffeine-fueled fire. I don't even know if it would destroy his body, if we're successful at killing the bastard." He wiped his face, closed his eyes, and took a breath before he focused back on me. This time, he patted the surface of the table. "Come on up so I can take a look at your hand."

I climbed up on the table and stuck my bloody palm out for him. I kept my breathing calm, even though his iodine flush stung like a bitch. His sigh told me enough. Fear crept into my bones as his gaze rose to mine. "You need to cauterize it?"

His lips turned up at the edges. "No. But you do need a couple stitches since I'm not sure we have enough of that liquid bandage left."

My shoulders sagged in relief, and I glanced up at the ceiling. "I can take stitches."

"I know you can. But this delays any more bleach runs." He met my gaze. "I might have to be the one to do the next one." He reached into the box he had put on the table, and pulled out a needle and some suture thread.

"We talked about that." I looked at the medical cabinet instead of what he was doing with my hand. The stab of the needle into my flesh pulled a wince, but I remained still.

"No. We talked about me not being able to walk there with a crutch. We never talked about me flying into the stairwell." He continued stitching me up without looking at me, as if his concentration on my hand was more important than the subject of our discussion.

My jaw dropped. *He flew over the city once and now he thinks he can fly out of a hole in the ground and still be all stealth-like.* "Flying in is one thing and I'll agree that will be the easy part. It's the exit with the bleach I'm worried about."

"I can carry three or four backpacks at a time without issue." He glanced up at me as he tied off a knot in the suture thread.

With a snip, the pull on my flesh was gone, but a dull throb remained. "And launch from a stairwell without making noise?"

He slathered antibiotic ointment over the sutures, cooling the sting in my skin. After he wiped his hands clean, he ripped open a square bandage and pressed it to my palm and secured it with a roll of gauze that he wrapped around my hand. As soon as he finished, he met my gaze. I saw resolve in his eyes, and I clenched my teeth together. I wanted him out there as much as he wanted me galivanting through the streets.

"We've got backpacks, bleach, and a stairwell. We can test it out." He collected all the dirty crap he had dropped on the floor and tossed it in the incinerator.

I hopped off the table. "I'm not thrilled with the thought."

"Welcome to my world." He didn't wait for me. He crutched to the door, hauled the backpacks over his shoulder, and left me to my own devices.

Dragon Dawn
Chapter 25

I FOUND MIKHAIL IN the lab, hunkered over his table as he formed and molded a half circle of steel big enough to cover half a basketball. He set it in the cooling vat. Steam hissed out and he waited until it slowed; then he pulled it out and placed it on a fireproof tray.

"What are you doing?"

"Making the bombs so I know exactly how many more bottles of bleach we will need."

I swallowed hard at the size of the shell he just made. *If one the size of a marble nearly blasted the door off the steel room, what the hell would something that big do?*

He must have caught my wide-eyed stare because he glanced at the half round. "That's for the big one that I plan to set off over Times Square. This one will do the most damage. The others will only be as big as a baseball."

I guess that made sense. "So, we will have twenty-one bombs just hanging around." The nerves in my stomach jumbled.

He just nodded and continued working the next half circle. "What I need you to do is bring me all the bleach in this building." He glanced at me. "I'm not sure if some of the cleaning closets on the lab floors have more. You can grab what we have in the apartment, too. Line them up on that wall." He nodded to the wall near the elevator, where he had already lined up the ten bottles I brought back. He had one at his workstation that he had used for the bomb tests, too. "Somehow mark the ones that aren't full as well, so I know. I don't want to make any faulty assumptions."

I nodded and went to collect all the bottles in the building, including the stash on fifteen, which I would save for last since the lab was closest to fifteen and exhausting myself further wouldn't do either of us any good.

I skipped the first floor because the night still shrouded the city and lights were a no-no in the storeroom. The apartments garnered three bleach bottles that I found between linen closets and under sink spaces. Of which, only one was opened. The office spaces only seemed to have some generic cleaner, and nothing bleach-oriented, which brought me to the labs. I dropped the bottles I had off in the lab where Mikhail was, physically separating the full bottles from the partials.

"The partials are going on this side of the door," I said as I put the one partially full bottle on the opposite side of the door from the rest.

"Thanks," Mikhail said without looking up.

"I'll be scrounging on the other lab floors." I didn't wait for a response; instead, I did just that. With all the cabinets to open and inspect, it took a good amount of time, and I could feel the weight of the evening dragging me down. For all my searching, I only found two full bottles and two partials on those floors. Although there were plenty of industrial cleaners, bleach was scarce here, too.

I brought the four bottles down to the eleventh floor where Mikhail was making the bombs, and then headed to fifteen to collect the rest of the stash we had amassed. Twenty-nine jugs took me six trips and by the time I finished, I leaned on the wall next to the door.

Mikhail glanced up at the growing collection of bleach bottles. So far, we had thirty-three full bottles and four partials, if I included the one on Mikhail's desk.

"How far did you get?" he asked.

"I skipped the first floor but got through floor fifteen." I wiped my forehead.

"Go get some rest. I'll be up in a few." He gave me a soft smile. "We can hit the other floors tomorrow."

I wasn't going to argue with him. Besides, my hand throbbed. I glanced down at my palm. No blood seeped through the dressing, so it was just normal healing pain.

"I'll take a look at that in the morning to make sure it's healing properly." He nodded toward my hand. "If you want some pain relievers, I have some in the medicine cabinet."

"I know. I straightened that up while you were gone."

"I noticed. Thank you, by the way."

"For?"

He waved at the bottles. "For cleaning the apartment. Alphabetizing my books, organizing my closet. And not freaking out on me."

"It was not easy to keep my mind occupied."

He snorted a laugh. "I can't imagine. You were only gone for a couple hours, and I was a fucking basket case. You went three days, and outside of me finding you sobbing watching *Marley & Me* while eating my ice cream stash, you had it together."

"As much as I hated it, focusing on my worry wasn't going to do me any good." I lifted my shoulders in a quick shrug. "So, I just transferred all that nervous energy into my obsessive, compulsive need for order and accepted that it was out of my control until you either returned or they paraded your body around the city."

He cocked his head. "How? How can you just let go like that?"

I chewed on my lower lip as I mulled over his question. I kept eye contact with him. "I guess I chose to trust you. Trust that you wouldn't do anything that would put you in harm's way. And

660

I chose to believe you would be back." I waved at him. "And here you are."

His hands lowered as he put the sphere he was working on down on the desk. "That makes me a complete asshole."

I cocked my head. "Why?"

"Because I doubted you would stay true to your word the entire time I was gone."

My exhaustion twisted into aggravation. "Yes. That does make you an asshole." I turned and marched out the door and up the stairs before he could make any sort of rebuff.

I needed distance and sleep, and not to see Mikhail's fricken' gorgeous face right now. I slammed the penthouse door behind me and headed to the main bathroom. I found the pain relievers and took two before I brushed my teeth, stripped, and climbed under the covers.

But as much as I wanted sleep, my brain just kept tumbling over his words, his expressions, and the fact that I would not be able to recover if something happened to him. So, I knew the fear he felt today.

He didn't follow, or if he did, it took him a hell of a long time to get up the twenty floors to the penthouse. But when he stepped in the bedroom, I flipped on my light and glared at him.

Mikhail had lost all the fire and fury that had him growling at me in the medical bay. He took a seat on the edge of the bed with his back to me. "So, I need to work on trusting you out there on your own." He waved absently toward the window. "The way you put your trust in me."

I did not expect him to concede. Especially after his dictatorship comment.

"Yes." I glanced down at my hand. "And I need to trust you in the same way."

He glanced back at me. "I am not capable of silently taking off in a stairwell with more than a backpack of bleach." He chewed on his lip as he met my gaze.

"You tried?"

His nod confirmed it. "So, either I figure out how to deliver the devastation we need to the leviathans with the bleach we have, or I trust that you can make another two trips out there to get us the minimum of what we need."

"We need twenty more gallons?"

"To make the bombs, yes. But we also need a couple to load up our spray bottles. Otherwise, we're vulnerable out there."

I glanced down at my hand and sighed. *Two more trips.* The thought made my stomach cramp. I forced a smile and a nod. Maybe I'd feel better about it in the morning.

Mikhail tossed something on the bed and then headed into the bathroom for his nightly ritual. I stared at the fingerless gloves. Their weight registered as I picked them up. Heavy, durable, and the palms seemed reinforced somehow so I wouldn't rip the stitches on my injured hand and my other hand would remain perfectly intact.

I put them on the nightstand, shut the light off, and curled on my left side, facing Mikhail's side of the bed. When he slipped under the covers, he gave me a small peck on the lips.

He wrapped his arms around me, just holding me to his chest, and kissed my forehead. When he didn't make any further advances, I glanced up at him.

"Sleep. We both need it," he said with a voice loaded with exhaustion.

I shifted so he was spooning me and snuggled into his warm embrace. If tomorrow night brought the same perils as tonight, I was going to need this rest.

Dragon Dawn
Chapter 26

HE WRAPPED MY HAND with new bandages. His frown pulled at the corners of his lips. His eyes held all the trepidation that coursed through my veins. He had spent the day in the lab, building out the parts for the bombs, and only needed the rest of the bleach now.

"Did you figure out a way to trigger the bombs?" I asked to get our minds off my next trip outside.

"I think so. When you get back, I'll need to tape you screaming."

I raised my eyebrow at him. "Like horror movie screaming?"

He smirked and met my gaze, nodding. "It's how I plan on getting them to Times Square."

"What about the dragon blood? Wouldn't that be more effective?" I didn't really want to scream into a microphone.

"I already told you. I'm not willing to part with that."

"If you insist on taping me screaming, I insist on using a little of the dragon blood. Just enough to bring them running along with my screams." I stared him down. "Besides, don't we want the serpent king to come, too, and not just the leviathans?"

He chewed on his lip as he finished wrapping my hand. He grabbed the glove and slipped it over his patch job. "Point taken. Your screams won't bring the serpent king, but dragon blood will. He wants to see me suffer, and he knows I'm the last one."

"So, you'll use the dragon blood?"

His gaze rose to mine. "No. I'll use my blood. It smells different than full dragon blood, and he knows the difference between the two." He crutched to a cabinet and pulled out a needle with a tube at the end of it, and a glass jar.

I went to say something, but before I could, he jabbed the needle into his arm and put the end of the tube in the small glass jar the size of the ones I used to have to pee in at the doctor's office. When it was half full, he yanked the needle out, covered the jar with a screw-on cap, and dumped the needle and tube into the incinerator shoot. Then he put a Band-Aid on his arm and smiled at me as if this were all so normal.

"That ought to do it." He picked up the canister and waited for me to get down from the table. "Do you want me to wait in the lobby for you like I did last time?"

I swallowed. If he hadn't been there with the door open for me, I'm not sure I would have made it inside without being attacked. "Yes, please."

Relief smoothed out some of the unhappy lines in his face. "When you get back, we'll have to test the triggers and make sure it transmits to multiple locations down the line. I have an idea, but I need to test it out a few times to make sure it works. Then we can figure out when to do this insanity."

I chuckled. Insanity was the right word for it. It was more like a suicide pact than waging war.

"I've got something for you to wear under your clothes that should help protect you a little more." He headed for the door. "That way I can be sure you won't get stuck with some random piece of glass or building debris."

I followed him up to the twenty-ninth floor. He handed me the jar of blood and then went into the gun room. In the cabinet in the center, he opened a pair of double doors and rummaged inside. When he pulled out something that looked like a one-piece pair of long johns that reminded me of the ones the villain usually wore in the old Westerns, with the back flap, I started to laugh.

Mikhail hung it on the wall and went to get a sword. When he came back, he thrust the sharp end of the sword at the fabric. It just bent inward and rebound. He then sliced from shoulder to waist and again, nothing happened. He glanced at me, dropped the sword, and tossed the fabric to me.

I caught it and inspected the light fabric. I found nothing that indicated he had just basically hacked it in half.

"That will also keep you from burning up when we go after the serpent king."

I glanced up at him, surprised at the effectiveness of the fabric. "What is it?"

"Stronger than Kevlar and much more heat resistant," he said. "It was an experiment. That was made for my wife." His lips pulled down at the edges. "But she never got the chance to wear it before they pulled her apart."

"You were taken by surprise." I studied him.

He let out a scoff. "It won't happen again."

I believed him, and followed him to the penthouse to get into the gear I would need to do this bleach run.

"We need to do two runs tonight," I said as I slid the bleach bottle into my belt.

Mikhail didn't speak; he just pursed his lips at me and picked up a pad and a pen. "We'll see how the first one goes and go from there." He tucked a strand of hair behind my ear and ran his fingers along my jaw. His attempt at a smile did not work and he turned away, bringing his hand down to his crutch.

"Mikhail?"

He stopped and glanced over his shoulder.

"I love you, too." I said the words that he hadn't, even though they were glazed in his eyes and by the tenderness in his touch.

That half-smile that warmed me appeared. "I choose to believe this isn't goodbye." He headed toward the door.

I slid on the black beanie, tucking my hair underneath it, and grabbed the backpacks, bow, and quiver full of freshly dipped arrows. The scent of bleach surrounded me as I climbed down the thirty flights with Mikhail.

We did the same wait until the sentry passed before he cracked the door and looked both ways. When he turned back to me, I captured a quick kiss, lowered the night vision goggles, and took off onto the street. This time, my feet were surer in the direction and the twist and turns in the alleyway maze. I found a suitable spot to hunker down and wait out the sentries walking this grid.

The ground did its familiar tremor, and I waited. Only one sentry passed by. I cocked my head, questioning the pattern. There had been two last time. I went to take a step and movement in the shadows across the street from the stairwell had me pausing. I adjusted my night vision goggles and stared at another leviathan hunkered low, just staring at the opening.

My heart clanged in my chest. I was less than twenty yards away from that beast. My brain registered the distance and the wind tunnel that blew down the street. The only way I was getting in that hole was if I killed that thing. But I would have to wait until the next sentry passed to give me the most amount of time. I crawled to the alleyway entry slowly and stayed in the shadow as I brought my bow and arrow to the ready. If I missed, I would only serve in pissing this beast off.

Thankfully, Mikhail was right: they couldn't see shit.

I waited, and the sentry passed again without giving the leviathan in the alley a glance. I aimed for its eye and let the arrow go. I'm not sure the beast saw it at the last second or not, but its head dropped to the ground a moment later.

I waited a moment. When the beast did not move, I made my jaunt into the stairwell. My last glance showed just a small amount of the arrow sticking out from the middle of his eye. Most of it was embedded in the leviathan's brain. Hopefully, the sentry would not notice on his next pass.

I took out the spray bottle and sent mist behind me as I made my way down the stairs. At the bottom, I started packing just as the ground trembled above. There was no pause in the footsteps, and they faded again by the time the packs were full. I overstuffed them this time, because if I ran into trouble, it would be the last trip out here. With my quiver saddled on my front and fourteen bottles in the packs, I climbed the stairs, relying on the adrenaline pumping in my blood to fuel me.

I needed to be out before they came back, and I didn't wait for the sentry to pass again. I knew I only had a limited window and climbed out as quickly as I could. The ground shook in earnest, and I bolted into the alley, hunkering down in the shadows as I caught my breath, moving into the maze as stealth-like as possible.

Halfway through the maze, the muffled leviathan's voice reached me. "How long are you going to stare at that hole?"

Damn it! Why couldn't he have passed by one more time? I picked up the pace as much as I could without juggling the bottles in my backpacks. The weight wore on my muscles and keeping my step light became difficult. I needed to move, to get to Mikhail's building before this idiot called in the cavalry.

I did not hear the next words, but the irritation was clear in the tone. I was almost to the narrow alley across from Mikhail's building when that high-pitched sound reached my ears. I froze in place as the ground rumbled underneath me. The sentry that walked the path the alley came out of turned in the direction of the cry, then he took off toward the next road. I glanced at Mikhail's building. And with the monsters running toward the bleach hole, I had a window.

At least I hoped I did. I bolted, praying my footsteps were not louder than the siren getting farther away by the second. I didn't even look as I took the corner. I ran. My heart thumped in a near heart attack pace and my feet now slapped the thundering pavement. The door opened and I dove inside. Mikhail slammed the door and grabbed my arm, hauling me into the stairwell again. But this time the light was on and my eyes slammed shut under the brightness. I tore the night vision goggles off as he shut the door.

I fell forward on the stairs, my breath wheezing as the weight of the bleach seemed to crush me from behind. Mikhail tore the backpacks off me and turned me over. His frantic eyes took me in, scanning me for any sign of injury.

I started laughing silently because I knew we were too close to the entry for me to be guffawing like a maniac.

Mikhail whispered, "What the fuck is wrong with you?"

I just shook my head and rolled over, crawling up the stairs because I couldn't walk. Not laughing the way I was. It was either laugh or sob, and now that the adrenaline started to fade, my muscles began to quiver from overexertion. I was sure I threw my back out with the weight, but I'd deal with that in the morning.

"What happened?" Mikhail finally asked when I collapsed on the landing of the eleventh floor.

"There was a leviathan camped out in the street across from the stairwell. One sentry walking, the other watching."

He looked at the bags in his hands. "How did you get down there for this?"

"Arrow to the eye. Killed the watching one instantly and the other just walked by him the first time. The second time, he did not, but I had already filled the backpacks and made a run for it by the time he came around again. This time he said something to the one lying in wait. I was already halfway through the maze, and I guess instead of continuing on his grid, he checked the other leviathan." I took a deep breath. "By the time I got to this side of the alley, he gave the distress call. Then I ran like hell once our sentry passed by."

He stared at me in horror.

"We can't go back again," we said at the same time.

I nodded up at him as every muscle in my body decided to yell in unison. Man, I was going to need another one of Mikhail's massages before this day was over.

"How many bottles did you get?" He unzipped one of the bags. A bottle nearly tumbled out and he caught it.

"Fourteen. We are short." I gasped at the air around me, trying to satiate my body's need for oxygen. Thankfully, my breath had stopped that high-pitched wheezing. The near-hysterical laughter hadn't helped. I propped myself into a sitting position and peeled off the quiver.

"We haven't looked at the floors above fifteen. Maybe we will get lucky and if not, some of the bombs won't have quite as much bleach as others. I'll figure it out and make do with what we have since we don't have the time to search out more bleach." He headed inside to drop the bottles with the rest.

I climbed to my feet, ignoring all my aches and pains. *Only the living felt the bite of overexertion.* The alternative was far more depressing to think about.

Mikhail stepped back out in the hallway with a recorder in his hand, like the one he had used in our trial to show the tribune the serpent king had ill intent. He slid it in his pocket. "Let's go see if we can find any more bleach bottles," he said. "I'll take the lab on sixteen, and the medical floors. You can look in the cabinets in the spa and the gym. I don't think there's any in the bowling alley or in the billiards room, but I can meet you up there as soon as I'm done with the lab and medical floors."

I nodded. The idea of outfitting in a hazmat suit wasn't on my to-do list today. I started the climb to the seventeenth floor, going slower than Mikhail and his crutch.

He paused at sixteen and deep creases of concern appeared on his forehead. "Are you sure you're all right?"

"Yes." I offered up a tired smile that I hope quelled his worry. It must have been convincing enough as those lines smoothed out and he disappeared through the door, leaving me to climb another flight to the spa.

I did a thorough search of all the cabinets and closets, and found a total of one bottle in the cleaning closet. It was unopened, and smaller than the other containers, but it was bleach. I set it on the stairwell and headed into the gym to do the same. One would think the gym would be the place to find bleach, but there were only items that combined cleaning solvents with bleach, not the pure thing like we needed.

I sighed and headed up to the bowling alley on twenty-one. I opened the door on the bang of a ball on bowling pins and looked up as Mikhail turned toward me with a smile. All the pins down the alley were being swept away and reset by the machines. On the table near him sat another bottle of bleach.

"I've still got it, even with only one leg." He crossed to the table and put his hand on the bleach. "I guess they did use this stuff to clean here. It's not quite full, though."

"Did you find anything in the labs?"

"Yeah. An unopened gallon jug and one with only a small amount left. I brought them down to ten and grabbed the one you found on the way."

"So, we're up to seventeen?"

"Yes, but the one you found in the spa was only a half-gallon. Although, if we add that to one of the opened containers, I'm sure we can reach at least eighteen bottles with a little to spare. This is the best we're going to be able to do, and I can work with a deficit of two jugs. That will give us enough to fill up that spray bottle on your hip to mask our scents when we try to set up the bomb." He hobbled toward me with the jug in his free hand.

"How are we going to do this?"

"We'll just have to load a couple of the containers with more shrapnel to make up for the missing liquid."

"We still have the first floor of office supplies to look at once the sun rises," I said.

"I'm not sure there is much down there, either, but I'll check it out after I get you to scream in this recorder in the theater."

"Excuse me?"

He pulled out the recorder and wiggled it. "I need your best terrified scream. And it needs to be long and loud and convincing. One that will bring those mothers running."

"Can't you just pull it from one of those horror movies in your movie stash?"

He shook his head. "I can't isolate the scream from the background soundtrack. My stuff isn't that sophisticated. Come on." He led me to the door and opened it for me. He did the same thing I had and left the bleach on the landing before heading up two floors.

"Why the theater?"

"Because it is fully soundproof, and with the monsters searching the streets outside, I do not want to take any chances." He opened the door to the theater and turned on the lights. "Plus, this place has phenomenal acoustics."

It took me only three tries to get what Mikhail truly wanted. And his prompting of closing my eyes and making me envision a leviathan catching me really helped. But it took the last ounces of energy I had.

"Go get some sleep. I'll be up in a bit. I'm going to check the first floor and then transfer this into a bigger recorder that has a remote to turn it on and see if I can figure out how to trigger the bombs when it shuts off."

"Why wait until it runs out of batteries?"

His tilted smile greeted me. "They'll smash it, but not until the serpent king orders them to shut it off."

"How can you be sure they'll all be there?"

"With the smell of my blood, the serpent king will send in the troops before him, just to make sure it isn't a trap." He glanced down at the bleach in his hand. "At least that's the theory I'm betting on."

"That's a risky bet." I yawned.

"This whole thing is risky. But if we want any sort of life, it has to be done. Now go, before you fall asleep on your feet and tumble down the stairs." He pointed up the steps.

I stood on my tiptoes and planted a kiss before I trudged my way to the penthouse.

Dragon Dawn
Chapter 27

THE BED DIPPED AND I turned, blinking at the brightness of the room. My gaze dropped to the clock, and it didn't make any sense. *If it was three, why was the sun shining in our bedroom?* My gaze jumped to Mikhail's exhausted eyes.

His eyelids dipped closed.

My muscles cried out as I rolled toward him. Everything hurt. I must have groaned because Mikhail's eyes opened wide with worry.

"Holly?" Even his voice sounded haggard.

"Just sore. Why is the sun out at three in the morning?"

His worry transitioned to the crow's-feet of a smile around his eyes. "It's three in the afternoon."

I blinked at him as my sleep-addled brain grasped his comment. "You let me sleep for fifteen hours?"

"I did not *let* you sleep. I was busy finishing the bombs and testing triggers and delivery protocol while you pretended to be Sleeping Beauty. I also got everything to the roof in preparation. Tonight, I need to fly them to a closer destination because we can't go back and forth from here to set them in place. But right now, I need sleep."

"I need a hot shower to loosen my cramped muscles."

"Wake me at sunset," he said.

By the time I got to the bathroom door, he was snoring.

The shower loosened the knots in my back and legs. When I stepped out of the heat, the entire bathroom was filled with steam. I wiped a streak of the mirror clean enough to brush my hair and twirl it into a messy bun. I grabbed clothing out of the closet, and Mikhail didn't stir, so I went into the living space to make myself some coffee and toast.

On the island counter were pages of notes, and I glanced at them while my coffee brewed. His detailing of how the bombs were to be set up and how he planned to trigger them left me confused. It was so elaborate, the likelihood of failing was pretty damn high.

He also identified the building where he could bring the bombs for us to get them set up, along with the set-up plan. Ten blocks. Twenty bombs. I would have thought that would be pretty self-explanatory, but instead of setting them all up on the street level, he planned to have half of them at ground level and the other half up high enough to do maximum damage. But that meant he would have to tie them off either on streetlights or on the buildings themselves. It did not give me the warm fuzzies for this plan.

The farthest bomb would go first in order to keep the leviathans in place. Then the others would follow immediately. His plan was to fly down Fifth Avenue to get behind the leviathans and let his fire loose. And Mikhail had written *coffee* in large letters and underlined it at least a half dozen times.

What he did to the Museum of Natural History would be nothing compared to what he was planning to do to Broadway. I wasn't sure the city would recover from a wound like that, but it was the only way to annihilate the leviathans and have a go at the serpent king.

I decided to make my way up to the roof and see the bombs for myself. I hunkered down out of sight and stared at the six large canvas bags next to the side wall of the building. Four of the bags carried the small bombs. Two of the bags had bombs with clips on either side of the transmitters, along with uniform lengths of rope. Those were the ones I would bet Mikhail would hang from the buildings or lampposts. Two had only bombs with transmitters and no rope or clips. Those would be placed at the base of the buildings opposite of the ones that Mikhail hung. The last two bags had the larger bomb with the same clip ties, but much longer lengths of wire curled up in the bag. The last bag had remotes wired together that would trigger all the bombs when the frequency rang through Times Square. In the same bag, the recorder I screamed into sat next to the remotes, along with an amplifier. The glass jar was also among his preparations.

Damn. The man had been very, very busy during the fifteen hours I was in my sleep coma.

But it was the massive collar and breastplate with four chains hanging off it clipped to what looked like a heavy-duty leather belt that gave me pause. Mikhail would have to be in full form to wear that sucker.

I sat down against the door, letting the chill in the air wrap around me as the sun dipped low on the horizon. If this was the last sunset I would ever see, I was going to enjoy it in the fresh air. The sky turned twilight, the pink time of night where the water almost looked turquoise just before it became that deep blue of night. Reds and purples painted the clouds in various degrees of color, and I sighed at the beauty.

In a way, I did wish Mikhail was here with me to share this stunning sunset, but on the other hand, I was glad I got to see this. It reinforced my need to get this done and get on with my life, or get on with my death. Whichever fate was in store for me, I just wanted to move forward. This perpetual hold was starting to drive me batshit.

Well, not all of it. The sensual encounters with Mikhail were about the only things that didn't leave me on edge. No, those left me completely lethargic and wanting to just snuggle with him until the world disappeared.

When the twilight sky dipped into darkness, I got to my feet and slipped back into the stairwell, flipping the light back on so I could see the stairs. I climbed down to the penthouse and cooked the steaks he had left in the refrigerator.

I glanced at the door, anticipating him to be standing there, looking expectantly at me as I prepared our meal. But the doorway was empty. Considering the amount of work he had put in before falling into bed, I guessed even the smell of steak wasn't enough to break sleep's hold.

As soon as the meat registered rare on his meat thermometer, I took them out of the broiler and set them on the stove. Then I went into the bedroom and took a seat on the bed next to him. I ran my hand over his back gently.

"Time to start waking up. Dinner is all set."

Mikhail turned his head toward me, and his eyes fluttered open. "Need more sleep," he mumbled.

"You're the one who told me to wake you at sunset. I actually let you sleep a little longer than just sunset, too." I continued to rub his back. His muscles relaxed under my fingertips, as if my touch heated him from the inside, loosening the knots.

He opened his eyes. "If you continue to do that, you are going to put me back to sleep."

I removed my hand. "Dinner is done. I'm eating." I swatted him on the ass, hard enough for my palm to sting. "Get your lazy ass up." I stood as he glared at me with a hint of a growl.

"How'd you like it if I spanked you?"

His words gave me pause at the door. I glanced over my shoulder with a smile that I knew he loved and just shrugged before I headed to the meal while it was still warm.

I put the steaks onto plates, along with some mashed potatoes that I found in the pantry. Of course, they were the dried version that you add water to, but they still tasted good loaded with butter and steak juice. I didn't bother with any vegetables.

The toilet flushed and then the cadence of Mikhail's crutch approached the kitchen. He climbed up on the stool and pulled the plate in front of him.

"Thank you."

"What the hell is that giant collar doing on the roof?" I asked through a mouthful of potatoes. "And couldn't you have come up with a simpler approach to setting off the bombs?"

His lips tilted into a smile as he gave me a sideways glance and cut into his steak. "We need the time to get them in the range of the bombs, otherwise, we won't get them all. So, unless you have a better idea that can't fail, I'm all ears." He devoured the steak as if he hadn't eaten in days, then swiveled the chair in my direction as he wiped his lips on a napkin. "Nothing?"

"Why not use a remote to detonate it?"

"You have to be close to the bombs to do that. This way, the frequency that is emitted after they kill the recorder is the trigger. And that frequency carries for miles. It is not short range."

"Oh." I hadn't thought about the range of a remote.

"Plus, we want to drive them closer to Times Square by setting off the farthest bombs first. With a remote, the likelihood is the one over Times Square will detonate first and then it's mayhem."

Shit, he had put a great deal of thought into this. "What about the collar and chains?"

"I didn't have time to make a proper riding saddle, and since you are going to ride me into the fight, you need to be secure on my back. I can't have you flying off, so I've got a belt for you to wear that clips onto the end of the chains. It will ensure you will stay put."

"You've thought of everything."

He huffed a laugh. "It still has a thousand things that could go wrong, but it is really the only option we have. The bombs themselves won't be enough. I need to burn them to ash while they are vulnerable." He pushed his plate across the counter and hobbled around to the sink.

I stared at his shirtless arms and chest as he washed the dishes. Something about seeing him do all this domesticated shit really turned me on.

His gaze moved from the dishes to me, and that quirky smile appeared, and his eyes sparkled. "While I'd love to live out whatever fantasies are going through your mind, I really need to get that stuff upstairs across the city. And then we both need to rest up, because tomorrow night is our target to get things set up out there."

I blinked at him. Even with all our preparation and talking about taking out the leviathans and serpent king, apprehension filled every muscle. My mind kept thinking of excuses why we should hold off, but that's all they were. Excuses.

He turned off the water and reached for me. His warm palms swallowed my hands and he stared into my eyes. "I promise, if we make it out of this alive, I will scratch that itch of yours."

"What if I want more than that?" The words slipped out before I could stop them.

His slow grin lit up the entire fucking room. Damn him for being so incredibly delicious to look at when his smile reached his eyes. "I will give you whatever you want. Gold, diamonds, guns, swords, sex—whatever you desire. It is yours."

"I don't want things, Mikhail." I was not interested in stuff. What I wanted was a life with him. I wanted to figure out a way to have his children and not die from it. All the things that matter in life, those were what I wanted. Not material possessions.

His smile persisted. "You already have my heart, Holly."

I licked my lips and pulled my hands away, looking down at the counter. A new and unnerving fear bit at my insides. We'd been running for our lives since we met. Living on adrenaline. *What happened when that adrenaline faded and there was no life-and-death threat hanging over our heads?* Although I could never get tired of the man before me, could he tire of me? Especially considering I would age and die?

He leaned his elbows on the counter so he could catch my gaze. "What are you afraid of?" His soft voice caressed my spent nerves.

"What if after this is all over, you find...you don't want me?" I forced myself to meet his gaze.

He shook his head slowly. "That will never happen."

I rolled my eyes. "You don't know that. When I get old and frail..."

He put his hand up. "Holly, I'm in love with you. Your heart. Your soul. Not your physical body."

I scoffed at him. That's what all men said. *Baby, I love you for who you are inside.* But then when the woman gains weight or cuts their hair short, men changed their tune.

He stood up. "We can talk about our insecurities after all this is over. Right now, I need to go get all of the stuff upstairs delivered to the top of the Wall Street Journal building, which is as close as we are going to get to Times Square."

"Why not on the building where the ball drops?" I asked.

"It's in the blast radius."

I blinked and wondered how much of the city would be devastated by this and prayed that people were not hiding near there. "What about collateral damage?"

"I am sincerely hoping that people have vacated that area." He swallowed and headed toward the door in just sweatpants. "If not, they'll be collateral damage."

"What?"

He turned at the door and his face pinched in aggravation. "What would you like me to do? Announce that we are planning to wipe out the leviathans and attempt to kill the serpent king?"

My skin heated in irritation, but I took a deep breath, tempering my tone before I spoke. "I get it. I just didn't think there would be other casualties."

He closed his eyes and hung his head. "There are always unintended casualties when you wage war. But the alternative is complete and utter annihilation."

"I know. I just..." I wasn't sure how to appease this uneasiness inside me.

"You're just stalling."

My gaze snapped to his, and my mouth popped open.

He chuckled, but there was no humor in it. "I'm fighting the same thing, Holly. I would prefer to be here with you, doing sinful things together, but we cannot hide here forever. Because if we do, they will kill every last human on Earth." He pointed outside. "Neither of us want that. And stalling just means more people will die."

Leave it to Mikhail to cut to the quick. I nodded. "Do you need help upstairs?" I changed the subject because I couldn't focus on the pending offensive without breaking out in a cold sweat.

"No, but if you want to come up and watch me fly off into the night and help me reload the bag when I return, that would be nice." The tension in his shoulders relaxed a fraction, and he opened the door, holding it for me like a gentleman.

"It's going to be a long night, isn't it?" I asked as we trudged up the stairs.

"Yes. It is going to be long and exhausting, but at least I'm flying high enough to not really be noticed, especially since there is no moon tonight," he said just as we reached the landing. Mikhail turned off the light, dousing us in darkness. He pushed the door open and waved me out on the concrete roof.

"I wish it was overcast." I glanced up at the stars in the sky, wondering whether the monsters below would see Mikhail this time. But I shoved the worry away as he handed me his crutch, swung the first bag over his head, and transformed.

"See you in a few." He launched into the sky. Instead of dipping down, he flew higher, staying near enough to the buildings that he seemed to merge with the shadows.

I laid the crutch down and waited with my heart thundering in my head. My gaze drifted to the collar. *How the hell did he even get that thing up here?*

I sat with my back to the door and my legs drawn up, waiting for Mikhail to return. This wasn't going to be an easy night. He had to make this run five more times, based on the bags. Again, my gaze landed on the collar because we had proved how unprepared his shrunken form was in handling something of that significant weight.

I stood and crossed to it, reaching down and taking a grip of one of the chains. When I pulled, nothing happened. I placed the chain back on the ground, cognizant of doing it as quietly as possible, then I slid my fingers under the edge and tried lifting with my legs. I got the thing about a half inch off the ground before I settled it back in place.

Mikhail would have to be in full dragon form to fly that sucker across the city. That thought terrified me, especially on a night where the stars painted the sky.

The crunch of claws on concrete pulled my attention behind me. Mikhail landed a few feet away from me and cocked his head as he looked from me to the collar and back.

I opened my mouth, and his wing came up over his mouth, signaling for me to be quiet. I tilted my head, listening. The faint tremble reached all the way to the roof, and I peered over the edge. Three leviathans patrolled together, but each one was at least twenty paces behind the other.

I sat down with my back to the ledge and stared at Mikhail. I twirled my finger, hoping I was conveying my question right. *Had they increased their numbers everywhere?*

He shook his head and strapped on the next bag before pointing toward where the stairway holding the bleach was, and then he pantomimed a big square.

So only in this area. That made me feel better, but it also made Mikhail's takeoff and landing all that much more harrowing. Yes, he was no bigger than a large eagle, but still, the skies were not full of birds, so one flying the same pattern would be suspect if they paid any attention to the world above them.

After he took off with the last bag, leaving only the collar and harness behind, I climbed down to the fifteenth floor and grabbed a tub of ice cream and two spoons. We hadn't eaten since the steak, and my stomach was making noises. This was the only thing I could think of that would satiate me enough and provide the sugar crash I would need to sleep with all this angst pummeling my insides. Especially considering we were executing on the plan the next time the sun set. Besides, I was having a craving.

The skies lightened from the deep blackness to a warm, deep navy, and my heart pounded in my chest. I surveyed the sky in the direction of Times Square, squinting to see whether I could make him out against the near twilight sky.

A noise behind me made me jump, and I spun, nearly dropping the spoons. Mikhail stood in human form, reaching for his crutch. He put his finger on his lips again.

I rolled my eyes and pointed toward the ground near the stairwell, facing the eastern skyline as opposed to the western sky. He silently hobbled and took a seat, and patted the space next to him.

I slid into the spot he indicated and handed him one of the spoons as I peeled the top of the ice cream container off. I took a healthy spoonful and offered the container to him. He took a heaping spoon of ice cream and grinned at me. Even with the light dancing in his eyes, I could still see the dark circles under them.

He needed the sugar rush as much as I did. We silently stared at the sky as it bloomed into the colors of the rainbow before the sun crested the horizon, painting everything a stark yellow compared to the soft tones it had been moments before.

He sighed and took the last spoonful of ice cream, gobbling it up before I could protest. I pouted and dropped my spoon into the container and then stood, helping him to his feet before we slid into the stairwell.

"Thank you," he said as we descended.

"For the ice cream?"

"For everything tonight. Including the ice cream. It's been awhile since I've enjoyed a sunrise. I had forgotten how glorious they were, especially sharing it with you." He leaned toward me and grabbed a kiss before punching in the code to the penthouse. He headed directly into the bedroom, and I diverted, dropping the empty ice cream container into the garbage and the spoons into the dishwasher before following him.

He stepped out of the bedroom in just his underwear and crawled under the covers of the bed. I hurried into the bathroom and did my business, brushing both my hair and my teeth before joining him in the bed.

My heart raced and I moved closer, planting a kiss as if this were my last night on earth. I did not want to waste a moment, but Mikhail pushed me away.

"I'm not doing this now." His stern look made me pull back. "I am not acting like tonight will be our last." He shook his head. "I will not do that to either of us. Instead, I will take a rain check, because damn it, I need the motivation to make sure neither of us gets hurt." His hard gaze met mine with all the stubbornness of a wolverine.

I swallowed hard. I wanted to feel him against me. I wanted time to explore our bodies, to satiate this insane need that welled up inside me. I captured his lower lip between my teeth before I kissed him with as much demand as I could muster.

He kissed me back, pulling me against him, and then he broke the kiss and swiveled me, so my back was against his chest. His arms wrapped around me in a tight hug, holding me in place with little effort. His hot breath tickled my ear.

"I promise, Holly. I promise when we get back, I will make love to you until you cannot walk. But tonight, I am holding you and dreaming of our future together."

"Mikhail," I whispered and kissed the crook of his arm, running my tongue up his bicep.

He squeezed for a moment. "I am serious. I need sleep, despite both our libidos going into overdrive right now." He kissed my neck. "I will be even more exhausted if I give in to you, and I need every ounce of focus tonight so I don't make any mistakes."

I sighed, giving in to his logic. "Fine." I squeezed his arms as the exhaustion claimed me. By tomorrow at this time, we would either end the war, or we would trigger the end of our lives.

Dragon Dawn
Chapter 28

NIGHTFALL.

I stretched and rolled over, glancing out the windows as a bank of clouds brushed the sky in various colors of the sunset. A quick glance at the clock and I laid back down. We had less than an hour before the night would be here in earnest and our hourglass of time sucked downward in a merciless countdown.

"Mikhail." I shook his shoulder and yawned. "The sun is setting."

He pulled me closer with a soft groan, as if he did not want to let this comfortable moment go. Still, he glanced out the windows. "At least it's cloudy. Let's just hope it doesn't rain." He wiped his face and then stretched beside me. He rolled out of bed, grabbed his crutch, and headed into the bathroom.

I closed my eyes again when the shower went on. Mikhail's fingers trailed down my arm and I blinked up at him, fully dressed.

"You fell back asleep. I've got clothes for you at the end of the bed and food is cooking in the kitchen. We need sustenance to get through tonight."

"Okay," I said through a yawn. I went in the bathroom to take care of business and brush my teeth before grabbing the protective shell he had me wear to get the bleach. I slid on a pair of warm sweatpants that he put out, along with a soft sweater. Gloves, the katana, and what looked like a replica of a comic book hero's shield sat on the edge of the bed, and I carried the items to the kitchen.

"What's this?" I held up the shield.

"It should protect you if the serpent king spits at you."

I blinked at the container on the edge of the counter that Mikhail poured an entire carafe of coffee into. Then he restarted the pot.

"I'll be peeing all night if you give me that." I pointed at the thermos.

"This isn't for you."

"Oh." I blinked at the size. If he only had a cup when we were in the museum, this amount of caffeine was likely to raze the entire city. My glance moved to the bag of coffee tree cherries next to the thermos, and then I locked gazes with Mikhail. "Are you trying to destroy all of Manhattan?"

He pushed a plate piled with steak and eggs toward me, along with a freshly brewed cup of coffee. His plate was nearly double the size of mine. He came around and took the seat next to me.

"I need that kind of fuel to do the damage we are planning. We need the leviathans to turn to dust."

"Is that what you drank when you took out the nuclear bombs?"

His knife and fork paused as he looked at me. "No. I only had a small carafe of coffee for that."

I waved at the excess.

He didn't dignify my motion with an answer. Instead, he dove into his food with all the focus of a jeweler setting a diamond. It was only after he finished eating that he spoke. "Imagine the monsters as a thousand and one nuclear bombs." His gaze slid to mine, and he pointed at the canteen with a raised brow.

His argument transmitted loud and clear. I slid off the chair and cleaned up while Mikhail made sure everything was in order. Then we doused ourselves in bleach and headed upstairs with another duffel bag slung across my shoulders, along with the katana.

Night blanketed the city, with thick clouds above.

Mikhail unclasped the collar and laid down, positioning the chains and the belt so they were on the center of his back. He nodded for me to come closer.

"Put the belt on," he whispered.

I straddled him and tightened the belt around my waist, giving him a thumbs-up. He transformed large enough for the collar to not fall off if he leaned down, but he was not nearly full size. Still, he would not be mistaken for an eagle at this size. I gripped his spikes and stifled a gasp as the pounding of leviathan feet reached my ears. Mikhail lay flat, putting his head on its side and I followed suit, grabbing hold of his back and stretching out between the grooves of his spikes.

Low clouds drifted over us, cloaking us just when we needed it the most. Mikhail climbed to his feet as mist surrounded us and then launched straight up into the thicker clouds.

My heart lurched in my chest at the sudden jolt as we lifted off. The mist dampened my hair, and I swallowed hard, hoping it didn't dull the bleach we had all over us. That was soon forgotten as he flew out of the clouds and the dark world below came into focus. If I could have let out a whoop, I would have. Wind whipped through my hair and my cheeks hurt from the near maniacal smile I sported. My adrenaline zoomed through my body, making me tingle as both fear and excitement gripped me.

I did not dare speak until we reached the building where he had deposited all the things to complete this crazy operation.

The low clouds provided us with the cover we needed to set the bombs up, from Broadway to Times Square: Twenty small bombs at one-block intervals. One at ground level and the other on the streetlight across from where we zigzagged the ground bombs. And the granddaddy of them all strung up over the triangular space above Times Square.

It took us most of the night to get the placement right and the amplifier hooked up high near the ball that used to drop every New Year's Eve. The cold penetrated through me as I stood at the railing, looking down. All I could smell was the bleach that penetrated us. Mikhail's dragon form was only big enough to transport me and not his formidable form that we would use to burn the monsters with.

Even so, we had been cautious, running the routes that a hawk nesting near Times Square flew. And in the fully cloud-covered sky, we blended perfectly with our surroundings.

Mikhail set the transmitter and the chain of remotes up behind the ledge we stood on. They would send the signal to the triggers of each detonator, making the bombs explode when the right frequency shattered the area. Then he grabbed me and the recorder and amplifier that served as our trigger, and jumped.

Using his wings, he dropped us gracefully behind the broken steps that once sat on this side of the square. He set up the recorder and amplifier that had my screams in a constant loop and handed me the remote. Once this puppy was turned on, the detonator would go live.

We were betting on the leviathans crushing the device, which would set off the chain of bombs.

To ensure they came in a massive rush, he set the glass jar of his blood on a ledge high enough, so it was sure to break when it fell. Then he tied a string around it and attached the other end to the amplifier switch that would flip via remote. The minute that switch flipped, it would yank the jar off the shelf, shattering it.

If the scream didn't get the leviathans into a single space, his dragon blood would. It was such an elaborate setup with multiple points of failure. But we had been diligent in poking holes at every last detail, enough so that neither one of us believed it would fail.

But theories were very different than the actuality of bombs, and I had a moment to doubt all our work. But that went to the wayside as Mikhail's talon gripped me around the waist and he took flight back toward the Wall Street Journal building, where we'd hide out while Mikhail downed the canister of coffee and the bag of coffee plant cherries we brought with us for this event. It was far enough away not to be included in the damage, but near enough to have a bird's-eye view of Times Square.

Mikhail landed on his single leg and then shifted back into human form and pulled me into an alcove that gave us some protection from the whipping winter wind. He wrapped his arms around me, and his body pulsed enough heat to warm my frigid bones.

"Do you think it's enough?" I whispered.

"We only have one shot at this, so if it isn't, we're truly fucked."

We had barely gotten what we needed of the bleach from the stairwell without being caught.

However, we still had the rest in the stairwell and the storage room at Penn Station if all went south at sunrise.

"And you are sure about killing the serpent king?" I captured his gaze.

"Holly, I'm not sure of anything at the moment." He wiped his face as he scanned the city below us and then met my gaze. "If this one isn't the primary..." Worry laced his citrine eyes as they searched mine.

"If it isn't the primary, we're equally screwed," I finished his statement. Killing the primary serpent king would kill all of them. But no one had been able to harm that thing. Even if we killed the leviathans, if we failed at beheading the serpent king, then he would just call more monsters from other places to rid the city of us.

"It was only lore," he whispered.

"Yes, but wasn't everything else true about the other monsters in that book?" The raid on the library had brought us necessary intel in the ancient tomes he brought back. It had information about many monsters, including dragons, and everything written about dragons had been spot-on. So, we were assuming the details about the Hydra had been just as reliable.

A reference book Mikhail found at the library had indicated that a certain kind of ancient steel could kill the Hydra by beheading it, but like the old Greek mythos, if you cut off the head of a subservient serpent, two would grow back in its place.

We both prayed that the serpent king in New York was the primary one.

The ancient katana that I used to kill Troy was made of that specific steel mix, so it would be up to me to slay the beast from Mikhail's back without injuring either of us in the process. It was ballsy at best and suicidal at worst. But, as Mikhail had said multiple times, it was the only way to win this war.

THE sky lightened enough for me to see the mangled city in grizzly detail. I hadn't seen it from this height and the scarred landscape saddened me.

Mikhail reached for the thermos of coffee. As he unscrewed the top of the canteen, he met my gaze. "Ready for this?"

I strapped the belt around my waist. The harness that would keep me on Mikhail's back. Chains hung from the leather, and I'd have to attach them to the collar we had sitting open on the roof once he shifted into his full form and put on the cast-iron collar. After securing the belt, I slung the katana over my shoulder and picked up the shield he insisted I carry.

He didn't want me hit with the serpent king's spit. That was also the one thing that could bring Mikhail out of the sky. He could survive it, but he was sure I would be decimated if I was hit.

Mikhail tilted the thermos to his lips, gulping down the contents. He closed his eyes, and I actually saw every vein in his body broadcast white light under his skin. He held the container away from his mouth as the last few drops fell into his open maw. He licked his lips and opened his eyes. Citrine glowed with flames of white and blue, and he smiled.

"Cold coffee tastes like shit." He set the can down and gobbled up the small bag of coffee tree cherries next. "So does this." But that didn't stop him from eating every last one. He pulsed with the power filling him and nodded toward the square. "It's time."

He went to the line of triggers and set them all into the on position. The bombs were now all active and just waiting for that certain frequency that would set off the blasting cap in the C-4.

My heart quickened as he moved over to the collar and then laid flat on the roof. His transformation took a blink, and then he fastened the collar with a clang of metal on metal.

I climbed on the back of his neck and clasped the chains into place. Four of them held me fast so I didn't have to strangle him with my legs. This way I could kneel between the hard crowns of the scales on his back instead of having my legs dangling over his shoulders and subject to the heat of his fire.

"Remember to bank when I swing. Otherwise, I'll hit you with the blade."

Mikhail nodded his massive head. "Turn on the recording."

I pointed the remote and a moment later, my screams echoed off the buildings. I thought I heard glass shatter, but I couldn't be sure at this height. Mikhail sniffed the air and nodded, confirming our dragon blood container had shattered as expected.

It took a moment, but then the stampede started. The footfalls sounded like thunder, and they came primarily from downtown. But there were others careening from the rest of the island, right to the center of Times Square, right to the amplifier and Mikhail's spilled dragon blood.

The horde came into view, with the serpent king in their midst, and their roars of frustration reached us at our remote vantage point. All of a sudden, the screams cut, and that high-pitched soundwave rang out, making me cover my ears.

I held my breath as my heartbeat counted through the seconds. Silence fell on the square below and I stiffened, thinking somehow they had nullified our bombs. But then the first explosion rocked the city, farther down Broadway. Then, like a chain reaction, all the bombs exploded, one after another, sending bleach and nails and anything sharp we could find through the air with deadly force. When the bomb over Times Square exploded, the noise was deafening, silencing the screams of the injured below.

The serpent king hissed at the wailing leviathans, but he was no longer in control of them. Some lay dead and the others stumbled around, injured by both bleach and projectiles.

Mikhail pushed off the building and banked down Fifth Avenue, coming around the back side. The moment we passed where we set off the first bomb, he turned onto the next street. As we took the corner between the buildings onto Broadway, Mikhail let his fire loose.

White fire brighter than anything I had ever seen spewed from Mikhail's mouth. I squinted and held the shield up to block both the brightness of it and the heat that blew over me the moment he let his destruction loose.

The writhing leviathans turned to dust; so did the facing of the buildings we passed. Some buildings toppled over seconds after we went by. Mikhail flew high enough to remain out of reach of the monsters, but low enough to turn them to ash. If they survived Mikhail's fire, the buildings toppling over on them would slow them down enough for us to end them.

The serpent king spun toward us as we neared Times Square. I pulled out my blade and held it at the ready. Mikhail continued aiming at the masses of leviathans, and dust of the dead thickened the sky.

The serpent king spit at us.

Mikhail aimed his blaze at the creature. The gray ball of wetness coming toward us sizzled and turned to steam before we reached it. He aimed fire at the rest of the leviathans and then dropped low, banking below the serpent king's head, giving me a shot at its neck.

I dropped the shield because I needed two hands for this. I gripped my katana tight, swinging as we flew by while Mikhail blanketed the area with his white flame.

The serpent king's howl filled the air, and I glanced back. Mikhail shifted around as we took a second pass at the serpent king. His head hung at an odd angle. In order to finish him off, Mikhail would have to almost fly upside down.

Fire still shot from Mikhail like an endless deluge, and this time as he passed the serpent, its jaws clamped shut on the tip of Mikhail's lower wing. Mikhail roared as he struggled to break free.

I was close enough to the serpent's neck to swing again, but this cut was lower on his throat than the other, so it did not sever the bastard's head. Although, my slash made his grip on Mikhail release, sending us careening toward the closest building.

A hiss filled the air behind me, and I turned. The serpent king's beady eyes were locked on me as it shot forward. Its neck hung from a strand, and I spun, throwing the katana on its edge, aimed directly at that strand holding the two pieces together.

And then I ducked down, wrapping my arms around Mikhail and stretching my legs out flat on his back. Closing my eyes, I waited for death.

Mikhail's side hit the building, exploding glass and metal with it. He crashed through the floor, taking most of the office furniture with him to the other side, littering the street below with glass and debris. His claws scrambled for purchase, and he caught the edge, dangling us from the building. I didn't scream. I only stared through the ruined building at the head of the serpent king wedged behind where we had hit. Beyond its head, its neck swayed and then fell in slow motion into the blaze below.

"You did it!" Mikhail grabbed onto the metal frame and started a slow crawl down the side of the building until he reached the street.

I turned and glanced at the wing that the serpent bit and gasped. It looked raw, as though it had been burned in his fire.

He folded it in and hobbled back toward Times Square in an odd three-legged gait. He wanted to ensure no more monsters were alive. A squeal sounded behind us, and he spun, opening his mouth to shoot flame. But he paused at the sight of a baby leviathan whose body was mostly charred. It crawled along the road toward us, mewing.

"Kill it," I whispered as a thread of fear gripped me.

"Go." Mikhail pointed toward the water.

It stopped moving and blinked, as if the command perplexed him. His gaze moved to me, and he bared his teeth in a feral snarl.

"Damn it," Mikhail swore under his breath and then sent a plume of white fire at the thing. It went up in a puff of smoke.

He continued his limp toward where the most concentrated force of leviathans had been. Ground zero...Times Square. Neither of us recognized where it began or ended. White dust filled the silent space. Nothing survived, which meant the bombs we set off did their job and Mikhail's fire wiped out any evidence that leviathans existed in New York City.

And the body of the serpent king lay smoldering on top of the ruined earth. I could not fathom how the thing was still whole, with the heat making me turn into a sweating machine.

Mikhail took a deep breath and blew out a pyre that rendered its body to dust. He looked up at the building that now housed the serpent king's head.

Mikhail inhaled again.

"Leave it."

Smoke snorted from his nose, and he turned his head to catch a glimpse of me. His eyes widened.

"You're bleeding," he said as his gaze scanned me.

I blinked and did a quick check of my current situation. I had minor cuts from the glass on my left forearm where my protective undershirt had hiked up almost to my elbow, leaving my skin exposed. Beyond that, I was right as rain. Nothing was gushing; it was just dripping as if I had been caught by a barbed wire fence. "Well, when you crash through glass, it's bound to happen. But I am nowhere near as injured as your wing." I pointed at his molted appendage.

He turned back toward where the head was lodged, ignoring my assessment of his condition. "Why don't you want me to burn it?"

I cocked my head as I studied the hacked neck that was visible. "We should bronze that fucker and set it up at the shoreline as a warning to any other monsters that may decide to rise from the deep and try to stamp us out."

He snorted a laugh.

"I'm serious."

"I know you are. That's why I'm laughing. But I don't think that is nearly enough. What we need is a statue of *you* with that katana dripping with serpent blood in one hand and that head in your other. That would deliver the message you want better than just a severed serpent king head."

"You think?"

"Yes. You deserve that type of immortality, considering I truly believe you just saved humanity." He moved back onto stable, unblemished ground. Ground that I could walk on since most of Broadway and Times Square was that white-hot trench of burned earth that, if I stepped on it, I'd turn to dust just like the leviathans.

"That's missing something, though." I unhooked the chains and slid down off his shoulder and down his good wing until I landed next to him.

"What's missing?"

"You. You need to be a part of that statue."

"No." He squared himself in front of me. "I caused the near extinction of your kind and the total extinction of mine. And aided in at least one more species' demise. I do not need to be immortalized as a hero. But you. You are."

He yanked a streetlamp out of the ground, severing the wires before propping it under his injured wing as a makeshift crutch. He nodded for me to lead the way. I picked up two of the chains dangling on the ground, hauled them over my shoulder, and started toward downtown to our home.

"At some point, we'll have to come back here and see if the katana survived," I said.

Mikhail glanced back toward Times Square, as if he were going to backtrack.

"It will keep." I pulled him forward by the chains, toward the last promise he now had to deliver on.

Dragon Dawn
Chapter 29

THE BURNING BUILDINGS IN Midtown, along with the sudden absence of ground-shaking footsteps, brought forth many of the survivors in the city. They crawled out of the subbasements of buildings and stared at the dust and white-hot devastation of Mikhail's fire.

They gawked at us as we passed: the human woman leading the dragon in chains. I couldn't find it in me just yet to invite them along to a safer building. Not with the memory of the things the soldiers had done still at the forefront of my mind.

Trust in my fellow humans would return eventually, but right now, we both needed tending. Mikhail more than I, with the damage to his wing, but I also needed cuts and scrapes cleaned. And then we had to get the information out far and wide on how to destroy the monsters.

That was, if anyone was still alive in the other parts of this country and the world at large.

Even with the danger extinguished, the number of people who surfaced was still minute compared to how many had lived in Manhattan before the pandemic. Sadness stroked her cruel fingers across my skin, and I bit my lip as the first hint of true grief leaked out of my heart.

Without the terror of danger present on every corner, reality settled in. So many lives had been lost in this bloody and horrifying war.

"Please, Lord, let this not be all the people who survived," I whispered and looked to the sky. "Please let us not be too late to save the majority." My heart and mind knew that wouldn't be the case. Especially with the lack of people in New York. But I still had hope wrapped around me like a warm cover, and I clung to it like a baby clings to their blankie.

"If this is any indication..." Mikhail replied, glancing around at the sparsely populated streets as we hobbled toward home.

"I know. But I can still pray." I glanced over my shoulder at him with a glare that shut him up. If we could have taken to the sky to go home, we would have; then no one would have been the wiser as to who had stopped the beasts. And just like a highway accident, people just had to look at the survivors of the carnage.

He mumbled his agreement, allowing me to fall back into my reverie with every step. South of the rubble of City Hall was deserted, and I glanced behind us, squinting in the darkness to see whether we were being followed.

"No one followed. And anyone still in this area is deeply entrenched in their hiding places." Mikhail glanced around as well and gave an absent nod, as if confirming to himself that what he said was true.

When we arrived at his building, we both did one more scan of the streets. And then I punched in the access code. Even down here, the stench of burnt reptiles permeated the night air, and I crinkled my nose as I opened the door for Mikhail.

Mikhail dumped the streetlamp he had used as a crutch, and it rolled to the far sidewalk. We both stared at it for a second, and then Mikhail met my gaze. Without explanation, he shifted, shrinking into the tiny dragon that I had gotten used to being around. The collar he wore crashed to the ground, but this time, it didn't crash into him, pinning his small form to the ground like last time. The collar was thick enough to land flush on the ground. Thankfully the street was relatively flat; otherwise, we might have been running from a rolling steel barrel.

Mikhail hopped through the collar and over the threshold into the building.

"Should we do something with that?" I waved toward the collar and chains with the door still wide, and ambient light from the stars glinted against the metal.

The rustle of his wings had me glancing at his dark figure in the lobby. I think he shrugged, but I couldn't be sure.

"It won't fit through the door," he finally said and produced a flame on his front claw of his damaged wing arm. The flame barely lit up the area but it illuminated his face enough so I could see whatever dragon expression he was leveling at me, and it was not flattering.

"Thanks, Captain Obvious." I then glanced at the barren streets around us and sighed. "There has to be more people." I closed the door, glancing at Mikhail.

"Are you going to carry me or watch me struggle up the stairs?" he asked, as if my powers of observation had suddenly been nullified.

"I put a crutch in the stairwell for you." I waved at the door behind us. I could just barely make out the raised stairwell sign on the door in the low flame Mikhail held.

He lifted his damaged wing and the flame danced in response. He wasn't nearly as injured as he had been before. It was more burned than shredded, so I had no fear of him bleeding out in human form.

"And?"

"It's burned."

Was he whining to me about being burned? I crossed my arms and gave him the look that clearly expressed I was as unimpressed as it gets.

He took a deep breath and sighed. "Holly, I can't maneuver a crutch with a burnt arm."

I blinked and studied him closer. The wing that was injured did happen to be the one he'd need to use the crutch, but I wasn't about to let him off easy. "You are going to try logic so I'll carry you upstairs?"

His eyeroll was so pronounced it would have made a cartoon proud. "Will you please give me a hand?"

I clapped my hands together slowly.

He laughed. His sharp teeth glinted in the flame, but the aggravation swelled in his irises, creating a slow burn of yellow and red in his citrine eyes. "I'd bite you, but then you'll make me crawl up the stairs."

"Damn straight." I scooped him into my arms.

He nuzzled into my chest with a toothy grin.

I climbed the fifteen floors to the medical unit and entered. The only thing I took off were my shoes, and then I padded through the interior door and set Mikhail on the metal table.

"Grab me some iodine and bandages, too, so I can patch you up as well."

I glanced back at him as I opened the cabinet that had the last jar of dragon blood inside. He already transformed into his human form and was peeling off his shirt with a noticeable wince. I grabbed the dragon blood, a large roll of gauze, and instead of iodine, I chose peroxide and some antibiotic ointment with bandages. My wounds didn't need iodine; none of them were deep enough for stitches. They just needed to be cleaned out and covered.

His arm was covered with red welts and melted skin. It was far worse to look at than his crushed leg had been, and I wondered whether this is what my back had looked like after he burnt me. My stomach tightened as I approached. At least his injuries were localized to his arm.

"Is that what would have happened to me if the serpent king had hit me with his spit?" I set down the bandages and unscrewed the dragon blood.

He glanced at me with his lips set in a tight scowl. "You would have died. This shit would have eaten right through your skin and left nothing but petrified bone."

I bit my lower lip and took his hand, raising his arm from close to his body as I slathered a thin layer of dragon blood across his damaged skin. The bumps under my fingertips made my throat tighten on bile. I swallowed hard, forcing the vile taste back down into my stomach.

"Do you need to lay here until it heals?" I asked, trying to occupy my mind with something else until I had his arm covered in dragon blood and wrapped in gauze.

"No. This isn't the same as my spine." He reached over and pulled my chin, making me meet his eyes. "Take a deep breath. You look a little green. I can wrap it if you'd like."

"I'm fine." I jerked my chin out and finished applying the dragon blood. I wiped the excess back into the jar and screwed the top back on before I began wrapping the gauze from his shoulder down to just above his wrist. I patted the back of his hand. "Done." I stepped back, gaining a solid handle on my upset stomach. "You weren't hurt anywhere else, right?"

"Not that I'm aware of." He turned his back toward me, so I could make sure.

"You didn't even get a scratch from crashing through the glass." I traced my fingers over his smooth back.

He turned to me. "Scratches on dragon hide heal within minutes, so whatever scrapes and bumps I got from that were gone by the time we got here." His gaze dropped to my shredded jacket and he helped me peel it off.

"Another one of my favorites destroyed." I frowned at the comfortable leather jacket tossed on the ground as Mikhail swiped a peroxide-saturated cotton ball over my cuts and scrapes.

"I'll get you as many leather coats as your heart desires," he said while he blotted the cuts and then smeared antibiotic ointment over the deeper wounds and attached bandages where needed. My arm looked like patchwork when he finished. "I'll get you pretty much anything your heart desires."

"So you said."

"I made a lot of promises yesterday, didn't I?"

I smiled. "You promised me a future if we succeeded *and* made it out alive." I was not going to let him waffle out of that.

Dimples appeared in his cheeks. "I did. That's if you want this old dragon at your side."

"Mmm, I don't know about that." I pursed my lips and looked up at the ceiling, as if mulling it over.

He pulled me to his chest and planted a hard kiss on my lips. "You can figure it out after you help me to the penthouse." He swung his injured arm over my shoulder and hopped off the table onto his good leg.

Mikhail stuffed the dragon blood container into his pants pocket and followed it with the gauze, and then nodded toward the door.

"What, no mini-dragon to carry?" I swung my arm around his waist.

"While I'd like that, I don't want to waste the patch job you did. Especially with less than a jar of dragon blood left."

"Ah. But don't you heal faster in dragon form?"

"Yes. But it means if I shift, when I shift back, you will need to reapply the green stuff and re-wrap my arm. And honestly, I don't want to waste the time. We have more important things to take care of."

"Like falling into bed?" I asked as we maneuvered to the door. We hadn't taken refuge in each other's bodies since before the first bleach run, and I was antsy for his touch.

"While I would love to just screw around until we fall into a satiated stupor, we need to get the word out." He glanced at me. "If they don't go back to the recesses they crawled out from, we will douse every last one of them with bleach and annihilate them just like we did in New York."

"You're giving the leviathans a chance?" I drew back from him.

"I would prefer not to eliminate another species if I don't have to. But the message will be clear to everyone who intercepts it that bleach *IS* their weakness."

"How will anyone intercept?" I asked. Mikhail had explained that the leviathans and serpent king communicated on a different frequency. One that he hadn't originally been privy to with being half human; but Ricky had explained it to him, and he found it on the only satellite he hadn't destroyed. St. Clare Industries' satellite. He had been monitoring their activity ever since.

"I'm sending the message out on a repeating loop on all frequencies, so if someone has a battery-operated ham or CB radio, they will pick it up when the satellite goes overhead."

"Sneaky bastard." I smiled as we slowly maneuvered up the steps.

"Then I'll let you show me just how appreciative you are that I followed through on my promise."

His sideways glance along with the glimmer in his eyes made me want to rush us upstairs so we could get this business behind us and focus on starting a life together.

Dragon Dawn
Chapter 30

I LEFT HIM IN the den with a crutch and his computer, and went into the main bathroom to clean up as best as I could. My mouth tasted bitter and I'm sure my breath was just as deadly as any of the bombs had been to the leviathans.

I searched the closet and drawers for something to put on appropriate for a seduction and came up empty. Then my gaze rose to the box on the top shelf. The box of Mikhail's wife's undergarments. They weren't my comfortable style, but perhaps there was a sexy negligee in there.

I glanced out to the living room. The light was still on in the den and the clicks of a keyboard continued. I pulled the box down and brought it to the bed. Under the layer of thongs was a sheer baby-doll with matching lace panties. I pulled it out and sighed as I held it up.

I might as well be wearing nothing, but it did have delicate lace at the shoulders and hemlines. Although it was not my style, I was sure I would get an instant rise out of Mikhail the moment he saw me. I slipped it on and surprisingly, the flimsy fabric and lace did not itch. It was actually as comfortable as an oversized T-shirt.

I would have to take a second look at his wife's collection later. If she had things that were downright sexy that didn't bind or chafe or itch, then maybe my tastes would change.

I put the box back and slid the door closed. I glanced at the bed, debating whether I should lounge on the spread and wait for him to come to me. If I stretched out on the bed, I'd likely fall sound asleep and that would not do.

I wanted my dragon now.

I fluffed my hair and strode across the living space to the den, leaned against the door, and cleared my throat.

"I'm almost done," Mikhail said without looking up. "The chatter has been entertaining." He smiled and glanced toward where I stood. His eyes widened when they fell on me, and his fingers paused on the keyboard. He pushed away from the desk and swiveled the chair so he faced me. His irises turned from his normal citrine color to nearly blue as they ignited in hot flame.

"I was tired of waiting." I crossed to stand in front of his chair.

He looked up at me and grinned, pulling me into a straddle on his lap. "This is far more entertaining than the groveling of the leviathans."

"They are groveling?"

He nodded as he brought his mouth to my cleavage.

"Should I make you grovel?"

He glanced up at me with a wicked smirk and moved his tongue from my chest, up my neck to my earlobe. He took it between his teeth and nibbled, creating a web of chills through me.

"Do your best," he whispered in my ear before moving to my mouth, capturing me in a kiss that momentarily stunned me.

I went to get up, to gain control, but his hands cupped my ass tight enough so I couldn't move from where he had planted me. He was teasing me as much as I had hoped to tease him. He wouldn't let me break away, so I slowly grinded into him.

I definitely got a rise out of him. One of his hands slid over my thigh and between my legs as he broke the kiss and moved his mouth to my throat.

God, his touch ignited every cell in my body.

I made the mistake of glancing at the screen of his computer as his lips tickled the line of my throat. The leviathans weren't groveling. They were promising Mikhail a painful death the next time they surfaced from the deep. I pushed on his chest, sending him into the back of the chair we were in.

"That is not groveling." I pointed at the screen.

Mikhail looked at the last entry and shrugged. "That's not unexpected, but they were begging to stay topside earlier. I gave them the ultimatum: stay topside and die, or burrow back in their caves and go back to sleep." He removed his hand from my ass and used the scroll to move the text farther back in the conversation so I could see.

I scrolled through the text from the beginning to their last threat. They had groveled before they lashed out. "Did you transmit this entire conversation?"

"Yes. Anyone with the means heard it."

I sighed with resignation and met his gaze. Mikhail St. Clare outed himself to the world. Hopefully, they would see the hero and not the duplicity of his actions while under the control of the serpent king.

"Tell them I look forward to it, but understand, I, and any human they encounter, will be armed with bleach and the means to cut them down before they can launch any coordinated attack."

I moved off his lap and faced the computer.

Mikhail positioned the chair right behind me and spread my stance with his foot. Then he started to play with me again, but this time as I leaned over the keyboard, he sucked on my ass cheek and rubbed my clit in slow circles.

I fought to focus on the words I was writing, but it was difficult with Mikhail's ministrations. When I hit the Send button, I started to turn.

"Stay right there. Hands on the desk where I can see them, please," he said. But his tone wasn't stern; it was seductive enough for me to shiver and comply and even spread my legs wider.

I glanced over my shoulder at him, enjoying his pleasure play, along with the heated glint in his flaming eyes. He took his time, and when the computer dinged a response, both of us took a cursory look at the white flag that the leviathans raised, and then focused back on creating a heat between us that was all-consuming.

Mikhail groaned as his finger dipped inside my wet path. He removed his hands and spun me around, sweeping the keyboard and computer to the far side of the desk. He tore the underwear off me and propped me on the desk. Pulling the chair forward, he pushed my nightgown higher and lowered his mouth to my core.

Good Lord, the man's tongue had to be considered a national treasure. He knew how to bring me to the brink and then slow me down so the next wave was even more intense. My hands threaded into his hair as he played with my clit, teasing me in the most wicked of ways.

"Mikhail," I gasped and arched my back.

His eyes sparkled as he looked up from his quest. "Yes, my dear?" He cocked his head and humor lines crinkled at the edges of his eyes.

"I need you inside me," I whispered, my voice hoarse and full of want.

His finger slid inside me, and he dipped back down, continuing his manipulations.

"That's not what I meant."

He chuckled but continued his slow stroke with his hand, coupled with the fast flick of his tongue until I was nothing more than a quivering puddle of panting flesh.

He rose to his feet and hopped between my legs. When he pushed his member against my waiting path, I shivered with anticipation. He moved so slowly as he glanced down at me with eyes nearly as frenzied as I was.

His slow rhythm claimed my body, creating ripples of heat. He tore my top off and played with my breasts as he grabbed the opposite edge of the desk with the hand of his injured arm. Muscles flexed and he winced but did not stop his languid pace. He met my gaze.

"Holly," he whispered, his voice husky with need. "You challenge me in every way, every moment we spend together, and I want to feel this insane craving to have you as a part of me for the rest of my life." He plunged into me with more force.

I palmed his cheek and then pulled him to my lips, kissing him because his words accompanied by the ecstasy he created every time he touched me transformed my heart into something I never thought I could feel. Love so complete warmed me from the inside until I thought I would burst.

"Marry me," he whispered against my lips as he lost control, slamming into me like a battering ram, hips against hips as my body contracted with pleasure.

I tilted my head back and screamed, "Yes!"

And then he pulled out of me, covering my stomach with his seed before he collapsed on top of me on the desk.

Catching our breath was nearly impossible, but as soon as his trembling subsided, he lifted his head off my chest. "Was that a yes you'll marry me or yes because I finally pushed your g-spot?"

I let out a guffaw. "What do you think?" I said through my laugh.

"I think it was the g-spot." He chuckled against my neck.

"Maybe. Besides, I don't see a ring, so that proposal was incomplete."

"I'm going to make you a bronzed statue of the serpent's head. Isn't that enough?"

His tilted grin made me love him even more. Although, I was torn on a bronze statue or just putting that mother's skull with the rest of Mikhail's collection.

When I shook my head, he said, "Fine. I'll take you to Tiffany's tomorrow and you can pick out whatever ring you want. Assuming Tiffany's is still standing."

"I'm kidding, Mikhail. Yes, I'll agree to drive you batshit for the rest of your life."

He kissed me softly, but that soon transitioned to another heated kiss.

"Hey, babe?" I asked from under his mouth.

"Mmm?" He didn't stop tangling his tongue with mine.

"Can we at least move this to the bedroom? I'd like a softer cushion under me," I mumbled while still trying to continue the heart-warming kiss.

He chuckled, maneuvered off me, and grabbed his crutch off the floor, hobbling toward the bedroom with the solid muscles of his backside drawing me to follow.

I sighed at the realization that I'd follow that ass anywhere.

The End

Thank you for reading Season of the Dragon.
Please consider leaving a review!

About J.E. Taylor

J.E. Taylor is a USA Today bestselling author, a publisher, an editor, a manuscript formatter, a mother, a wife, a business analyst, and a Supernatural fangirl, not necessarily in that order. She first sat down to seriously write in February of 2007 after her daughter asked:

"Mom, if you could do anything, what would you do?"

From that moment on, she hasn't looked back.

Besides being co-owner of Novel Concept Publishing, Ms. Taylor also moonlights as a Senior Editor of Allegory E-zine, an online venue for Science Fiction, Fantasy and Horror, and co-host of the popular YouTube talk show Spilling Ink.

She lives in New Hampshire with her husband and during the summer months enjoys her weekends on the shore in southern Maine.

Visit her at www.jetaylor75.com to check out her other titles and to sign up for her newsletter for early previews of her upcoming books, and release announcements!